T0146679

TO CAST A FLY

A Novel

Douglas E. Templin

authorHOUSE®

AuthorHouse™ LLC
1663 Liberty Drive
Bloomington, IN 47403
www.authorhouse.com
Phone: 1-800-839-8640

This book is a work of fiction. People, places, events, and situations, are the products of the author. Any resemblance to actual persons, living or dead, or historical events, is purely coincidental.

Published by AuthorHouse 09/30/2014

ISBN: 978-1-4969-4008-7 (sc)
ISBN: 978-1-4969-3947-0 (e)

Library of Congress Control Number: 2014916570

ACKNOWLEDGEMENTS

It is with much gratitude that I once again thank long-time friend, Julie Garston Mattson, accomplished Newport Beach, California artist, for her patient observations and commentaries as she read the first draft, as chapters were submitted. Urged to continue despite the need for much revision, I wrote and rewrote as a fledgling writer must, because she liked the story, the characters, and looked past the crudity of the initial product.

Her encouragement and critiques, proved likewise invaluable on my first published novel, *Red Star on the Sail.*

I thank, also, the teams of back surgeons who opened and closed most of my spine seven times over five years, which eventually permitted work at the computer. I was thus given leave to write full time for days, weeks, then months and, finally for two pain-free years, to complete the first, this novel, and my third; soon to be published, *A Shot at Aaron.*

Finally, to dear Jacqueline, my housemate and devoted love, for catering to my insatiable desire to complete my last two works while convalescing at our small horse ranch in the mountains above Lake Elsinore, California, and for her undying support during the aggregated nine months spent in various hospitals.

—Doug Templin

CHAPTER 1

Michigan

He rubbed tired eyes, first the left and then the other, opened his window periodically, and shook his head often, to maintain a decent level of vigilance. A nagging, circuitous array of pros and cons; his bundled thoughts seemed naught more than insoluble swirls of confusion.

So disorganized and shallow they were; Mike could not decide. Would a one eighty and a turn toward home, stop the torment? An idea he negated and followed too many times that evening; he grew tired of repeatedly transiting the same terrain, given his whimsical changes of mind. It seemed that each segment of several miles, or period of fifteen to twenty minutes, fostered a recurrent urge to stop. He would think about it, and then reverse course, north to their cabin, or back south—the easy way out—to their home, where he began the trip at the end of a tiring workday. Mike Gladdock resisted the latter urge as it strongly conflicted with a deeper and more compelling desire.

I simply must continue, his internal voice finally concluded, *and at the least, try to enjoy this badly needed five-day break from work. I'd be freed, too, of the nauseating—though well meant—sympathies from bereaved relatives and friends.*

Mike Gladdock's thoughts turned audible as if she listened. "How can I possibly savor this otherwise lonesome, nighttime drive, as I did in our past, without the cheerful company, our lively conversations, and her happy chatter of the river? Should I bite the bullet and press forward, despite the pain from her absence?" He shuddered with the notion that he could be so indecisive.

Michigan's open spaces soared by, though in a seemingly dismal and definitely disappointing blur. Stubborn snow patches, on the upswing as the miles rolled north, offered assurance that the toasty days and balmy nights of an early summer, while they loomed with possibility, might take their time to ignite.

Deciduous trees along the line where forest darkness began, glared in his headlights like weathered barber poles; they stood defiant, and still refused to dance in their brilliant yellow-green, spring clothes. Something far more severe birthed Mike's apathy; not just the weather-borne dither of bursting buds, or the lazy recession of winter white's every trace.

Meg died the week before. His loving wife joined the great beyond.

The emptiness that gripped so tenaciously, and that alone, forced the deviations from his usual wild-eyed anticipation during the commute to their place in Oscoda County. "So much sullen brown everywhere," he muttered aloud, "and all those bland grays that crowd the evergreens—outside thermometer too close to the thirties—a faster jump to more pleasant conditions looks awfully doubtful."

For the first time, Mike felt the physical pain that he would face again and again, until denial could be supplanted by the stark reality of her passing. Entirely different from the norm, it was his only venture in many a year without Meg, to their erstwhile cozy, second home. While they stayed there over the occasional winter weekend, they better used their pride and joy for longer breaks, during the other seasons. While there, the couple passed countless days on and about their beloved Au Sable River.

Farther back than his memory stretched, Meg was with him, cuddled alongside. Head on his shoulder at times, she kept him awake with stimulating colloquy, slept lightly, or she hummed to music he played at high volume, to keep alert in the abject darkness of the smaller byways. Mike leaned forward, tried to nudge aside painful reflections, hugged the wheel with both arms, and peered cautiously through the low blanket of mist that clouded his visibility.

Moisture droplets collected, slid to the side, and distorted his view of the road ahead, as fast as the sweep of wipers erased them. An incessant cadence, the hypnotizing flip flapping hindered concentration more than he liked, and to his greater disdain, encouraged drowsiness. He squinted and blinked more often than normal, while his mind worked hard to expunge itself of so many unpleasant distractions. No matter, he could not disconnect.

She took that turn for the worst, just up and died … so fast … she did. Why the deuce did I think I could do it alone, so soon after her demise? I might have avoided wallowing in this huge muddle, this stack of unsettled feelings, if I delayed departure a bit longer. Weekend warriors—hunters and anglers by the droves—soon to crowd highways and byways, would have reduced the woeful solitude and worked to dispel the unpleasant sense of impending despair that engulfed his thoughts.

Six foot-three, bare heels on the floor, to many he seemed a virtual tower. That included the loss of nearly an inch of his younger height to a congenital spinal curvature that just began to take its toll. The past year or so, Mike's body frame bent some from back pain, after cutting firewood or mowing. Broad chest and rock-solid arms, however, almost masked the ailing spine, and his abdominal musculature still rippled. Beneath his comparatively youthful physique, Mike's sixty-two years stayed fairly well concealed. Almost wrinkle-free, though pasty from the paucity of sunshine through the long winter; his complexion looked healthy and ever rosy-cheeked. Curly, brown and receding some, Mike's hair was long enough that it ruffled from beneath the red baseball cap that stayed glued to his head while in Oscoda County. His personal flag, the Detroit Tigers fixture topped off normal weekend attire: faded Levis™, a plaid, long-sleeved woolen or cotton shirt—depending on the season—and laced woodsman's boots. Adorned with ever-present lenses,

Mike's face seemed somewhat hollowed from its younger fullness, but his grin was genuine, broad, and natural, and he used it often, along with his magnetic laugh. Soft of voice and compassionate to a fault, he lived to hunt and fish for the myriad bounties offered by the region in which he was born, raised and, surely, would die. Deer, game birds, trout from river fly fishing, and salmon caught deep water trolling in nearby Lake Huron, kept his freezers and those of friends and relatives, well stocked with meats of the seasons.

Who would succeed in his footsteps? Mike wondered, as he massaged his right temple with stubby fingertips. He did that to stay attentive while driving at night, when he often ruminated over the son who never came along, to whom he might have passed the lore of his native woods. He hoped for a boy after the first daughter, and suffered only slight disappointment with the arrival of Jennifer, his younger girl. Just twenty-seven, a graduate of Michigan State, she moved west not long before, to teach high school French in Northern California. He sorely missed her, for she did enjoy her fishing when a youngster. Judith, his eldest, lived close by, with husband and two kids, but never shared Mike's passions for the outdoors.

While proud of and devoted to his two girls, Mike's thoughts drifted to further speculation about the son he never had. He glanced in the darkened rearview mirror. His wrought and saddened expression, a window to his troubled soul, likely brought on the continued musings.

Brilliant, just like Jennifer, Mike Junior—we'd have called him— tallest in his class; would have played ball as I did. Certainly, he would have been a fine fly angler by the time I finished with him, and a one-shot hunter by the age of twelve, as I became after Pop's endless coaching. Oh, Jennie liked the woods, but her penchant for the chase, probably just to please me, never quite matched mine. Didn't like shooting game ... always cried when we approached the dead animal. "Poor thing," she'd say, no matter their excess numbers would starve during our long Michigan winters. I wonder what Jennifer's doing out there tonight? If she only knew how Mom and I ... dern, how I do miss her.

The last thought startled Mike from nearly ramming a doe and her fawn as they nimbly, but boldly, crossed the black-as-pitch, double lane road ahead. Since he turned off Interstate 75 to the more isolated eastbound State 55, he sighted dozens of the graceful animals that grazed on barely emergent grass along roadside margins. Preoccupied with diversions, though, he missed these two until the last few seconds.

Tires screeched, the front end slid sideways over the moist pavement, and the car shuddered to a fast halt on the shoulder before he collected himself. When the dust cleared, he looked in all directions, and assured no impacts occurred.

"Jesus Crisp! That was close … too close," Mike shrieked loudly, as if Meg sat with him in the front seat. "Did you see that scrawny fresh born stagger behind its mother? A tiny one, spindly little legs; it looked so innocent." He rarely swore, especially in front of her. Mike almost apologized as he turned to his right, expectant that Meg awoke from the commotion. Meg was not there, and would never again go north with him. *Can't believe she's gone! I never anticipated feelings like this. So blamed eerie—thoughts so out of control—well beyond my grasp.* Paused a few minutes to recover wits and watch the unconcerned deer saunter into a thicket on the other side of the deserted byway, Mike shook his head in disbelief, how oblivious the animals were to their near-death experience. *There might have been suffering, or death could have come quickly. We are here for such a short time, to plow along and do what we can to survive.*

He stopped the turmoil of dissociative thoughts for a few moments and took some slow, deep breaths. The brief digressions helped him organize ideas as they burst forth and merged with his inventory of older, more troubling reflections. *Two well-placed and quick shots; they would have died without warning … no advance worries … no grieving family. Why is it that some beings suffer and others do not? Why are some taken before their time, and others, not? Why did my love have to hurt like that? If only she. …* He suppressed the internal taunting again, as he did every minute since the funeral, when forced acceptance of her demise spawned the new and inescapable truth.

How can I separate myself from the sadness and not relive her loss, day after day? Strangely, though, it seems she's here—smack dab with me in the front seat. He glanced to the passenger side, sensed her presence, the warmth of her body against his, even the familiar aroma of her perfume. Cheeks dampened, however, with the sight of three inanimate grocery bags stacked against the passenger door. He became acutely aware, once again, of the vacuous space which surrounded him after she died.

Mike loved Meg's medium length, wavy blond hair. He chuckled at her habit: having it highlighted every forth Wednesday at Bonnie's Beauty Center, her cousin's shop, a short walk from home. He often waited for her there, after work. So many things he would miss: child-like dimples when Meg laughed, her bright and inviting blue eyes, increasingly notable forehead wrinkles that, of late, bothered her, but added character, he thought; the turquoise sweatshirt she usually wore to the cabin; and the faded tennis shoes she dyed to match.

Before leaving home for this solo vigil, Mike hastily grabbed a dishtowel to wipe his eyes, after an upset that erupted when he noticed the neat stack of her folded clothes. Garments for the cabin, she kept them together in the hall closet, to permit quick breakaways whenever they left at the last minute.

A set of oncoming headlights spurred his thoughts. *Have to get on the move, back on the highway, keep on going, and spend some good time at the cabin.* He feared that, if he didn't and right away, he could dissuade himself from using the retreat they painstakingly built over the years—a future retirement residence—where they would have whittled away the rest of their lives. They both referred to the place as "Up North," from the day escrow closed in August 1975. Jennifer was but a toddler; Judith just finished first grade.

He started the engine after the close animal encounter and slipped Meg's favorite CD into the player. Singing as best he could and the tap of his left foot to the classics in Elton John's, *Greatest Hits,* raised his awareness. The music allowed him to focus on needed projects: things he could do to spruce up the cabin, prepare for fishing, and most importantly, to determine whether the Morris shack at the end of the old dirt logging road, might still be for sale.

Perched right on the Au Sable, old man Morris' property—a piece of imaginary heaven, ever there were such a place—captivated Mike since boyhood. His brother Wayne and sister in law, Nell, still lived nearby in the small town of Tawas, where they were raised, at the Lake Huron shore. Streams of local gossip wafted through the small grocery store Nell managed. Rumors hinted that Morris heirs might sell, after the family patriarch's recent death. When she realized their excitement at the opportunity, Nell struggled to get Mike and Meg inserted at the top of an interested buyers' list. "Could I actually go through with it now, without Meg?" Mike queried himself loudly. Then he buried his words, and went on to himself: *the excitement, anticipation, and the allure; could they come anywhere close to our dreams, without her participation?*

Mike and Meg always admired the oddly shaped slice of land, probably no larger than ten acres or so; they never checked. What counted was the enviable and isolated position it occupied, deep in a dense and verdant section of the Huron National Forest. Poised on a bluff, just shy of twenty feet above the meandering Au Sable—midst heavy growths of poplars, red and balsam pines, maples, firs, oaks, and yellow birches—the shack, as they called it, stood above a bend in the river that harbored huge brown trout. First taken there by his father, as a young and curious boy, his dreams of eventual ownership were born.

He grinned broadly at a pleasing collection of memories that flashed before him as might a two-act play at the old opera house. *Pop always described it as, "Da big pool ... only bend in the Au Sable, scooped by God, dee-rectly." He claimed it was the deepest one for miles in either direction.* Mike's musing turned to the old man who died more than twelve years before. He lapped at the clear remembrance, however, as if yesterday—the first time he put eyes on "the shack" and the enchanting scene it overlooked.

"Dere she is, Mikie, da spot where you'll fish from now on," his father said proudly, with an unchecked grin. They scurried down the bank to the first growth fallen cedar tree that allowed the bend to retain its depth, even in low water times. "You will never see a better series of fishing spots dan these. Dat one dere," he continued excitedly, as he pointed to the largest just below the shack, "dat's da one to dream about from now on … probably as long as you live."

Mike gazed with relish at the enormous log, stripped of its bark, bleached near white, and devoid of branches from countless high-water lashings. He viewed it immediately as the perfect throne on which to seat himself for a day's fishing.

"I blanched and refocused—crestfallen, though," he said loudly, and to his surprise, "when Pop assured me; big browns that hunkered in the nearby depths would spot my silhouette, long before I thought of climbing out on the dead tree."

His father's words rang loudly as he further reminisced. "Me Boy," he said back then, with the patience of a good math teacher, "you'll only catch Mister Brown by sneaking quietly down da river, upstream from the pool." He thusly referred to each brown trout landed, before he released lucky ones to endure for another season. "Den ya works down current; through da rushes, you will sneak unnoticed. Dat's where you'll learn to drop your fly. See dere?"

His father pointed to the wide girth of water plants, behind which grew no intruding willows or saplings. "Dat's where dey be a waitin'." Mike's head cleared with the sprouting of more vivid pictures: dusk, cool, still night air, and swarms of mating caddis flies fresh from their hatch. They came in clouds from protective trees, and flittered down to hover *en masse* over the water. He felt the sloshing, rancid-smelling muck as he stepped, softly as possible, through the reeds. New waders the old man gave him for his birthday that April left him proud; the sacred fishing secrets of the Gladdock family were about to be shared.

Awestruck, he watched his father, a burly laborer, though consummate gentleman fisherman, deftly tie an artificial caddis about the size and color of those that swarmed, to the end of the near invisible monofilament leader. The old man spoke softly, almost to himself, while he instructed his spellbound boy. "Now, swing your fly rod in an arc, Son. Stand straight and tall. Picture your hand, the center of a big clock. Point da rod tip over da river, to two-o'clock, swing it back to ten, and wait for da the fly to slip behind you." Mike felt the same tingle that excited him at the time.

"Now bring da rod over da river to two o'clock again, and let out da line as she stretches. "Dat line is heavy, but ya handles it as if a feather … keeps it from dropping to the water behind you and splashing. Mike watched without a blink, while his father repeated the action several times until, in the most beautiful arc he ever witnessed, the fly swung back at least forty feet.

Nary a sound, it leapt forward again, over the low willows. Like a shot; the floating line moved forward in a rolling circle across the eddied surface, and fell quiet. The tiny lure fluttered for a moment—live flies buzzed around it—then dropped and bobbed in a circle of expanding ripples. The seasoned fisherman explained, too, the danger of whipping the line in the back cast, and how that could pulverize the fly into a "dusty puff," he called it. "No dusty puffs allowed 'round here," he insisted, after which he blew bilious clouds of pipe smoke that hovered about him like ground fog over a frosty winter meadow. Mike still remembered the unique, sugary scent the freshly exhaled smoke imparted to the placid air.

The boy marveled as his mentor carefully twitched the tip of his feather-light, split bamboo rod, and imparted live movement to the fly. It vibrated on almost dark water and drifted like the real thing toward the sleeping log. He remembered gasping for breath when a black-spotted, yellow-orange and silver crescent shot into the air, a full two feet downstream from the vibrating feather insect.

Mouth agape, down the fish fell upon the fly. His father's pole sprung with the load; the fish swam for cover, and the old man set the hook soundly, with a gentle heave backward, as he took up slack line with his free hand. "We gots 'em today, Me Boy," he whispered, "yippi-eye-yay."

The fight began, and, on it went, as the sun settled behind the trees on the opposite bank. The new moon bloomed in the east, to the cries of two loons that basked in the oncoming dusk, on an upstream pond more than an eighth mile away.

An enlightening experience, that evening dished out everything Mike might have imagined about fly-fishing, and much more. Rare moments with his father, and others like them as years passed, he would never forget. Hopelessly snagged with the esoteric method of stalking the wary fish that night; never again could his father go to the Au Sable without his new and enthusiastic *protégé.*

Driving grew easier with the busy imagery that charged his senses. Mike reflected affectionately of the old man and breathed deeply, as he often did, to regain composure. Thoughts raced from that first fishing trip to the day he introduced Meg to the river … the very venue where he witnessed his first big one hooked and landed. As his father coached in his youth, Mike showed Meg the subtleties of hooking *Salmo tutta,* the brown, in that revered section of quiet backwater. So quickly, she learned to cast; she perfected the hard fought art, too, of proper fly selection, its size, color, and action, before its proper placement in the water. She took to the new set of skills like a pro. Mike questioned her in jest at the end of their first season fishing together, "Why in the name of the Holy Father did I teach you to catch more fish than I do?" He chuckled aloud at that memory for, deep down, he teased half seriously that his pedantic efforts proved almost too successful.

"I can't help it if I'm a fast learner," she quipped, then warmly nuzzled him in gratitude.

Mike wanted those days back. *The present is a danged nightmare. How could I have lost my best friend so early in our lives?* She became his closest companion for the hunting and fishing he cherished. His queries then turned to sacrilege and darker, while silent, wanderings. *Why did He take her like that? Has He no heart? Why did He make her go through so much torment while she withered away … a mere shell of herself?* Mike felt guilty when he blamed the Almighty, but for reasons not well understood, it made him feel better, added more purpose to Meg's life, and clumsily explained why she left it for the next horizon.

Maybe she's fishing right now, as I drive north alone, and feel sorry for myself. Yes, she is off to catch Jaws, when I think of her, the river, and fishing in the pool at the bend. He had to laugh at the many years they struggled to entice the one thought to be the largest trout in that part of the watercourse. Its almost grotesquely overreaching mandible offered good cause for the name.

They spotted the large fish one quiet morning, in a slow cruise, just below the glassy surface, about the same time as the first shark movie's release. Meg tried to entice it with everything in the creel and then some. Since the oversized fish first taunted her, she tirelessly worked the pools below the bluff, "With the tolerance of Job," Mike joked.

The polka-dotted lunker sported numerous flies and lures as facial décor, vestiges of many a fisherman's futile attempts to land it, once hooked. A skilled line-breaker, its oral jewelry became the easiest means of its identification, when the trout swam the quiet eddies or surfaced to feed voraciously on pockets of insects it gobbled down every evening during the hatch. Well into late river darkness, heavy slaps on the quiet pools from Jaws, and other monsters like it, echoed through the forest, and titillated the spines of the most bored of stalkers.

Caddis flies came and went each year in a few short weeks, usually toward the last of June. Fly fishing during those times delivered the most excitement and birthed the best hook-ups. For the remainder of the season, the larger fish in the river fed more on small crustaceans, minnows and crawdads, and were not so easily coaxed to the top. Mike and Meg then turned to their boat on Lake Huron, for summer salmon fishing.

He swerved to regain his track along the narrow highway's broken centerline, which brought forth more thoughts of the old Morris shack. Two-storied, at least two upstairs bedrooms, a well-equipped kitchen, propane heating, and a large stone fireplace in the living room; it seemed to offer all the amenities of a comfortable city home, including a full basement. They were never invited inside, but when owners were not around, he and Meg often helped themselves to dreamy window peeping, as delusions of future ownership kindled and fired in their minds.

Though a convenient distance from the nearby town of Mio, the twisty half mile-long driveway, almost overgrown with forest foliage in spots, appeared inaccessible to all but locals, and received little use. A makeshift cable gate at the Old River Road junction and large "No Hunting" signs deterred most motorists, even all-terrain vehicle drivers from the area. It appeared to be private property at first glance. Authorities admonished the Morris family, however, never to lock the gate without risking confiscation of their lease. Mike knew that.

Years before, he checked with Forest Service acquaintances about the purchase of a similar site on which to build along the river, in the same area, but was barred by a twenty-year-old moratorium that precluded new subdivision and construction. The coveted cabin would always stand out there by itself.

Since his father first took him, Mike ignored the signage and the gate. *Like Pop, we had squatter's interest, as far as we were concerned. We grew so derned accustomed to parking in the Morris' cul-de-sac.* He respected owners' privacy only when he saw their car at the shack. Those times were rare in the preceding ten years, which permitted fishing at the bend almost as often and whenever Meg and he wished.

Many more deer stopped on the deserted highway margins, the farther north he traveled. For some of the stubborn ones, he leaned on the horn to persuade movement. Except during hunting season, he found fascination just watching the tawny figures, and never tired of the activity through the summer months when he and Meg spent so much time at their getaway. He grimaced visibly, when he viewed the isolation he would soon experience, bouncing along back roads, and searching adjoining fields, using his high-powered spotlight, without Meg as his spotter.

Deer scouting evenings were special. She prepared gourmet finger food, and a carafe of hot coffee. We went on patrol before dusk settled over the rolling hills, sometimes for hours. They took note of evident population changes, and reveled at the rare sights of well-antlered bucks as they escorted new fawns from hidden game trails. *Wasting time? Idleness?*

Sure it was, most certainly. We often had no other distractions to keep us from animal spotting. Both of us craved the time thus spent: no phones or television; quiet talk, stillness, and just our closeness.

He felt the sudden movement of icy air about the nape of his neck. Earlier, he closed all the windows. His head suddenly cleared; it had to be her. Meg summoned him from his laments, as real as she ever was. Provoked, almost shocked by the sensation, he pulled his black Suburban toward the grass-fringed shoulder, pressed his foot to the brake, left the engine running, and tried to collect himself. Outside, darkness, isolation, and the forest stillness reigned.

He buried his face in his hands, and rubbed his forehead to clear what he discerned, when Meg spoke. "Michael," he was sure he heard her whisper, "the Paul Bunyan Café is just ahead, and they'll be open, Honey. Let's get you up to speed with fresh coffee, and a quick dinner. It's late, you know, and I won't have to cook."

Speechless, Mike shook his head in full disbelief. His mind ran at double speed. *She's here, dang it. All that sadness, just a terrible dream? We'll be together, once more, first night of the season. Another habit I will have to break: the usual pit stop for dinner. We ate there so many times for so many years ... a tough reminder.* Sometimes he begrudged the expense of dining out when the girls were young, and spare cash rare, but Meg would not settle then, for him to pass the small restaurant. She wouldn't permit a drive-by that night. He pictured her sleepy gaze, head against the passenger window, while she coaxed him to the roadside eatery.

"All right, My Dear, we'll do it." Mike had no options. He smiled, reached over to pat her thigh, and noted directly ahead, lights on the hilltop restaurant, less than a half-mile away. "I ... I just want to tell you that. ..."

An ear-splitting screech of tires that viciously burned on pavement, cut through the tender words his heart prepared to unleash. Staccato horn blasts penetrated an intervening instant of silence, and the deafening skidding continued. Mike squinted into the rearview mirror. Dizzying headlights flashed from low to high beams, and approached too fast from directly behind. Helpless—hands frozen to the wheel—Mike saw a toxic massacre about to take place in the milliseconds that followed. "My God," he screamed. "Look out Meg … look … get ready … look out!" He reached out his right arm instinctively to keep her pressed to the seat, locked his eyes closed, and prepared for the worst.

CHAPTER 2

———◆———

Time whisked backward, along with his reflections. Mike turned sixteen just four and a half weeks before. "As sure as my real name is Marcos Gladdoski, damn it all … your license is headed down da drain. You won't drive anything—anywhere—anymore—anytime!" Mike never saw his father so angry. "You can just walk 'round town for three months, and dat's it, Sonny Boy! Driving is all done." First generation Polish, the old man changed the family surname to Gladdock before marrying, to eliminate the ethnic twang. He usually found it easy, though, to expose his old country toughness.

Earlier that fateful night, Mike planted the family's 1953 Chevrolet pickup on the shoulder, but not fully off the lightly traveled roadway—for which his father issued many a stern warning—while stopped at Meg's house to see her to the door. They finished the last of too many embraces on the porch, when a speeding sedan rounded the curve from the west, its engine locked in a frightening whine. Absent any sign of a braking effort, the old blue Oldsmobile's driver lost control. The car slid on mist-dampened asphalt and smacked into the rear of the Gladdock truck, just off dead center.

Incredulous, Mike stood motionless, arms tight around Meg. They watched steam gush from beneath the crashing car's hood that sprung open with a creaking groan. Shattered head and tail light glass clinked to the pavement in a symphony of reminders that something terrible just happened

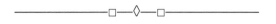

Solemnly, they stood in the small bathroom, for the showdown. Thick yellow paint curled in large peels from the cracked ceiling over the shower. Blotches of black mildew proliferated where plaster was exposed. Mike stared upward, then down at the white hexagonal tile floor, rust-stained and in need of repair. *The house was in shambles,* he thought, *but Pop won't get my help with it this summer.* Moist towels, different colors and disheveled, hung from the loosened towel bar. Spots of dried toothpaste bejeweled the badly chipped, dark green counter tile. The old man's arm extended dramatically over the toilet; Mike's almost new driver's license dangled between thumb and index finger. He puffed on his knurled corncob pipe as he spoke, and gritted yellowed teeth on the amber plastic stem. Lips, likewise stained from a life of heavy smoking, bore shady brown colorations at the corners. Mike would never forget the scene. *Clad only in undershirt and shorts, Pop was tired and he meant business.*

Mike's mother stood close by, though helplessly, hair freshly curled in short ringlets. Attired in a blue, floral-print dress—a wet dishtowel draped over her forearm. She looked concerned for Mike, over the tops of thick hexagonal glasses. Hands folded across her protuberant abdomen, she stayed silent, and while she looked detached, she watched with apprehension and a mother's empathy, from the hallway just beyond the door. Mike wished his folks and their small house in East Tawas would disappear from the face of the earth at that moment. Three months, no driving, spelled an impossible eternity.

He longed for little else but his permit to drive, for more than a year before that night. Assured it would be a ticket to escort Meg, the piece of paper granted him a more hip decorum at school functions and it might have been a ticket to fish in the woods, by himself.

Mike dreamed of the freedom it offered, yet before disbelieving and weeping eyes, it awaited a simple drop into oblivion. His carelessness may have been good reason to sacrifice the coveted license, but he burned with temporary hate toward his father, when the new permit fluttered downward as if a falling leaf, to swirl away in a vortex of flushing water.

"Daddy, I'm sorry," he said; his uncontrolled sobs interrupted by hiccups. There was no question about his determined father's resolve. He knew better than to argue, beg, or plead. He was in the wrong and deserved punishment.

Mike's senses bolted back to Highway 55 as fast as they took him from it. Braced for a collision, he writhed over repercussions of his youthful error, opened his eyes, and looked protectively toward Meg as the smoking tires shrieked and the vehicle closed in behind him. The smell of burning rubber stifled; the noise deafened, but no impact ensued as he anticipated. An older, bronze, Ford Excursion; he noticed the model immediately. A long-time General Motors employee, Mike disliked Ford's overgrown Suburban clones. The large SUV sported a temporary paper license in the rear window. It pulled to an abrupt stop along his left side. Secured to the roof rack, a green canoe covered a half dozen suitcases. When the passenger window whirred down, Mike dropped his window calmly, in hopes he could defuse the situation without an exit.

"Ya dumb sowmbitch! What the burnin' hell y'all a doin', stopped out in the middle of the road like that, for Christ's sake?" The male driver barked far louder than necessary. Stretched forward to look around his female passenger, who stared ahead and said nothing; the other driver let Mike have it again. "Ya damned bumpkin. Drunk or something? Jesus, you could have killed all of us."

Mike looked out his window at the pavement below his door. The guy drove too fast, but Mike did err. A careless stop in his haste, he did not pull completely off the road, and by quite a margin, too. His father's past admonitions rang too clearly for Mike not to offer, at the least, a passive apology. He then turned up his palms, nonchalantly hit the button, and closed his window. He kept his cool as the Ford spun its tires, and raced into the dark. Its Washington D.C. license frame explained the driver's curt and rusty attitude.

It wouldn't have ended like that in the old days; no second thoughts; no resistance. I would have jumped out of the car, first to initiate the attack through his window, when the jerk would have been the most vulnerable. Brother Wayne with me ... well ... would have beaten Mister Smart Arse to a pulp and asked no questions.

Fisticuffs came naturally to the Gladdock boys in their younger years. Never to turn tail on a scrap, they practiced pugilistic moves more often than necessary.

That was another time. It seemed so long ago; Mike easily reflected how bellicose he and his brother could quickly become. A shouting match evoked a slugfest in seconds, and usually, with little provocation. Patience granted by age, however, he was pleased it took as much as it did, to act out his anger. Very soon after they met, Meg worked without relent on that facet of his personality.

Mike wanted her with him in the worst way. He recalled opening day of school in the eighth grade, when he first took real notice. She assumed her lady-like persona through that summer and wore a yellow short-sleeved sweater over a white blouse, with a ruffled lace collar; when she walked into Mr. Kelsee's English class in the fall. *Seemed just overnight that she wore lipstick, had breasts, and legs, too, that glowed like marble sculptures below her short plaid skirt.* Meg metamorphosed into a veritable princess in just over two months. Though he knew her before, as nothing more than a noxious pest, she smote him that day, and he fell hopelessly in love.

Born Margaret Mary Kinder, the youngest of three, Meg was second generation German. *Those large blue eyes, her gangly tussle of bright blonde hair, full lips, and high cheekbones; a smile that devastated, severed all protective resistance I mustered toward the opposite sex.* Mike's guard deflated with the sight of her. No matter his antics, though, and the clumsy means employed to attract her attentions, he was just another nuisance male at first glance.

Meg's parents owned the butcher shop in East Tawas and since she spent much of her after school time, while she studied or worked there; it evolved into one of Mike's regular stopovers. He had to detour more than a country mile to make the call while walking home following after-school athletics. At first, he received few of her attentions. The added trek, though, became an obligatory part of his schedule and one, without which, he feared he could end up on the back burner. He worked at it voraciously until she found him irresistible. It was a rare evening when Mike was not easy to manage on arrival home, after spending but a short time with Meg; hence his folks paid little mind to his late arrival for dinner.

If he turned up after school with his typical surly and combative attitude, especially after the demise of his driver's license, they jokingly suggested he take a walk to the Kinders' store for a "Good boy transfusion," his father called it. Later that year his folks grew to love Meg as if she were their own, and the two became an inseparable pair.

"Gol dern it! Such good years they were. The summers …" he spoke aloud, again, to his surprise. He took a deep breath, and saw humor in his patent smile with the clear recall. "Long summers at the lake: swimming, canoeing down river; such great times." Sobered by his carelessness, he ascribed his distractions to the strange conversation with Meg just before the Excursion appeared.

He drove slowly, not wishing the memories to drift, but the "Bunyan" lay just ahead; yellow marquis lights flashed on the huge arrow-shaped sign in front. To his great consternation, parked in the next space, sat the bronze Excursion with the brand new green canoe on top, and the D.C. license frame.

What now? Do I go in and face the music? Will those out-of-towners recognize me? Have I enough self-control to avoid a confrontation without Meg the mediator by my side? What can I say, but surprise the couple with an apology, for heaven's sake? He was roaring too dern fast, but I stopped well on the roadway.

The café door swung wide with a nudge of Mike's right arm; it banged sharply against the stop, and at the same time, a bell that hung from the jamb accented his arrival. Like the movie lawman who entered a disrupted barroom in old western movies, glances from the waitress and the six patrons at the counter fast turned his way. For a moment, he stood by the door, a self-styled spectacle. *They're likely wondering why anyone would drive this lonesome road so late, by themselves. I wouldn't look so odd if Meg were with me.*

Two locals in soiled work clothes seated next to one another, turned heads back toward the kitchen and resumed their conversation. The young man and boy, a chair away, continued with their homemade deep-dish apple pies. That left the couple at the end of the counter for him to survey. Tables were empty at that hour.

Has to be them. Mike looked vexingly toward the couple. *He's the one who swore at me; the big shot over there with the crispy army fatigue jacket, and matching cover.* Mike ambled to the counter and sat in the red vinyl covered chair next to the boy. He noticed stiffness in his back; a creeping numb feeling that extended part way down his left thigh, and a newer pain that persisted through the preceding hour of his drive. He looked to his right again, to size up the couple from the Ford.

The man appeared about fifty-five. No visible stubble and attractive, he seemed solidly built, and sat unusually straight in his chair. *Jackass! What did he do, shave in the danged car? Look at that bull neck.* Thick and muscular, extra skin piled in folds against his collar. Unlike so many locals whose hair extended to shoulder level, his was close-cropped in the back and around the ears; the dark brown was graying. Sideburns cut high and neatly squared smacked military.

Mike noticed the tightly laced, spit-polished combat boots, into which his baggy camoflage pants were stuffed. A *derned redneck, that's what he is ... a smart-mouthed, military redneck from Washington D.C. Maybe on leave from some paper pushing, creampuff, high paying, do-nothing job ... up here to vent frustrations on us.*

"Hello, Ina," Mike uttered softly to the lone waitress. He tried not to attract any more curious glances. "Only coffee, but, would you shoot a little of that sweet whipped cream of yours on top for me; just this once, please?"

"Why, it's Big Mike! Just this once, huh?" she laughed. "Finally came north to check out the fishin', did you? Where you two been?" She looked tired. Her starched white cap slipped to one side and coffee stains marred her wrinkled pink gingham dress. She wore tennis shoes with thick soles, one of which, with loose laces, slapped on the floor when she shuffled behind the counter to pour refills.

"Where's the boat, Mike? Been expecting to see you two parkin' it out front, whenever you passed by, due most any time now. And how's your Meg doin'? She asleep in the car?" Will you be at the cabin for a while?" Ina gnawed on gum as she spoke, and it crackled noisily. Mike found loud chewers irritating. He did not know how to open the soreness in his heart, and sheepishly looked at the verbose server. He squinted, as if that would bring forth lost words to fill the pregnant silence.

Mike's aimless gaze caught her attention; then she froze, worried she offended him. "Hey, I didn't mean anything by. ..."

"No, no," he said and quickly waved her off, "no offense at all. Meg is … she's … ah … dead, Ina," he said more loudly. "It … it ah … yes … happened last week. I've lost her … lost my dear heart to cancer, I did." Mike nodded his head while he foraged clumsily for more words, as if to prove the point, and stared sullenly at the wall when he spoke again. "We thought she was doing well there, for a time after the surgery and all, the radiation … chemotherapy." He removed his glasses and wiped his eyes with a red print kerchief jerked from his back pocket.

She stared, listened with shock; her jaw dropped open; she could not respond.

"Died at the hospital in Flint, at McLaren Medical Center. You remember; she spent time there earlier. They were heroic but she just couldn't fight it any more." He could see that theirs was the only conversation in the room; the other patrons eavesdropped as best they could.

"I am sorry. You two were such nice fixtures up here. Such a fine woman. I loved her smile, the soft way she spoke to people, and her enviable dimples. You were so lucky to have a real woman, yet one who loved hunting and fishing as much as she did. Always looked forward to hearing of her conquests when you two stopped for dinner on the way home, Sunday nights, mostly. What are you going to do?" She stopped the queries as suddenly as she began them. Ina realized Mike's hurt, his difficulty to speak, and turned to the couple from the Ford to pass them a check.

The man in army garb took a good look at Mike as though he recognized his voice, not his face. He and the woman got up and strode toward the door. A few steps closer to Mike, he spoke gruffly, with the same thick drawl, "Hopefully, Buster, y'all have a little more driving courtesy the rest of the night; more than you showed us back there. You've got a real problem, Soldier."

The stranger's gray eyes glared and his forehead wrinkles smoothed. The two grimaced at each other for a moment. Then the woman—very attractive, and far younger, maybe ten or more years, Mike thought— tugged at the man's elbow and gestured him toward the exit. Mike's pulse jumped; he felt a pounding at his temples. His hands shook and adrenalin pumped like it did in former times. He said nothing, though, closed his eyes to gain composure, and swung the chair around to the counter. Yet trembling, he nervously slurped the rest of the whipped cream from his coffee.

Mike felt the same cool, wisp of a breeze on his face again, as he did in the car, before she first spoke.

"Just ignore him, Dear." Mike could swear he heard Meg say with confident calm. "Pay him no mind. He's just a stupid wannabe from the city. We've seen plenty of them come up here, make trouble, and think they can get away with it. He probably has a Confederate flag tattooed on his rear end." Meg's unusual yet helpful words came to him as if she were there, and, as quickly, drifted away.

Mike gestured to the waitress with a wave of his hand. "It was nothing, really, Ina. I stopped back there to rest a bit, and stupidly left half the Suburban on the roadway. "The guy sped from behind like a bat out of Hades and dern near ran right over us … I mean me. He stopped, cussed me up a streak, and down the other, then took off like a band of lightning again."

Tires in the parking lot driveway boiled in the gravel and interrupted his tale. Mike heard rocks fly and impact with metal—probably his metal, he thought—but he stayed seated, felt beaten, and ashamed. The Ford plowed onto the road and the skidding continued while its engine roared into the distance.

"A-hole!" Ina said, just above the refrigerator's purr. She looked at Mike sympathetically, "Big city nutball."

Mike smacked down his coffee money and a dollar tip at the register, stretched his hands high, sighed deeply, and exhaled a whispered reply. "Thanks Sweetheart; always great to see you."

"I'm so very sorry about your wife, Meg … yup … she was the best. If there is anything I can ever do, just stop by. I'll probably be working here 'til I drop dead in my tracks," she quipped before thinking. The waitress fluttered a hand past her blushing face, blinked her eyes, and bit her lower lip in embarrassment. He moved to the door and, with a clink of the bell, melted into the parking lot.

Gol, how many times will I have to go through the pain of explaining details to people who haven't heard? The immediate future will unfold to so much more sympathy, I can hardly stand the thought of it. Mike grumbled at the mud splatters on the right side of the car, left by the vengeful Excursion driver, but smiled, too. The rude gesture would have caused an uproar in younger years; he might well have reacted more violently. "Gol derned coward." He slammed the car door with a bang.

The drone of his oversized lug tires, and the dotted yellow line that streamed toward him from the almost invisible road ahead required more of his attention than he wished. Still, he found space and drifted back to the final days Meg spent at McLaren, Room 303, where she passed the last two weeks in rapid deterioration. He hardly recognized her, the way she changed from day to day. Notable weight loss, disappearance of the usual cheer in her eyes, and her blue-white skin color, belied shallow assurances she might have been doing better. IV feedings failed to support her emotional or physical needs for sustenance. She always enjoyed her meals. A hearty eater, however, she managed to preserve her youthful figure through the years, with little difficulty.

During Meg's final hospital stay, Mike stopped at the hospital for long visits over lunch, and late each afternoon, too, after the whistle blew at the GM pickup truck plant in Flint. Supervisor of Electronic Installations—his handle since the sudden, but long-predicted closure of the Buick plant in June of 1999—he gave thirty-eight years of his life to the assembly line, before he became a plant electrician. Not long after, the foreman's job opened, a slot he filled upon his predecessor's involuntary commitment to a mental health facility.

Alcoholism on the line was an ever-present threat to assembly workers—more the rule than the exception, it was said. Extensive overtime hours, coupled with intolerably repetitious duties, predisposed plant workers to substance abuse and other work-oriented personality disorders.

Mike remembered the day he began union-sanctioned counseling for his own well-seated drinking problem at the early but still serious stage; it took its toll in his relationship with Meg and the children. He shuddered at the thought of so many late night homecomings before which his crew and he drank and played pool after work at one of the bars outside plant grounds. Too often, he forgot the late hour and the number of drinks consumed.

Week-by-week, month-by-month, his indiscretions increased, until Meg finally sent him reeling. A steamy Friday, the date remained indelible in his memory: June 24, 1977. They planned an early departure up north to the cabin. He arranged for departure from work at noon to help Meg pack. Fly-fishing on the river filled their agendas. The caddis hatch was in its prime.

Mike argued that morning with the union steward for his group. The men were promised overtime work in the ensuing weeks, but management withdrew. Ben Artiff was not at fault. The steward was only the messenger, but Mike lit into him with a vengeance until they threw blows just outside the production line. Mike received a citation that, he feared, would affect his chances of advancement. He attended night school classes to prepare for the higher position, became morose over prospects of losing it, and fell easy prey to the heavier boozers in the crew. Beer began to flow at lunch.

Drunk beyond measure and hours overdue, he managed to navigate his way home, but found the house dark and unoccupied. That never happened before when he poured himself in the door at an inordinate hour. A sobering note on the kitchen table explained it all. He knew the words by heart:

Dearest Mike:

You broke your promise for the last time! The girls and I have left and will move permanently up north to the cabin next week. I spoke with Attorney Bellows in Flint. He assured me this afternoon that, if necessary, he will prepare a Restraining Order to stop your visits without the court's approval. You and your drinking have caused this, Mike. Nothing else can be blamed; not work, me, Jennifer, or Judith. Start a program Monday or kiss your family farewell. I am so very sorry, but I'm left with no choice, in the girls' best interest and mine, too.

Love always, Meg.

CHAPTER 3

Mike swerved the Suburban when he saw a porcupine wobble over the shoulder on the other side of the road, and was stimulated to review some vivid recollections that revisited his consciousness. He froze from the shock as if levied the day before. The brief note Meg composed nearly killed him. Her stern warning became the turning point in his life. He signed a Standard Commitment Agreement at work that week, and his Alcoholics Anonymous program began. Not once, thereafter, did Mike succumb to so much as rum flavored cake. His distaste for the effects of alcohol persisted to the moment, as he wound his way north—his first stay at the cabin without her.

Memories of his scare that night, he might have carved in stone. Faithless, he stood in the kitchen, lighted only by a single bulb floor lamp in the adjoining den, and read her words repeatedly. Yet sickened in retrospect over the hurt he caused, Mike pictured her sadness while writing the thought-filled, brief, yet punitive missive. Amazed by the strength she garnered to call the shot as tough as she did, with two small children, a dog, and a part time job; "Her courage, Meg's unlimited guts gave her the confidence she needed. Such a trooper, an unbelievably strong human being, Meg answered every challenge."

Wandering thoughts snapped him back to the highway. He slowed the car and gazed affectionately at the spiny, arch-backed animal. Such an odd design, he thought, *its muscular tail of quills dragging behind like a sack, as it patiently plods its way along the road; no apparent concerns.* Small, beady eyes glowed in his lights; the porcupine turned toward the car before it changed course into a heavy clutch of berry bushes. Mike enjoyed the docile, slow moving creatures, despite their lethality to aggressive hunting dogs, from whose pain wrought noses local veterinarians kept busy in the summers, extracting the tenacious, sometimes life-ending quills.

He pondered the last deer season opening day with a welcome grin. He approached the blind he left in the same spot year after year, in the center of a clump of five brushy red pines. It appeared an animal was at rest on the pile of old horse blankets he used for padding. He moved closer, saw the quills of a very large porcupine, and yelled, instinctively, to scare the intruder away. He saw no sign of movement, crept still closer, and finally recognized from the smell that the animal had long been dead.

A spiteful hunter—evidently resented his blind's choice spot along a well- traveled deer trail—shot the poor creature, and tossed its remains on Mike's blankets. Not satisfied with that, the culprit took everything of value Mike stashed for the winter. Angry at the unseemly incursion, after disposing of the mess, Mike restored the lair to its former comfort level and took a nice buck from it that season.

Not far from the site lay the most formidable array of blueberry vines in the area, clustered in season with their succulent, purple fruits that begged instant ingestion when ripe. Mike cringed. Another special time with Meg saw its last. Early in the summers, it became a ritual, an ingrained habit since they began dating—berry picking to their heart's content in the open glades beneath the conifers. A can of whipped cream, coffee, large cereal dishes and spoons, and Nirvana was easily touched.

"That was, until stomach aches ensued, as they always did," Mike growled aloud, fired by the recall of a particularly severe one he experienced after eating too many of the irresistible morsels. *Oh, those blueberry pastries! Gol dern! Where will I ever get a pie like those she baked?* The recipe, from Meg's mother, was never duplicated by anyone. *It'll be impossible to go there, too. How could I do that without her? How can I eat until I get sick? I did it partly for her, so she could laugh and chide me about it later.*

He remembered a portion of the poem he wrote for one of her birthdays to memorialize the uniqueness of the berry experience:

We went to pick blueberries in the woods today,
We often stopped to look for them along the way,
When, all at once, Meg called out, 'twas certainly no surprise,
She always saw them first, what with her eagle eyes.

"There they are," said she,
"They're waiting near the car.
They couldn't be much closer; don't you see?
"We didn't have to go so very far."

Quickly piling out, each staked their boundary lines,
We couldn't wait to savor this tempting, newfound prey.
We dropped down to our knees and fell upon the vines.
Would we maintain this pace for the remainder of the day?

We pummeled on the lacy green, where the luscious royal jewels ...
("If we eat too much, would we be breaking rules?")
Of the verdant forest floor could easily be seen.
"Are there more around the bend?" She screamed.

More verses came forth, but he lost the beat when the Highway 65 sign sparkled in the headlights at a dip in the road, less than two hundred feet ahead. He slowed quickly, and with a slight squeal of tires, made the left turn north, a marker for the final ten miles. "Tomorrow, I'll clean up the yard, sweep the pole barn, and vacuum the house thoroughly, as Meg would have done. I'll spend the day tidying and, if there's any space in the afternoon—yes, I'll drive to Tawas to see the realtor, or pay a call on Nell and Brother Wayne."

More than anything, though, he longed to explore possible availability of the old shack by the Au Sable. Mike imagined its comfort, the feeling of isolation, snoozing in a rocking chair on the Morris cabin's private front porch. *The added expense of another property has not really been on the agenda, but there is nothing to keep me in Flint...without Meg and her friends. I would sell our house in a heartbeat, to purchase the shack. That would work. I have to try; so green with envy, I've been, far too long.*

Though lonely without Meg, it would feel like a kingdom. Never again would he have to worry about an interruption to the Morris family's privacy, even though the river was publicly accessible along the bank, below the bluff. He had to have that beautiful piece of property. He had to do it for Meg, too. Mike wound down the last hill to his cabin, breathed a sigh of relief, turned into the gravel driveway, and stopped by his front steps to unload.

Lots to think about tonight, maybe too much. Why did I insist on bringing everything the first trip? I won't fish this weekend; just short of opening day; hardly time to sleep, with the long list of things to do. It'll take me twice as long without Meg's help. She did so dern much, and now, it's up to me or it won't get done.

He sat still in the car and gazed at the dark cabin. Pain sulked in his heart. It seemed strangely lackluster, forlorn and blank, being there alone. *It seems so wrong to be here without Meg.* He shivered from the night's chill, and the isolation.

Sure glad I never took her good company for granted. She would wonder what I did out here, just sitting, an hour or more. An owl's plaintive hoot broke his musings. The call was answered with a higher pitched refrain, one hundred yards away or more, "Probably the female," Mike muttered with a shrug. He piled up grocery bags and gear for the first trek up the steps to the front deck.

The round, steel table for outdoor summer dining, almost unrecognizable, piled with shards of pinecones; served as a trash can for the busy squirrel nest in a crook of the maple directly above. Dried leaves and pine needles padded the faded deck planks. *They'll get a coat of the red stain I brought.* He kicked a pile of browned, throwaway newspapers stacked against the screen door, fidgeted with the lock with biting hesitation, flipped on the light, and stepped inside.

Tossed back and forth by the mild breeze, the hanging lamp over the door cast dancing ochre shadows on the front grass, which already grew long. It promised extra difficulty to mow the first time; the steeper slopes beside the parking area fostered a greater sense of obligation. "This is not going to be easy, gol dern it," he said. He started to climb the steps with a heavy stack of books, un-read magazines, and bed linens.

They fell from his grasp when he lost footing on the dew-dampened third tread and tumbled to the grass below. "Damn 'em; sons of my britches; hell's afire with 'em; dagone it!" Mike sat on the bench he built into the first landing, buried his face in his hands, and shed some tears for Meg, for himself, too, in the lonely, self-serving moment; embarrassed, and critical of the stern language he used.

Mike zipped his jacket, tipped one of the patio chairs from the table, and brushed away the debris. Paused to settle his upset with hot coffee, he grasped the large mug tightly to warm his hands. He breathed slowly, regained composure and revisited the first trip to the cabin during the previous spring when Meg fell on the stairs, in the dark, at about the same time. She carried an armload of his hunting supplies to the front door. He heard a crash from the basement and could tell from the cacophony that shotgun shells, pistol ammo, and his reloading rig fell victims. He listened intently.

Astonished ears picked up an unimaginably stinging song of four-letter epithets that wafted through the front door and slithered downstairs to his location. Fearful she was hurt; he worried, also, about the equipment she dropped. By way of the language, though, first of its kind from her in years, he debated whether to stay out of the firing line, or rush to her aid.

For the best that he stayed away, she ended up in an uncontrollable laugh at herself and the spontaneous release of such strong words. Profusely apologetic, and exhausted from the long night of unpacking, she fell into his arms shortly after for a lengthy and memorable session of late night romance.

Meg did have a sense of humor compared to none, gol dern it! I feel like cussing a blue streak myself, as she did that evening. Meg thought it so funny. Seems but a short time ago, yet it's been a year. She was sick through much of last fall ... never did get loose of it ... poor thing. He poured a second cup of coffee and tasted her soft lips. He felt the warmth of her old sweater when she hugged him from behind, and whispered for him to come to bed. The smell of her perfume, the one he bought for her use in the hospital, filled his nostrils. He asked the store clerk in Flint for the newest and most alluring fragrance. She let him test it on his wrist; he liked the scent immediately. Meg cried when he un-wrapped it for her. She felt unworthy of a thoughtful gift at a time like that; a decisive moment for both of them, which signaled mutual awareness that her horizon for survival noticeably narrowed.

"We'll get that shack, damnit," Mike asserted for her ears, knowing she would forgive the slander. "We'll talk sometime, too, from the old Morris shack porch, surrounded by swarms of caddis flies, while they find mates, and head for the river pools. We will not accept a substitute for that property.

Sheepish from his denial, he sagged into silence and continued the stream of disarrayed thoughts. *The girls and grandchildren were so distraught during the memorial service. Could hardly stand it. I felt as if I lost the entire family, somehow, that afternoon. Things weren't the same when we gathered at the house for dinner afterward. The girls seemed different; everyone did. Did they blame me? I've got to get through this. I have to get past the sadness and the guilt I feel. Can you help me with it, Meg?*

"Can't you please help me?" he then pleaded audibly and startled himself with the sudden desire for chatter. He felt a nippy breeze around his neck. It whirled and lightly disturbed the clump of leaves at his feet, then stopped abruptly.

He froze when he heard her say, "Go on inside, Dear, just trot upstairs. The water's hot by now. I'll get your shower ready. Only one more trip from the car and we have everything. Pay no mind. I'll fetch it. Now, go on; go on in before I take a switch to you," he heard her poke laughingly, from behind the door. Just go on now, upstairs with you. Think of me when you snuggle under the down comforter. Night-night, Mike."

He looked around wishfully, and though he found himself alone, he felt comforted by her words. Was it an illusion or was she there? Years of AA counseling taught him ways to detour around many tangles, one of which he took to heart early in the game, shortly after his rehab program began. That discussion broadened his understanding of perceptions. He recalled the night well. A therapist led the group, composed of men and women toughened by years on the assembly line, too much drinking, and innately narrow minds.

The session focused on the subject of reality, He learned with some resistance, to accept what one apparently experiences at a given moment as the product of what is there, blended with and through the filter of a lifetime's experiences. The sum of all the input, he slowly learned to accept as reality, as opposed to exerting willful efforts to change one's perception or hide from it. No more dodging delusions thrown on by liquor or even attitude; he discovered a new gospel. He finally became comfortable with the newly discovered notion that one person's observations or evaluations could well be illusory to another.

Mike marveled at the discovery, too, that each person's editing processes, furthermore, were capable of altering events they saw before them, to permit as many different reality views as people present. He took that to heart, too. It allowed him to see things from alternative viewpoints, to become more empathetic, understanding, and tolerant of others' behaviors. He grew more aware of his own in the process.

Strength in his relationship and improved communicative abilities with Meg ensued as a result, and the foreman job opened as added reward. His curt, impatient attitude slipped from its former precarious forefront, and he ceased fist clenching as the first step of misunderstood intentions. People said he looked different after that night, and later encounters on the subject. He loved Meg even more for luring him toward the discoveries, and she slowly learned to trust him again.

Mike thought, as he pulled covers to his head, that it might have been easier to accept her demise if their relationship soured like the marriages of so many middle aged friends who only stayed together for their children, or, later, for economic reasons. *If only we had no common grounds outside the children and grandchildren. If we had not done so much … practically everything together, from church to hunting and fishing, it might have been a more pain-free separation, and I wouldn't hurt like this. I might have felt relief at this very moment.*

He awoke to soft glows on the master bedroom walls, canary-white tendrils of the waxing gibbous moon in its transit across the crystal sky, filtered into skeleton shadows by bare tree branches just beyond the window. It could have been a Halloween scene, painted to frighten the onlooker, and frighten Mike, it did. He rolled over with a start, looked at the clock he forgot to set, then at the macabre shadows, and sat up to establish his surroundings before he dropped back. "Have I been sweating, for heaven's sake?" he asked, and patted the pillowcase. "Was I crying? It, it's sopping wet."

His watch read 1:45 AM. He slept less than two hours, and languished at the time that remained to pass the night. Then the dream, which awakened him, merged with his consciousness. He wasn't crying. He perspired in abject fear. Aghast at details that came forth, he remembered he decked himself out in full fishing garb: old chest-high waders, willow creel, a coffee Thermos™ in his small backpack, and his father's old nine-foot, split bamboo rod with the red aluminum automatic reel.

A large landing net dangled from his waist. Meg made the meatloaf sandwiches he stuffed into the side pocket of his vest. The other pouches, he crammed with all his needs for a few hours' fishing along the riverbank. Very dark in the shade of densely foliated evergreen trees; no one else was in sight. He sloughed along the shallows, and paused every few steps to cast a caddis fly. The real ones still swarmed wildly over the calm, pewter river surface. He heard fish—good-sized ones, he knew—feed greedily in their jumps into the still air.

A move to deeper water, he increased his back cast for the longer stretch. A nibble teased his senses, then another and, WHAM! A bruiser with an empty belly struck hard. His drag whined, he whipped back the pole to set the hook and, with all the self-control he could muster, sighed long and loudly. The line slacked. *The gol dern leader broke. Probably my knot on the fly,* he thought. *Maybe the leader was defective. The fish wasn't that big; pound and a half, possibly, no larger.*

Mike hesitated, reluctant to continue, but strained, nonetheless, to dig further into the dream. Thoughts ran more freely. He felt a sudden tug at his waders, and the strong, silent pull of the current around his legs, when the sub-surface, undercut bank gave way. He slipped in water to his neck; his waders filled, and the swirling coils of the Au Sable took him in tow.

His trusted friend, the river, showed surprising anger. Mike did not swim strongly, and with the gear he carried, might have been as much lead. For a short time, he felt the bottom bounce along, and then nothing, as his head slid slowly below the surface. He coughed reflexively; water filled his nose, mouth, and then his lungs.

He caught sight of Meg, perched on the large log that bordered their favorite pool. She gestured solemnly, said nothing—but waved her hand with arm extended, as if she rode a parade float—while Mike helplessly slipped beneath the icy darkness. As he sank downward, startled, he disavowed the last view of her. A sardonic grin spread across her face.

He awoke panic-stricken, when she pirouetted happily around, skipped like a young child, up the bluff, and darted across the grassy meadow to the shack.

What the devil was that about? Why would she flush the grin and such a sinister one at that? Why would she have been happy I drowned? Why did she do nothing to help me ... just let me sink? He knelt on the pillow, propped elbows on the window ledge above the headboard to gaze at the moonlit trees, and briefly sought the unusual prayer for consolation. It felt phony and disbelieving, if not blasphemous. "How can God, to whom I now appeal for help, be the friend I need?" he asked the night sky. "He took Meg from me. There was no discussion, no terms, no questions or warnings; absolutely nothing prepared me for this loss.

"Why do I ask for your help now?" he continued, in search of answers that were not there. "I have no understanding of all this, no matter the priest's contentions that Meg, 'Will be doing God's work,' he claimed, 'for the rest of eternity.' "What about me? Gol dern it! What about my loss? Doesn't anyone give a good bucket of stove bolts about that, beside Big Mike?"

A hearty shiver, he wondered if he could ever fish alone on the river with Meg gone. The soothing wave of apathy that followed, made the answer easier to see. "Considering the possibility something could happen, as it did in the dream, what's to live for now?" He questioned the stoic pines outside, before he dropped back to the security of the heavy quilt. "Meg walked off and left me there. Why should I care about life at this point?"

CHAPTER 4

Meg's words in the hospital, taunted him, the final day of fourteen in the last admission. The weather turned cool that afternoon, but the diving sun's glow provided welcome, though transient warmth to the corner of her room where he stood, next to the window, as they talked. He looked coldly, though, at the parking lot, keenly aware that he would not take her to the car in a wheelchair as he did after prior stays. Soon he would walk out by himself, maybe with one or both girls, and would not return to visit the following day at lunch hour.

At last, alone, absent the distractions of a roommate, a brief opportunity existed for more frank conversation. "Sweetheart," she said weakly, but with her usual charm and beaming smile, "will you go to the river soon? Will you go for me? You won't neglect our Au Sable, will you? Just because I won't be there, I don't want you to turn away."

Mike remembered the awkward feelings. He needed an escape, some time, and distance to respond. "How can I ... without you?" he finally replied. "What does the danged river offer me, in your absence, that the gutter in front of the house in Flint doesn't provide? It can't be the same up there, if you're gone for good." Filled with feelings of futility, even contempt; his eyes wetted and his lower lip quivered uncontrollably while he continued.

"Sure Dear, sure. I ... I ... can't let that out of my life, as I'll have to do with you." He looked hopelessly at prospects of losing her, even though they thoroughly discussed her imminent demise. "The river is a part of me," he went on, "a big part. I could never step away. I'll do everything I can, to preserve our memories; that, I assure you."

"You're just saying that to please me," she said with dimples still aglow, but feeling a bit patronized. "Speak to me like you mean it. You will go back, for me, and fish this season at the bend, won't you? Try again this year for old Jaws, that big hunk of a brownie we've never landed?"

"I will." He wiped his cheeks with the back of his hand, but it was not enough. He reached for a tissue. "Yes, I'll keep after the old son of a buck. You know I will. I'm worried I won't find the woods the same, if you don't get well and come back with me, if you. ..."

She interrupted and scolded him lightly. "We've been through this before Honey. I'm not going home, and you've agreed not to burden me with something I can't accomplish." Meg lay there, looked plaintively at the ceiling, arms flaccid, veritable drains to the intravenous catheters that bypassed her inoperable esophageal blockage with life-giving nourishment. She no longer swallowed solid food. The oxygen cannula draped loosely beneath her nose hissed slightly as she exhaled against it. She whispered almost in synchrony with the heart monitor's throbs, "I want you to go up north as soon as possible after I. ..."

Her eyelids briefly slipped closed and she inspired with difficulty. He stepped to the bed and grasped her hand. "After I go, I want you to hop right on to the cabin, clean things up for the season. Clear out my clothes and let the kids decide what to do with them. Continue our dream for the Morris place ... the shack. You go through with it for our family. Promise me, OK?"

She changed the subject once more and rambled on to things more mundane. "Don't forget my dry cleaning ... lots of stuff there. You can work on the boat ... get things shipshape for the lake. The grandkids will enjoy it more this year." Mike lost control again, but kept it hidden inside.

It was too much to face—not knowing when it would come—when she would slip from his grasp. Maybe he would be too late to be there in her last moments, he worried.

"Honey, stop it. You cannot keep on like this. Let's talk this through," she said strongly. "The river is your. ... She closed her eyes and ceased speaking for nearly a minute. Her mouth dropped, and then she snapped to her senses, as if shaken by something. "Honey, I just had the most terrible premonition today. I saw you … that is, I saw you … oh, never you mind now … probably the morphine."

Meg fell silent, and when she collected herself, sharply admonished Mike to be careful driving, to be cautious when he waded into the deep river water, and to stay wary of impending bad weather when he took the boat on the lake.

"You must be careful … alone … by … out by … yourself."

"What do you see?" he quizzed her anxiously. "What is it?" He waited with anticipation while she closed eyes and contemplated a response.

"There was a frightening image, something happened to you, not sure what it was exactly—some sort of thought about you joining me … but … but way too soon. So creepy; I felt a cold chill, and the thought stayed with me for what seemed a long time. Something came up which I have never before seen or felt … ever!" I saw you in an accident, maybe with the car or in the water. Don't know what to think, but I'm frightened, Mike. I would not want anything to happen. You have a full life yet to lead, even if it is without me."

He stared at her paled eyes, wordless for a reply, leaned forward quietly, and hugged his wife.

Lucid, yet confused, she seemed genuinely affected by the experience; however, she went on, this time to shed jollity on whatever she alarmingly visualized. "My Dear, there's one more point before you go home. Should you manage to get hold of the shack—if it proves to be for sale—may you soak your head in the big pool forever, if you ever take another female there … teach her how to fish as you did with me so long ago. I'd turn away and never come back."

Mike, in his unmitigated remorse, took what she said much too seriously, earnestly wondered what provoked her to speak that way. It wore on him after he left the hospital that night. Headed home, he spun her words repeatedly, and concluded with the mistaken, but very real perception, that she wanted him to die also; to join her in the beyond they both called the hereafter. The priest, too, used that word at the funeral. At that moment, it sounded far too comfortable.

He returned from his deep reflections, back to the bedroom. *That's where my spooky dream must have originated, from her comments that day at the hospital. I could have taken them to heart. The mind does conjure confusion sometimes. Why did she just walk away as I drifted down river? Doesn't make sense; she would never do that, or would she?* He warmed with the sun's early climb above the distant hill to the east, but his blood ran cold.

Just after the turn into the driveway at home on her last night, he received the dreaded cell phone call. The clerk in the hospital nursing office explained that Meg lay *in extremis*. He rushed to her bedside and waited there but briefly, before she let go. "Don't forget, Sweetie," she said, as her hand fell limp in his. "Enjoy our Au Sable River for me this summer, but don't you dare. ..." She smiled, though feebly. The monitor ceased its rhythmical pulses. The steady hum that followed, signaled her departure.

He stayed there more than an hour before he paid heed to nurses' pleas, that he return home and rest. Her last few seconds, the toughest in his life—were far worse than the early morning of his father's demise. Younger then, and more immune to hurting inside, he nearly keeled from that experience, too; the loss of his mentor for the ways of life, and the outdoors. His father, prime source of Mike's strong moral code, poured the foundation of his integrity, his work ethic and, to his own frequent regret over the years: the resolute stubborn side he inherited.

———————□—◇—□———————

Chores done, Mike packed his spotlight, two cold-cut sandwiches, a Thermos™ of steamy coffee, and some cookies for later. He pointed the Suburban north for the twenty-mile trip to the Au Sable. No time to call the realtor about the Morris shack, as busy as he was all afternoon; he planned afternoon deer spotting along unpaved roads not far from the shack, and a dusk dinner on the bluff above the river bend, to watch hungry browns jump to feed.

The long way, northeast through the small town of South Branch, allowed passage through many thickly wooded sections. Sparsely housed, they were replete with grazers. He drove slowly beneath an overcast leather sky, frequently paused to smell the emergent spring and to scrutinize the many deer that stretched their legs in the gusty breezes of day's end.

A group of the animals entered a clearing from the forest margin. They seemed small, even timid, and hungry as he supposed they would be after such an enduring cold winter. Cautious bucks waited longer than usual to show themselves, and stayed hidden in the cover until their smaller counterparts assured the way was safe. *"The cowards. They will always do that ... allow their naïve little ladies, even fawns, to be the guardians of their own safety. Typical males,"* Meg would have joked, *"boys are all alike; they push their families into the hunters' realm before they step onto the grand stage themselves."*

Gol dern, I do miss her out here. Mike lamented, as he scanned a group with binoculars. A brute of a buck shook its rack at another nearly his size, in the company of several females that fed on traces of fresh leaves. Meg usually searched field margins while Mike drove slowly along rutted dirt roads. When she pegged an interesting subject, she'd exclaim, always in the same way: "Mike, Mike! There, there! Stop. Stop! Quick, now quickly!" He laughed at the duplicitous words she employed for emphasis, whenever excited.

Mike dropped the binoculars to his lap, grasped the wheel with both arms, and leaned his head forward, to rest his chin on his hands. A cold, aimless stare, he peered into the bowels of thick, scudding clouds, afraid of what he would see. He exhaled deeply and sighed, closed his eyes to the immediate vision of a memorable spell of lovemaking they talked about for years afterward. For some reason, though, it never quite repeated itself after that day. Such a keepsake, they seemed unwilling to allow subsequent levity to replace it.

Several summers before, it happened not far from where he stopped. Darkness fell. "Probably about nine o'clock," he surprised himself, when he spoke aloud. "Meg brought that blanket and the chaise cushions from the cabin."

Later she admitted that she felt increasingly heated with amorous designs since she arose early that morning. They approached a clump of trees, closer than most to the secluded dirt road and she beckoned Mike to stop. Meg rushed out of the car, bid him to stay inside, and unloaded all the accoutrements herself, including a picnic basket, with dinner.

Curious, he sprung to the birch grove when she called minutes later with an unusually seductive voice. "Mike, Honey; I've a little *soirée* planned," she said. Poised like a nymph of the glen, she sat, stark naked in the center of the blanket, summer flowers in her hair, a sparkling lemonade in each hand.

Mike did not anticipate the unusual welcome, and hesitated so long, she had to summon him with curled index finger as though she called an undisciplined child. She had his clothes off in a flash, and left him with a collection of memories that spurred his libido whenever he later thought about it. Meg took pride in the "picnic," she later dubbed the interlude whenever they nudged one another about it. A mischievous grin opened with his wonder, what provoked the appetite she displayed while she experimented with amorous positions to which they were not accustomed. The thought of doing anything else in the fields after that memory, seemed anticlimactic. Anxious to check the river anyway, he made a beeline for the turnoff to the Morris shack. Close to an hour of daylight lingered, to absorb sounds of the forest, and songs of the rapids just above the bend.

The power company finally has a stout gate across their access road. He slowed to admire the new addition at the last turn-off before the Morris path that lay just ahead. *Must have received a budget increase this year. Maybe my phone calls and letters did some good.* He recalled the old gate's dilapidated state shortly before hunting season opened the previous fall, when he angered at ruts left by off-roaders who passed around it.

He complained bitterly. Unauthorized use of the easement allowed unrestricted penetration into that section of National Forest, and unduly threatened the deer populace in the area. The new yellow steel pipe barrier, fringed by chain link fences that extended to the heavy tree lines, blocked access on both sides. He drove on, grateful for his proactive stance.

"Good Gol a-mighty," he exclaimed aloud. He skidded to a stop at the small clearing on the left, where the dirt path to the Morris shack opened to the paved road. He backed up in disbelief. Yes, to his rear lay the large granite boulder he kept nicely white washed, and the nearby utility pole. Both assured it was the turnout he wanted. "There's the derned tower, the boulder with my paint. It's the right place, all right, but, what in the name of heaven is going on here?" He checked the mileage on his odometer—one point six miles from the yellow gate— just as it lay, always.

"Who. ...? What. ...? What the Sam Hill is this? My God, what's happened here?" Certain his glasses were clean, he rubbed his eyes, in doubt of his senses, rolled down the window, and leaned outside for a clearer view.

CHAPTER 5

———◆———

The new sign nailed to a large maple that fringed one side of the narrow turnoff, sent him reeling. The only break in the dense thicket along the road in that vicinity—brazen—it smacked insult, grated Mike like non-melodic trends of a dissonant fugue, endless bars of Stravinsky to the ears of a Mozart lover:

SOLD BY
RED PINE REALTY
We have other listings!
Give us a call and see.

The spanking-new posting was shock enough, worse than a painful jab to the jaw. The real injury, though, came from a smaller, more carefully prepared panel just below, that fostered the upheaval and churning he felt deep inside:

Attention!
This is now private property!
No trespassing, hunting, fishing or, vehicular traffic!
Brig. General Homer Payton Claybourne, Owner

The mailbox, bright red no less, secured to the other gatepost, brought him to a hotter boil. Newly installed, four-inch diameter steel pipes set in concrete, supported a ranch-style gate of rough-sawn poplar.

Someone padlocked it. Mounted in the center of the gate, a fancy, gold-leafed, carved wooden sign read:

CLAYBOURNE FARMS

Mike stayed in the car, virtually stunned by the sight. *The gol derned path has been graded. The gate ... what the hell's afire ... and who is this Brig. General Claybourne? What's he done to my, to our old diggings?*

"Meg," he called desperately, "Meg: some help here!" Mike turned off the ignition; the engine ground to a halt. Powerless, unable to contain himself, he poured coffee, and awaited guidance or direction. His hands convulsed. He needed something, some words to steer him through the offensive discovery. Angry beyond description, his fists chenched white, arms grew stiff, and his toes curled involuntarily. *What the devil do I do now? Do I sit back and let this SOB, this scoundrel, whomever he may be; take over my entire existence, my only reason to live? Should anyone have that much power? I've seen the maps. Dern it! This is our National Forest. What does this Claybourne think he is doing? I will not give up my river, not without a danged fight!*

A quick glance in the rearview mirror when a truck rounded the curve and its lights glared; he saw his face contorted, beet red with fury from the surprise. His usual pale-tone cheeks flushed, and the lobes of his ears nearly glowed. He felt the hum of a strong pulse, packed up by an adrenalin rush he barely controlled. Terribly frightened with the level of his upset, he counted heartbeats as the second hand of his watch ticked fifteen. "Thirty—five ... times four ... that's one hundred forty. Good grief ... one hundred forty ... twice normal. I would have to split logs for thirty minutes to muster that heart rate.

"This'll kill me; it surely will," he screamed to the stand of trees before him. "I can't take it. First, Meg goes and then he takes away my river. Don't steal the only thing left for me, the only thing with meaning. Leave me something." Mike's knuckles glowed even whiter from his grip on the wheel. He withdrew, poured a second cup of coffee, and found his arms and hands still trembled, weakened from the shock. More shakes, chills and lightheadedness followed.

No less than seething, he could not recall such an alarmingly steep temper level since Brother Wayne and he, in their mid twenties, were hopelessly drunk in the Pine Bough Inn. A duo of truckers condescendingly scoffed at their tale to the bartender about an almost mythically huge buck they shot. One insult after another passed back and forth, until the Gladdock brothers lost it and Wayne dealt the first punch, a stinging smack to the jeering drunk's jaw. The loudmouth did the unthinkable, and remarked negatively about Wayne's long, blond hair.

Much taller than his stocky brother, Mike lunged for the stricken chap's larger companion, and knocked him to the floor with a powerful swing. Without relent, while holding him pinned, Mike punched the man into total submission. The beers he consumed urged continuous pounding, and his persistence increased with the number of blows. He soon became unaware of the damage he caused.

"Bro … Brother … Brother … hey … don't maim him! Hey," Wayne screamed. "Goddamnit, knock it off Bro. You'll kill the poor sucker in cold blood." Wayne slapped cupped hands on Mike's ears to startle him from the beating he dished to the near-unconscious victim, whose face bled profusely. When pulled off the near limp remains of the former smart talker, Mike began to sob, realized the heights his outburst took him, and how dangerously close he came to inducing irrevocable harm. Wayne usually finished their altercations. Nell, Wayne's fiancée at the time, and Meg stood outside, petrified at the outburst. Both threatened to end the relationships in the event of a repeat performance.

Recall of the incident from the perspective of an older man, far more learned in the ways of self-control, startled Mike. He relived his sudden and all-too-familiar temper losses, spurred by the shocking sight at the roadstead. It took many deep breathing minutes to regain composure.

Memory of another fiery tantrum filled space in his worried mind. About nine years old, otherwise robust and daring as a boy, Mike arrived home early that Friday. Crestfallen, he lost much self-esteem from a repeated beating he suffered at the hands of Billy Hoodman, the school bully. Smaller than Mike, but more aggressive, Hoodman propelled himself to the enviable position of campus tough guy. He overpowered once again that lunch hour, and Mike's relatively new bike and the cycles of others, became targets of his intimidating actions.

Billy took a year's rubber off the tires, while he endlessly skidded on the pavement in front of the cafeteria. Awe-inspiring in the eyes of anxious onlookers, many laughed unsympathetically at the hasty despair the bicycle suffered.

Mike angered with the degradation, made worse by the bully's sarcastic cackling, but his supplications to stop, fell on deaf ears. He had to halt the abuse, and landed a surprise smack to the stomach, then a cut to the left cheek of the teaser, which forestalled any retaliation. That night, though, he received a new set of tools to prevent such ridicule, after relating his humiliation to the old man, who paid dearly for the new bicycle at Christmas time.

Marcos "The Beef" Gladdoski, an amateur prizefighter in his post-teen days, won many a bout during the depression, when he ventured into the din of Detroit's east side bars to earn extra money for the family. "No Gladdoski needs to take crap from anyone," his father said, his way to console young Mike after the bicycle incident. "Does ya understand dat, Son?"

They sparred for several hours behind the garage until Mike's punches were unarguably honed to a fine edge. He left the tutoring session with renewed vigor, a burst of needed confidence, and a left jab that later became legendary.

The following Monday afternoon after school, his nemesis made a big mistake. Hoodman tried to abscond with Mike's bicycle again, and prompted the freshly coached boxer to turn the tables. The beating suffered that afternoon bordered on brutal. Mike lashed into the former aggressor with everything his father shared, though he added to the equation, a yet unseen and freshly discovered determination.

Crying as he did so, he swung fists in a blur while seated on his victim's chest, until several classmates pulled him away. Still he struck the shocked, bloodied, and very frightened opponent.

Pushed to intolerable frustration by the ominously worded signs, Mike pondered over the old but stirring memories of physical violence. He thought about his reactions to the challenges beforehand, and how reticent he was to enter each fracas, until taunted beyond his resistance level. *I don't like violence. I don't even like it when I feel violent, as I do now, and I don't wish to become a violent person again. If only I could find a way to calm down inside.*

"I'd like to kill the man who set up this gate," he then growled to his surprise. The arteries over his temples swelled. He rubbed them and flushed red again. "This, this Claybourne, bought the property out from under me. The gol derned realtor sold me out, too. Don't I matter at all? Nell said I was at the top of the list. What happened to my name? Did someone just toss old Mike out the door? Who got paid off here?"

Must calm down and try my pulse again. It had better be back to normal. Fingertips on his wrist, he counted the seconds. Again, his heartbeat remained strong. Too rapid for his inactivity, the fiery pulse confirmed uncontrolled emotions. *I'll drive right over the derned gate, up the road to the shack and, if anyone is there, we will just have it out. What I would give to hear their story, the tale of this guy's purchase of 'Claybourne Farms.'* His teeth ground together; Mike took several more forced deep breaths, counted beats again, and rethought the impracticality of trespassing.

Don't want to tear up the Suburban to satisfy curiosity. Nothing gained by doing several thousand dollars of front-end damage. How about the winch? I could wrap the cable around the post and tear it out. The gate must be illegal anyway. He checked the forest margins past the posts, decided there was insufficient room to drive around, and dismissed that mode of entry.

More than an hour of rumination, while he wrestled his upset, darkness finally enveloped the woods and ushered in a modicum of calm. *It's too late to do anything. I'll go to the Forest Service first thing in the morning, see if they know about the security gate this general whatever has installed. Best I do that, than take matters into my own hands at this hour, and in my state. No telling what I would do.* Mike felt pleased with himself, and his ability to transform thought processes from vengeance and contempt, into acceptance, however temporary.

Back in the car, he poured the last swatch of coffee. The tremors in his hands mediated; strong pulsing in his chest subsided, and the facial blush nearly returned to its usual pale. Mike scuffed nervously at his moustache, reset his glasses, and rustled his hair.

A light breeze encircled him, and he cooled more. The tight grasp on his wrist quickly became apparent. Expectant of her appearance as before, Mike waited for Meg's words. Tears alighted on his upper lip and fell from his chin.

"I am worried about you, Mike, very concerned. I saw your festering anger, that Big Mike madness of so long ago. Oh, I sensed your fear, hurt, the rejection you must have felt when you drove up to that hideous gate." His chest heaved, though more slowly, once she spoke, and his eyes dropped closed. He feared looking her way. "Who is this guy, and what does he think he's doing?" she asked. "Can he really get away with this? You'll look into it for us both, won't you? You can't let him take it from us."

Mike's composure remained tenuous. *I will not. Derned tootin', I won't. He's not going to get a piece of this Michigander's life without good reason. Nell and Wayne will have some ideas. I will see them right now, tonight.*

"Now, don't you let yourself cut loose, like you did that evening at the Pine Bough. I'll never forget that. Promise me, won't you?"

He nodded patronizingly.

"Promise, Mike? And, you watch yourself, too, with that wild-eyed brother. The two of you—angry at the same time, same place—spell trouble."

"I'm calm now," he said, while he started the engine. "I'm settled, and, yes, I promise." Mike turned back toward the south with accelerator floored in a rubber-burning mockery of the daunting signage. "Sure, I'll take care of it; I most surely will." The comforting touch on his wrist loosened and slipped away.

CHAPTER 6

"You should a plowed right through the goddamned fence! For Christ's sake, what the hell's the matter with the fricking idiot?" Wayne bellowed. His brother's face soiled to maroon, as deeply as did Mike's—a common trait both inherited from their quick-tempered father. Wayne stretched his big arms wide, from his perch on the tattered gray leather chair that faced the river stone hearth in his living room. He never mediated his use of epithets as Mike managed to do, and he was a little beyond his normal after-work alcohol level, to make matters worse.

Wayne finally quieted, contemplated for a half minute, and then smiled broadly. His face turned childishly cherubic—cheeks still rosy and dimpled—his usual countenance. "We should take the old Jeep right now and just friggin' run it right on through. To hell with what might happen to the old jalopy. I still have the snow blade on the front end. That would do, wouldn't it?" he asked, as he snapped the top off another beer. Wayne shifted his cowboy hat back and to the left, to better see Mike, who stood by the fireplace, arm propped on the red oak mantel.

Wayne's hair, usually uncombed, corn kernel blond, but close to gray around the edges, fell just above his shoulders. His yellow straw Stetson, soiled from many a year's wear at the garage where he worked, became a trademark. Usually seen with what most thought a four or five-day beard, his overused razor insured the ever-present stubble. Several years junior to Mike, he had no post-high school education, which, despite good intentions, left him woefully inarticulate, insensitive, and impulsive. Liked by most locals, though, he always added jollity to a gathering, and was always quick to join any foray in behalf of the underdog.

"We can't go and do that, Little Brother. It will not work! Jesus Crisp, do we really need jail at our ages?"

Wayne's understanding wife, Nell, interrupted sarcastically. "Well, you both got a free ride to the pokey after that night at the Pine Bough. You sure haven't forgotten that. Everyone in town heard about the beating you gave the gravel truck driver. Made the papers the following week; columns featured both your mugs.

"Don't you remember?" Nell tossed good common sense into things before they got out of hand. "Anyhow, Wayne, you couldn't hit a fly at your age. My heaven, your bad knee would cave in anyhows," she added with a cheerful titter.

Wayne knew she was right. He underwent stomach ulcer surgery in January, which forced a month's work lay-off; the tricky left knee was next.

"So, how ya doin' this week, Honey?" Nell queried Mike. Sympathetically, she noted his unfocused gaze, how his eyes saddened from Meg's death, and tried to settle things by changing the subject. "Is it real tough without her? Have ya gone to the cabin yet or did ya go straight to the Morris place?"

Mike appreciated her empathy. A gentle woman, and, though not particularly attractive, she was a much kinder person than Wayne deserved. "No, no … stayed here last night," Mike answered. Flashbacks of the unpleasant dreams clouded his response. "I was there, Meg's gone, and it was tough. I am beat down from all the work we would usually share on our first day up for the spring. You know how that is."

Nell continued, "Well, the sale of the Morris property was quite a … ah, surprise … went fast … right after the old man died. The agent said there would be a waiting list, but it was pre-sold, ya know. I gave him your name last fall, but he kept no list, he finally said." She continued with hesitation, fearing the story would further upset Mike.

"Apparently, yes; the man who bought the land fished there years ago and remotely knew a family member. A while back, he expressed interest in buying at any price, if a sale ever occurred outside the family. The younger Morris daughter … only kid left in the area. No husband and a rack full of kids to take care of, so, keeping it wasn't an option for her."

"That led to the probate attorney making contact with this character. Whoever he is, paid cash … right away, he did," Wayne filled in solemnly. He pressed air with his tongue through the space between his upper front teeth. The *thweeth—thweeth* sound he made, always irritated Mike. A habit Wayne exercised when angry or fearful, it stemmed from his dipping days. Nell included no tobacco chewing in her list of pre-marital requisites and the dips, at least, succumbed to a quick ending.

"What did it sell for, Nell?" Mike asked. He ignored all else that was said, including Wayne's mock spitting.

"No word, 'cept he stole the place for a ridiculously low figure."

"Damn him! That was yours, Mike … *thweeth, thweeth* … just plain yours," Wayne interrupted, "the sonofabitch, the lousy, stinking sonofabuck. I hate to tell you this, but. …" He stopped, looked worriedly at his wife, then to the floor, and turned back to Mike who paid more attention with Wayne's dramatics. "They're going to live out there full time, the no good slickers. They will never navigate the path in the deep winter snows. City types; what are they thinkin', for Christ's sake?

"They'll be marooned when it really packs up, won't they?" Hail from out of state somewhere, from what we heard. Jesus, Mike, everyone sort of knew you and Meg … I mean you … oh … just can't get over her being gone." Wayne looked at Nell for help.

"Don't worry about it, Brother. I do the same thing with Meg, and her absence. I was with her when she went, but she. …" Mike blushed at the admission. "She's not really gone, seems to be with me, shows up, and talks to me sometimes. I'm not imagining it." He caught hurried and skeptical glances the other two exchanged, and continued. "Oh, I know it sounds crazy, but when I hear the voice, feel her hugs … this strange breeze blowing around before she speaks; well, I can't just ignore her when she surprises me like that."

Wayne and Nell sat spellbound a few moments, and then Nell replied. "No matter if it seems strange, Honey. Just go with it. You go right along with it."

Wayne looked strangely at his brother, for he was not particularly self-aware and hadn't a clue what his own thought processes really were. Still a problem drinker at times, and hopelessly irresponsible most of his employed life, he worked irregularly as an auto mechanic in a sloppy, run down garage at the outskirts of town, since army discharge in his mid-twenties.

Wayne's singular accomplishment in the military, if not anytime before, or after, was the attainment of high rankings in marksmanship. Selected for sniper school, which he completed at the top of his group, years of daily practice in the enviable specialty bred him well for the hunter he later became. He indulged in the art as often as work and family allowed, and quietly ignored rules to poach an off-season animal here and there. Mike forgivingly turned his head from Wayne's irreverent indiscretions. The victim of too many overindulgent years, yet hardy by any standards, Wayne still cut an impressive figure, spoke with an intimidating and arrogant air, and considered loyalty a lifetime maxim, perhaps to a fault, for those he loved.

The Gladdock brothers stuck close together while growing up, like their father and his older sibling, and remained united in their anguish over Mike's loss of the Morris property. Wayne also pictured Mike owning it someday. It would have given him access to the surrounding land for deer, most any time the fancy struck. "After all, it would be Big Brother's," he boasted to hunting friends, who licked their chops with envy at the thought of such an opportunity. "Abundant acreage of that fertile forest would provide more venison than we could ever eat."

Mike thought angrily about the signs, the gall exhibited by the new owner and, worst of all, the idea someone would live at the end of the Morris' dirt road. Even if the gate eventually came down, it would not work for him. His love of the area expanded with the Morris' reduced use of the shack; it was available much of the time to Meg and him. The limits of brown trout they took, in and near the pool above the fallen tree, filled his visions like they loaded his creel over the years.

The vast and endless supply of caddis flies, natural food for the spooky swimmers, further haunted his thoughts. There were other stretches of the river where the curious paucity of insects resulted in a corresponding absence of fish. Never, though, did that happen in the big pool or, for that matter, in the shallower ponds just upstream, where the river's course swung more to the north.

"No fear, Big Mike; we'll get the suckers. Mark my words. They haven't heard the last of the Gladdoskis," Wayne said with his crackly, country-style voice. For added emphasis, he used the family's Polish surname as their father did, whenever frustrated or angry. "They won't get away with closing that road, either. How could they, with you, my brother, in such a state of despondence.

"Ya see my trusty Mark V Sportster hanging up there on the antlers?" Wayne dramatically turned his gaze to the hunting rifle. "I'd put the sonofabitch in the scope's crosshairs if he ever threatened to shoo me off the property." Mike knew Wayne's pride and joy well, and loved shooting the old Weatherby himself. Every year Mike had to watch his brother spur his choice of deer to a wild run, and then, while on the go, drop it easily with a perfect shoulder shot. Wayne never missed the most difficult moving targets.

"Aw, c'mon Waynie, knock it off. I know that derned rifle in your hands is the epitome of accuracy, but it's for game—not people—for cripe's sake! Don't even talk like that. Your sniping days are over, and they have been for forty years."

"He's a barrel of hot air. Ya know that, Mike," Nell interrupted with a bored expression. "All smoke and no fire." They laughed, Wayne opened another beer, and the modulation of his boasting increased proportionately. "I swear, the bastard's not going' to get away with this. I'm only concerned because you deserved the old place, Mike. No one else should have access to it. You know that and so do I, by good God a' mighty. If Meg was here, she'd say the same thing; now wouldn't she?"

"Yes. Yes ... she'd ... she would, Brother. Oh, yes she would," Mike admitted, "but she's not here, and that may spell trouble. I have no one to reel in my temper. You're certainly not going to be of help, with your talk of putting a hole in the feller's head. I wish you'd quit thinking like that. I shouldn't have come over and fired you up like this."

Wayne stood slowly, wobbled a bit to gain his balance, reached for the rifle, and lifted it from the mounted deer head. He handed it carefully to Mike, who loved the feel of the finely designed piece, a .300 caliber specimen of perfect balance and craftsmanship. One of the better guns made, it served as the quintessential deer rifle. Mike pulled back the bolt and a live shell ejected. "What the Sam Hill are you doing? This thing's loaded!"

"One in the chamber, three in the magazine, Mike. I always keeps it on the rack like that: shoot-ready. If I sees a good one down there by the fence, he goes to the freezer. It's my property all the way to the creek, and I'll do what the hell I want with it. *Thweeth, thweeth.*"

Mike shook his head in disapproval as he stood to go. He thought ill of Wayne's bad habit, to bag game out of season. "OK, you two; I think I need to head for the cabin. It's late and I've had less than a perfect day. Sorry to keep you up so late … do appreciate your homework on the Morris place, even if it didn't pan out in my favor."

Cradling the Weatherby in his arms like a baby, Wayne stood in the dim off-white light on the full width front porch, and waved, until Mike turned onto the paved road outside the fence, and headed west.

"Nellie, my dear," Wayne said, when he turned toward the open screen door, "I just have something of a fightin' urge to handle this situation for Brother. He's in a peck of hurt. When he found the Morris place out of reach, it was like loosin' Meg all over again. We just couldn't tell him on the phone or, God forbid, at the funeral. I'm real worried about him, all alone up there at the cabin, and that to think about. What's he mean, Meg spoke to him, touched him, and all? More than a little creepy, isn't it? He isn't goin' crazy, is he, Nell?"

Wayne patted the powerful gun before restoring it on the deer antlers and, this time to his wife's concern, whispered, "Yup, this baby's goin' to do some talkin' while that smart-assed, frickin', thieving out-of-towner does some walkin'. We're just going to have to get ourselves all real nice and acquainted, now aren't we?"

CHAPTER 7

———◦◆◦———

After the time spent with Wayne and Nell, Mike's inner tensions were only minimally relieved. He lay in bed and stared blankly at the ceiling, deeply concerned that Wayne, loose cannon of the clan, might do something unpredictable. He knew how easily his well-meaning kin could generate troublesome contempt from within. *Such a lovable, harmless guy, but a few booze bullets in his gun, and he's not so cuddly. He's downright scary; that's what. As he used to be: calm as a sleeping cat one moment; next, a raging, searing, out-of-control Bengal tiger in a cage.*

Dancing figures in the Julie Bird painting Meg hung on the bedroom wall, unlighted by the cloud-veiled moon and barely visible in the dark, seemed to Mike a forlorn duo—not as they were when they beckoned Meg that summer day at the gallery in Laguna Beach, California. She said the vividly draped couple, while abstract, reminded her of unabashed gaiety, frivolousness, and carefree fun, emotions she and Mike ignored too often in their hectic schedules. Meg insisted they played too hard, and too much for decent working people.

What did she meant by that? Why did it take on such a negative connotation? Why was playing too hard, a problem? Isn't that what we're supposed to do in our leisure time? What is leisure time? Have I misunderstood its value? He waxed philosophical, craved intelligent discussion, and sorely missed Meg's contribution, the way she challenged him to think about feelings and deeper truths. When they did talk seriously, it was usually brief, just before they fell asleep, entwined in each other's arms.

Mike felt the hint of a breeze; the curtains tossed about behind him. There were no open windows. Zephyrs of cold air awakened his senses.

He snapped his eyes closed with her softly whispered words. "You never got what I meant when I suggested we ease off the play, did you, Dear?" Meg asked. Owing to Wayne's earlier concern and disapproval, Mike feared her reappearance in a way. He draped the quilt over his head with slightly trembling hands. Yet with interest piqued, he listened from beneath the covers while she continued.

Meg spoke with a determination rarely demonstrated. "You were always an achiever, a performer, a nose-to-the-grindstone kind of guy, to an awful fault some of the time, I must admit. Yes, you rushed to relax. Michael, you actually hurried to gather us all up, drove non-stop to the cabin, and then you would build, build, and build. First the cabin, then the barn, garage, the basement, and, finally…who knows? Was that really relaxing? No! Not for a moment, certainly not for the rest of the family, it wasn't a kick-back pace."

He stayed covered and withheld reply.

"Sure, here and there you'd take breaks," Meg went on, with continued persistence, "but that would be a three hour drive to scout animals, fish for several hours, work on the deer blind, reload rifle and … shotgun shells, tie flies or something else animated, and compelling. You know what was missing, don't you? We didn't talk as much … sit together … think … chat about intimate needs. OK, call them, 'girlie things,' as you or dimwit Wayne might have argued.

"You rushed from one activity to another. The passion with which you approached everything else, prevented a closer relationship between us. Yes," she went on, as if he disbelieved what he heard, "yes, it's true. Wasn't your intention, I am sure of it; but you pressed onward, and involved yourself in so many things. Your days and nights offered but rare spaces for feelings, or contemplative thought.

"Oh, I joined right in, failed to heed the signs, so I can't complain. I am in a position, though, to help you with your life, so you're equally comfortable with silent, unanimated, and uninvolved moments, hours, maybe even days, or weeks. It's time, Mike, smell the flowers … just this once.

"Only now, from the universe beyond, do I see the folly of our ways. Don't you remember our 'picnic' several summers ago, when I got the feeling, spontaneous intimacy was long overdue, there by the side of the dirt road, behind that grove of birches? Surely you haven't forgotten that, Michael," she teased lightheartedly.

"Don't you remem. ..."

He could not help breaking in, but he did reply submissively. "Do you know, I was just thinking about that, tonight," he replied, "on the way to the river, right past that very spot?" *How I wished you were there with me, and how deeply I missed you. Did I ever wish we took more breaks like that? I can only. ..."*

"Sure, I know you wanted me at that moment, but. ..."

"How did you know what I was thinking, Meg? You scare me. I was on my way to the bend, to watch some hungry browns jump to feed."

"Oh, I knew. I'll know your most private thoughts. If only I understood before," she sighed, "back then, it could have been more fun to talk about, to discover just between the two of us. You enjoyed me there, helpless, and buck naked, didn't you? Just the flutes of bubbly lemonade and my silly smile?" He pictured her on the green blanket, surrounded by tall spring grass, wildflower blooms all around her, face aglow in the dusky sun.

"Why didn't we do that again and why not before? Why didn't we treat ourselves regularly to that kind of intimacy? Do you have any idea what we missed? Think how imaginative we could have become, if we considered expanding sexual experiences together, as important as developing our economic base, the size of the house, our cabin up north, and the toys we accumulated.

"Along came the boat and obligatory fishing on the lake. Did that ever eat into our time! We became slaves to the preparations, time out on the water, and the clean-up that always followed. All of it carved great swaths through available hours we might have had, to develop closer emotional ties, for a better balance of our inner needs.

"We hid from it, Sweetheart. I know you didn't miss it at the time. Men don't always feel that absence; but I know you do now, or you will soon. Look at your thoughts since I left this earth. Only now do you think of intimate times, when we talked frankly, not about politics, work, Jennifer's welfare in California, Judith and Fred, the grandkids; but us; our special, personal needs. Isn't that right?"

Mike remained mute, but unhesitatingly agreed with what he heard. Drops slid from the corners of his eyes, down his cheeks; he continued listening.

She ran wild with her solo audience, and maintained the vigil without losing a breath. "I wonder what would have happened between us if you initiated the closeness of which I speak, if you wound down the commitments to your many, many diversions. We haven't begun to talk about golf, My Love. That's another story.

"I could have stymied your efforts," Meg went on, "discouraged you from sticking your neck into more things. Too many times, though, I wrapped around distractions the very same way: night school, kids' interests, the fervor of our off-work projects, my relatives, and the rest. The rest … your … oh, your drinking was the rest: the single greatest barrier to our really loving one another the way we might have, during those important times."

What is she going to do, punish me for the rest of my life for my past excesses? I know too well, how sadly that affected my availability, how I hid from myself, how distant my willingness to see and feel my aliveness became.

Meg's talk continued, "I appreciated the change in your choices when your recovery began, and I knew you worked hard for the steps you took. You became more sensitive to my needs, to your own, those of others, and you backed off some of your more compulsive behaviors. Yet, we still kept up the morning-to- midnight distractions, didn't we?"

Mike felt an urge to respond again. "All right, those years are gone. What can I do to make it up to you? Is there anything. …?"

Sharply, she cut in, tried to make it clear. "Honey, it's no longer for me that you do anything in your life. It's for you and those with whom you relate. Very important you learn from this; it's why I am here. Remember, though, I am only the messenger, not the one with the ideas. If I could claim copyright to the solutions, I would have brought them to your attention years ago. Alas, I have just received the wisdom.

"It began at MacLaren, in the final throws of my struggle," Meg went on, "in the chill of that hospital room, without you there. A stream of information flowed as if floodgates opened. I was too weak to share the discoveries. Then I left you, without a shred of a notion where I was going."

Mike remained mystified with the time that passed, the depth of this strange conversation, and how admonishing it seemed. Yet he stayed calm, relieved, and energized by her frankness, and her views of some of the shortcomings in their lives. It was at her risk, he reasoned, for he might have reacted defensively, and with well-practiced retaliation.

Certainly, he felt an internal shove to make her wrong, to raise his hackles, employ his ego, but that would have ended the session. *Gol dern, she isn't being paid to help me, to make my future more forgiving. Give her a break, Mike.*

He felt a soft finger press to his lips, to restrain him from speaking aloud. "Nothing needs to be said, Sweetheart, and you don't need to build defenses. I am not condemning you. I want you to learn. It's my job for now. Your frothing anger tonight at the river … well … ahem … quite worthy of condemnation, it was. You nearly boiled over—steam arose—you were so red hot. Just think of the repair cost to the Suburban if you followed the urgings of that inner voice, and rammed the gate. Maybe you should listen to mine for a while, not your own.

"Mind that brother of yours, too," she warned sternly. "I watched with worry, when he held his rifle like it was an old friend, ready for a new task. Be cautious of him. You know how I love that man, but your Wayne: alcohol, anger, and that gun of his—a sure fire recipe for no-good pie, My Sweet. As your daddy used to say, 'Ya doan wanna eat a piece a no-good pie, if'n ya doan have ta. Just ya leave it in da pan for da next guy.' She relayed the very words his father frequently spoke, in his inimitably gruff voice, and with the same accent, drawn from his Polish parents. An uncanny caricature, Mike remained quiet and humbled.

Suddenly, he felt lips press to his, familiar lips that found his throat, his sensitive spots. Warm breath poured over his body. Ecstatic, he relinquished resistance, succumbed to the writhing above that held him down and enveloped his consciousness in dreamy tremors, which his past connections and preoccupations with projects would never have allowed.

Mike opened his eyes, expectant to see her there. He sensed a tickling eddy in the room, and then heard her faint, parting words, "Take good care and feel, now, what you pushed aside so often, so you can appreciate the value of taking time for seemingly foolish spontaneity."

She's right. We did miss so much, but, why did she just discover this? Why didn't she share it with me before ... before she. ...? If Meg felt she missed so much, why did she stay with me? I certainly wasn't boring, but I wasn't exactly intimate, as she correctly pointed out tonight. I thought for so many years that it was my job to keep things interesting for her and the family. Where was the lesson plan that specified intimacy as important as our many outside activities ... more important than hard work and being honest? Do I get any credit for integrity?

His thoughts felt disorganized, defensive, self-serving, though searching. They cried for reasons, for rationale, explanations about who he was; his behaviors that seemed uncaring, and selfishly motivated, since Meg's recent intervention.

"Was it Ma and Pop, and the covert ways they employed to express love, who gave me a jump start to the avoidance of closeness?" He asked aloud. "Never saw them hug and cuddle like Meg and I did every night before we fell asleep. We were way ahead of the folks that way.

"When did I hear Pop tell Ma he loved her? If she sensuously gestured to him, he'd change the subject like a busy news anchor, at least if we kids were in range." Still he viewed his marriage as comparatively blessed with affection, compared to his parents, and how distant from one another they outwardly seemed most of the time.

Mike lapsed quickly into deep repose, uncharacteristic of his nights alone since Meg's demise, no upsetting dreams to plague his rest. There were no further visions save a curious, lingering scent of Tre'sor™ perfume, and the smile she wore after her lustful and convincing gift.

What the devil? Who's, who is calling up north at this hour?" Mike yelped at the startling phone rings that nearly sent him through the headboard. He reset the clock on the radio before retiring, and knew the time was correct. "Gol dern! It's five AM. Who's calling so blamed early? Still pitch black outside." Quiet reigned, except for beginning warbles of a few vociferous blue jays, and the trills of smaller songbirds fresh on the scene from winter vacations to the south.

"Yes, this is Mike. Hey, that you, Wayne? What the dickens? Is everything OK?"

His brother intercepted quickly. "Hey big guy, get the hell out of bed. We're going over to the Morris shack, right now, before I gets lost in work."

Mike sat up. Wayne kindled his immediate attention. *What's he up to? That's not like Wayne, unless he's going hunting, for cripe's sakes!"*

"Last night after you left, I went out to get some beer, and, by the time I realized it, I did the run to the Old River Road turn-off. Don't ask me why … just curious as hell to see that roadstead for myself. You're right; the signs, new gate, the locks, were much more than maddening. Beside myself, downright furious, I was. Well, I gets out of the Jeep and checks the padlocks. Did you do that carefully?" He gave Mike no time to answer. "Did you assume they were secured?"

"I … they looked as if. …"

Wayne broke in anxiously, "Yeah, they did appear locked at first glance, and I was about to drive off like you did, when I thought I saw fresh tire tracks over the tracks I figures you left on the turn-off. Big wide Firestones, they were … a heavy vehicle, loaded truck, I figures.

"So, I goes to the gate and finds both padlocks. Guess what, Bro. They were unlocked. I opens the gate, turns off my lights, and I creeps along a nice cushion of new gravel." The new aggregate started at the first turn, fifty or so yards into the trees. Well, I sees one hell of a big buck standing there in the center of the path, like he paved it himself." Wayne had Mike's wide-eyed concentration.

"Well, he just stands there, ears a wiggling, at full attention, just looking at me. But the goddamnest thing … I realizes it's not a white tail, but a mule deer. With ears like that, he was no *Odocoileus virginianus*. It stood larger, like the mulies we took out in Colorado—nineteen ninety-five, wasn't it? 'What the hell's a big stocky mule deer doing in our woods?' I asks myself. All of a sudden, I sees its eyes didn't blaze from my lights. Real blank, they looked like those of a highway road kill a few hours old. So I sets the brake, off go the headlights, and I gets out. I leans against the front hood, looked around, just to study things, when the dirt road illuminated as far back as I could see.

A circus, it was, Mike. Why, there were floodlights every hundred feet or so, and as far as I could tell, well into the woods. The damned path is fully lighted now. What is that going to do to our deer? "Wait a minute, there's more," Wayne continued excitedly, nearly out of breath. "Then I sees the fake deer is on a track of some sort, embedded in a strip of concrete that spanned the road. All of a sudden, it starts to roll slowly, toward the right side, into a nest of poplar saplings. Behind the track, I sees a heavy stainless steel cable that hung between two four-inch diameter pipes. That was locked up tighter than a drum with a weird key lock, big enough to have been used on the front gate at Fort Knox. This thing just smacked military, big time.

"Didn't know what to think, so I just stood there, leaned against my front bumper until, after a few minutes, the lights on the path go out. I'm a thinkin' that behind the buck's eyes might be a camera, video recorder, and I do not want the car identified. I bee-lines it backward and goes for home where I belonged. This was freaky, Big Bro, real weird. I want to go back, come daylight, though, and check things out a little more carefully. How 'bout it? Think we should?"

"I hardly know what to say," Mike replied, angered by the high-tech accoutrements already installed by the new Morris property owners. "I'm not sure it's something we should do. Yet, the land is as public as City Hall or the library in East Tawas. Why not, then? We need to verify that this whacko hasn't placed his hands on some government-backed lease we don't know about, that allows blockage of public access. I dern sure do not need a jail sentence for trespassing. And I am certainly not going to see either of us with a thirty-ought-six slug in the head.

"It is Friday, isn't it? How's about us eating breakfast at Paul Bunyan? We'll run on to the ranger's office in Rose City as soon as they open. Donnie ought to be there. We'll get the story from the horse's mouth, before and not after we become low-cost rifle targets. I'll buy, and we'll do some deer scouting on the way. Shall we meet in thirty minutes for chow?"

Wayne grinned at the excuse to get out of work for the morning, and he pictured the biscuits and gravy atop the ham, eggs, bacon, and sausage breakfast special that made the café famous.

Mike lay back a few minutes to reconsider what he heard. The final insult, his heart throbbed heavier the more he recounted Wayne's strange story. He had to get to the bottom of it before giving up on the dream. The wildflowers in the crystal bud vase on the dresser fluttered. Feathers on the stuffed golden pheasant poised on the bureau, vibrated slightly.

"Dear," her soft voice beckoned. Meg returned again.

He was not yearning for an arms-open welcome. *Will she tell me not to go? I already know it's unwise. I used my noggin, tried to head Wayne off at the pass. She would be proud.* Mike pulled the down pillow over his face and breathed slow and deep to relax. Streams of erotic memories veiled his senses from the session the night before, when she employed techniques so unlike those normally used to satisfy his desires. The experience overwhelmed him, and drove home the significance of perceived reality if ever before he doubted it.

"I'm proud of the way you handled Wayne this morning. He has always been protective of his big brother, hasn't he? I want you to be very, very careful, My Dear. Go ahead; do as you planned, but make sure this new owner hasn't some packet of government papers to keep the public out, before you tread on his tracks. Think, as you proceed, how you might feel if you had legitimate control of the land all the way from Old River Road to the shack. It could be possible. The guy might be a weirdo, outside the loop as far as local folks are concerned, perhaps unwilling to allow hunters on the property. That's not our way up here, though how could he know? Do the right thing, Sweetheart. I trust you … always will."

Daylight's fingers climbed the outside bedroom wall and crept through the high windows over the bed. Mike peeped from under the pillow at the signs of first light. Meg left as abruptly as she appeared.

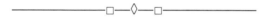

"Damn, I knew it. I knew there was something real illegal with what I saw, something very wrong. Do you thinks I understand at least a little; do ya Donnie?" Wayne persisted as he, Mike, and Chief Ranger Don Johanssen studied the topographic map of the Huron National Forest that lay under plastic on the big table. They stood in the lobby of the Oscoda County Regional Forestry Service building. Photos of last season's largest trophy deer and fish filled the expansive bulletin board behind them. Somewhat ironically on the opposite wall, many legal notices called attention to bovine tuberculosis cases recently documented in the area.

Painfully aware of the threat posed to the massive Michigan deer population, Mike knew of the frightening disease that spread originally from dairy and beef cattle. He lectured frequently to hunting clubs as a representative of the Quality Deer Management Association, to promote the best ways to curb such an epidemic. His wandering eyes found a new posting, pinned over a stack of older ones, on which a running tally of verified cases was kept. Briefly distracted from Wayne's monologue, he noted six deer were validated as infected that fall, in Michigan's Upper Peninsula, alone. *That's a far cry from the seventy thousand animals killed by cars on the highways in our state, but if the sickness ever got a serious hold, hoof and mouth disease in Europe would pale by comparison. Worse, most folks don't even know about the problem; nor are they aware of minimum cooking temperatures to kill the bugs in un-suspected but contaminated meat.*

"Hey! I'm talking here, Brother. Don's been kind enough to help, and what are you doin' but reading legal notices? Would you pay attention, please?" Wayne asked firmly. He sounded too much like their father in the old days, for Mike's taste.

"I got a little past the horizon there. Sorry, Donnie," Mike said apologetically, while he ignored Wayne's scolding. "Thanks for taking the time with us." He was immersed in thoughts of Meg, and the interest she would have shown, were she there. Long-time friends, he and the ranger hunted farther north together on many an opening day. Don enjoyed access to a coveted list of private landowners who allowed hunters they knew to use their lands, and he willingly shared it with Mike and Wayne. "So, what's the deal with the Morris property, old buddy?" Mike asked.

Johanssen flipped through the large canvas-bound book that contained government land leases in the county, but he expressed little confidence that he would discover anything by his efforts. "I don't know who the new owner is, off hand. I can tell you there has been no special permit issued to install wiring, lights, a phony mule deer or a damned gate where he did; and that means at the road, or around the place. Are you sure you weren't smoking something funny last night?

"No leases were altered over the preceding year to suggest the changes to the Morris place conformed to the law. "See here," Don went on, and pointed to the map, specifically to the upper reaches of the Au Sable River. "The south shore, mostly undeveloped, enormous parcels, with few structures, are the older leases. The Morris lease, for example, begins at the road, outlined in dark red; then it expands, sort of a piece of pie, into the woods, back to the old power line road. That's the area. You did all that hell raising about public access through the broken power company gate last summer. Remember? I helped you in your pleas, but it almost got me fired. All the drum beating around D. C., for a six hundred dollar gate, its cost when headquarters eventually granted approval. A bitch of a job, but we saw it through and got it done!"

"You know you were glad I intervened, gol dern it. Our good ranger; Mr. Proper over here," Mike snapped with a wry grin, and turned to Wayne, a tight squint to suggest he let him in on a secret, "Nancy that he was, our ranger couldn't do it. He called it ah … a 'political obligation,' to keep his big mouth shut, if memory serves me." He elbowed his old schoolmate. "How many times before the new gate, did your people have to drive back to the swamp and weed out illegal hunters and stuck four-by-four drivers? It was turning you nuts and you know it. Are we getting too old to recall that far back? Have we been in for our annual government physical; better yet, a recent mental check?" he persisted cheerfully.

"All right, all right. Let's get back to the problem at hand and that is: what to do?" Don replied. "I can tell you the presumptuous bastard has lots of nerve to do all this work without application for a permit, much less with no property rights beyond his lease perimeter." The ranger tugged authoritatively at both tattered lapels of his service-issued, overly tight, olive drab nylon jacket. "As a matter of fact, the lease must have been recently negotiated, because the book still shows Leland T. Morris Trust as the lessee. See, right here, it's shown."

"Well, if you don't have current information on file, what's to stop us from going out there, just like we always did, with old man Morris' implied permission?" Wayne asked defiantly. "Never, not once, did any member of the Morris family tell Mike or me to leave. They knew we respected their woods, their privacy, and they also knew we had the damned right to use the path, at least to their property line…all along the river shore, too. Hell, Mike usually picked up trash other fishermen left. Old man Morris sure never bothered. Our daddy taught those frigging Morris grandkids to fish the river."

"Well, if you're asking me for approval to trespass, I'm not giving it to you. Knowing what you now know, why ask? I didn't see you troublemakers today and you never asked. How is that for being neutral? I will call you, Mike, if the papers do come through. It usually takes a while after a transfer. You would like to know who the owner is, wouldn't you? Meantime, I'll make some inquiries; see what I can find out, before I stick my big nose where it doesn't belong.

"No more rumbles in the forest, before I retire, if you please. I've done a few too many things with the Gladdocks, many of which I would sooner forget. He patted them both affectionately on the shoulders and concluded, "I've got things to do, people to see; it's almost coffee time, and you two are buying.

"By the way," Johanssen went on, "I did hear a rumor that some big shot from D.C. was on a quest for available leases around the river, even upstream as far as Grayling. He's looked for very isolated parcels as far as possible from paved roads; e-mailed our forestry offices all over the place, drove realtors nuts. He even made threats, and threw out innuendoes when agents failed to accommodate him. So far, he hasn't contacted this office. Hey, hold on. Josh just drove up." Johanssen left Mike and Wayne alone in the office to digest his words and hurried to the parking lot.

He returned quickly and went on, "I take it back. Josh says there was a guy in here recently, talking big and loud, a braggart who sounded like he might have been in the military, either past or present." He spoke about the importance of property rights, and how he'd 'blow off anyone's head or plug anyone,' who intruded on his land. Josh ignored him, but noticed he looked in the map books at the desk, right over there.

"If the feller did what he was told, he should have signed the register, this book, here."

Mike thumbed through the last page in the register and saw just two names were logged the entire month. He froze into a blue stare at the second entry: *Brig. Gen. Homer Payton Claybourne.*

CHAPTER 8

Let's park at the power company road, by the yellow gate. Then we'll cut through the first heavy stand of trees to Morris' path." Mike whispered but his words flew rapidly. Fingers quivered; he was concerned for their safety, based on what General Claybourne apparently said to Josh at the Ranger Station. "Wayne, we have to be careful; we could be on real thin ice here.

"Why would anybody go to all the trouble and expense Claybourne did, if he weren't up to any good? Donnie's office might be the last to find out. Wouldn't our nosiness make for fine epitaph copy on a couple of headstones? I can see the words now, carved in white granite, nearly covered with un-clipped weeds and grass:

The two Poles buried here,
stuck their craws too far
into another man's affairs.

"I don't care what happens," Wayne said. He bit his lower lip. "Let's find out what's going on back there. What's the need for that lighting I sees last night; the mechanical deer, a mulie at that, wiggled his ears and looked about as real as it could look, there in the dark? Except that, it's the wrong species for our woods, for Christ's sake! Can the damned fool think we're that stupid? Doesn't he realize that deer's head is sure to be blown off on opening day, by every lazy hunter wishing to bag an easy one, straight off?"

"All right. Let's get quiet, remember where we are, and get a going. Wait a minute," Mike said. He leered crossly at Wayne. "You're not taking that gol derned thing. What's the matter with you, Brother? You're not sixteen. You're sixty years old and you know better."

Wayne spun the cylinder on the Colt .38 snub-nosed revolver he removed from his briefcase, jiggled it in his big hand, and argued only faintly.

"Whaddaya mean, leave it here? No way, Mike. Under the present conditions, I won't go without it. If I'm to help you here, I'm covering my butt, and covering it well ... *thweeth, thweeth* ... yours too, ya numbskull. If you don't have sense enough to protect yourself, I'll do it for us. How's that? *Thweeth, thweeth.*"

"I won't be walking back there to get us in a gun battle." Mike's forehead stretched tightly, and erased most of his wrinkles. "You think I'm crazy?" He grabbed Wayne's arm firmly, to hold him by the parked car. "Meg would have a kitten if she knew I was doing this, and ... ah, she knows ... she'll know ... can't explain it, but she's here, with us, right now. I can feel it." He waited for her to come to the rescue, to prove her aliveness for Wayne's benefit, and to unleash more sage advice. He looked into the trees, along the brush line, and along the road in both directions. He listened intently, but heard and saw nothing. The forest stood listless--no familiar breeze, and no signs. *Where are you when I need you, Meg? I'll need some direction, yes, a little help managing Wayne. I need you to speak with him.*

Wayne turned his head partly away, but looked from the corners of his eyes, so concerned he was with Mike's comments. *There he goes again, as if Meg is around.* Wayne could not help worrying. "All right," he finally sighed with resignation, "if it makes you feel more comfortable, the pistol stays here. Damnit, if anything happens, don't say I didn't warn you." Begrudgingly, he replaced the gun back in his briefcase on the front seat.

They walked into the stand of densely packed trees that closed off the budding blue sky, and almost blackened the moist forest floor below their feet. Leaves from millennia before, at all levels of decomposition, perfumed the damp air with a sweet pungency, and left little else for the nostrils to savor. Eyes feasted on the monochromatic vista. It seemed a stage set in shades of warm grays and beiges, from last season's fallen foliage, to witch's hair on the conifers, upward to the barren trunks and on up to limbs still dulled, and not yet painted with much spring green. Mike, particularly, perceived the woods' muteness, a familiar and well-defined still, punctuated only by the calls of a few darting birds.

Already overwhelmed by the environment he savored, he whispered reverently, in keeping with the soliloquy offered by the fresh atmosphere in which they found themselves. For a moment, he forgot their mission. His gaze moved upward to the forest canopy as he walked. "The buds, Brother: God's green blush, are almost here. Look!" Mike appreciated the forest's beauty much more than Wayne; he always did, and always would. Family members insisted he inherited his mother's sensitivity to nature. Supplanted by her honesty, before pain pill addiction consumed her, it was one of her few gleaming virtues.

"See there, Wayne. Poplars began to erupt first, as usual, greenest of the lot. Birches, oaks, aspens, maples, and beeches will pick up their yellow-green feathers most anytime. Can't wait; every year is different, isn't it?"

Both men trudged with noiseless steps, first on their toes, then slowly transferred weight along the outside edges of their feet, to the heels, as their father taught them. "It was da way of da Algonquins," the old man reminded countless times, to move without breaking so much as a twig, when they walked the forest carpet and stalked game or prepared an attack on another tribe. Whatever they sought was unaware of their presence until too late.

"Jesus Mike, you'd think you never before saw a tree, and, what's the matter, now? You walked right over that fresh deer trail. You said nothing about it. Looks like it was used lots during winter, doesn't it?"

Mike saw the acorns, a favorite deer feast, amidst the dead leaves; the rubs, polishes, and gouges on saplings at antler height—vestiges of the fall rut. He saw the many droppings, too, on that narrow cut through the thicket.

For the moment, though, the signs were not as important as the hunting instinct. *What is happening to me? Wayne's right. Why the sudden interest in trees? Why didn't I see the rutting signs? Here we are, on a nice game trail, funneled to a smaller one, and I go right past the evidence. What a spot for a stand, up in that big maple. An unobstructed bow shot down here … perfect view.* "I was just looking up at the high crook in that maple. Nice place for a perch a good bow shot from there, eh?"

"Shhhh," Wayne muttered harshly. "Shhhh, we're coming up on the Morris path, little more than a hundred yards ahead, I thinks."

They traversed nearly a mile into the forest but Mike was oblivious to their progress. He wished Meg would help him with the dilemma they faced. "So, what the heck are we going to do now?" he asked Wayne helplessly, palms turned upward. A quizzical look crept across his face.

Wayne stopped in the midst of a step, and held his right foot above a cluster of dry twigs on which he was about to tread. He put his index finger to his mouth, the universal sign for, "Be quiet." He halted just as suddenly. Both wore camouflaged outer garments. All but invisible, a deer or even the wary turkey might have mistaken them for landscape. Behind his younger brother by ten feet, Mike drew a breath, held it and crouched forward, ever so slowly.

Both heard the car approach. Wayne heard it first and reminded Mike of his superior auditory senses by pointing to his ear and spreading a pompous grin. Dropped to their knees, into the underbrush as the sound neared, they could tell when the crunching of tires stopped. The vehicle reached the un-graded dirt just inside the new gate.

"Gol dern. It's the Excursion! It's the car." Mike almost shouted, while he tugged impatiently at Wayne's shirt. "Derned if it's not the army guy, the feller in fatigues at the Paul Bunyan the other night. That's the Excursion with the roof rack, very same one. I thought we were going to fight. I can't believe it. The jerk has to be Claybourne, himself."

Wayne looked at him, completely puzzled and was lost for words.

"It all adds up," Mike continued, "the arrogance Josh mentioned to Donnie this morning that man who bragged about his military background. Yes, by gosh, it's coming together."

The SUV stopped. The beefy man, who spoke to Mike in the café, got out, took a key from a ring on his leather-sheathed brush pants, opened the lock, and swung open the gate. Seated on the passenger side was the same woman Mike saw before. As though under a spell, the duo watched the Ford idle through and stop again, for the female to secure the gate.

"They'll be gone for a time," Wayne said anxiously, relieved they were not seen. He spoke non-stop in his excitement. "Let's figure an hour, at least, if they're headed for town. Did ya see that fancy Browning .270 BMS on the gun rack? He certainly has money if he treats an expensive rifle that way. Who, in their right mind, would keep a custom-engraved, five thousand dollar rifle that visible in the car, even in this part of Michigan? So, tell me about it. What happened on the road Wednesday night? He's got a paper D.C. car license, must have just bought it."

Mike related the story as he followed Wayne through the closely packed trees, then along the fringe of the dirt road to the gate. Angrily, but curiously, they milled about the new fixtures. "Look here," Mike called, "check this lock … 'U. S. Government,' stamped here, on the back."

Stooped to examine the track more closely, Wayne eagerly relayed his findings. "This thing is quite complex; it's wired for everything but damned sound; maybe that, too. When I first sees it, the ears and tail moved. They're wired to servos in his head, and here's a remote switch. Take a look, Mike, with a whir and the snaps from two relays, the deer rolls to the center of the dirt path; its ears turn and flap, just like real ones."

Mike wisely ducked behind when Wayne pointed to its eyes, and intimated again that within the stuffed deer's head might be a fancy security camera. They watched in awe as the mannequin traveled twice across the dirt path, and returned to its hiding spot behind a cluster of poplars. Carefully, they swept over their footprints with a switch Wayne cut from a fir tree, then moved back into hiding, and hiked swiftly toward the old shack by the river.

The roar of the rapids below the big pool wafted through the forest cover, and whetted Mike's affections for his favorite fishing spot. A pleasant and familiar sound, he could already taste the humid nights—insects swarmed above his head—when Wayne grabbed his forearm, and pulled him, away from his fancies, and into the brush. He heard the soft whirring sound toward which Wayne pointed with index and second fingers, back and forth from the noise to his eyes, until he understood.

A video camera oscillated in a one hundred eighty-degree arc, from high in a birch tree beside the path, and just above one of the floodlights. They watched for a few minutes, jaws agape, as the recording device swept one way, then the other, while it thoroughly scanned the road. At the moment it swirled in their direction, they backed farther into the thicket, and safely out of view.

"That was close. We had better conduct our observations from the other side, out of the camera's eye or Mr. Big Gun from D.C. is going to figure us out all too soon. This is getting a wee bit heavy, Wayne. I have the strange feeling we shouldn't be here, now or at anytime; not until we get Claybourne's property rights figured out, at least."

"I maintains it's a public road. We already know the river is public. So, next time, though it'll take us longer; to hell with it. We'll come up along the south bank, or we can paddle the canoe downstream, now can't we? There isn't a damned thing he can do. "*Thweeth, thweeth,*" Wayne spat air between his teeth.

Twelve more floodlights and cameras mounted above, progressively frustrated the Gladdock brothers as they moved stealthily inland, parallel to the road and toward the river, well within the obscuring tree line. "Brother, if I'd known we were going to whack our way between trees like this, I'd have worn my brush garments. This is ridiculous," Wayne scolded, and poked his finger through a new tear in his shirt. "I can't get over the expense of the electrical work. It's unbelievable. What the hell's he afraid of out here? Makes you wonder, doesn't it?" He scratched his chin through the two-day old beard, fringed with white.

At least three distinct barks broke the silence the brothers enjoyed. One, more deeply pitched than the others, sounded much stronger. Mike heard them first. Big ones, they were running fast, and on a mission. An expert in canine behavior, Mike trained many a hound and retriever to serve his hunting needs. Anyone invited to work with his animals was among the privileged few. His yellow and black labs were the best, at work from a duck blind or in the field, when they pointed quail, grouse, woodcock, or pheasant. They did just as he asked, with subtle hand movements and faint whistles. He loved dogs, but there was something about the determined, if not strained bay from those in the distance, that provoked him to question their purpose.

"Wayne, if this guy talks of blowing someone's head off, in casual conversation with a ranger, and is this concerned about his security in the gol derned woods, his doggies may not be the friendliest in the world. I don't like what I hear. They're not barking just to make noise, or yipping out of loneliness. The mutts sound large, Akitas, Rottweilers, Dobermans, or even Shepherds, trained killers, maybe. This is not good, Brother; dern it. They are moving fast through the trees … back and forth across the dirt path … might be trained trackers. Can you tell?" Goose bumps arose on the nape of his neck.

Wayne nodded in agreement and without another word, the two looked at each other fearfully, crossed the dirt road, and tore off at a run toward their car. Wayne had presence of mind to remove his outer shirt and throw it into the branches of a birch, hoping their pursuers might linger there for a distracting few minutes if they came that way. Mike gathered several handfuls of deer droppings, crushed them in his hands to renew the scent and scattered them around the same tree.

Both stopped in their tracks, despite increasingly louder baying behind them.

"Oh, Mike, look here; a damned foxhole, regulation, frigging U.S. Army foxhole, if there ever was one. It's a straight rifle shot to the gate from here. I dug enough of the damned things in the military to know. This is no garbage pit or the start of a well. It's a two-man hole, for a machine gun emplacement, freshly dug … sandbags and all. You know

General Patton didn't approve of these things." Wayne digressed while they stopped to catch their breath.

"That crazy, egotistical general considered them a defensive maneuver, swore to his superiors that defensive tactics never won wars. Wonder how many more might be back there? Makes me curious about mines, too. How would it be, to have our legs blown off by an anti-personnel device in our own damned woods?"

The brothers stiffened at the thought, but the baying became louder, closer and more intense. They resumed running, this time more fearful of the terrain they traversed. It sounded as if the animals purposely spread out to cover more territory and faster, when, to their great relief, they crossed the last game trail, and reached the Suburban, panting though they were, from the reality of an imminent attack. Wayne recovered his breath.

Mike fumbled for his keys, and spoke between deep inspirations. "Dern; they're almost on us … too close for my taste. I can't picture myself torn to shreds out here and no one, not a soul would find us until there's nothing left but bones to identify. Close, close call, Brother."

Headed west toward the river bridge, at a good clip, they passed by the Morris path apron and caught sight of three unusually large Rottweilers, whose warning voices fortunately gave them away. They snarled and paced back and forth by the gate, "Look at that huge male. He's all mouth, shoulders like an African lion, back all bristled like the real thing on a hunt, and he looks hungry."

"Maybe he does, Wayne, you're right; maybe he does," Mike answered with resignation. "I take back everything I said about your pistol. Would have been nice if I didn't object, eh? Let's stop in the parking lot by the bridge, pour some coffee, and talk about what happened a little more."

"Did you know; a foxhole was touted in military manuals as one of the recognized methods of avoiding death in a nuclear blast, because of dirt's alleged radiation-filtrative properties?" Wayne asked. "That bit of BS wisdom was imparted on us by our government during the Cold

War. I remember. I was twenty when Nikita Khrushchev met with President Kennedy in Vienna.

"We GI's thought we'd not need foxholes and palm trees to hide within and snipe. Maybe, it was over, we thought. Hell, Big Brother, you were talking about marriage then; remember? It took you two years or so, didn't it, to get the guts? Then the Cuban missile crisis heated things up again, and back came the reality of digging in as fast as we could. You got married in sixty-four, right? Man, did you ever do well, with your deferment.

"Hat's off to you. I certainly didn't believe in the idea of killing, but they made it seem so easy in training, with all the propaganda. Only problem: who to kill was more than perplexing. Who were we were supposed to hate and then eliminate, without conscience?"

"Dunno, I never felt like I wanted to kill anyone. Just haven't been placed in that position, Wayne."

"Well, they sure got us going against the Viet Cong. We needed to hate them and, too soon, I wanted to shoot the first one I saw. Got the opportunity on each of my early missions. We digs in, climbed trees, stuck ourselves on hilltops … whatever gave us the best views of our targets. It took measurable time for bullets to reach the targets, oh, so long after the blasts, because of the extreme distances. Then I starts to realize, I didn't really like the idea of whacking someone with whom I had no personal gripe. I needed anger, a grudge, some sort of purpose; otherwise it seemed so senseless."

Wayne became visibly agitated while he continued, "The Battle at Ap Bac took care of that. January 2, 1963, not so long after I got there, the bastards got me good, didn't they? They popped up in that paddy like cupie dolls at the County Fair shooting gallery and fired at us with everything they had. We were such sitting ducks in the chopper, flyin' so low. A round zinged through the open door, went through my arm and killed the poor boy next to me. I didn't even know his name. Next thing I knows, we, and God knows how many other Hueys full of troops, were shot the hell out of the sky. Then we dug in like moles to avoid the intense enemy fire until more air support arrived.

"I knew I didn't like that Mekong Delta as soon as we began flying over it, but our damned advisors said the South Vietnamese 11th Infantry Regiment needed help." Wayne pulled up his shirtsleeve and exposed the deep, jagged scar close to his shoulder, as though Mike never saw it. "That, my good brother, got me discharged, to prematurely hunt and party with you. Don't ya remember?

"My coming home, lucky to be alive, was your downfall, wasn't it?" Wayne chuckled, and reminisced inside over their reunion and how they tore up the town for months thereafter. "You lasted until the wedding in '64 when you and Meg … sorry to mention her, Bro. There I go again. Oh, you couldn't handle me back then, could ya?"

"You couldn't handle yourself. Ha, my brother Wayne became his own worst enemy, didn't he?"

"Hey, hey, here comes that so called general, I think. Look, look, he's toting the canoe on top again."

Over the centerline, the bronze SUV spun around the curve too harshly, and forced Mike to swerve to the right, to avoid contact as it sped away. "Seems the jerk's after me; I can almost feel it." First, he dern near rear-ends us, er me, on Highway 55 and now, on Old River Road, we come too close to a head-on."

"It's a damned good thing we left when we did," Wayne said. "We can thank the attack dogs for that. Claybourne wasn't gone near as long as we figured, and would have driven right on us, if we poked around the shack. The next time we snoop, we better do it with a little more planning."

"Wayne, do you think we're going back? Do you really think so, after the dogs and all? This seems out of our hands. I simply have to reconcile myself to the loss of the property. It's a past tense which Meg … Meg." Mike stammered, "Meg and I will not forget … ever."

Wayne removed his pistol from the holster, fingered the grip, then the barrel as if it were the affectionate softness of a woman's hand and snapped back, to Mike's astonishment. "This little baby says we're not backing out of what we started to do, Brother, 'cause it's not our style. My sweet little six-shooter says she needs some exercise and doesn't like what just happened to us." He opened the cylinder, checked that it was fully loaded, and flipped his hand briskly to close it with a loud click.

Mike skidded at the last moment after he crossed the old steel bridge and rolled to a stop at the edge of the soft turnout on the river's north bank. He spoke a few minutes after they got out and contemplated the stretch of river that extended east and west. "She is beautiful. Our late spring Au Sable River is just about perfect," he said almost in desperation, while he nonetheless smiled at the sight. "Look how high she is." Leaned against the right front fender they sipped coffees and gazed longingly at the tannin-stained water that ran deep beneath the bridge. "Oh, to cast a fly," Mike continued, "and stop this madness. Wouldn't it feel good to slip on the waders and simply go fishing?" He raised his voice with each utterance, finally yelled, looked upward and asked for Meg's support. "I want nothing more than … to cast a fly."

Now, with Claybourne there, they'd have to fish from the more inconvenient north bank or bring a canoe to access their spot on the south side. At least they would be fishing and not snooping. Both agreed they had enough of curiosity for a spell.

Caddis flies or not, damned if we won't fish the big pool tonight!" Wayne yelled as Mike drove off. "To hell with those dogs!" He turned to the house and muttered, "Yep, just the three of us will be fishing." Yours truly, Big Mike, and this here revolver will be along for the ride in my back pack."

CHAPTER 9

"There's just enough clearance over the shoals. We'll traverse to the south shore, where it's deeper. Paddle like Algonquins," Wayne cried elatedly, above the roar of the bumpy water where they launched their canoe for the mile-long downstream run to the big pool. They dug in and pulled hard; the slender canvas over wood canoe slid easily across the shallows, and finally settled in deeper water along the deeply undercut south bank.

Exposed tree roots hung from the crumbling bluff like drying pasta and the loamy soil sparkled with seeping ground water. So fragile was the edifice, even patches of bright green sphagnum moss and clusters of new ferns hung precariously and negated any bank fishing in that area until the level dropped. The sun began to slide but the stubborn dusk allowed fishing for an hour or two.

That time of day offered the most potential.

"Pull over to the bar in the center. Let's think this through, Brother," Wayne said. He shifted his paddle to the starboard side along with Mike. The bow of the canoe pulled to port and into the center of the course, toward the narrow sand island where ample shrubbery could hide them at its downstream end. There the river stretched about forty feet to either side.

"Think what over, Wayne?" Mike asked in a whisper. The keel found solid ground and the canoe nudged to a stop. "What now?"

"I just want to regroup, make sure we know what we're doing, where we'll go if those damned dogs show up when we're casting out from the spit below the shack. Aren't we headed there?"

Mike was silent but his thoughts were far from idle. *Meg … where are you? He thought. I need your words of wisdom … want you fishing with me tonight. It's the first night of the season, but I'm not excited without your company. Doesn't seem right. Somehow, I feel deceptive, yes, selfish.* He continued to ignore his brother's query. "Mike," Wayne called again, "did you hear me? Don't you think, before we gets to the shack, that we should have a plan, in case the animals hassle us? The general could be there, for that matter. I brought a couple pounds of venison scraps; we'll feed 'em a little, and begin the start of a long and enduring friendship. It might help for later, when we come back and sees what's going on around the shack."

"You won't trespass on the Morris property again, will you, Sweetheart?"

Mike nearly jumped from the canoe when he felt that same gentle wind that rustled at his back.

"This doesn't look good to me, Honey … not safe at all, and with Wayne getting himself agitated; it doesn't bode well for you to be nosey. Don't you agree? Now, Honey," she persisted meekly, and sensed his reticence, "don't you feel likewise? Tell the truth to your Margaret and never mind your childish brother."

I agree and I told him so already. There will be no more sneaking around the Morris property. Someone's going to get hurt.

"Are you really fishing or just casting around for information tonight?"

"Oh," Mike surprised himself by speaking aloud, "we're fishing. We just stopped here on the bar to talk it through … a plan of action. Yes, we're fishing." He swung around, pointed to the poles and gear. Wayne sat on the stern thwart, mystified at what he heard.

"Hey," Wayne called sharply, "who the hell ya talkin' to? You didn't answer me and now you're talking to the river. Are you all right, Bro? Really, are you OK? Brother. …?"

"Yes, yes" Mike said, "I was talking to her." He dropped his head in embarrassment. "I told you I would. She's here with us, to fish tonight. It's fine. I'm fine, I assure you, I'm just fine," he finished in a stutter.

"Yes, all right. That's good. I think that's good. Nell said it's good, too," Wayne replied patronizingly, but with enough respect that Mike was satisfied to continue.

"Wayne, Meg doesn't like the idea of us snooping down at the shack. She feels a danger and, if she knows what I am thinking, maybe she knows about the danger, to us, I mean."

"No danger here, Bro," Wayne asserted confidently, as he withdrew the pistol from his fishing vest. He fingered it admiringly and his wide, ruddy face beamed.

"Let's just fish tonight—no guns—no playing detectives."

"Agreed."

"Now, Little Brother, put that piece away and let's hear your plan."

Wayne suggested they beach the canoe in the grass that extended nearly to the river's center, upstream of the big log. He thought the aggressive dogs, even if interested in them, would not venture that far from the bank, once they realized the water on that side ran swift and deep.

Mike expressed confidence that they would be secure. His retrievers, Yellow and Beau, never trusted the soft, sticky mud that grabbed at their feet below the water plants. They always waited patiently for him in the shallows below the steep bank.

Around the last bend and adrift with the current, they passed the gnarled, overhanging cedar that signaled the upstream border of the Morris clearing, and paddled to the outermost margin of the shallows.

Mike stepped into the cool muck; waders strapped high to his shoulders, and sloshed away from the canoe into deeper water up to the waist to begin his first casts. His insides turned warm, and his face glowed as he followed the fly in its backward flight the first few times, to gauge the point where the pole tip would stop before he coaxed the line forward. The whirring sound duplicated when his brother—also an envied handler of the fly line—worked his rig toward the faster moving water. So dark it became, that the tiny lures at the end of the fine leaders were no longer visible. "Hey, one on the rise over there … a small brownie, it looks like. See … see?" Mike whispered excitedly, and pointed to a subtle disturbance just above an eddy in the current.

"Jesus, I saw the damn thing. Don't wake up the dead over there." Wayne already directed his line to the spot and payed out enough slack.

Completely overtaken by the rampant hell of loud barking and snarling from directly behind, commotion shattered the tranquility they had captured.

"Fetch!" came the next salvo into their silent world, followed by three huge splashes that roughed up the solemn river's surface directly before them. Fabric training decoys popped upright in the placid water and three Rottweilers bounded into the stream after them; one cut directly across Wayne's fly line, as it lay extended, in wait for the attention of the brown he stalked.

Harsh commands echoed through the trees behind them. "Go get the birds, boys … Ace … over there. King … out … out boy … left … good boy. Jack … in the water with you."

"Goddamn the sonsofbitches! Get your stupid dogs out of the river, ya dumb bastard! Are ya out of yer cotton-picking mind?" Wayne threw his pole down in the weeds and cast non-stop epithets while Mike stood aghast at the scene: three big dogs that paddled and growled furiously in the river current, directly into the area where they fished.

Wayne thrashed his arms wildly, screamed at the top of his lungs, and kicked the water like a mad man. He threw down his hat, then his backpack, and cursed again at the voice that directed the animals. "Get your damned fool dogs the hell out of here. This is a trout stream, you fucker, not a blasted dog training pond." His screams bounced from the steep bank up river, across the shoals, and reverberated into echoes through the still woods. Mike angrily joined the protest, and yelled almost in unison. The brothers watched, and stared at each other in veritable disbelief, as the dogs paddled back to the bank. Each proudly delivered a decoy to the bluff top.

The dogs' interest in the game, however, lapsed as quickly as it began, once they became cognizant of the Gladdocks—two sitting ducks. Wayne and Mike then found themselves objects of the largest one's fancy. The fur on the male's back sprung up and his mouth full of oversized teeth glowed. He barked and taunted furiously, as he did when they narrowly made their escape from the woods.

Non-stop and incessant, it was all business. The big dog's two cohorts joined in and the three challenged one another to approach the brothers, a step at a time. They advanced, barked, growled, backed up, and advanced again. They sank deeper and deeper into the soft river grass the closer they inched. Wayne withdrew his gun, clasped it in both hands, extended his arms and cocked the hammer back. He pointed it toward but above the nearest animal, smallest but most fearless of the three.

"Oh no, Brother; don't fire … don't do it. We'll be in deep trouble. Please, Wayne!"

Wayne's hands shook. The lead dog was nearly upon him. Wayne's face flushed scarlet; his teeth gnashed the unlighted cigarette between them. "Thweeth, thweeth," he spat angrily. "Get the damned animals away from us, ya bastard," he yelled, "or they're dead meat."

Mike saw Claybourne first. The general stepped to the edge of the bluff, down river eighty feet or so from where they stood, an M-16 rifle in his hands. He held it at waist level, pointed at Wayne, and his finger curled around the trigger.

"Look up there, Bro. We have company, but don't move. Just look, real slow like."

Wayne turned eyes upward, saw the man, decked in army cap and fatigue jacket, baggy fatigue pants stuffed into his regulation boots. He didn't look happy.

Everything went white for a short but confused time segment, as Wayne's mind regressed. He spotted the Viet Cong regular. According to earlier briefings in camp, the area was clear, but they were everywhere—up on the rise above him, and his South Vietnamese infantry escorts. Well concealed on a hilltop for a three-day vigil, Wayne and his spotter's orders were to pick off designated targets whose coordinates they received via radio. It was a job for the sniper and he was ready.

He swung his pistol from the snarling dogs to the enemy; he could see them: dark skinned with floral painted faces, attired in green pajama uniforms. They peered from behind palms and hanging vines. The survivor would be the one with fast reflexes; the one to shoot and kill first. Countless admonitions he received in training rang clear, and flashed before him, fresh and imperative, as they were forty years before.

He squeezed when the first Charlie appeared in his sights. The recoil lifted his big hands several inches and he squeezed again. A second loud report reverberated through the jungle. He heard shots in the background, a machine gun, probably a fifty caliber, along with automatic rifle fire across the vacated paddy behind him. A grenade or two punctured the sticky mist and the bap-bap-bap-bap of a prowling chopper added visceral confusion to the enmity he experienced.

More dog barks and a woman's panicky cries sounded out and broke his brief regressive spell. He and Mike simultaneously dove for cover behind a large, partly submerged cedar log. Five quick shots rang out from the bluff, and there were more screams.

A woman's high-pitched yell spilled over the river: "Homer! For God's sake, what are you doing? Stop the shooting over there. Stop it, now! What the hell is going on, Homer? Homer?"

Bullets hissed over the log where Mike lay. One struck his only protection with a heavy smack and sent shards of bark in flight over the tall grass. Then silence reigned again, save the racket from the barking animals, which were nearly on top of the Gladdocks as they lay prostrate in the water, frozen in fear.

This isn't happening. It couldn't be. Jesus crisp, must be a dream ... not in my river ... my spot in the river. It can't be real. Mike knew the familiar sigh of bullets when they passed nearby. He heard them whir through the trees more than a few times, during most deer seasons.

Unthinking city types posed frightening risks; they'd shoot at anything that moved in the distance—deer or otherwise. However, this was different. The shooter was at close range and aimed to kill.

This old log saved our necks. We'd have been poked full of holes in the first volley. Mike settled into the muck as deep as he could. Wayne pawed the grass in search of the pistol he dropped after his second shot, when the rifle fire began from the bluff.

"Just leave it; no more shooting. Let's wait to see what's happening up there,"

Mike admonished, "the woman is going nuts. Listen, Wayne."

More hysteria resounded above them. "Are you crazy? Have you gone completely off your rocker? What the hell are you doing with that rifle? Homer, you can't shoot that thing around here. Look at the cabins up the river. Someone is going to get hurt." Her screams bounced easily over the water. Another shot rang out, but this time no bullet passed in the Gladdocks' direction. "Give me that thing; you've lost your senses. Give it to me, now," the woman continued to scream. Another shot blasted out and then quiet returned to the bluff.

The brothers lay still as statues. They both shivered in the cold water, but stayed immersed at least ten more minutes before they emerged from their protective shelter, collected their fishing gear, and rushed for the canoe. They pulled it from the reeds, got aboard, and furiously paddled for the mid-river current; out of sight to safety, around the big log and the noisy riffles downstream.

The canoe scraped roughly on the north bank's gravel apron. Both men gasped deeply for breath, to regain what composure they could from the ordeal. Seated in the bow, Wayne dug his paddle into the sand tied the bow line to it and bent over the rail. He leaned on his elbows to recover his senses; removed his jacket, wrung out what water he could, and threw it, disgustingly, into the canoe. He shook the offending revolver in the river water to cleanse it of mud and dropped it into his creel. "I should be putting a damned fish in there," Wayne slurred, while he gasped for air, "not a mud-covered gun. What's that psycho's problem, Mike?"

Long blades of muddy river grass hung from Mike's glasses. He buried his head in the sticky silt when shots broke out from the bluff. Black slime draped from the bib of his waders and his hat drifted downstream. He turned slowly toward Wayne, squinted, and spat dirt from his mouth before speaking in the style of Oliver Hardy, the early black and white movie comedian he admired as a boy.

"Well," Mike quipped—he planted hands on hips for added drama, "this is another fine mess you've gotten us into, Wayne." He never lost his sense of humor. "You and your derned fishing expedition on the Au Sable." Both laughed, relieved to have been spared injury, except to their pride—what little was left of it. "Scared as I've been in one hell of a long time."

"Good thing the Looney Tune can't shoot, Brother. We would be full of holes if I had that M-16 of his. Yes sir, floaters on the way to bloat on the beaches of Lake Huron. When I saw him standing there in the classic fire-at-anything position, that was it for me. I had a 'Nam flash back before I could react otherwise.

"Certainly my instinct to survive took over before I thought further, and I just fires. I didn't aim to hit the sonofabitch, just put them over his head for emphasis; that's all. I wouldn't have shot the dogs either, unless they actually attacked. Then, by God, I'd have placed them lower, I would."

"Remember when you got your first BB gun, Wayne?" Mike asked. He changed the subject with an ear to ear grin as he looked to the trees to spur his memory and to calm himself from the hasty exit they made. "How we dreamed of those Daisy carbines, drooled over ads in the Sunday paper and every comic book we ever read at the grocery store. You were ten. I received mine two years before.

No longer did I have to share shots with you. It seems like yesterday, doesn't it?" Mike continued, with a deep laugh, "We were lizard hunting at the edge of the woods, by Mr. Morgan's pumpkin field, along that dry creek. I was ahead of you, by a few feet. You cocked your rifle for the first big shot, said something about a bird on the ground, and the next thing I knew, I was hit in the head, just behind my ear."

Wayne's face reddened with the embarrassing recall. "I fell over, thought I was going to die, started crying, and you panicked, dropped the gun, and ran all the way home, before I recovered from the shock.

You told Pop you killed me. Mike laughed again, louder the second time. "Must have been your first taste of blood, eh?"

Wayne had no problem bringing back the incident. The event haunted him for weeks afterward; became an indelible vision. He thought he lost his big brother, best pal, and, worse, feared the inevitable withdrawal of his newly gifted gun. "Like an army medic in battle, Pop rushed to the scene and removed the embedded BB from your very superficial wound, before walking us home. You cried no end."

"Once I realized I would live, as I lay out there and waited for Pop to arrive, I cried more for you, Wayne, than from the dern wound. I knew he'd take away your Daisy for heaven knows how long. He placed it in the locked cabinet with his rifles for most of that summer.

"Sure taught us a safety lesson, didn't it? Mama was always convinced we'd blind ourselves before we were fourteen and she was of no help to quiet Pop that afternoon. Imagine the implications if that were the .22 rifle he gave you on your fourteenth. I'd have been a dead duck."

Both cringed at the shuddering thought. "Didn't we love those guns? They were both Model 111-40's weren't they?

"Yup, they gave us more pleasure, I think, than any rifles or guns we've had since." Wayne replied. "Sure as hell got us in continual trouble. Remember the Halloween night we took potshots at old lady Olanski's front porch light? After the noise of the first wake-up shots that smacked the front siding … heh, heh." Wayne's laugh was contagious. Mike chuckled with him and nodded at the remembrance.

"She swung open the big red front door and damn near took the next two shots in the face. Caused us no end of nightmares. She told Pop everything, but we always got our revenge. Every time the old biddy tattled, we pulled another shenanigan to fire things up and justify our next prank. Kind of makes ya think about the two of us, now, in our sixties, here on the river, lucky to be alive after a genuine shoot-out. We're doing quite the same thing. Will we ever grow up?"

"I'd think the County Sheriff's Office has been called by now. With all the shooting, Wayne," Mike said more seriously. "Maybe they'll come out from Mio, see the gate, and do something about it without our intervention. Ahhh, such sweet revenge, it would be.

"Think we can cover your warning shots, from our fear of the dog attack? They were getting awful derned uppity, and they were off his property. How can he excuse that near miss when the log took the slug meant for my chest. That was attempted murder. Do you think we should report it ourselves, exactly as it happened?"

The temperature of the night air that encircled the brothers suddenly dropped, and the willows above them vibrated in a strange way. "Mike, what in goodness' name was that frightening display of childish behavior up there at the Morris place? You might have been killed." Mike shook from the cold and from her stern scolding as well. He was about to reply when she broke in with more. "I thought I told you; I warned you. I saw the danger when you two came up here tonight. Maybe it will be unsafe always, I don't know. You disregarded everything I said, Honey."

Meg's tone of voice softened, she realized Mike's concern with the provocative series of events, and seemed pleased at how he and Wayne calmed themselves with the humorous stories they related. Such reminiscences averted the need for retaliatory action, most certainly not how they would have reacted in earlier years. "I wanted you to have that property," she said. "I can't visualize it not being yours, but the possibility may be behind you, Mike."

We didn't go there to cause trouble. We went to fish. Then he spoke aloud. "Our lines were already in the water, our flies drifted toward the big pool when the derned dogs bounded into that beautiful quiet, right before our eyes. They messed up everything. Shucks, we paddled nearly a mile downstream from North Road, so we wouldn't encroach on the property. We just wanted to fish."

Wayne heard his words and added, earnestly, to assuage Mike. "That's right Meg. We went to fish. It was my fault the firing began. The fellow's dogs. ..." He caught himself mid-sentence and wondered whether he, too, lost his marbles. "C'mon Mike, let's paddle back. We've a ways to go and it's getting late. I've had it for the river tonight. Pitch black anyhow. We can sneak by on the far side."

Meg continued, "Now, Mike, you go straight on up-river and stroke like Indians, just like you taught me. Make not a sound as you cut with those paddles, and don't splash, boys. Be careful. Do I have to watch you every minute?" she teased softly before her voice disappeared into the darkness, across the riffles and over the quiet water.

Wayne shoved the canoe into the current and jumped in close behind Mike. They pulled hard, without so much as a dripping noise, and stayed close to the north bank where the current that faced them stayed mild. The paddlers made slow way around the talons of the fallen log, then gracefully passed across the big pool to the shoals on the other side. They snuck beneath the overhanging cedar and out of sight to the west.

"Hey," Wayne shrieked too loudly, though they moved well past the Morris place, "the canoe's half full of water. There's a hole up here. Look, a bullet hole—river water coming in like a faucet—must have started as soon as we shoved off. He grabbed an overhanging sapling, cut a small twig with his skinning knife and wedged it in to stop the flow. "The nerve of the guy to shoot at our boat. He did that on purpose, just to be sadistic. It was ten yards from our position, not even in the firing line, was it? Now, why did he go and tick me off like that?

"Incidentally, what do you suppose happened up there when the woman started to scream? Two more shots followed the ones that splashed 'round us. You heard the others, didn't you?"

"Wayne, I was so scared when the log shattered in front of me, I wasn't conscious of anything but keeping my body submerged. There were more shots, however, I heard no more pinging around us, now that you mention it. What did she say again?"

"Oh, you heard her. You said so to me. You've forgotten already? She yelled like a Banshee. 'Put down the gun; stop the shooting. What the hell are you doing.' she keeps sayin'. Then *BAM,* I hears more yelling; sounded like a tussle and then another, *BAM.* It got real quiet. When the dogs ran up the bank, it gave us time to get in the canoe, and paddle out. I was nearly spaced myself, so I don't recall all the details."

"You … you … don't suppose. …" Mike hesitated.

Wayne filled in the blank space. "That he shot her, or maybe she nailed him? Do we know what happened? No! Did someone get shot in a struggle for the gun?" Mike withheld reply, but he knew what would come next.

"We're going back," Wayne insisted. "We'll head down river and find out what did occur, right here and now. Maybe one of them's a layin' out there on the bluff, deader'n a doorknob. What went on? Shouldn't we call the cops while the body's still warm? Ask Meg."

Mike would have summoned her, but Wayne was right. They had to verify Claybourne and the woman were both alive before going home. No further discussion, the canoe spun around, and they pulled heartily with the current, toward the south bank, invisible in the settling pitchy mist.

CHAPTER 10

All four wide-tread tires dug in, spat mud, and shot gravel far behind. They spun wildly and the back end swung from shoulder to rut-cleaved shoulder. The general's Excursion roared through the woods at too fast a clip for the twists in the serpentine path that lead to the gate at Old River Road.

Homer Claybourne was not at the wheel. He lay supine on the rear seat, close to unconsciousness. His right upper arm, numbed and awash in blood, pulsed from a slashed artery with more gusto than the hurriedly wrapped bath towel could mask. Virginia Blakes, the driver, and Claybourne's companion, unused to the heavy vehicle, barely held it in control.

Forty years old, younger than the injured man by eighteen years, and proud of her un-tinted, yet jet black hair, she hailed from Arlington, Virginia. Divorced from her n'er do well, navy gunner's mate ex-husband, Virginia vowed, never again, to allow love or good sex to interfere with the possibility of elegant living. As her first marriage ended, she swathed herself in wealth, jumped from man-to-man and bed-to-bed. Virginia managed to live quite well with many upper crust, though temporary partners, while she milled about the party scene with their well-heeled friends and business associates.

She never had a healthy fund to call her own, however, and that kept her restless. Always on the hunt for something more, accurately characterized her motivations. The only daughter of U.S. Army General Rodmend Blakes, Retired; Virginia did her best to surround herself with as much pomp and finery in military circles that a normal person with reasonable expectations could tolerate. Shy of normality, she required more than was immediately available, or offered. Spoiled beyond repair, and in the early stage of the aging process, she wondered how long her innate beauty would last; a haunting verity that reared its ugly head in times of upset.

She accelerated on a short straightaway, glanced in the rear view mirror, turned her head to the side to assure her hair remained tightly pulled, and fingered the clasped bun in back. She pressed knees to the wheel to hold the car steady, and fluffed the silk scarf around her neck. Tugs at the pockets of her pale blue corduroy blouse, uplifted her small though youthful breasts, bare beneath the soft fabric. Hands returned to the wheel to face oncoming ruts, and, in a rougher section of the narrow road, Virginia looked to the rear to check on her rider.

Claybourne's eyes remained closed. She shrieked, "Homer! Homer? His eyelids quivered. "Has the bleeding not stopped? I am so sorry." He appeared more pale, somewhat whitish, she thought. "I shouldn't have tried to take the rifle away from you."

"Damn it! Stop the blubbering. It's only a flesh wound; no bones damaged, thank God. It wasn't entirely your fault. If you just didn't meddle. Don't ever pull something like that again, you hear? Keep your fool mouth quiet at the hospital, doctor's office, or whatever facility we can find in one of these Yankee hick towns," the general said rudely. "That kind of talk, for Christ's sake, and you'll get one or both of us arrested, even jailed. Who knows what the cops would do to a couple of out-of-state types from the south, one with a bullet wound, blood pumping like sixty?

"You've got to get yourself together or else," he gasped twice with difficulty, "or someone's going to get arrested. Y'all hear, now? You hear me, Missy? Listen, Ginny." he went on, though with less fervor, and then tried to placate her. Claybourne sat upright and loosened the reddened towel long enough to survey the damage. He winced and pulled it back more tightly with his free hand, once he saw the throbbing rush of crimson return.

"You'll let me explain what happened," he insisted. "If I pass out or have to go under anesthesia, simply say I was cleaning the gun. You didn't see it occur." He yelled sharply from the pain when the Excursion jumped from an unseen dip. She turned the wheel instinctively, and the left side of the car brushed noisily along boughs of a fir that overhung the path. "Damn it! Be careful, Virginia! This is my nice clean Ford. Sure, I bought it used, but it's like new and I don't want it scratched up, looking the same as every Michigan deer hunter's pick up."

"Why did those men yell and scream so, at the dogs? There was commotion down at the river. She ignored his admonitions. "Homer," she asked, "why did they shoot at you, at us? My God in heaven, it sounded like a war movie out there. ..."

"A war movie?" he cut in sarcastically and curled again from his wound. It sounded like a movie, you say? Christ, it sounded like a war, not a damned film. God knows, I've spent enough time listening to the real things, in my day."

His eyelids fell and thoughts jumped back. *May 13, 1965--Phuoc Long, Vietnam: I was a wild-eyed lieutenant, fresh out of West Point and training. North Vietnamese artillery and ground forces brutally attacked my Special Forces camp. Americans died in the intensive clutter of mortar, sniper, cannon, machine gun, and grenade launcher fire. I thought it would never stop.*

He pulled his body through tall elephant grass that afternoon, limp from wounds to both calves, left forearm, and the right side of his head. "I fast discerned the difference between movie tactics and the real thing," he continued on, then turned inward with his memory input. *The dead, our dead were everywhere. They had to be crawled over, rested upon, hidden beneath, in my effort to move toward sheltering trees at the edge of the clearing. Some trees we stupidly crawled toward, held VC snipers, tied into their top branches, well camoflaged and near invisible. They waited patiently and fired all through the daylight hours, at anything that moved. No medics, no medical supplies ... only what we carried. I had my cigarettes, smoked all of them, and didn't give a damn if Charlie saw me after a while. You ask if I know about shooting?*

Shattering his reminiscences, Virginia continued, "I was in the cellar and heard a pistol fire—a .38 or .45, I thought. Daddy and I used both at the range. Then your M-16 fired and what a racket that made. I had no idea what the devil was happening outside, so I ran up the steps. There you stood, poised like you were blasting a trench full of enemy soldiers. Why were they firing from down at the river?"

"Oh, the guy was reacting … to … by … ah, he … they. …" Claybourne tried to answer, though timidly, and stammered further, "dogs … went for them in a big way, they did, and they … would not relent.

"I'd have been scared out of my Yankee wits, too. The intruders didn't realize our big babies are all talk and no action. They did look determined and mean, however, so one of the men popped a warning shot to scare them. I lost control, completely lost it, when I heard the shots. Hard to imagine; two men trespassing on our property, shooting at our animals.

"'What the hell is this?' I asked myself. 'They're good dogs, and they're here to guard the place.' So, I unleashed a volley over their heads, hit their canoe with one, but in recoil, one round damned near got the tall fellow behind the fallen log, in the grass." He gestured toward the river with his uninjured hand, and bounced when the car struck a protruding rock.

The general groaned from the jarring. "Slow this thing down, will you. You'll throw me through the roof. I sure was relieved to see the guy get up and run for the rushes. Could have killed him, and then where would we have been? Already, it's become serious enough. I'm close to losing my arm; we have a shooting incident to explain, and our privacy to maintain. This is not good. We'll argue that they were vandalizing our property if a police inquiry follows."

"It's my fault," Virginia said; she sobbed, over the results of her interference. "I shouldn't have grabbed for the rifle. I wanted no more shooting. I will not stand around, and watch someone kill or be killed and take no action to halt the mayhem. I didn't spend close to twenty years as a surgical nurse for nothing, Homer. I'm a lifesaver, not a taker. "I am so sorry. Please don't hold it against me, Darling. Please, I'll make it up to you; I just wanted to keep you alive."

"You're in this for the millions; you know it as well as I do; so, don't, 'Darling' me too awful much, Sweetheart. You're not in it to be with old Homer for the rest of your upper-crust life. I've known of you since you were a thieving little teenager in the suburbs, and I've seen enough of your manipulating, ass-kissing daddy to last a long time, too. Aren't we in, both of us together, for the millions?"

Virginia shrugged affirmatively though with a futile expression, pulled the car to a stop and awaited the gate's opening. Impatient, she pounded clenched fists on the wheel as the concealed motors whirred. "Please don't talk like that. It was you. You reached for the muzzle when I grabbed for the rifle. I could have been shot just as easily," she retorted.

"Don't insult me or my father. You're in this as deeply as we are. We need to watch each other's backs; you said that yourself, when the idea was first broached. We'd better make the big bucks we're counting on, millions, I say, considering the risks taken, and the filthy, stinking men I've had to put up with so far."

"Hey, I'm bleeding now because of your craziness. Let's get this crate on the main road and start hauling. I don't need to rehash your complaints. This will work itself out; mark my words," the general muttered, but struggled to speak clearly. "We'll play it through and must exercise the utmost tolerance for whatever is necessary, as we pander to our goals. Please forget my upset right now. I've a gaping arm injury and it could be a long-term problem. I've got to be in my strength for what looms ahead; you know that, Virginia."

"Oh, I'll play the game; don't you fret, General Claybourne. I'm a committed contestant, especially with these stakes, and I'll work the board to the very last man," Virginia continued with the sudden cool of a seasoned professional. "You need not worry about your Ginny, Homer. Worry about your back-stabbing military cronies, not me."

Once on the paved highway and more composed, she again checked her hair, wiped dried tears from her eyes, and organized her thoughts for the tasks she faced. They had to find a hospital; the general's arm needed treatment as quickly as possible.

Still, Virginia Blakes worried. *The missiles will be here all too soon. The place has to be safe from intrusions like this. Well beforehand, we need to familiarize our security people with the confusing terrain around the house. I have to find out more about the men Homer tangled with tonight. They could be our first real threat. I won't have our long-standing efforts, the chances we have taken, allow any room for failure. No one will compromise our plans.. My remaining youth is out on a limb and Daddy's future, too. No one, including Homer, will stand in my way.*

Virginia pondered her new mission, by far, a more stressful one than she envisioned, filled, though, with the most financially rewarding potential, beyond anything she imagined. Legal or bordered on the illegal—in the past—she undertook either method to advance herself. This would be the crowning glory, however, and would assure her return to Arlington, if ever, in high style. She could cover up the embarrassing bankruptcy, and the close shaves she had with the law.

Virginia had to forget Paul Lonzzi, the brisk and handsome Italian, ten years her junior, to whom she was engaged for nearly six months— her last fling, though the least redeeming—before Claybourne. Lonzzi charmed himself into the town's wealth and charity scene, and led Virginia, at first unwittingly, into a con game that involved the sale of thoroughbred horses, all but ready for the glue factory. Prices paid for the lame and unproductive animals, mostly by naïve Florida retirees, set the plotting couple up for a healthy level of spending: jewelry for her, cars and fancy clothes for him, and lots of travel for them both. The seed money, though, came from a small inheritance left by her grandmother.

Lonzzi ran with that, and everything else moveable, including almost all her personal possessions. He disappeared in the midst of night when the law began to close in, and left her alone to face family, friends, and the authorities, with whom she had much explaining to do.

Criminal fraud charges threatened and there were a few lawsuits. Her father sympathetically intervened, though, and hired locally revered counsel, Colonel Junior Patton "Buzz" Jennings—noted defense attorney for the Washington D. C. political crowd. She scraped by relatively unscathed, and with little injury to her already jaded reputation.

While in the process of cleansing herself, Virginia found herself surprisingly receptive to Homer Claybourne's overtures of friendliness when they were formally introduced a year before in Florida, at the Ft. Myers Officers Club. She allowed her injured ego to begin healing beneath his seemingly strong and immediately protective wings that night. After a few dances, too many drinks, and token small talk with the attending military gentry, the two escaped across the street to the darkened Summerall Field. High up in the bleachers, they talked for hours in the warmth of the evening, before she lured him to her condo on Key Boulevard.

Both needed companionship, to avert loneliness. A bond quickly developed. Claybourne, a two star general, seemed well schooled in societal mores. He appeared financially well heeled, and was about to retire from the army. Younger, lively, and fun loving, Virginia presented herself as a catch well beyond Claybourne's usual imagination and was, important at the time, larcenous enough to fill the unique position her father sought. She and General Blakes, in turn, needed someone just like Claybourne as an accomplice, in their efforts to finalize the bloom of a huge fortune.

Claybourne's fifty-eight years left him youthful in appearance, tight, strong and active, save the emotional scars from Vietnam that plagued him too often. Deep brown eyes, rugged facial features and nice teeth, he exuded self-confidence. Though contemptuous at times, his brash sense of humor drew him as a regular invitee to military social functions, for the wooing of unattached females—that is—before he met up with Virginia. Their encounter in Arlington that summer stemmed an intense relationship that led to a merger of households after three months of continual dating. She moved into his downtown, two-story home, not far from her condominium.

Travel, golf, tennis, expensive nights in the city, and lots of time for romance, urged Virginia to quit her nursing job in surgery at Arlington Hospital, where she worked with a prominent heart team. She missed the camaraderie and the excitement, but not the high stress level her position required. Initially, life with the general was good, she thought.

Claybourne stayed quiet, and held the towel to his bleeding arm while she drove.

Yes, life is good, except for Homer's rages, aftermaths of his dreams, such horrible ones, all the death, and suffering he experienced in Southeast Asia. The memories will always plague him and, if I'm in the way, they could eventually envelop me, too. Damn it! Sometimes I think I've been there myself. I despise Homer when he takes his army nightmares out on me. How I can hate the man, at times.

She called to him, and interrupted contained emotions. "We're getting close to Mio, Homer. We'll get you medical attention in a few minutes, I hope. Are you able to move your fingers? I'm worried about bone, tendon, even nerve injury. It's a real mess in there and I couldn't see much through all the coagulated blood." *What use will he be to me as a cripple? He's on his own, that's what! I've spent eighteen years working hard as a scrub nurse. I'm not switching to geriatric care quite yet.*

Claybourne responded faintly, "I'll just let the doctors sift it out, I guess. I can move all my fingers, but they feel so numb, and the hand is almost white. Suppose that's because of arterial damage, higher up my arm."

"Of course," Virginia replied. She turned back to look at him. "There's a severe tear in the basilic vein, brachial artery, possibly both— very large vessels in there. One of them took the hit. Those vessels funnel blood up and down the arm … major suppliers."

"I don't care what the hell they're called. I just need patching up. I want you to be sure these hick doctors up here can do the repairs or I'll have to go south to Detroit, I suppose, to a large facility. Remember! Don't be stupid. Keep your big mouth shut when it comes to reports on what happened. Just keep the jaw buttoned tight. Do not be a volunteer."

"Homer, I'll not repeat myself. You keep up with the condescension, and you'll make me sing like a canary. Why do you insist on degrading me like that?" Her fine eyebrows arched and her unblemished forehead suddenly bristled with ripples. Blushed from anger, Virginia stopped the car with a screech of tires. "I want that talk stopped this instant," she went on with increased irritation.

"You'll drive me away with your lack of trust. It's all you can do to be nice to me lately, since we moved here, in fact. Now, cut it or I'll take off for home as suddenly as we got together in my condominium that night. You do remember, don't you? I'll say, 'to hell with you, with Palestine, and the whole damned plan. To the devil with all of it,' Homer."

The general sprung up, reached forward with his good arm, and clasped the nape of the young woman's neck in his large hand. Fingers squeezed slowly, but vise-like, as they inched part way around to her throat. He bit his tongue, then growled menacingly, "Virginia, you're in with me to the end, up to this pretty white neck, you are. There will be no leaving and don't you forget it. 'You're here until this little war is over, completely finished, and we have our money. Afterward, you're still in it up to the waist. You take off beforehand, you could disappear, you know. It's that damned serious. You do understand the terms? Now, y'all remember the agreements you made, Honey Child." He held the grasp to drive home his point until she flinched from the pain, then released it abruptly and shoved her head forward for emphasis. "Now get us going and clam up!"

The approaching lights at the edge of town eased her mind some, but she was was frightened, shocked, too, with the sudden flare of his temper, and the threatening remarks. For more than two months, he grew increasingly physical. She knew it was too late to withdraw as a participant in the carefully planned mission. Almost imprisoned, restrained against her will, and close to hopelessly servile, Virginia became fearfully cognizant that she played in the big leagues, for big stakes, woefully unprepared. She went to bed with a relentless player, to whom the answer, 'No,' could never be uttered. Choice no longer remained an option. Running away, her most familiar response to unpleasantness when the heat turned on, would not be a remedy this time. She already went too far, and would have to see it through.

I've made poor choices with men in my day but this one is beginning to pale all others by comparison. Who does he think he is? If it weren't for the time I spent with those slobs, the obnoxious, chauvinistic Palestine

Liberation thugs in D.C. two months ago, Homer wouldn't have this game to play. He went fishing and I was the lure, just plain bait. They pawed me, fondled, tore off my clothes, and poured liquor over me. So awful it was!

She trembled at the remembrance. *I was but a piece of meat. They did what they wanted. I thought it would never end and I had to put up with Homer seated there, watching, probably getting his kicks. He acted as if I were nothing ...naught more than an item of entertainment for his business prospects. What animals! How can men be that way?*

Virginia perspired heavily and grew quiet with the stunning recall. She cleared her cheeks of tears with her shirt cuff, and pulled into an all-night gas station at the town's outskirts, to ask directions from the attendant, who leaned perilously back in a rickety chair by the outside pumps. He told her there were no critical care centers in town, that the two family medical offices were closed nights. "Best bet, Miss ... yup ... best bet is to head west. By the way, you familiar with the area here?" the toothless man inquired, while he shuffled to the front and rear, and enviously drooled over the Excursion. "Best idea ... head west and. ..."

"Hey, we're in a heck of a hurry, Mister. West on this road, you say? What's out that way?" she asked.

"Well, Grayling ... yup ... City of Grayling ... that's what. Ya go to the next corner, slip to the left and head down to seventy-two. Stay on ... hey that guy in the back ... he OK, ma'am? Appears he's a bleedin' like a stuck pig. Why, he is bleeding, isn't he?" The attendant opened the back door and stuck his head in for a closer look at the reclined general.

"What the hell do you think you're doing?" Claybourne seethed. "Get out of here; we're in a hurry." A clamp of toughened fingers snapped down on the curious man's shoulder helped him sit up again. The attendant squawked in surprise and withdrew from his grasp. He peered through the open front window, and screamed at Virginia, "Now, you go find the damned highway yourselves. Get out of here before I calls the cops, he squawked through the dust cloud that arose from spinning tires, and surrounded him in the pale light. "I'll call 'em. They'll be here in. ..."

CHAPTER 11

———◆•◆•◆———

The Excursion's gone," Wayne whispered. He and Mike crawled cautiously over the dew-dampened leaves at the edge of the bluff, noses to the ground. They felt safe, with no signs of activity after they beached the canoe and waited on the sand bar below. A red 1957 Chevrolet pickup was parked next to the barn. Table lamps in the front room of the shack threw just enough light on the bluff for them to find their way.

"The big car is gone. The general must have taken the Ford when we paddled upstream. Must have left in one hell of a hurry, too." Wayne continued.

Stone quiet prevailed around the path's end, but for muffled whines of the three dogs. "Sounds like they put the animals away, more 'n likely in the cellar. Should be safe enough to prod around for a minute or two, I suppose," Mike replied. The two stood at the edge of the clearing until they felt assured no one remained. "The dogs must be contained. You have the bag of meat, right?" Mike asked, "just in case."

Wayne patted his wet jacket pocket in acknowledgement. "Ready to toss in their direction when we starts a running." He swung his small flashlight back and forth, as they shuffled to the clearing. Wayne dropped to his knees for a closer look, when he reached the spot from where Claybourne fired at them. "Mike, Brother, lookitey here, on these pine needles. It's blood, isn't it? Damned if someone didn't stop a bullet. My God, it's quite a puddle here. Look over there ... more spots. Someone was spoutin' like a pump." Wayne crawled again, in a widening circle, and searched the fallen leaves, while he spoke apprehensively.

Mike, too, bent to the ground for closer scrutiny. He patted a moistened spot with his finger, held it beneath the light and rubbed the sticky red paste in his palm. His eyes, glazed and widened, showed the fear that churned inside. Stomach muscles gripped in tight contracture. "It dern sure is blood. Could be from one of the dogs. Good heavens, Wayne, could you have shot one of them? Is that possible? We're in real deep stuff, if you did; tell you that right now. You don't shoot a person's hunting dog, dern it, you just. ..."

"I tell you it wasn't me," Wayne interrupted. Remember, I only fired twice. All three dogs were down by the river, coming at us. Then came the rifle fire in our direction, and finally, the last two reports we only heard. Didn't see who fired them. Those shots rang out after the woman carried on so, correct? Wayne, too, shook as he spoke.

"Yes ... yes," Mike affirmed, "after her screams. Maybe the rifle brought blood; but who was injured? Was it an accident? The general is certainly a weird character, sure acted psycho."

"Here are two shell casings, standard M-193 ammo for an M-16. It must be a model A1, early issue, 1965 or thereabouts," Wayne said. He took his from here; both shells dropped around the blood stains." Wayne walked to the bluff's edge and found more expelled shells that sparkled in the yellow glow of his penlight. "No sign of any other firearm. These casings are all the same, from his carbine. Such a good gun for combat, it was. I got a brand new one when I arrived in 'Nam but used an M40-A1 for sniping, with its longer barrel and larger slugs. The newer .223 caliber projectiles for the M-16 were fast, but too inaccurate for us long distance snipers."

He fingered the casings and stuffed them into his pack. So many years ago, he still remembered the first station to which his freshly trained, four man sniping team was taken when he arrived at Viet Nam's sprawling delta. Their nest was a rock outcrop that sat well above the plain. It overlooked a narrow pass through which Communist patrols passed in early dawn hours, to hide in the shelter of tunnels or the nearby hilly terrain, during daylight.

The enemy groups operated mainly through the night, and their activities had to stop. They caused far too many U.S. casualties. Available sniper shots required pinpoint accuracy at distances up to one thousand yards. Wayne stayed well barricaded, covered in weeds from the area, and waited on a ledge where, supported by the bipod, his rifle, at the ready, stayed solidly positioned.

The first group we saw; I can picture those two sawed-off little ranking officers in front. Then, I sees the one toting the thirty-caliber, who appears in the crosshairs, walking confidently, bent slightly as he passed under some low-drooped fan palm leaves. My finger squeezed slowly. I waits for the blast, the kick, and the time it took for the strike. It seemed like forever."

Mike's call startled him from his wanderings. "Brother! Wayne," Mike called, eyes afire. "here's an M-16, propped against the maple." He picked up the short-barreled carbine, removed the twenty-shot magazine and pulled back the bolt to expel the chambered cartridge. It dropped by his feet. He handed the piece to Wayne with a satisfied grin, and watched while his brother examined it.

"Yup, this is the A1, all right; just like the one I was issued. He counted cartridges left in the magazine as he snapped them free. "... Nine, ten, eleven and the one you ejected. That's it. The madman fired five at us and then, the two final ones. This guy knows what he's doing," Wayne said sternly, and cocked his head toward Mike. "He loaded it with nineteen rounds, not the twenty it can handle; the mark of someone familiar with the gun's tendency to jam, with the magazine fully packed. Guess he's the rare general who knows his small arm weaponry. Wonder what he did in his later years with the army? Let's mosey over to the house and see what we can see." Wayne readied himself to dispense chunks of meat to the dogs if required, and motioned his brother to follow.

Mike propped a cut log below the large front window, stepped on it cautiously, and peered over the sill, into the living room where two table lamps burned shyly in the far corner. "Same wallpaper as before, Wayne, different furniture, and a huge desk by the window. He ties flies, Jesus crisp, in the very same spot I would have set up my worktable; gol dern him. He's got an expensive tying vise there, feathers, too, hackles he'll need for the caddis flies. He's after brownies, I guess, getting ready for the hatch. He must know a little about fly fishing; leastways, he has the gear.

"I get furious when I think this could have been mine, really heat up inside. I can't ignore the growing drive to mess with him." The impacts of Mike's tightly clenched fists on the clapboard exterior reverberated through the building. The dogs sang with panic in their voices. They were contained safely in the cellar as the men suspected earlier.

"He's got a computer on the desk, must have left it on. There, hand me that other stump. I'll just lean over and see what's on the screen." One hand pressed against the window casing while the other stretched to the overhanging eave as Mike arose. Thus supported, he balanced on the stumps and stepped to the sill. While he held himself close to the wall, he had a closer look inside. "The screen has … looks like … yes … a Department of Defense logo at the top," he called to Wayne, "I can see it fairly clearly. Looks like a personal memo or a letter beneath it, but I sure can't read it with these glasses of mine. D.O.D, eh? What's he up to, Brother? You want to try?"

"Wayne jumped up, placed himself against the house wall similarly, and looked curiously inside, cheek against the glass. He wiped condensation from the surface with his shirt cuff, squinted to look again, and read the small type. "P-A-T-R-I-O-T M-I-S-S-I-L-E-S," he read the letters one by one, turned to Mike and said more loudly: "Patriot Missiles! That's what it says under D.O.D … Patriot Missiles and below that, text of a letter, a memo, or something. Those little babies operate ground to air, against other missiles or planes, don't they?

"I have read that, In the past, we've sold them to the Israelis for their air defense systems; was in the paper a few months ago. I was provoked and asked myself, why? Why must we add fuel to the fires? Aren't things burning hot enough—especially right now, with the Palestinian suicide bombings, endless rocketry—then retaliation? Why do they need more firepower?"

Mike held the light. Wayne prepared to step down when a crash resounded, and he cried out. The window, against which he leaned, explosively gave way when he began to fall and reached for support. Glass shards flew everywhere, inside the house, and out. The large man fell with a groan to the soft flowerbed below, more than lucky he wasn't sliced to ribbons. Only his pride suffered. A few seconds passed before he spoke, from a supine position upon newly planted annuals. "Gheeze, wha, what the hell happened?" he uttered. "The mud on my boot was slippery. I guess, I. …"

"Now you've gone and done it." Mike was miffed, unconcerned for the moment over Wayne's well being. "First we shoot at someone in their own front yard; now we're committing a gol derned burglary. What'll we do to top this little escapade? If we get out of it in one piece, we'll be doing well. You OK?" he finally inquired.

"Sure, sure. Just flattened the flowers. So much for those daffodils and tulips."

"Let's get out of here before we do anything else we might regret," Mike pleaded with urgency in his voice, and darted toward the bluff. About to descend to the canoe, he glanced toward the shack and saw Wayne had removed his boots.

"What the Sam Hill are you doing, Brother?"

"I'm going in, that's what. We're here aren't we? Let's find out what we can about this crackpot? May as well do what we'll be accused of having done. I'm in for a look-see around. You stand guard and watch for lights down the path." He broke away remaining splinters of glass from the bottom of the window frame, stepped on the stump, and then to the sill. Wayne slipped easily into the room, and moved straight to the computer.

Mike stopped in his tracks and crouched to the ground, unbelieving and bewildered at what he watched. He was quick to picture himself behind bars at the tiny Mio City Jail, and then state prison, after trial and conviction. *We'll probably be sent to Saginaw Correctional Facility in Freeland. What a God-forsaken place.* Could he bear the thought of friends on the outside, free to fish and hunt with the passing of seasons; while he counted the years going slowly by?

Might he get paroled in five, maybe three years as a first-time offender? Would he be able to deal with the twenty foot, double fences, topped with layer upon layer of razor wire, the armed guards, high security, and cell doors with ports just large enough to pass meals? He got a good look at the place on a TV program that featured Michigan's prisons, and never imagined he would be a candidate for admission. "We're finished, really done," he said aloud. Mike shook his head and squinted fearfully toward the darkened dirt path to his left.

He saw Wayne's head just above the window ledge, blue-lighted by the computer screen. A cooling eddy whistled down through the maple trees above where he knelt in the shadows. His clothes dripped river water, and he shivered from the new chill.

She spoke as clearly as she did in the bedroom, late in his first night at the cabin. "Michael Gladdock. Michael Jules Gladdoski! "What in the names of all the saints are the two of you doing? You cannot be participating in this! Wayne is inside the shack, and you've been shooting at the new owners. Am I to sit back and say nothing? Your judgment today and tonight—the choices you made—slipped to a level I'd not have believed possible. I'm as disgusted as I was in your drinking days, when you needed someone to shield you from ill-advised decisions. You might as well be drunk as a skunk, right now. Yes, just like the old days: no rules and no standards to uphold, just because I'm absent from your life."

Mike bristled, said nothing in his defense, and continued to shiver.

"I feel as I did the time you stood up the girls and me. We were due at Daddy's birthday party. Surely you recall, don't you?" She gave him no chance to respond and followed up without taking a breath. Mike's guilt reeked.

"We waited on the front porch, faithful you were upheld at work. It rained that day, off and on, and twisters were in the forecast. The kids didn't want to take shelter in the cellar; you were soon to arrive. We took our chances on the porch, fried in the late afternoon heat and humidity. Jennifer's crying between squalls and the rapping thunder didn't help. No Mike, Daddy, no calls."

He pictured Meg—she shook her fists like a prizefighter—the dressing down he faced and wisely let her rant go forth.

"You promised we'd be there for Dad's surprise. That was at four o'clock. We waited and watched the kitchen clock hands spin to five, six, seven, on to eight thirty, and it began to get dark. Still, the girls wanted to believe their father cared, that he would be home in time, as he promised. You did come, Michael. Yes, you did," she rambled, deep in sarcasm. "Showed up at 9:30, past their bedtime. The party broke up about then and we were thirty minutes away. You recall, don't you?"

I would not have predicted this rampage, not ever. Doesn't Meg recognize I've tried to pay for mistakes like that, by releasing the demons that held me so tightly, by paying homage to my obligations, and by adhering to a decent course of conduct since I joined AA? Or, am I to be haunted forever by my errors? Do I ever remember? Do I recall my low feelings? He dropped his head in shame without reply, and wrung sweating hands together in frustration.

"Now, don't start feeling sorry for yourself. Try to experience what you put us through that evening. It wasn't just that night. There were so many other broken promises. Family parties, when you did arrive on time, you, Wayne, and your mother got so drunk that the Gladdocks looked like fools in the process. I became an accessory, just being your wife. Do you know how humiliating that was, as the incidents increased? Do you remember the night when you nearly connected with the swing you took at. …"

"I didn't connect, thank God and his mercy. All right, all right, Meg. That's the last straw. Don't I look upset enough to you, Dear? What's the matter? Don't I appear guilt-ridden enough to show you I'm not feeling proud? Yes, I went completely out of whack when I drank."

Eyes closed, he related the words aloud, when Wayne approached from the shack, wide-eyed with excitement. He looked battle-worn. Blood from glass cuts dried on his hands and forearms. His boots were mud-encrusted. Clumps of dirt from the flowerbed soiled the back of his jacket. He wore an ill-fitting fatigue cap. Pointing proudly to it, he broke Mike's musings with Meg. "Spoils from the enemy, Bro. You like my new U.S. Army hat?"

"You just took that, stole it from the house, Wayne? You think that's OK?"

"Say, you weren't talking to … to her, were you? Is she being pissy with us, for the … oh, hell … for everything that we's done tonight? Any self-respecting woman would be, for Christ's sake. It's certainly understandable, I figures. I'm not happy myself, except for what we's discovered here in the Morris shack in Oscoda County, Michigan…a byte of new history. This is simple, country Michigan, Mike. There is stuff floating downhill that beats 'em all, if I'm right about what that computer seems to suggest." He spat noisily between his teeth.

"Thweeth, thweeth. I may be a damned low-life auto mechanic from East Tawas, but Daddy didn't breed me stupid. You know that and so do you, Meg." He raised his voice considerably and spoke with notable derision when he looked upward, into the overhanging trees.

Mike, still in shock from Meg's tirade, didn't react immediately to Wayne's pronouncement. He stared blankly, unfocused, into the darkness, and bobbed his head in several apathetic nods, without making eye contact.

"You really do look beaten." Wayne went on. "I probably seems the same, but I was inside and risked my backside for both of us, to see what I could see. I saw lots, Mike. Yep, I did see plenty. I told you I read 'Patriot Missiles' from outside. Well, I wasn't imagining that. The words appeared in the caption of a letter beneath it. I printed a copy and have it here in my pocket. It sounds like this guy, the woman, and missiles to the Palestinians are mixed up together, right here, in our woods. "The Palestinians, for heaven's sake, Mike; do you know how far away they are from here?" Wayne jogged his eyebrows up and down and cocked a wry smile. "Wouldn't it be cute if, suddenly, Arab troublemakers had the ability to shoot down Israeli jet fighters, helicopters, missiles and bombers? Wouldn't that change the state of Middle East affairs? Today they throw stones at the police, fire unsophisticated rockets, sacrifice a suicide bomber here and there, and tomorrow, they fire missiles and drop Israeli planes from the skies. Think of the interesting shift in power. Sure would give our administration fits to explain, wouldn't it?"

Both shunned interest in Arab politics over the years. Absent any direct effect upon their lives, neither came close to understanding the deeply rooted issues, but Wayne forced Mike's attention. It made sense when he reconsidered the story.

Mike read the somewhat cryptic text aloud while his brother held the paper beneath the dimming penlight:

General Abdul Shal al Badiza
Palestine Liberty Outdoor Equipment Corporation
Re: Patriot Missile Carnival Ride

Within several weeks, Operation Eastern Star *will be ready to execute. Home Base is to be the site of final negotiations and arrangements. It is well out of the way here, isolated, and free of possible surveillance. Forty crates are being readied as we correspond, dimensions about eight feet by two feet square, making up twenty units, total, when assembled. The 'P' cylinders come complete with ninety-kilogram warheads and on-board electronics. They will be of the new PAC-3 design with advanced guidance.*

One launching station, holding four units is now available. Later, possibly an additional station can be procured if all goes well.

Finally, and this presents the only logistical problem for shipment, the order will include an AN/MSQ-104 Engagement Control Station. You have already employed the three personnel trained to operate it. The ECS will fit within a small semi-trailer and is completely self-contained, but for the needed power supply.

The price appears to be firming at twenty million, yet to be finally determined. Communicate through this e-mail address hereafter; we are out of Virginia for good,

now. Finally, we appreciate your interest in our envied
recreational products.

Cordially,
Vibrant Outdoor Toy Company
Homer P. Claybourne, President

The men turned and their eyes met when Mike finished reading. He was filled with questions. "Sure doesn't sound like they're selling carnival rides, does it? You left no indications that you printed the letter?" You're sure, Wayne, no mistakes? Did you scroll back to exactly what we read from the window?"

He expelled a hiss when he thought of Wayne's tumble from the ledge, and the shattering glass. "What about the dirt? You didn't leave traces that you sat in the chair at the computer, no signs at all? Wayne, this is important. If they think we've stumbled on anything, M-16 rifle fire won't be the next artillery Claybourne uses. Who was the recipient of the letter? Who do you think they are?"

"Jesus," Wayne laughed, "I'm not as stupid as some might think. I left everything except the window, regrettably, just as it was when I climbed inside. Set a brick just inside to suggest it was callously thrown through. Now, let's get the hell out of here, up the river to the car, and home to bed. We'll figure out how to process all this information when we get some sleep, and can think more clearly. My Lord, it's two o'clock in the morning," Wayne said. He picked up the M-16 as if it were his, whipped the sling over his shoulder, and shuffled toward the bluff.

"Not a soul hears about this, not a solitary soul, right?" Mike demanded with some trepidation, knowing his brother's proclivity to boast of his adventures to willing buddies. "Not even Nell, agreed? Is she going to be worried about the late hour?"

"You know she knows, that on hunting or fishing nights, no arrival times are specified. It's a long tradition in our family. I don't ask questions on bingo night, and she leaves me to my devices for nights in the woods. At least she's confident we're not in the bars as we might have been twenty or thirty years ago. She knows I'm safe from. …"

"Get the devil in the canoe, quickly, now," Mike warned. "I just heard the dogs growling. Sounds like they're up from the cellar, maybe coming outside." The men ran for the riverbank, pummeled down to the water, launched the canoe and with a few deep strokes, moved upstream to safety. Not far behind, the general's three hounds roared along the south shore until the bank rose vertically from the water and prevented further progress Their angry baying rattled the forest's stillness, while the brothers slid out of sight, upstream and around the bend.

CHAPTER 12

———◆◆◆———

Greatly relieved she made it, Virginia Blakes bounded through Grayling Hospital's automatic double doors, which hissed open as she pushed the wheelchair over the rubber matting. The darkened hallway close to the entrance, so unlike big city medical centers where she worked, struck her as appealing, absent the myriad patients usually seen, practically stacked on top of one another, in long waits to hear their numbers called. Familiar hospital scents filled her nostrils, however, and helped control heightened tensions. She found the coral, taupe and putty wall colors pleasantly soothing, even attractive, beneath the white fluorescent lights. So different from the boring, sterile look of most hospital corridors she had seen, the environment felt friendly, almost inviting. Light beige vinyl floors glistened as they received a fresh coat of wax. An enormous rotary polishing machine twisted and pulled at the hands of the diminutive janitor who barely held rein as it hummed back and forth in its final mission for the night. Otherwise, save the synchronic clicks from a nearby computer, it was terribly still. That spelled minimum staff, maybe the lack of medical personnel on duty. Her temper fused when she visualized an impossible wait, after the long and harrowing drive.

"We need a trauma surgeon … STAT … please," Virginia panted to the bespectacled clerk at the desk. "He's got an injury here and it's getting worse. Lost lots of blood, too much for his own good. We've come a long way, didn't. …" Frightened and pale, she was short of breath from pushing the general up slope in the wheelchair she found in a far corner of the parking lot.

Claybourne assumed the color of a canned pear. Though conscious, his head slumped over on his left shoulder. He still held tightly to the blood-soaked towel wrapped around his right upper arm. His dark and usually compelling eyes, lack-luster and forlorn; spoke fatigue, and weakness.

"Is there a surgeon on duty or on call? Please, I can't make him travel any further tonight. We'll need someone with vascular experience. His axilla is a damned mess … maybe the brachial artery … basilic artery or vein … wide open and pumping. Just as soon as pressure is relieved, his blood just pours."

She puffed as she spoke, noticed the curious eyes of two green scrub-attired women who passed by, then bent forward and anxiously awaited a response. The clerk got up from her perch at the cluttered desk, nodded philosophically, and whisked Claybourne and his companion into a cubicle.

"Now, what do we have here; how'd this happen, Mister ah. …?"

Virginia started to answer for him. "Well, we … that is, he had his rifle out there … outside the house, of course." She smiled nervously. "He loaded … oh, and his name is Homer Claybourne."

The general sparked to attention and interrupted with a shout. "Damn it! I don't need anyone to speak for me. I'm just as capable as ever to talk in my own behalf. Now, now, shut up … er please, be quiet for a moment here; allow me to take care of this," he whimpered. "My name is H-o-m-e-r P. C-l-a-y-b-o-u-r-n-e," he said methodically, "… Old River Road, just Old River Road—no house number yet. That's Mio, Michigan, out in the boondocks," he continued with a feigned grin, hoping to ease tensions. He gestured in Virginia's direction and continued, "She is beat; she's frightened, and she's been driving these lonely roads for too long."

"Yes, and the injury, Sir, a chain saw, I suppose?" the clerk asked, after her other queries were answered. "How did you do it?"

"My rifle," he replied quickly, lips pursed from a rasp of pain when he sat up straight. "I shot myself. It went off by accident, caught me completely by surprise. Believe it or not, I was cleaning it up after target shooting, thought the magazine was empty," he lied with a perfectly straight face. "I'm a retired army general and should have known better." He opened his wallet and displayed the Pentagon ID card as he spoke.

"I was trained to place nineteen cartridges in the magazine," he went on, "to prevent jamming. I know, or so I thought, I loaded exactly nineteen rounds. Somehow, I mistakenly placed twenty in there and didn't count on the last one being in the chamber. It could have jammed; I could have died, defenseless, if I were in combat, just by that stupid error." He shook his head repeatedly to illustrate the lack of rationale to his actions.

"Oh, out here, especially during hunting seasons, we hear all the stories, see lots of deaths, too, from the, 'empty gun,' I can assure you," the clerk replied, unconcerned with the general's shame.

Claybourne looked from the corner of his eye at Virginia and winked. *The clerk bought the story, so I'll stick with it. Sounds logical. That they have so many accidental gunshot wounds will ease explaining the incident to the doctor. What else is new to this part of the world?*

"I work, or worked, with a cardiac surgery team in Arlington, Virginia … nearly twenty years as head scrub nurse," Virginia offered without solicitation. "If there's anything I can do to speed things up, I'd be glad to help. I'm fresh off the job. I quit to move up here, to Michigan, to … be with him … with Homer," she muttered with too much hesitation.

It's OK; that's all right, Ginny. They know what they're doing," the general said, while he forced a tight smile again. He reached to her with his free hand, grasped her wrist until he knew it hurt, and squeezed harder to curtail any further flow of unneeded commentary. Virginia grimaced, felt a rush of bitterness surge through her body, and withdrew her arm from his grasp with a jerk. She fell silent, angered to the core, and pouted openly.

Lips pursed, she turned away, rolled her eyes upward and side-to-side, so the clerk could catch her intolerance, and then glared back toward Claybourne. *You treat me roughly and it'll come back to you—double, I promise. That is the only course of conduct I find utterly unforgivable.*

Brutality, roughness and public disrespect are outside the bounds under which you may operate with me, Mister Homer Claybourne. I told you before and my father warned you from the outset. You don't deserve the distinguished title of general when you behave like that. She knew her stare conveyed the unspoken message, for he reflexively extended his hand, patted hers gently, and gestured an apology.

"C'mon, Ginny," he whispered, "c'mon, I'll be fine, and so will you. Now, be a good girl for me." He swung back toward the clerk's desk and continued, "She's a highly trained surgical assistant, but you wouldn't know it, as excited as she is over this little wound. I've had combat injuries all over my body that caused me far more concern in the past. At least there weren't any North Vietnamese hiding in the bushes tonight."

He lifted his pant leg and showed the attendant the deep furrow in his right calf. She looked on with disinterest. "After I got this one, I had to play dead for several hours. They'd have found me and blown off my head. "No," he continued, and blinked his eyes several times, while he grimaced from pain, "this arm is nothing by comparison, but it hurts like hell."

"Yes … now Mister, er General Claybourne, we have to report all gunshot wounds to the State Police. It's the law, don't you know?"

The general stiffened, pictured police interrogations and Virginia's unchecked blather. She could easily volunteer inadvertent contradictions. There could be suspicion, maybe a detective's call at the house. An abhorrent vision, he felt panicky, considering what would soon, and very quietly, take place there. The up-coming deliveries and negotiations, he vowed, would settle their financial needs forever.

"You'll be getting a call from the cops, no doubt, if they're not here by the time you fix to leave. Though, I will note the wound was self-inflicted." The clerk laughed. "I don't mean to suggest that you were committing suicide, hardly in the armpit, so I'll add that no perpetrator was involved, not really a criminal matter. If you will just sign this form, everything is explained. See here, I've added that you were cleaning the … by the way, what type of gun was it?" She poised her pen to complete the entry.

He swallowed hard, remembered he spoke of the twenty shot magazine, and all but branded the gun as a military piece. Claybourne hoped the type would not spawn added interest. An M-16, U.S. Army model A-1; I use it for plinking at cans, targets you know ... more a toy than anything else at this point." He sensed her cooling curiosity and was relieved when she stood up.

When the clerk abruptly turned and pushed his wheelchair, he grimaced from the sudden movement 'through swinging doors into the first curtained examining area. She chuckled over her own husband's never-ending quest for the elusive multi-forked buck, as she turned to leave.

"Chuck, ah, Doctor Washton should be with you in just a few minutes," she finished cheerfully, and drew the peach colored curtain around him. "We have only one other patient to see, ahead of you."

Claybourne felt drowsy from the 80 milligram pre-op Versed, given IV, and his pain level markedly decreased. When he blinked his eyes and reopened them, he tried to focus on the large surgical lamp directly above, but could not do so. He saw double and it turned like a top. His tongue felt thick. It sloshed in the way of speaking clearly, when he tried with futility to respond to the doctor's questions.

"Are we ready, people?" The surgeon had asked.

"Sure, I'm ... ready. I ... want to ... to ... get this repaired ... fixed quickly, if you don't mind. I've things to do ... many important things." He slurred, then stopped the talk to crack a beamy smile, as if he downed several of Virginia's devastating martinis. His injured arm, secured to a padded board, stretched out to the side, while the other sported an IV catheter and dripped a late snack of Propofol, saline and water to supplement gaseous inhalation. He shivered from the cool temperature in surgery, the wound hurt; he quivered and allowed his eyelids to drop closed.

"We may be here for a while," he heard the doctor say, "so, everyone, take care of personal needs that may soon cry for attention. Could be a tedious dissection and repair. Too much jellied blood to wash him and look around in there, before we put Mister Claybourne to sleep. Is the anesthesiologist ready?

The general grew increasingly giddy from the pre-operative medication. His thoughts easily slipped to the night he first met Virginia at Ft. Myers. General Blakes, her father, did not count on the instant mutuality of attraction. Strictly for business, she was there in her father's behalf to broach the idea of the secreted business venture. A raving beauty, he saw her poised at the bar with her father and two friends. Awestruck, Claybourne saw stars. Eye contact began the very moment he entered the room; she smiled whenever he glanced in her direction, and that was often.

Not only was Virginia the youngest available female at the club that night, she was certainly the most attractive. Claybourne could not restrain himself from staring. When she smiled, her lips spelled sensuality. Her hourglass figure inspired and her ebony hair glistened. Stunningly attired, Virginia wore a sequined blue strapless gown that just brushed the floor around her black Gucci heels. Her right leg, tanned, slender, and muscular, beckoned from beneath the revealing slit that tugged his teased eyes just above mid-thigh.

Blues and light rock tunes intermixed—supplanted by good Scotches they both quickly devoured—worked well to reduce tensions after introduction. They talked more than an hour, and became well acquainted, before he asked her to dance the first time. While on the prowl, most importantly, Virginia was there, on a mission, to search for opportunity, whether business or romantic. Feeling very vulnerable that night, he wanted a woman. It was inevitable that their desires would mesh.

Well aware of the man's impending retirement through her father's detailed briefing, she viewed Claybourne's military connections, active lifestyle, financial condition, and his quest for a new business venture, with bubbling enthusiasm. She found him extremely attractive, if not irresistible in his dress uniform, embellished with as many ribbons as her father accumulated in his many years of service. The two generals, close friends and long time co-workers, served together in the Pentagon for years. Claybourne and Virginia Blakes shared a common denominator from the start.

Drifting in and out of the placid pools of drug-induced slumber, the general recalled how young she looked that night. He suffered interminably as chatter intensified, because of their age disparity, with concerns that his advanced years might bar any romantic interest on her part. His trepidation soon cleared when she alluded to her preference in dating, "gentlemen who had the benefit of more experience than naiveté behind them."

Later in the evening, she broached discussion about a project she and her father discussed. She called it the, "zillion dollar gold ring on a fast moving merry go round."

Claybourne, relaxed in his twilight sleep, recalled the warmth of her sly smile while he revisited the exact words she used. "Daddy and I have something we would like to speak with you about," she confided, with her lips pressed close to his ear as they slow danced. "A vein of brilliant gold is waiting to be mined."

He worried about perspiring in his excitement, and felt the incipient wetness on his neck, beneath her tightly clasped hand. Worried that sweating might deter her interest, he suggested they sit for a tune or two, to continue with talk of the proposed venture. However, it did not matter; she found herself more than content, to plant sensual kisses just the same, as he held her body tight to his chest with muscular arms.

"This proposal, ah what I'm to discuss with you, admittedly bizarre, a long shot, multi-million dollar project; but it's a real one, with certain and immediate imminence, and the pipes have been laid to prove its potential."

"I'm all ears for anything that smacks big bucks," he remembered saying, curious beyond reason what she might have up her sleeve.

She put her finger to his lips, pouted, and hissed a sexy, "Shhhh, Homer.

Across the room, let's dance over there; we'll talk more freely." Arm arched high, with the deftness of an instructor, he swung that way and allowed her to pirouette close to the wall, well away from the bar, where they were more alone, and well away from the prying ears of others. He held her close. She wrapped both arms around his neck and they continued to dance, face to face, though at half the music's pulse, that she could continue.

"You and Daddy, you've such intimate knowledge of Patriot Missiles. They're within your section's budgetary controls, and you dispatch them as necessary. We have discussed the possibilities of these little 'sparklers,' as Daddy always called them, possibly to sell the units … ah … outside, ahem." She paused and watched his eyes carefully, for a flutter that might show doubt, as a dancing couple moved too close.

"There is already a plan to vend them," she went on, "er, ah, outside the system, far beyond the reach of U.S. Army's talons. Daddy wanted me to mention this to you tonight, knowing you would find the topic, ahem, ah, yes, oh, more than casually interesting."

"Interesting? Enticing would be a better word, absolutely enchanting." He laced his words in a broad, confident smile and allowed her to lean back as his hands slipped to her hips. His eyes swept from her face, to her neck, her inviting breasts, and flat stomach, and then he brought her back in close. "Your lips, those piercing, sexy eyes and body perfect. I came close to not coming tonight, and would have whipped myself silly, had I demurred. What's more, I sense a good brain rests comfortably beneath that shiny black hair. Am I correct?"

"Yes," she replied spiritedly, "I've a God-given head on my shoulders. Though, I must say, there have been times when, perhaps, I haven't used it, let's say, in the right direction."

"Now, why hasn't Rod, your daddy, ever said anything of this to me … this bizarre design?"

"He's been retired for so long, he was rusty on the contacts, except for the absolutely necessary factor: customers … potential buyers. That is the key. You must have discreet and desperate buyers with unlimited funds, and passionate desires."

"Are you saying," he asked in an excited whisper, while he scanned the crowd with suspicion, "that we're talking about …" and he whispered into her ear, "… a foreign power, group, or nation with no business owning Patriots? We cannot be talking terrorist organizations, can we? Jesus Christ, what the hell has Rod been doing? We're both under military employment until we die—our pensions, you know—pledges of allegiance. Are we talking criminal…?"

He looked pensive, suddenly distant, and disbelieving. He wondered about a set-up, being baited, entrapped. He'd seen enough of that in recent years with so many media reports of military secret sales, and the aggressive Congressional rat chasing that followed.

Virginia was more than convincing that night. A creepy but curious overlay enveloped the physical attraction he felt, given the chance to make millions. He acceded to the discussion of square two. Despite her mention of something that far below board, the illegal sale of Patriot Missiles, and the high risk of exposure, he listened greedily. He took Virginia at the end of the evening, and snapped with lust at the romantic bait she cast.

"Let's talk about those Patriots, the glorified sparklers, and get the plans moving forward. I'm willing to take my chances. I've taken nothing but risks for my country, all my life, and what thanks did I get? I got sued for divorce. Is that the gratitude I get, being away so much of the time in my active years?" Confused and cloudy, he still spoke softly, but with more intensity.

"What kind of gratitude was that? I skirted death so often it became routine. I don't earn as much as half the fresh college graduates get to start. What the hell kind of. …"

"Homer, Honey, quit the mumbling," Virginia admonished, "you're coming out of the anesthesia. Her lips pressed to his ears and she went on, more sternly this time. "Shut the hell up. Do you hear me? Shut up! You were talking about Patriot Missiles, about Palestine and who knows what else, while you were here in the recovery room, coming out of the anesthesia. Jesus Christ, Homer! I'm telling you, clam up about all that. What else did you say?" *My God, if Daddy overheard, he'd kill Homer on the spot. We can't afford distractions like what happened tonight, and such loose lips, too. I don't dare tell Father.*

"It's nothing, Ginny ... nothing at all. We're ... I'm waiting for the anesthesiologist to arrive." Claybourne still reeled from the after-effects of anesthesia. "The surgeon's here ... scrubbing now. I saw him, but I'm not going through it without an anesthetic, and I'd better. ..."

"Homer, snap out of it! Your surgery is complete. The doctor said everything is fixed. Your arm will be as good as new, though awfully sore for awhile." She grasped his good hand in both of hers and shook it, to sharpen his wits. "You missed disastrous injury by a mere centimeter— nothing short of miraculous. The bullet tore up some musculature, but bone, nerves and vessels escaped permanent injury by a stroke of luck. The bleeding came from the brachial artery, as I suspected, a small tear the surgeon easily found and closed. The muscles were a disaster."

The general went out again, and his mind wandered aimlessly, back to the dance floor and that first night with Virginia. He felt her cheek press his shoulder, her hips against his. He laughed at her sensuous smile. He didn't recognize the Elvis song that blared, but he wanted to dance again.

His own yelps from the darting pain in his arm startled him back from the fancies. Claybourne lifted his head, grabbed the gurney rail, and tried to get up. "Ohhh, its sore, hurts like hell." He saw her standing there. "We were on the floor, moving to the music," he said, more clearly this time, "back there at Ft. Myers. We met that night, do you remember? You approached me with the ... the business plan; we went outside to the bleachers—talked in the moonlight—then kissed and held each other."

Virginia wanted to feel for him, to reach out with the affection she lavished upon the general in the early stages of dating, but he pushed her too far in recent months, worsened by added pressures of buying the property by the river, and as final plans for the treasonous escapade matured.

"I'm sorry this injury happened, Homer. I've apologized for my part in it. I was worried about cross fire, that the shooting might escalate. I had no choice. I had to grab the gun from your hands.

"You were going crazy," she said, with business in her eyes. "I … I thought you were losing it, completely. I won't take chances like that, not now. Nothing will avert the trails we have cut and the millions we stand to make. She looked around the room, to assure they were still alone. The horror of the encounter with the Gladdocks dropped with a pall of fear, and the threat of exposure. "You talked too much in there—too much about the deal—far too much. For your own good fortune, Homer, I hope no one made sense of it."

Eyes glazed over again, then lids dropped closed; the general fell back into slumber, dreamless this time, and absent the imagery he enjoyed earlier.

"So, General Claybourne," Virginia continued as if he were prepared for more admonishment, "don't you tell me to clam up in front of others, ever again. You may have set up diversion of our Patriots, and you may have arranged transport to where they now rest. Your usefulness, though, will soon end. Mark my words, Buster. Mark them well.

"There will be no more Claybourne-instigated barriers to the finalization of our plans. I'll not be cut out of my millions by you or anyone else." Frustrated with his lack of comprehension, she gritted her teeth, leaned close to him and whispered, "I said, 'the next time you're brought in here, I won't be the chauffer and it could be with a well placed, gaping, and irreparable chest wound.'"

CHAPTER 13

A loon broke the midnight calm with its mournful whine. Similar cries followed, some nearby, some barely discernable from afar. Intermittently, the calls sheathed the rumble of the river and its untiring symphony with mournful counterpoint. No longer anathema to Homer Claybourne, the forest still failed to supplant the more familiar clatter of the city. He missed Arlington, its honking horns, smoke-belching buses, trash trucks, jackhammers, and the constant roar of commercial and military jets in steep take-off climbs.

Comparatively vast, the unusual quiet of the Au Sable and its surrounding woods brought him from a shallow sleep. Fraught with concerns, he tossed and turned, to find a comfortable position for his arm. Soft voices of the woods seemed laden with an almost bothersome and inexplicable truth, a haunting certitude that sliced its way into his conscience. So important, and heeded all his military life, he allowed that guiding force to bend, to become jaded, since he united with Virginia. He felt temporarily troubled because of it. Money became the pry bar to unearth new and lower standards of ethical conduct, in great departure from his former patterns of patriotism and integrity.

Virginia looked deceptively innocent beside him, hair tossed loosely about the bed pillow, childish face barely lighted by smiles from the emerging moon. Yet, beneath that apparent probity, he knew, rested an un-tamed wildcat, with few scruples, hidden claws in wait for the chance to rip into bellies of the unsuspecting. He wanted to trust her. He grew to love the woman, to be sure, but the cunning accumulated as a trained warrior over his entire adult life, kept him from completely letting go. *It would be too dangerous to do that with this little slicker. No! Suicidal would be a better word. She's far more than just a danger. Ruthless? Cold-blooded? Merciless? They all fit like a glove. Why must I remind myself almost daily, to look behind with every forward step I take?*

She loves me in many ways, I'm sure of it. God forbid, I'm not the easiest man in the world to live with or love. We're going on two years. She says she adores me and a part of me wants believe that, to completely succumb to the notion; but my darker side, the soldier in the battlefield, won't trust the little imp farther than I could throw her.

What did she mean by that comment in the recovery room? She assumed I was asleep, and said something about the next time I came to the hospital it could be with a shot in the chest. What was that about?

Blakes, her father ... such a fine reputation he enjoyed through his career.

When, along the way, did he allow greed to shift his focus? Has he skimmed off the U.S. Army all this time, while I've stupidly struggled, and worked so hard beside him? How could I not have known? What made him pick me for this project? How could he have been so sure of my potential for such larceny? Apprehensive from his dimmed wanderings, Claybourne shuddered from the possibility that he might have been included simply as a needed scapegoat, an expendable member of the team to take the rap when his usefulness expired. Might he be the one to take the blame? *They could murder me right out of the scenario, just as quickly as I was invited into it. I'm sure not his family. Could she do that to me? Would General Blakes? Will she stay with me? She's such a little liar, a manipulator of the highest order. Look at her part in the thoroughbred horse caper. Virginia's hands were as filthy as those of her con-artist boyfriend. She's damned lucky she wasn't lynched in Arlington. That her father extricated her without question, and put her in our operation, suggests her dubious ilk has deep and solid family roots. This solitude and the woods have summoned me to think tonight, to consider covering my rear flank—minute-by-minute—day by day.*

Almost as if it knew his confused thoughts, the loon's whine again severed the blackness when it popped like a cork to the surface of the big pool, shook its black hood free of icy water, and swallowed the minnow

125

that dangled from its arrow-like beak. The persistent bird, speckled on the back, fluttered its large wings, hovered above the surface, and settled back on the water, to alert moral senses of the wary once more.

General Claybourne tossed, rolled and turned in unsuccessful efforts to find comfort and induce sleep. Concerned with his aimless musings, he focused on the more important facets of *Operation Eastern Star*, as Blakes dubbed the caper, in true military fashion. It seemed forever that the two generals spearheaded Patriot missile development and deployment by the army. They fought side-by-side, and advocated massive funding for the new-technology, though problem-fraught ground to air missiles. Testimony like there would be no tomorrow, before Armed Services Committees of the House of Representatives and the Senate, both lobbied tirelessly, too, with the Secretary of Defense, and his staff.

They saw the program through testing and low-level use. Eventual proof of Patriot missile efficacy, followed by significant reworks, led to refinement, and the reasonably effective status the program eventually enjoyed. Like proud new fathers, Blakes and Claybourne bragged long and hard at high-level cocktail parties, about the 1990 Gulf War launchings—more than one hundred fifty of their prized, though horribly expensive, ground-to-air weapons.

Early use of Patriots against incoming missiles wasn't foolproof. Continual performance deficits failed to convince many tough, scrutinizing members of Congress. But the army did not give up. Its key people continued prodding Raytheon, the manufacturer, to improve and upgrade sophistication of the system's software. Blakes and his staff remained at the forefront, steadfast in their advocacy for increased budgeting, with each administrative change in Washington. Those working at the Pentagon knew that relentlessness was the way to get the Department of Defense new money for old projects.

God, how we fought! How we got ourselves pummeled, even disgraced so often by lawmakers, clueless about present and future military needs, and the need for our country to update warfare tactics. We were so patriotic, so believing and trusting of the system, yet we both developed deep-seated resentment over the poor economic returns from our jobs. We were educated.

Our schooling never stopped and, for so many years, we placed our lives on the line for our country, in combat exposures, too, through our younger days.

"When did I reach the point that I could be so quick to compromise my long-standing beliefs in our army? When did I start disbelieving in high ethics, for the sake of earning extra money, enough to care for myself when I'm no longer employable?" he asked sleeping Virginia, softly, but with determination. "When you said there'd be millions in what was, clearly, a very shady deal, I jumped on it. Why? You little snake," he snarled, loud enough to awaken her. "Blakes used your lovely face and that delicious body to tease me. Lust took over and placed my neck in the snare, didn't it? Isn't that how it worked, My Love?"

As he spoke those words, the general felt his good hand creep uncontrollably toward Virginia's throat, thumb poised over her peach-pink larynx. He stood ready, at the behest of his passions, to cut her air supply, forever. Her body would wriggle, while pasty hands grappled at his face; but the loud crackling sounds of the fragile cartilages crushed in her throat would so frighten her, that she would just look, wide-eyed and unblinking, at his indifferent expression and search it for mercy. Then her eyes would close.

Claybourne recalled vividly, many years before, the morning he used just such a hold on the Viet Cong recruit, laden with three M-16 rifles lifted from bodies of dead American soldiers or, worse, from struggling, wounded men who needed the arms for protection in their final efforts to survive. So long ago, yet it could have been yesterday.

He pulled himself through dripping wet, insect-infested vegetation. A loathsome patchwork of leeches accumulated on his bared skin, harbored by viscous muck that bordered the small river course where he slithered. He stayed well out of sight, in search of the source of deadly rifle fire, behind a small rise in the levee. They lost too many men from that enemy position. The sweet-smelling shoulder-high grass, a bright verdant green, blended with the early sky: stinking hot, and a vibrant tropical blue. His first challenge to a real hand-to-hand tussle, he and Arturo Romeri, a young lieutenant starting a second tour, were the only ones uninjured that day. After an eon of serpent-like ground-level squirming, AK-47 and M-16 slugs screamed and hissed just above, their quarry lay just ahead. Shrapnel rained, too, from endless enemy mortar fire.

They flipped a coin. Romeri won the toss and stayed back to cover. Claybourne began the approach from behind to make the kill or, at least, to die in the attempt. The general squirmed with the grizzly memory.

Before he knew it, Romeri heard the grotesque noise of the surprised V.C. soldier's throat cartilages collapse beneath the general's sinewy hands. The surge of Claybourne's dagger through the gasping man's green cotton garment followed. It slid just below the sternum and into his heart, for the final blow. One long gush of air, and no subsequent inspirations told Romeri the gunner suffered almost instant death. Claybourne's kill permitted the platoon's advance and saved its remaining numbers.

That same sense of desperation reappeared, filled the general's thoughts, when he remembered the shock he felt with the VC's head slumped in his lap. The dead man's wide-open eyes woefully pleaded for help. Once again, he felt the almost overbearing urge to squeeze. Virginia's external carotid arteries pulsed silently, barely visible on either side of her trachea. He felt the beat of a strong pulse, but it was his own, suddenly fortified with the same rush of adrenalin that took him through his first life or death altercation. *Is this combat again? Am I at war? Is this a 'must kill,' like the major said in the meager cover of that rice paddy?*

Virginia's lips rumpled softly with an outgoing exhalation, eyelids flickered; she buried her face in the pillow, and sleepily stretched arms to reposition. His hand jerked reflexively away from her, as if snapped by a strong rubber band and Claybourne's thoughts returned to the bed. Eyes watered slightly; he looked at the beauteous woman he grew to love, and to nearly trust. An ugly image formed. He pictured her in the aftermath of his clamping grasp, eyes bulged from anoxia, neck deformed, skin dimmed to a gray-blue. She lay unresponsive.

Good God, what the hell am I thinking? First, we steal our government's missile batteries, and arrange to sell the works to an unpredictable buyer with few scruples, and then I fantasize about killing my partner's daughter.

She's the current love of my life. Get your head together, Homer. Get some sleep. He checked his watch, opened the bottle of pain pills on the nightstand, and quickly swallowed one with a mouthful of saliva that surged with his musings.

Dazed and unfocused, the general stared coldly at the pale blue ceiling Virginia embellished by hand painting faint gray-white clouds. She worked tirelessly before they completed the move. Virginia selected the light green and blue striped wallpaper, which he had to admit, looked more than pleasant. He turned again to his companion. This time he looked at the sleeping woman with contradictory affection, appreciation for her efforts that made their new surroundings comfortable.

She seems so peaceful, unaffected by this turmoil. Even the shooting incident, the curious presence of those two intruders from the river, has slipped her mind. The dinner, that meal she cooked tonight … memorable, at worst. Where, in the woods of Northern Michigan, could I get rack of lamb served with all the trimmings? The mint jelly, foie gras, *and delightful salmon hors d'oeuvres … have to go to Arlington for a meal like that."* Claybourne patted his yet-full stomach. *The Paul Bunyan Café definitely doesn't have European cuisine on their menu. They simply fill empty bellies with potatoes, gravy, and over-cooked meat.*

He grumbled, paused in his thoughts for a few more moments, adjusted his sore arm in the sling, and thought more about the night he and Virginia stopped at the remote eatery on Route 55. He sprang to a sitting position and barked crisply, "The Paul Bunyan … yes, of course! That's it … why the backwoods jerk looked so familiar. Even in the dark, down there by the river, I sensed we'd met. That's where I bumped into him."

Claybourne recalled the brief encounter with Mike at the restaurant and the passive attitude his adversary displayed. "The dummy just gave me that stupid-looking, palms up routine, rolled his window, and, then, the big brush-off. There, in the café, he simply let me walk all over him. What a wimp. The girl, that funky waitress knew him … said something about his having a boat. He has to live close by, maybe near the lakeshore. What the hell was his name? She called it out when they talked, didn't she?" he asked sleeping Virginia. "What was it, now? It was monosyllabic, a short one—common, too, like John, Bob, Mike, Jim, Mac, or something basic like that. No matter, I'll do a little detective work as soon as I can drive. The waitress seemed goofy enough, and should volunteer everything I need."

His thoughts whirred ahead. *I am very curious; what the devil he and the cohort who fired his pistol at me, were doing near our house. What were they doing with firepower? Were they just fishing? They said they were, both yelled at me to curb the dogs. Both were fly casting when I sent Ace and the other two. They had all the gear and cast like pros.* He remembered Wayne's perfect posture, the fine parabolic curve of his bamboo rod in the back cast, and the extreme reach of his line, once thrust toward the deep pool.

Claybourne recalled his streak of awe, if not jealousy, at the finesse Mike and Wayne displayed. Irritation with their skills spurred unleashing the Rottweilers. "The dogs began the ensuing fury, but the men shouldn't have been there, damn it. I bought this land with all the trappings and that included the bank down to the river's edge, according to the realtor. On that basis, the men were trespassers," he whispered, though with less confidence, that his overly protective attitude was justified.

"I did not know who the men were. I'm new to the area," he loudly rationalized. "Maybe they were casing the place. What if burglary was their motivation to be so far back in the forest?" He fell quiet and continued his deliberations.

For all I know, they're CIA, FBI, Department of Defense investigators chasing leads, getting ready for a sting. I could go to Leavenworth, spend the rest of my life sewing army uniforms, not wearing the damned things. It's far too late to change coats now.

Blakes, maybe even Virginia, would kill me if I put a stop to the accumulation of gear it takes to assemble a battery, a completely functional Patriot launching pad, and tracking station. Blakes would say, 'kill the bastards,' and he'd see to the wasting of all others involved. He's desperate for this project's completion and his manipulating daughter is even more determined. I should have taken out those two meddling locals when I had the chance, the sonsofbitches. I damn sure will if they show their faces again.

"Hey, wait a minute," Claybourne called loudly. Virginia groaned and then rolled to the edge of the bed, otherwise undisturbed. "I left my rifle out there, propped it up against the maple tree by the bluff. I didn't see it when we parked in the *cul de sac*, back from the hospital. Did she bring it inside? I'll have a look downstairs."

He moved about carefully, winced from pain, for the first few steps. He tried to shield his arm from as much motion as possible, so carefully he descended the stairs to the entry. His gun rack leaned against the knotty pine paneled wall near the base of the stairwell. He did not yet take the time to mount it, above where it sat. He noted the missing gun straight away, the M-16 from which he took the shot. "The damned thing isn't here. For God's sake, she could have brought it in the house for me. I bled like a faucet and couldn't carry it. I calmly placed it against that tree. I distinctly recall, now. The wound seared, burned something awful at first."

He trudged out in the black chill, and searched the deep mat of multi-shaded amber leaves with a flashlight. The M-16 was not to be seen, anywhere. "It's gone. Damn it! Those snooping sonsofbitc. ..."

"Homer? Homer! Homer? That you out there?" she screamed from the bedroom window. Virginia wore no robe. Her uncovered torso flashed a sensual silhouette, back lighted by the pale yellow glow of the nightstand lamp with the print shade she brought from her condo in Arlington. The outside floodlight flashed on, and cast the brilliance of daylight around the clearing.

He saw the shadow of a revolver in her hands. It had to be his Colt .45, the one he kept loaded in his top dresser drawer. *What the hell is she doing with it? Isn't it obvious, I'm outside? Is this the opportunity she's waited for, an excuse to get me out of the picture, now that my inside contacts have produced the Patriot battery from so many different components?*

Claybourne's mind moved like a Grand Prix race. Thoughts tore in front of one another, like the big cars when they dart forward on the straight runs. He stood still, wished she'd not turned on the bright light that found his pale gray bathrobe like a road sign. He looked down and realized his prominent visibility. He might have been a theatre marquis. He wanted to dive behind the tree to his left, but his arm hindered such evasive movement. "My damned arm," he called, "don't shoot, for Christ's sake!"

"Homer, is that you down there? What the hell are you doing in the dark?

Get the dickens back up here. Are you crazy? I nearly took a shot. I'd have hit you dead center, too. You know how much I've practiced with this pistol," she yelled. He saw Virginia release the hammer, yet still she leaned out the window. When she set the pistol down, he slowly moved from behind the tree where he sought refuge.

Assured Virginia's hands were free of the weapon, he high-tailed it for the house, crouched like an advancing field soldier, until he reached the door. His older M-16 lay in the gun rack, but the newer one he used on the Gladdocks, was definitely missing.

"Maybe I did bring it in the house," he said to Virginia. She waited downstairs. His eyes quickly searched the room for the gun as he turned to her. She looked devastating in the nude; she blushed, and he continued to stare longingly at her body. "You look so luscious, this damned arm … couldn't if I wanted to, Virginia. It aches so. Maybe those responsible for the break-in stole the gun. I saw the fishermen paddle west like scared mud hens. They wouldn't have come back with the dogs, the shooting and all. Would they?" he questioned hesitatingly. "Could the window breakage … might it have been them? Did the dogs do it? There was so much glass outside, I just assumed the animals. …"

"Wait a second, just a damned second," Virginia cut in. "If there was a coincidental burglary, why would they have taken only one rifle? Doesn't make sense. Is anything else missing?" she queried.

"We're sitting on a big pot of money—millions My Dear—between the two of us. It's enough to get anyone excited, real envious. Perhaps someone in our own net located us. The payoffs I arranged, recipients could feel the money insufficient, once the gravity of the operation became completely apparent. It's not impossible that we're looking at intrusion from within our ring of close confidants."

"But Homer, you've done an excellent job hanging a severe criminal offense on everyone's head, should they blow their cover, or try to bust ours. "Furthermore," Virginia continued, as if she rehearsed day and night beforehand, "you were careful to involve each participant enough that, if caught individually, they would be thought responsible for the entire scenario. They were well informed about individual exposures. They don't yet know this hideaway. No one has been told yet. Your house in Arlington would be the site for surveillance, not this place. We've kept ourselves on the straight and narrow. We're only the unseen masters—not the vulnerable players on the board. It's so foolproof; I'm so anxious to see the money," she giggled childishly. "Together, we'll have six, maybe eight mil, Darling … all cash … overseas financial centers … unmarked … no U.S. banks involved, right?

"That's it, and we launder what we wish through our buddies at the bank in Arlington, for a small percentage, a very small share, indeed." It felt good to discuss details. Many of the components would soon arrive from the warehouse in Texas, to be prepared for flight to the East African coast and onward to final rendezvous in Syria. "Let's go back to bed for whatever we can milk from the rest of the night, and when it's light, I'll look more carefully for the rifle. It must be outside, somewhere."

Virginia's fingers gathered the floral print sheet and white blanket just beneath her chin and fell quickly asleep. He remained propped on two pillows, gently stroked her silky hair, then her forehead, with the back of his hand. Patiently, Claybourne withdrew the covers and exposed her torso to the new morning's chill. Her nipples beckoned. Firm breasts invited his lips. He caressed and recalled the first night they spent together, when the loving extended through the next day.

How long would he be able to keep up the pace to which she became accustomed? How much time would his arm take to heal? Would she become impatient, and be inclined to look elsewhere for companionship? Usually he did not worry like this. It made him furious that he could feel vulnerable, nearly helpless, and to his dishonor, so dependent at that moment. Her body, still youthful and appealing, silently mocked him, prompted a rush of anger. He grew furious, fearful, too, that he became less attractive as he aged.

Debilitated and hurting, this was not the Homer he knew. He grew ever closer to convinced that he was not the man with whom she would stay, once funds were distributed. Ready for that, the general schemed to employ whatever means were necessary, to give her reason to reconsider.

Well prepared for the eventuality, Claybourne almost looked with relish, at the day she might tell him she was done. That he would have the opportunity to see her squirm at such a time was always a correlative part of his plan. He was not a man to relinquish control to anyone, anytime, anywhere. *She'll stay here in the woods; she will, when informed of the alternatives.* "You wouldn't want to leave your old Homer, now would you, my little southern cupcake? Heh, my Virginia Dear, now would you?" he blurted loudly enough for her to stir and roll towards him with arms stretched out.

"Can't you sleep, Homie? Is your arm hurting? I'm sorry you're so miserable with that sling," she purred. Anything I can do? Can I rub your back a little? Maybe a stiff dose of Glenlivet Scotch would help, along with that pain pill. The combo always works when I wish to sleep."

Claybourne thought about that as his mind wandered and recalled vividly, how a major, who worked beneath him for many years, killed himself by taking advantage of the synergistic effects of opioid-derived medication and hard liquor. Even physicians on the base who knew Barclay, he recalled, were willing to assume the death to have been an accidental overdose, with a liquor overlay. That would be an option, a foolproof way, most assuredly, to deal with the little vamp if he ever needed to do so, he pondered, and turned to Virginia with a sardonic grin.

"You know, that's a good idea. I'll mix the two, should knock me right down. I'll get a glass of the good old stuff. In fact, I'll take a couple stiff shots." As he ambled downstairs, he cradled the painful extremity with his good hand to ease the pain. Relieved by her idea, Claybourne sat at the bistro table in the far corner of the front room, and dropped a shot glass and bottle to the marble top with a bang. He admired the inviting space, its stained pine wainscot and blue-gray upper wall surfaces. From the start, he fell for the large river rock fireplace off center of the expansive picture window.

The general poured a nip of Scotch, and deeply whiffed the bouquet before he downed it with relish. "Twenty one years old when it was bottled and now …" he laughed, when he checked the label, "… twenty-five and perfect … liquid perfection, indeed, if ever there were one." He refilled the cut crystal glass to the brim, with patent recall of the previous spring, when he and Virginia toured Scotland.

They ended up in the Highlands for intimate contact with whiskey distilleries. Both enjoyed Scotch; their favorite became the revered Glenlivet, produced near the River Spey in Ballindalloch. Fringed by the barren Caerngorm Mountains, in the Livet Valley, they were enraptured with the picturesque scenery, the old white stucco houses with thatched roofs, and such memorable deep green, everywhere. Samples of whiskey at each distillery they visited, and making love alternatively, boredom was hardly a factor. "Ginny was such an animal on that trip. What's happened to her? Is it the forthcoming money or, or did I lose that old Homer curb appeal?" He spoke aloud, drank from the full glass with relish, and poured another half before he slowly climbed the stairs.

Virginia slept heavily. When he returned to bed, desire embroiled inside. He needed assurance that she'd accept him, that she would find him sensual enough to initiate the activity. That would not happen, he knew. It could not, until the arm began to heal. "Maybe then, he moaned, "we'll get back on line; damn the luck." *Damn the remaining details. Damn the delays in getting all the missile parts together. I have to make calls and update the status of things. Blakes will want to know. They ought to be loaded soon. They'll come here for temporary storage, and I'll need to assure the forklift's delivery beforehand. Where the hell is it? The rockets weigh more than fifteen hundred pounds apiece. We must have the lift. We ordered it three weeks ago.*

Drowsiness crept slowly, but it came stealthily, as his concern with details intensified. Claybourne felt the effects. Glenlivet's envied 1972 liquid masterpiece began to work, though he still found room for continued musing, and took full advantage of it. He relived some of the thrills experienced while he created the strategy, worked through the myriad supportive factors, and saw results culminate in the end.

Operation Eastern Star began with the discreet telephone call from Palestine to General Blakes. The Arabs wished a meeting, a clandestine encounter, to discuss "matters of great remunerative mutual benefit," as Colonel Abu al Badan of the Palestine Liberation Organization alluded. Blakes later informed General Claybourne that Abu al Badan came to the United States in search of a source for Patriot Missiles, and after a quick U. S. State Department rebuke, began to look elsewhere.

The P.L.O. colonel soon realized the source would have to be under the table, as illegal and treasonous as the sale of government secrets themselves. Armaments would expectedly see use in the strife against Israel and her allies. Subtle inquiries finally led the Arab to Blakes as the man behind the Patriots. Chairman Yasser Arafat contended that peace could better be attained and with more equanimity, if there were, in Palestine's hands, means of defying Israeli fighters and rocketry.

At the time, they employed bottles of gasoline, grenades, rockets, and encouraged terrorist bombings with futility for the most part, against the persistent Israeli arms, many of which were high-tech implements given by or purchased legally from the U.S.

P.L.O. advisors thought a small number of successful missile launches would present the image that they had plenty more. Israelis would jump to the peace table when they measured costs of downed fighter planes and missile destruction.

Claybourne remembered General Blake's words well: "Homer, Homer, Baby," Virginia's father said that early summer evening at Rudy's Bar, near the Pentagon. "Homer," he repeated, while almost too vigorously he shook Claybourne's hand, "we have before us, what I think is the opportunity of our lifetimes, and I want to include you, as Virginia suggested already. You were receptive, so here goes. She's crazy about you, damn it, absolutely nuts," he giggled, and clasped his old friend's hand once more. "We'll have to risk our goddamned necks—stick the bastards out on the line, and I mean completely out there. But, we can do it, well before. ..."

Blakes fell silent, and stared into Claybourne's eyes, in wait for his imagination to take charge. "Yes." After a long pause, Blakes continued, "Yes, we can; we will do it. We've done everything our army has ever asked us to do. We've a chance, now, to tell them what our needs are, and have the job done for us, if we plan things smartly. We will be the brains for a change, and they, for a shift, will be our grunts, and handle the dirty work."

A look back at that night kept Claybourne wide-eyed, and distracted from the pain in his arm. He remembered in September 1990, the United States sold two Patriot batteries to the Israelis for nearly one hundred twenty million dollars. The Palestinians grumbled. They were used in the Gulf War against Iraqi SCUD missiles. The U.S. Government felt deceived, however, as later, there were reports Israel sold the technology to China in a moneymaking venture. He remembered how Pentagon leaders spoke of that incident with disillusion, and how bizarre it seemed that a customer of such valued technology would stoop to sell it for the sake of a quick buck.

That led Blakes and Claybourne to the conclusion that money was at the bottom of war; not power, geography, or the control of people, necessarily. 1994—he mused further about big bucks for U. S. corporations and the United States Government—South Korea bought Patriot batteries. Later, other Patriot installations followed in Asia.

Blake's brainstorm for easy earnings sprung when the army replaced hundreds of Patriot Missiles in Asia, with newer technology units. There were operational defects in these early systems, far too many to repair on site. Nearly all the units were sent back for rework, to the Red River Army Depot in Texas and were kept in storage there. As systems became obsolete, updated versions replaced the older units in the many countries that bought them. The Texas stockpile of tested and updated missiles began to grow and the inventory became a forgotten child to the army paper mill.

That was the, "pot of gold," to which Blakes referred while he beamed excitedly at Claybourne that night. "They're just begging to be ripped off, Homer … and … we … understanding army record keeping as we do … well, who else could do it? We know the system; palms that need greasing, and how to get the goods transported. We've done enough of that over the years, haven't we?"

Claybourne remembered with a greedy grin, the enthusiasm with which he listened to his cohort's ideas. The initial offer from Palestine was five million. Blakes jimmied it upward to twenty. The Palestinians would be responsible for getting the missiles and launch gear out of the United States—not a small feat, in itself. That concession, though, relieved Blakes and Claybourne of the majority of their risk. The deal would give them ample funds to split three ways, for a tidy net take, individually, of more than five million. "Three ways?" Claybourne queried the general immediately, "and, who might the third player be?"

"Why, my daughter, your girlfriend, General High Density," Blakes answered sarcastically. "Where's your head?"

Claybourne acted irritated with the remark.

"She's … er … going to … ah … be needed as negotiations continue," Blakes said. The Palestinians, Homer … well … they like their western women and she … she can be counted on to do what is … ah … right in our behalf, my friend. She … she can always be trusted. Can you? Can I be unequivocally trusted?" Blakes asked rhetorically. Never did he appear more serious.

After much whiskey and many hours of idea sharing on the processes to undertake, they decided plans should move forward to the next level. Blakes took on the more risky aspects of the plan at the early stages: verify the claims of his initial Palestine contact, establish direct liaison with former leader, Arafat's high-level aides. His successor, President Mahmoud Abbas was to assure tender of deposit money, up front, before efforts began in the U.S. to collect assets. Two million would be required up front, in non-sequential serial numbers, to get inquiries moving, and begin the payoffs. Funds arrived immediately by personal messenger.

Claybourne's job: to use his contacts in the active army which were much fresher—to assemble the materiel. From the start, that promised to be a mammoth undertaking. Claybourne rolled to his right slightly, noticed the throbbing in the surgical site was further dulled from the whiskey and looked once again at his bedmate. His senses loosened. *She gets one third? What happens to her if we're caught? Not a damned thing, that's what. She has little risk. She will walk, could spill the beans on us … maybe just on old Homer … to avoid prison. We are in the army, abscond with government property and sell to a nation not exactly on favored status. We will be lifers, for certain, and she's out among them, to scam again. I have no patience for this, no patience whatsoever; you ungrateful little vamp. You shot me, damn it! You put me in this mess. Will I ever know that it was not intentional.* He grimaced as he looked at Virginia. *You think of crossing old Homer, even touch on the notion and you will end up as gourmet dog food—very nutritious—if not most attractive dog food.*

"Their coats will never look so good," he said lustily, until he realized she might be awake. He contained remaining thoughts to himself. *Why, they will shine for months with that pretty fat you carry in just the right places.* He patted her naked thigh, rubbed it affectionately and collapsed into a slumber filled with further plans for *Operation Eastern Star.*

CHAPTER 14

Perusal of the aisles in a grocery market, he thought, scored as abhorrent, more a womanly task. It did make him think even more kindly of Meg, however. Through all their years of marriage, she rarely asked him to handle that onerous chore. Not until she fell ill, that is. Mike recalled, then, how difficult it was for him to take over, mentally map out mysteriously obscure grocery store interiors, to make shopping trips as time-efficient as possible.

He exited the supermarket, drained and already bothered by inadvertent omissions. Foreshortened by the accumulation of comp time, he reduced another workweek to three days. Glad for the added time off once again, he left Wednesday evening, to allow time for leisure that loomed ahead. A quick glance at his darkened reflection in the rear view mirror, his eyes illustrated the momentary satisfaction he felt—mellow contemplation over the wide choice of activities available during the next four days at the cabin. "It's time to get organized for the caddis hatch," he iterated several times as if likely to forget. "I'm up for fishing … to relax for a change, just like Meg said. She was right, definitely correct about that."

He placed his cap on the seat, ran wiggling fingers through his hair, roughly scratched his scalp and slicked his curls back. Thoughts progressed, stimulated by the brief massage. "The boat should be dewinterized this trip—washed and waxed—but, it'll keep until after the brownies start bottom feeding … tire of jumping and packing themselves with flying bugs." He began to understand the joy of procrastination, a word he used minimally before, and he grew to like it.

"The browns, dern 'em," he continued, slightly concerned with the growing habit of talking to himself, absent Meg as an interested listener. "Why do I always dream of those little speckled teasers at this time of the year? Just look at how long they have vexed me. I can't resist the urge, can't help myself when I hear their call. They're chanting now!"

As always, when ruminating about the Au Sable, his mind ventured to the Morris shack, an inevitable and powerful draw. He sensed its approach as his mind turned idle, and that, too, became easier with the passage of time since Meg's demise. "River day dreaming," he jokingly called the process. It came more quickly with the slower driving speeds required while towing the boat. "Dern it! The Morris place has become such a different picture," he exclaimed, and shook his head in utter disbelief over what happened during his previous trip.

He recounted the regrettable incident at dusk. The shooting stopped. He tried to piece the sequence of events together, to understand why things blew so far and so quickly out of proportion. The entire event seemed surreal, especially with time to reflect.

Mike and Wayne heard the Excursion bounce into the darkness toward the main road after the last two shots, followed by a veritable quiet. *Gol dern. I still cannot believe it! Did brother actually go in there and screw with that computer? Fingerprints are everywhere, no doubt. Gosh yes, on the sill, the window frame, perfect prints on computer keys. We are dead ducks. He didn't even think of that, did he?*

Wayne did remove his boots, so no muddy tracks inside. It might have been dark enough that Claybourne could not identify us. The cops will do it easily at some point. As if breaking in was not enough, Wayne walks off with the general's M-16. Jesus Crisp, he steals his gun. What in the name of the good book was he thinking? We left evidence as plain as those enormous bear prints we saw while hunting along the margins of the river swamp last fall.

How well he recalled that chilly afternoon. Wayne, Ranger Don Johanssen and Mike, bow hunting for turkey, stumbled upon two sets of the largest black bear tracks they ever saw in the local woods. Shifting interest from the big birds to the thrill of chasing furry mammals, they spent the day clambering through cedar-strewn, swampy bottomland, along one musty backwater after another. The elusive bears were on a feeding rampage and left fresh signatures on many a large log they ripped to the core, in search of grubs, mice, and whatever they could find to fatten themselves for the rush of winter.

One of the bad-tempered animals, much too close when stumbled upon by the inquisitive threesome, did an about face. Only a small cluster of swamp oaks kept them separate. Straight up on a pile of autumn leaves, the bear stood, defiantly roared, and angrily pawed the air with both forefeet, in a threatening challenge. The ongoing game of chase then over; a curtain of serious danger dropped before them.

Wayne saved the day, Mike recalled, just as he did in their tangle with Claybourne. His brother's pistol rang loudly. Four fast shots—toward but not directly at the bear—buzzed through the deadwood thicket and dissuaded the frustrated male from further aggression. Dropped reluctantly to all fours, the bear roared a challenging growl, turned tail, and bounded away; its rear end dragged on the mottled forest blanket.

His companion followed in a fast, though noisy escape through crackling underbrush. Fortuitous encounters with the game that abounded in the local woods never ceased to fascinate Mike, a beckon call he heard loudly, as summer approached, and he afforded more time for the woods.

I should find a way to talk with those folks, to see what their plans for the shack might be for the long pull. If I do anything, I will outlive their interest in the place, possibly buy it from them and offer a fair profit if I have to do so. I will not leave this earth without tying flies in that front room with its picture-perfect view. He shuddered in his musings, though, and wondered about the significance of what Wayne saw on the computer screen. *Patriot Missiles! Hmmm.* He paused to consider the implications. *What the devil are they doing, toying with missiles? Why would people from Virginia, with their own lovely woods and countryside, wish to move so far north? Unless, unless they're hiding something or staying out of someone's way on purpose? In that event, our woods would provide perfect cover. They have no right to be shooting and, dang his dogs, to screw up the best fishing spot in Oscoda County. What if that general sends the Rottweilers down to the water every time he sees us, or others, fishing there for that matter? There are so many short-tempered woodsmen, many a lot more hotheaded than we Gladdocks. Disaster lurks. I can feel it.* He paused in thought for a moment, then quipped aloud, "What if I brought the Labs? "What if I took Beau and Yellow with me?" Mike felt confident his large animals could change the posture of things.

"Cripes, Claybourne's big dogs might make mincemeat of them. Beau would put up one heck of a fight, though, and my boy is far from passive. He would not turn tail and run, that's for sure. Might scare the two smaller females, which could keep the large one out of a prolonged tangle. Their squealing could persuade the larger one to retreat. Yes, we'll hike downstream from the shoals where we can cross on foot, just past the last cabin on the north bank and leave the canoe at home."

He slowed, to climb the final grade before the café. The heavy boat in tow, even his Suburban groaned on long grades. "Paul Bunyan is just ahead, and I'm ready for coffee. Lunch would help, too. Won't block the road this time," Mike mumbled, in self-mockery. "I dern sure don't need another confrontation with that creep from D.C. What an experience! If I didn't know better, I'd never believe it was anything less than a nightmare." *Add it all up: the Morris place sold out from under me, three Rottweilers spoil our fishing; gunshots, one almost split my skull; a bullet hole in our old canoe, and then a burglary. Stir in computer hacking, and Wayne, my own flesh and blood, off with a stolen M-16 rifle, half-full of ammunition. What a story it would make for the family some day, should we live through all of it.*

He laughed, felt proud that his sense of humor at that point in his life was still alive. Thoughts of his father left him in wonder, amused at what might have transpired in the altercation, had the old man been there with his spirited personality. "Pop … heh, heh," Mike chuckled as if speaking with Meg, "now, Pop … oh, what an example he would have set that night. He would have personally wrestled the dogs into submission before shooting became necessary, eliminating flying bullets and the anger that developed.

"He might have used that old horse whisperer trick, which worked so well with the mean dogs that used to chase us through Reynolds' Ranch." He remembered the short cut he and Wayne took as kids, when grouse hunting along margins of the sprawling cornfields. *Reynolds' big Shepherd, the one with the snag teeth … just plain didn't like any of us.* No doubt their taunting and heartless rock throwing drove the poor thing past rationality over the years.

"Remember that, Meg?" Mike asked sheepishly, when he turned again to the passenger side, fully expectant of her affectionate reply. "Pop put his hand straight out when the old dog got close. What was his name? Jake, I seem to remember. Cripes, that was fifty two, fifty three years ago." Mike chuckled as he spoke. "Pop smiled at the animal, made direct eye contact and, at that moment, moved his arm in a sweeping wave. Then he fearlessly walked toward the perplexed dog. Pop had a way that sure got attention. If he were with us the other day, and couldn't quell the Rottweilers, though, all hell would have broken out … a real war … a shooting gallery. And, Pop, never the quitter, not ever, would have fired until out of ammo." He went on with his reminiscing, grinning the while, ranting as if Meg, too, laughed. "I can just picture how it might have gone down with Dad there: Wayne and he, egging each other to a frenzy as they did so often."

Mike felt a twinge of jealousy as he continued. When it came to game playing, practical jokes, and laughs, his father usually worked more on Wayne, easiest mark in the family for a good time. "Brother, always the more playful one, the otter of the group; ready, anytime, to take absolutely nothing seriously.

"What's so different at the present time?" Mike questioned. "Wayne's sixty years old, going on sixteen, and still plays like a kid." He loved his brother's youthful personality but regretted, too, that his moves at the river were too impulsive to be repeated.

He saw only one car in the rear parking lot of the café. Relieved it was not the bronze Excursion, he pulled to a stop in front, got out and proudly patted the cover on the boat as he shuffled around it on the shoulder, and made for the door. The waitress chatted with a couple at the counter and didn't notice him at first. He slid four quarters in the old jukebox and, as Patsy Cline began to sing, *When You Need a Laugh,* Ina looked up. Meg usually played that song as soon as she and Mike arrived for dinner.

"Why, darned if it isn't Mike, Meg and the boat. And, where are the doggies? Oh, dear God, for the love of Pete. Oh, Mike, I am so very sorr. …"

No, no, don't mention it," Mike interrupted softly, unaffected by her forgetfulness. He grasped Ina's trembling wrist reassuringly and seated himself at the counter's end by the register. A good place to chat, she usually stood there to catch her breath between customers. "Don't think more of it. I've been doing the same ever since she left. It's lunchtime, nearly. How 'bout some roast beef and potatoes, Ina? Shoot the works and I'll skip dinner tonight."

His coffee disappeared quickly. While she refilled the cup, Ina leaned forward and whispered, "Say, you remember that loudmouth, the one from Washington D. C., who hassled you, a while back? Well. …" Mike's ears perked up as she went on. "Well, guess what? He popped in here, just this morning, about nine, and asked about you. What do you make of that? Wanted to know where you lived, your name, what you did for a living, the whole works. He acted real creepy, he was, yup, quite strange, a little too curious, and much too friendly for my taste. So I clammed up real tight."

Mike felt himself flush to a rosy hue. His heart leaped forward, eyes saw red. "What did you tell him?" he asked. "Did you say anything, anything at all?"

"Said I sort of knew you but not real well … lied that I always called you by the wrong name. You were so nice, you never corrected me. Then, then he asked me what I called you and I said. …"

"What did you say, Ina?" Mike looked concerned.

"Hey," the waitress said seriously, "is there anything you want to tell me? This isn't just about your little skirmish on the road is it? The man's arm was in a sling and he looked like it hurt. He cradled it in his other hand, real careful-like."

Mike's curiosity whirred. *So, it was him. Claybourne did take a shot. How the devil did it happen?*

"The woman, that same woman, drove the big Ford this time … came in with him for the lean breakfast, but didn't say much. I thought that a little odd at the time, too. She seemed like kind of a snotty little thing, a little bitchy, quite striking though: lovely black hair, sculptured body, and all. Boy, how nice to be thirty-five or forty, and in shape like that. So, what's up with these folks, My Dear?"

"Oh, there's a lot more, Mike replied, while he nervously wiped the corner of his mouth with shirt cuff. "Suffice it to say, the man is way out of reality, way out there, Ina. Did you know he bought old man Morris' place on the Au Sable? You know the house; the one by itself, out at the end of the dirt path, north of the power company gate."

She acted surprised. "Why, now I do. Hubby hasn't been fishing out there. I did hear from the Carlsons, though. You know, they're up-river and across quite a ways … some loud shooting goin' on. Someone was certainly doin' too much big gun target practice for their taste. Guess a bullet or two screamed through their river frontage trees. Pretty scary, huh? Suppose it was him? Hey, your crazy brother wasn't up there stirring things, was he?"

"Nope, not us," Mike lied, and panned a passive expression as he looked down at his plate and swept it clear of gravy with the last biscuit. "Thanks for the dumb act, though; very perceptive of you. He, Clabourne's his name, he's undeserving of Michigan hospitality, I can sure tell you that," Mike went on, and finished with a deep sigh.

Mike's curiosity whirred. *So, it was Claybourne who took a shot while we buried ourselves in the river mud.*

Ina reached in the register drawer and withdrew a business card. "The guy left this with me and said to call if I saw you. Said he'd make it worth my time, even tipped me ten bucks. I took it, too. Yes, that's his name: Brigadier General Homer Claybourne." She handed Mike the card.

146

"You're a sweetheart, my dear, a real sweetheart in my book," Mike said with more sincerity than he calculated beforehand. *I'll bring her a few flowers next time I pass through. Could have put us in real jeopardy, all right.*

Mike poured himself into bed after the long drive, exhaled deeply, stretched, and crumpled the pillows to elevate his head for a few minutes' TV viewing before he dropped off. The flickering glare illuminated his room with an eerie glow, mixed comfortably with the cool, moist air that streamed over him from an open window above the bed. A light drizzle fell. The drapes tingled, then ruffled noticeably, yet the birch leaves just outside remained stone quiet, save the patter of droplets that tickled them and rinsed away the day's dust.

"Hello, Darling." He heard the words clearly, as if Meg spoke, that he responded audibly.

"It's you, Meg, Honey. It's been a week. I thought you wouldn't be. …"

"You know you can't rid yourself of your Margaret, not that easily, you can't. I've missed you, Sweetheart; missed you lots." She always said that when he returned home from hunting and sometimes, too, at the end of a workday. "What am I to do with you and Wayne after that tirade on the Au Sable? Mike, I told you there would be big trouble. I meant what I said. Boy, did you delinquents find it? You dug up just what I said you would; now didn't you?" He shut the window part way. *How much does she know? I hope Wayne's escapades inside the house got by her. The rifle theft; she'll roast us alive over that.*

Ashamed but lonely, and in need of conversation, he apologized.

She cut in abruptly: "Who has the gun? You two cannot keep that rifle. It is not yours to take. Suppose it was used in a crime," she admonished. "Have you considered that?"

"Don't you think I know? Mike replied. "Wayne took it; I didn't."

"Well, he rode away in your Suburban, didn't he? You were the getaway driver. What was he doing for so long at the computer? Did he vandalize it, erase data? Just exactly why was he so excited when you left?"

"This guy, Claybourne, Meg; he's up to something that involves missiles. I read the document Wayne printed. He is selling some Patriot Missiles … yes that's the name … possibly to the Palestinians. Brother has the papers but we're not going to the police about it. We can't report it just yet. How do we know it's not some kind of joke, maybe a fantasy, even a game? If we went to the State Police and they found the man to be legitimate, we would end up jailed for trespassing and burglary.

"'So, Mister Gladdock,' they would ask, 'just how did you come by this letter about the missiles? Did you just find it there on the road all by its lonesome?' I can hear the cops now. We'd be up the creek. They would see right through us when our jaws dropped, with nothing to say for ourselves. The locks on jail doors are real big, not for me, though, and certainly not yet, anyway. We have a sense of duty to explore this Claybourne a bit more. He inquired about me down at the Bunyan. I don't like that nosiness, kind of scary. He's asking questions, managed to acquire the Morris shack. He does not deserve it and, now, he thinks he has control of the big pool. Well, he does not! We're not going to put up with the harassment."

Meg's voice turned from tolerant to sharp-edged. "Michael Gladdock, you must go to the police with this. You have to go. Do it immediately. They'll be contacting. …"

He cut in, "They've got nothing, nothing whatsoever to interrogate us about, absent our admission that we participated in a shooting and break-in. One or the other took a shot, a real bleeder it was. Apparently, it was Claybourne. He has a sling on his arm, Ina said, so it must have been him. That makes it all the worse. There was a lot of blood on the bluff, over by the big maple, where the swing used to be."

"I know. I know. Yes, I know the man was shot," Meg answered. "That doesn't matter now. What's important is that you and Wayne come clean of this and wash your hands of it. You mustn't get involved any further."

"But Claybourne," Mike insisted, "owns the place I've dreamed of my entire adult life. I still have faith we'll talk there, Meg—just the two of us—there on the porch. I could barely handle the shock of seeing Claybourne's sign on the gate and I want the place even more, now that the big-city sonofabitch, has his claws in it."

Mike cringed at his language but she ignored it, determined, she was, to keep him away from more difficulty. His left arm dropped to the floor below the bed. He tapped fingers impatiently but noiselessly on the carpet, bit his lower lip, and broke his stare from the ceiling. He felt compelled to leave. *Maybe I could excuse myself, drop downstairs for some ice water or orange juice. I could say that. ...*

"Michael, that that's not going to work. I know you're uncomfortable. I could be your mother nagging, reprimanding you like a child. But you have to realize you fellows acted out of character, shall I say?" she said, delicately as she could. "I'm frightened for you. The Morris place is starting to give me the heebie jeebies. It's so far back in there and. ..."

"Its remoteness makes it so ... so enticing. We both know fishing there is the best." Mike's thoughts charged ahead of his words. *Is she softening on the idea? I'll be danged if I will give in. I'll phone Wayne in the morning to see if he wants to go up river. We'll take binoculars and watch from a distance, who goes in and out of the property and what they do during the day. If they're up to no good, we'll find out and we will be better equipped to spill the beans. I am going to expose that underhanded southern boy, and his cute little lady friend, whatever it takes to do it.*

Mike curtailed his silent monologue, listened, and realized he showed too little interest in Meg's desire to keep him on center. The silence was pervasive. The cheering section of crickets in the canyon below the house was all he heard as his ears searched for more of her wisdom. Comforting or not, he didn't care. He did not receive enough of her. He remembered his recent and ethereal sexual experience and thought that another benefit of staying in touch.

"I'm just too insensitive. I'll never change," he lamented, discouraged with a sudden sense of helplessness. "She's told me; she's finally come clean with her frustrations and I see her concerns. I still need Meg, yet I shun her at the same time. Why? Why am I made up like this? Why can't I learn?"

He remembered how stubborn and inflexible his mother and father were during his formative years. *Maybe it's a behavior pattern that's cast in stone; nothing I can do about it.* He awaited her reply, and there was nothing. The curtains above his head wriggled on their hooks. He listened intently but the room remained deathly mute.

"Was I blinded all our married years, only to see through the fog once Meg's gone? Jesus Crisp! What a time to figure out how selfish I was." He turned silent and nervously tapped fingers on the floor again.

"Glad to hear you're thinking, My Dear," she finally whispered. "Keep working on that, for yourself, not me. Life will turn for you, I promise. It will turn when your ears open wider than that Gladdock mouth, that Marcos Gladdoski mouth you so unwittingly inherited."

"Meg? Meg? That you back with me?" Mike asked, frightened by the words he heard. "Meg? Please, stay here." When no response came forth, he pressed the remote button, turned off the cackle of eleven o'clock news, and covered himself to hide from further intrusion.

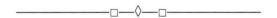

Chores complete, Mike resolved to drag his brother to the river. More surveillance at the shack might offer opportunity to see something they could take to local police. He waited patiently for someone to answer and gave up when Wayne's static-filled, antique answering machine cut in. A disappointment, Wayne and Nell were away—would be until Monday—on a visit to Nell's family in Lansing. *Dern. If I left such a recorded message in Flint, that I would be out for several days, the*

house would be ransacked, nothing left but the old dishes. Burglars would take everything.

How sweet it would be, to live in Oscoda County all the time, to get out of the city, the gol derned crime, and hurtful memories of Meg. Every time I look in a cupboard or closet at home, open a door, answer the phone, or see her clothes, my heart sinks. Guess I'll have to check out the Morris shack by myself, poke around a bit, and see what shakes. Should be at the river by mid-afternoon. I'll watch for a few hours until dark and try to get a little closer in at that time. Slow to replace the receiver, Mike still hoped Wayne would be home.

He threw the charged cell phone into his backpack along with two colas, some fresh vegetables, cold turkey slices, and whole-wheat rolls. He wrote Nell's brother's number on a piece of scratch paper and stuffed it into a side jacket pocket. *I'll call Wayne if anything pops. Need to keep him fired up, and tell him, too, that Meg is angry about the M-16. We should return it to the shack somehow. Let's see: binoculars, night scope ... my .357 ... plenty of firepower there.*

Mike pondered but a moment, walked from the kitchen, and left the holstered pistol on the gun rack by the front door. *Don't need guns tonight. I'll stay plenty far away. Even the dogs won't know I'm there.* Just the same, he filled two plastic bags with old frozen venison saved from a hunt several years before. The Rottweilers could be seduced with that. Wayne was right. Deer meat would endear him to the hostile dogs, if an encounter occurred.

Mike didn't wait below the crook of the tree more than thirty minutes before Claybourne's ebony-haired female companion walked from the front door of the shack to the pole barn.

His binoculars penetrated the distance perfectly. More than one hundred yards away, he kept himself well hidden by brush gathered for concealment—just upstream of the shoals, and above the opposite riverbank.

An occasional break in the surface of the big pool hinted the browns were getting itchy, though caddis flies *en masse* were still unready to taunt them. Not yet in swarms, a few clusters of the insects gathered here and there amidst the trees. Hence, it was easy to relax, take in the rustle of the fast water, and the afternoon's songbird calls.

A pileated woodpecker rattled bark high above, in the tree that concealed him. The bird's red crested head moved like a jackhammer and drilled with its stout bill into a beetle hole with hungry vengeance. One of Mike's favorites, he watched the crow-sized flyers often, when they worked the trees around his cabin. A flock of blackbirds—Mike called them grackles, as did his father—swooped low over the river riffles, and settled noisily, to gossip on the roots of a dead snag.

The woman returned to the house; she wore boots this time and shuffled them clumsily in the road's end dust. He saw the laces were untied. Such visible detail, Mike decided, he was positioned plenty close. She left the front door open, and carried two unusually large suitcases. One was brown leather, the other black, but they were of the same style, about twelve inches wide, with squared corners. Mike's eyes strained but he could not make out the gold embossing on the one carried in her right hand.

The Rottweilers bounded behind her, each pushed the other to enter the open doorway first. "Get the hell out of here, damn y'all!" the woman shrieked. "Homer, get these smelly sonsobuckeyes out of this house! Homer! Where are you?" The volume diminished to an inaudible lull when Claybourne appeared at the bluff. He came from the river, just out of Mike's view, and appeared fatigued from climbing the steep trail up the bank.

The general bent over to catch his breath, adjusted the sling in which his arm was suspended, and solemnly walked to the woman. Without further provocation, he lashed out with his good hand, smacked her with open palm in a stunning act of bravado, and simply stood there as if he expected a response. Spellbound, Mike watched with intense curiosity. She dropped her head, burst into a cry, and retreated inside.

Evidently, the general did not care much for her cursing at his precious dogs. Jesus crisp, that swing might have knocked Wayne or me for a loop. She is quite a beauty, but won't be for long if that's how he treats her. Moments later, she reappeared. She held a revolver with both hands—cops did that on TV—like she knew how to use it. The woman screamed; the general appeared frightened, and stood motionless in the clearing.

"Don't you ever do that again, Homer." Her angry words waffled through the forest. "Don't you ever. ..." Mike could only watch them speak thereafter; their voices settled and became inaudible in the distance. Claybourne appeared shocked by the confrontation, and gestured excitedly until she gave him the gun, and walked inside sobbing. He followed, shook his head and kicked at a pile of raked leaves in disgust.

Darkness ensued about 9:30, with no added activity to follow the short altercation. Only the upstairs bedroom light burned. He could see a shadow against the far wall. Someone was using the telephone. Enlisting the help of his night vision scope, he watched the grounds patiently, but saw nothing. Nothing, that is, until the dirt path lighted, as it did the night Wayne tripped the switch at the gate.

Mike went back to binoculars when the loom of approaching headlights over-lighted the green patterns in his night scope, and completely blotted out the images. A black limousine eventually swerved around the last turn and skidded to a dusty stop. The outdoor flood lamp on the shack snapped on, and cast its orange patterns and dark shadows on the clearing. Two strangely attired men alighted when the driver opened the left rear door.

Mike was unable to read the small lettering on the front license plate. *It dern sure isn't a Michigan license.* He dialed Lansing, shaking like a rattle, excited to tell Wayne. "Hi Betsy, it's Mike. Yes, oh yes ... sure, thank you for being there for us ... er, me. Thank you ... and, yes, Meg was a very fine woman. Please bring Wayne to the phone. It's quite important." Mike waited and watched Claybourne greet the bearded men who wore black and white checkered turbans and long, dark capes. They carried large leather suitcases, of the style Mike saw earlier in the young woman's hands, and were hastened to the house. The driver remained standing outside, rolled a cigarette and smoked it voraciously.

"Wayne … that you, Bro?" Mike whispered into the cell phone. "Sorry to interrupt, Hey, I'm up here at the shack … across the river … doing a little more snooping."

Wayne wished Mike called before going alone, but paused to listen.

"As I sit here, I've seen the woman pull a gun on the general and saw him slap her beforehand, real hard, Wayne, like he meant it and, now a limo—big bugger—just pulled up. Yes, yes," Mike continued breathlessly, "two guys got out dressed in Arab garb, I swear, and they carried in heavy valises. Earlier she retrieved two empties just like them, from the pole barn, and took them into the house. The front plate, I can see it now: red border at the bottom, white center section, and blue, or black along the top. Wayne, write this down, quickly … DWB 246 … got it? That's … DWB 2. …"

"Hey, hey! One second, the driver withdrew something from beneath his cloak, looks like an AK-47. Sure enough, it's a danged automatic rifle. He's holding it, looking around real suspicious-like. Oh, oh, one of the dogs is coming around the corner of the house, must have heard the commotion noise out front." Mike's breathing grew erratic and his heart leaped. "Did you get that plate? Could you call your buddy down at Lansing P.D? Ask him to check the license. Tell him, you were just curious, and say nothing of this to those big mouths, Brian and Betsy. Wayne, we don't want to go to jail or get ourselves killed. The limo driver looks like a soldier, not a chauffer. He's just gave the big male dog a swift kick in the flank; the poor thing disappeared around back, whimpered like a baby.

"Oh, oh," Mike called too loudly, "the men are leaving the shack. The suitcases look empty, the way they're carrying them. Yes, they are empty. What the dickens is going down? The driver just motioned Claybourne … and … and now the woman … into the back seat with the other two. They took off. What the heck? Have to go … try to catch up with them when they arrive at the gate. Must hurry and, yes, I'll be careful. See ya, Bro."

Wayne stared at the phone in disbelief, and listened to the dial tone for ten seconds before he dropped the receiver.

CHAPTER 15

"How could I have known?" Claybourne asked. He recklessly swung his good hand above his head while he paced in front of her. As a toddler might, in the midst of a tantrum; he threw his cap across the room, and stomped his right foot on the hardwood floor, to amplify the drama of his denial.

Virginia sat on the couch, just out from a long shower. Her hair was wet, looked tangled, and her nose had been bleeding. She patted her face with a bright pink towel, well spotted with blood, as he went on with his defense.

"Sure, they seemed serious and, yes, driven ... quite determined, I admit. But I thought ..." he lied, "... really thought they just wanted me out of the limo to ... ah ... to ... verify with y'all, what I had told them. I assumed they sought collateral assurance that we had more than a guessed shipping date for the missiles and equipment. After all, I insisted another two million be paid, per our original agreement, once we took possession of the launch electronics. Virginia, I didn't know the word 'ravage,' was on their minds. They seemed calm enough to me.

I'll not be responsible for the actions of a bunch of camel herding sons of. ..."

"You thoughtless ass, Homer! How could you? How could you let them take me, drive off in that limo, and ... and not know what they were going to do ... particularly after the last time they manhandled me so? That episode was part of the original solicitation, I agree; my slime ball father got me into that," she continued and panted apprehensively. "But that was enough. How could you do it to me tonight, especially? The way you swung at me earlier, Homer and then, what those men did to me, was too much to take." Her fists stayed clenched, knuckles blanched.

"I could blast your bulging belly full of holes; probably should have done so," she whimpered. "Homer, I have loved you and, foolishly, thought you cared for me. I fear, though, what you've become: a grotesque monster, a malignant tumor evolved from this intrigue—this backwoods roughness—grown so far out of hand." She stopped her crying and turned to him sternly, to continue. "No worry, though, I'm not stupid enough to cut out, not now, not before the missiles have been picked up and we have our money."

She raised her voice again, pushed her luck, and pleaded, "Don't you have any imagination? They were despicable, filthy slobs. Can't you guess what they forced to do in that short time you waited in the woods? You're a man. You knew; you understood their intentions. They were wild dogs. Do you want the shameful details? I'll spell it out, paint the repugnant picture if you wish."

He stopped pacing and withheld reply while his mind spun for answers. His sling fell to the floor. He unbuttoned his shirt and removed it. He dripped perspiration from the long walk to the shack. Claybourne contained his thoughts for the moment. *You're damned right I knew what they'd do. They're uncultured animals. You were brought into this because of your gender, and the fact that we were dealing with Arabs, who take their women, do what they want, whenever they get the urge.* In a way, Claybourne envied them. *You were the baggage they craved tonight; simple, ordinary baggage. You got in this scenario as the tramp you are and that's how you'll go out, too.*

"I didn't know; I'm sorry," he finally responded with a meager effort toward repentance. His eyes shifted too quickly. She watched them closely as he unsuccessfully feigned ignorance. "All right, OK, I could have guessed. I sensed they wanted you. I knew it wasn't about missiles when I got out of the limo. Their mindset was you. The bodyguard, chauffer or whatever the mean looking driver does for them, motioned me out of the limousine with a wave of his AK-47, ready to shoot my carcass full of holes. Y'all remember that, don't you?" he went on with his defense. "The guy said nothing, but the muzzle of his gun spoke loud and clear. aimed to follow instructions to the letter when he turned it my way.

"It was loaded to the gills and his finger was on the trigger, I might add. I'll concede, they were nearly slobbering, already drunk when they got here. But," Claybourne snapped like rifle fire, "you're in this because of your body—maybe a bit for your brains—but, certainly not your contacts. There's no other reason I can imagine. Your dear daddy volunteered you, sniveling little ingrate that you've become. Here you stand to make several million, and you complain about a chance to experience a little Middle Eastern passion?

The general continued admonishing without pause. "You're boring me with all this self-indulgence and the sad outcry for pity. You shot your Homer and you beg for sympathy? Ha! You're a big girl, a big one to talk. You were cognizant of your the risks; Rodmend and I have our own, and, there are, no doubt, many more to come.

"We're not out of this mess yet. If you think tonight's little *Arabian Nights* interlude wasn't exactly endearing, try sex against your will in a women's prison. Just imagine what those dominant beasts would do to that slithery little body of yours. You'd go public in a heartbeat." Virginia's shoulders shuddered uncontrollably. "So mind your self control and chill a little. Her eyes closed, she dropped her head, and tried to imagine the horror of incarceration if something went wrong in the operation's final hour.

Claybourne spouted without relent. "That's the chance you took, your part of the deal. You've no business bemoaning temporary indignation from a couple of quickies in the back of a Mercedes limousine. It couldn't have been any worse than your rather active younger days, I would wager." The general smiled sarcastically, licked his lips, and concluded his degrading monologue. "If my arm were healed, I'd likely have stood in line, too. It's been a while for your Homer, hasn't it?"

A cauldron of steaming hatred festered as she mulled his remarks. Claybourne could be dense and uncaring beyond belief. He picked up his hat and shirt and hobbled up the stairs. "C'mon Ginny," he called insensitively over his shoulder without looking back, "I'll give you a rub down. No worries, you've had your excitement for today."

Virginia's consciousness zipped back to the limo earlier in the evening. She pictured the eldest of the two Arabs. He grinned, showed his decayed, yellowing teeth, reeked of cigar smoke, and cheap whiskey. When he moved across the seat, and planted a wet kiss on her lips, she dared not shrug. The other man, probably twenty-five or thirty, groped beneath her loose blouse. Head back at his request, she remembered the bottle found her lips. She swallowed too much of the bitter liquor, then saw mostly blurs for the remainder of the distasteful experience. Her clothes were off in seconds, as were theirs, and the rest was tasteless pawing, and much else she hoped to forget.

Virginia rocked her head in deep nods to clear recurrent, unpleasant thoughts, breathed deeply and clasped her knees. Fingernails dug deeply into milky skin. She leaned back, and left four long scratches on each thigh.

Homer is nothing short of a lecher. How could he ignore my safety out there, and do nothing? Some clever words … anything … might have discouraged those filthy Arabs from such feverish behavior. My God, how can people act like that? To think of what I had to. … She thought again, though briefly, that she probably jumped into *Operation Eastern Star* a bit over her head, and as the subservient member of the team, to make matters worse. She could have guessed there were possibilities of exploitation, but the promise of so much money fast obliterated any apparent negatives.

Daddy did remind me: I was a female, and I should expect to perform a 'female's duties,' as he casually labeled them, from time to time. Look how he treated Mother. She was a doormat of the worst order. At least now, she has that horse trainer, William. Good for her; 'a man of great sensitivity,' she said. No wonder she found him irresistible. Daddy should take lessons.

She worried that her father's genes, replete with callousness, greed and unbelievable chauvinism, might have passed to her, considering how easily she was persuaded to participate in the plan, at the expense of her self-respect.

General Blakes presented the idea to her at the officers' club. He simply said, "Honey, you're going to like what I have to say, and you're not going to like it. There is good and bad news to this proposition, but when you come a running for the offer I'm about to make, don't look back. You must promise me that. You'll contribute a great deal to the cause—maybe a twenty million cause—with lots of just plain, Virginia." She wasn't then sure what her father meant, but, knowing his larcenous potential, and willingness to compromise things to suit his needs, she imagined the worst. She was right.

Virginia's first project was to spend the evening with two emissaries, low-level ones at that, from Syria—designates the P.L.O. sent to commence initial negotiations. That long night of drinking and unabashed sex, for which she recruited a promiscuous girlfriend, involved extremes in everything that transpired. The entire experience was regrettable, more than shameful, and she told her father that it would not be repeated. When the Arabs paid their initial deposit, though, it became too late to withdraw. She did not wish to be responsible for the failure of her father's last business venture.

Daddy didn't care about me—not a rat—for his only daughter. He should have allowed me to pull out when it got as sickening as it did. What did he care? His part only involved exploiting people he helped along the way, people he got into trouble while in the army. When he sieved them out of it, they fell to their knees before him, eternally grateful for his contrived effort. How many markers did he pull in the Pentagon, or elsewhere? Tearful, her face contorted; Virginia turned sinister and ugly. She then muttered aloud, "What would Mother think? What would she say if she knew? I'm so ashamed of all this, the way it's gone with Homer. What a pig he's become, or worse yet, a low-down skunk."

She failed to notice the general, as he crept softly down the stairs. He'd showered, walked barefooted, and was draped in a white robe with gold embroidered stars on the lapels. He heard her mumble from the top landing after drying himself, and descended the steps, cat-like, to overhear her words.

"What's that about a skunk? I don't smell it. Did the dogs turn up something?" he asked. "Did they, Ginny? Ginny!" he yelled angrily, "I'm talking to you."

"No, the dogs didn't turn up anything. They're outside where they belong. You're screaming again and I don't like it. Back off, Homer. Don't you understand?"

"Oh, my girl, you're just feeling a bit down. After the mauling you received, I suppose, who wouldn't? What's the matter; do you want more of it, and you don't like the urge? Is that it, my little filly? You slurped up the attention, did you? Yet you know you shouldn't have liked it." Claybourne actually thought himself humorous. His heartlessness went on without a break. So sick, he had no idea how he pushed her away—away from the operation and from him. He pushed her away from everything.

An aimless stare at the ceiling from her supine position on the couch, her eyes showed no signs of acknowledging Claybourne, who stepped into the room, tied the waist cord of his robe into a neat bow and approached her with renewed concern. He cradled her chin in his cupped hand. Virginia looked depressed and colorless. Her hair, absent its usual sheen, hung down, tangled; eyes seemed hollowed, dark circles hung below them like old theater drapes. She remained hushed as Claybourne sat on the edge of the cushion. His hand touched her forehead, fingers slid softly through her hair, and then he repeated the maneuver. This time he listened.

"Homer, we have to do something about our situation, about my involvement." She thought a moment and sighed deeply. "I do want out. I can't keep up with the need to service these demanding, bestial camel herders. This is … it's your," she stammered, "it's … just … the complete lack of respect. Your Virginia is not a machine for screwing the brains out of any man you might dictate. I'm educated," she pleaded and placed her hand upon his as he moved it about her head. "I enjoyed a long, and viable career as a nurse. You know I was well respected in Arlington medical circles, in high demand, and was very well paid for what I did.

"I dropped all of that to come here with you, because I believed I found an interesting man, with a military background like my father. I viewed you as a caretaker, too, for the rest of our lives together, and I saw myself as yours. She whimpered and then cried openly, close to hysterics, "It seems I've lost it all. My dreams for a long-term relationship based on strength and honor—and I began to believe in all of that—have shattered like fine crystal on concrete.

"Turn me over to the authorities, Homer; kill me. I don't care, not after what went on tonight. Keep the money," she went on, and again elevated the amplitude of her voice. You can have my three, four or five million, whatever it turns out to be. Then you just come up here and play with it until you're sick of counting green pieces of paper. Play by yourself all day, for all I care," she shrieked, "but, you'll do it alone. I don't think that's going to be real fun, here, the middle of nowhere. It will not be the picnic you thought! She sat up from her reclined position and recounted the last words but inches from his face.

Claybourne, starved for an immediate reply, just looked at Virginia. His glance swung instinctively toward the nearby gun rack, propped against the wall at the base of the stairs, and then back into her eyes. His surly frown sent a non-verbal, but clear message, he hoped, that he could silence her at any moment, and with great facility. One tug on a trigger, any one of them, and she could be finished.

Virginia, too, had visions of a shooting, as her glassy stare swung to the cluster of weapons on the rack. However in her mind, she was the shooter, not him. She could not sway herself from a strangely satisfying feeling that swelled from within, as she watched him topple from the bluff, and grapple at his chest, bloodied by all nineteen shots from the M-16 magazine. A slow motion picture followed: Claybourne roared out in pain, mouth wide-open, eyes ablaze, and careened head first into the deep pool at the foot of the bluff. Emotionless, she followed the patch of bloody water with more shots, until what was left of him drifted out of sight around the roots of the dead log, and away toward Lake Huron.

"Military Intelligence: what a farcical contradiction. 'Military lack of intelligence,' the department should be called. It's the epitome of oxymorons, probably of more imminent danger to our forces than the enemies themselves," Claybourne spoke through pursed lips, while the single edged razor cleaned two-day growth from beneath his nose. He scraped away the lather on his sideburns, finished the shave by deftly trimming them to perfect horizontals; and wiped his reddened face with a hot towel. The general prepared for the final trip to Texas, where he would personally supervise and confirm removal of components for the last six Patriots, piece by piece, from the base where the army spent millions to update them. Once joined with the others already absconded from the facility, and stored in a small commercial warehouse in Waco, his men could begin the slow process of reassembly and prepare the contraband for delivery. "The army hasn't a clue what's happened to them. It's too funny," he boasted admiringly to himself in the mirror. "You get to know how that system works, and then, how it fails to operate, after so many years' service."

The early phone call he received from his friend and operation participant, Master Sergeant Halsley Hinteroffer, offered encouragement. Still on duty, with two years until retirement, Hal covered all details from the Texas side, and received a quarter million-dollar payoff for his share. *Without him,* Claybourne thought, *it might have been impossible. He sure made mincemeat of the damned MPs and Intel on base, absolute mush. He took the greatest risk, too, more than the rest of us put together, and he's receiving the smallest share … the jerk … no idea what we'll be making. Small steaks for small fries, I always say. He thinks he'll be rich from the deal.*

The General combed his hair, then mused quietly. *I left no Claybourne tracks from Hal's direction; none that Army Intelligence could follow, anyway. The tracks, if any, lead just to him, then Washington, and directly to the Senate Armed Services Committee. From there, who the hell cares? Those Members of Congress will scatter like flies to nail each other if he ever talks. As usual, the Democrats will point to the Republicans and vice versa. I'll sit back with my fly rod, here on the lovely Au Sable River, and only imagine the turmoil as it unwinds down there. Hal could get nailed but I think he's covered his rear. How anxious he was to help, to show his gratitude for my getting him out of that scandal at Fort Bennings.*

"Little did he know that it was I who reported him to the old man, the beginning of his troubles." Claybourne sang the words while dressing to the nines in tight silk slacks, a black polo shirt and black Italian loafers. "All it took was a martini with General King, and assurance that Hinteroffer wasn't involved. 'My mistake, General, my mistake;' that's all I had to say," Claybourne laughed heartily. "Heh, heh, he'd have kissed my tail for the rest of my life. Such a perfect lever to get someone to help you; let them think you bent over backwards to get them out of trouble. Works every time … every single time."

Claybourne forged his career on the weakest underpinnings of his key men, wherever he could spot them. They would be the ones beholden to him, sooner or later, in some way, and he was not one to let them forget.

His flying agenda for the following week promised to be a busy one: Flint to Detroit, thence to Texas, and finally to the National Guard facility in Alabama for final arrangements—acquisition of the tracking and sensing computers and the battery assembly. "Communicators are complete: brand new AN/MSQ-104 unit and the M901 Launch Station … looks good. We could have done with an older setup. How they got them swapped for the new technology, I'll never know. Pappy Tapper, the old sonofagun, may be a lifer supply sergeant, but he knows his way around D.C., and any U. S. Army base in the country, better than anyone, I'd venture. He could smuggle nuclear weapons from beneath the snoopiest of Intel noses."

Before sliding them into the red manila folder in his open briefcase, the general grinned at the stack of printed e-mails, which arrived in the night. The end loomed in sight. "Very soon, very soon, indeed. We'll have everything in our barn, ready for pick-up, in exchange for final funds. We're almost home free; so very easy; I'd almost do it again," he sighed gleefully.

Virginia toiled restlessly in bed, disturbed by the glare of bathroom lights, and Claybourne's mutterings while he packed and dressed. 5:15 AM was far earlier than she typically arose since their move to the woods. "Homer, can't you do that without waking the dead? I'm bushed and really need the rest."

"Pipe down and go back to sleep, Dear. Your Homer is taking care of everything for you." He hummed a few measures of the Beatles' *Yesterday,* patted her back patronizingly and resumed packing. He stretched his injured arm high, and for the first time since the gunshot, felt only moderate pain. "I'll take the sling, but I'm not about to wear it if I don't need it."

Elated that full recovery appeared on the horizon, he could satisfy himself and Virginia, too, when he returned. *Should be able to perform inside of a week. I'd better be able bodied by then. I'll show her, I'm not all bad; bring back some perfume, maybe a little diamond, too. That'll soothe her anger along with the passage of some time. How could I have thought what I did last night? Where do these wild fantasies originate … taking her out of the picture? I cannot imagine acting on the notion. Well, damn it, she shot me and said she would do it again, too. Why shouldn't I have such feelings?*

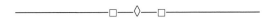

The Excursion engine labored when the SUV traversed the first set of deep ruts in the path toward the main road, then settled back to idle. He coasted and idled, alternatively, for several hundred yards along a smoother section, and then rolled to a stop. Claybourne forgot one not-so-small detail. "The two million the Arabs brought. I left the stuffed suitcases in the bedroom closet." He checked his watch. "It's going to be close; I could miss my plane if there's unexpected traffic."

"I must get the hundred fifty thousand to pay Hal, if all is well with the missiles. I'm taking a huge risk sending it as street checked baggage in the aluminum suitcase, but how else? Couldn't do it carry-on. I'd better hide what's left and the briefcases, also. I shouldn't trust Ginny completely, not now, in the final stages, considering her upset with the screwing she took last night and everything else that's rooting out her spurts of anger."

He nearly coasted back, soundlessly tiptoed up the stairs, not to awaken her. The bedroom door swung open. Claybourne stood paralyzed, almost unable to stand, so aghast at what he saw.

Virginia turned pearly white. Unable to speak, in disbelief Claybourne returned, she began to tremble. "Oh ... oh ... Honey," she stammered, "I ... I ... thought you left ... I ... ah, just wanted to count it," she said meekly—panic-stricken and fearful of his wrath. He found Virginia on the bed, strewn with bundles of hundred dollar bills—stacks and stacks of them. Both briefcases the Arabs brought, lay emptied on the floor.

"What the devil do you think you're doing?" The general snapped a steel grip on Virginia's right arm, and yanked her to the floor in a heap. "What, in the deepest pits of Hades do you think you're doing?"

CHAPTER 16

———◆◆◆———

Fire engine red, the 1957 Chevrolet pickup truck was a prize. Morris family members restored the classic for the old man's eightieth birthday present. While overwhelmed with the gesture, he had little time to appreciate the gift; its completion came too close to his final days.

The old classic, just another asset on the long list of accoutrements included with the river property when the estate sold to Homer Claybourne, it didn't see much use. The general abhorred trucks, considered them the silly pride and joy of backwoods rednecks, not civilized city people. Once he moved in, he disrespectfully parked it outside, between the shack and the barn, so indifferent he was to the expensive restoration. More important, though, the barn would see use as space to store the Patriot Missiles and accessories when they began to arrive.

While he traveled, the general left the Chevrolet for Virginia to drive, which pleased her no end. She handled the floor shift like a pro. "Daddy's old Model A Ford prepared me well for this," she said happily. She jostled the shift lever in search of low gear. "Let's see, lower left position … in the "H" pattern. Yes, I remember. That should be it … clutch down, a little gas, clutch back, slowly back … slowly. Now, a little more gas." She recalled with delight, the day her father allowed her to drive his antique four-banger for the first time. Just sixteen, she never forgot the dripping heat of that August day in the Virginia hills, and the time he spent with her on the dirt lot behind the abandoned packinghouse—a perfect site for driver's training.

The radiator on the old Model A coupe boiled several times with the extended low speed operation but her father expressed surprisingly little concern. Quickly, she learned the art of the manual shift, and found the new driving experience so exciting, he allowed her to carve endless furrows around the tract by herself, for the rest of the day. She never felt closer to him.

"There ... oops. ..." The truck jumped forth, startled her from the recollections. It stopped, with a jolt, and then juggled, bump to bump along the path a few yards, before its motion eased as she gained control. "Got it ... smoother, now. That's it."

The woods began greening and the pervasive scent of leafing trees could not have been more invigorating. It felt like the lovely, sun-drenched morning it was, despite the pain that stung her wrist, the one Claybourne viciously grabbed in the bedroom, the night before. Yet fearful of that, and his frightening verbal lambaste, also, she looked forward to her first day alone. She pleaded for her life and, stuck in bone-chilling fear, finally convinced the general that, in a silly, child-like way, she wished only to play with the bundles of cash. It wasn't easy to satisfy the general that she harbored no designs of making off with it.

Virginia recounted the general's terrifying tirade repeatedly. "You... you thieving little alley cat," he screamed as she lay on the floor beside the bed, where he pulled her, petrified he would kill her immediately, knowing he could easily do it, and with little reflection. "You dirty, sneaking little con," he yelled, with his big knife to her throat. "How could y'all think of getting away with this? I should tell Rodmend. He'll probably take you out himself, his only daughter, notwithstanding. He'd come right away. That man is far more determined ... greedier than I could ever be."

Crying in hysteria, she begged him to listen, to believe that she was dutifully responsible, that her intentions were innocent, and not malevolent, as he suggested. Claybourne remained beet-faced and livid through her many explanations, unfazed by the pleas. Until cooled down after more than ten minutes, his hand remained clamped around her tiny wrist, afraid she would escape with the briefcases if cast loose. When he finally relented, the general shamelessly admitted his own inclination to do much the same when they received the first deposit.

"Such piles of money, huge sums like that, can turn an adult into a child. Any of us, I guess, would be vulnerable to the urge," he finally stipulated, to her surprise when his composure returned. "How many people in the world ever have the opportunity to play with so much? I think I understand; I guess I do. Yes, I wanted to feel free to do that myself." Her terror eased when she heard those words.

He released his grip, and sheathed the threatening knife he held. To her fortunate deliverance, he was late, and after hurriedly removing funds to pay Hinteroffer, Claybourne left, behind schedule to catch his plane at Bishop International Airport in Flint. Before departing, though, he hung the money-filled briefcases in the rafters of the pole barn, away from prying eyes, and sticky fingers.

The Chevrolet pickup ground its way toward the gate. Virginia felt liberated. "He's gone … at least a week." She squealed the words with hands clasped on the wheel, and tossed her shoulders back playfully. "I'll have run of the place, to sunbathe nude by the river if I wish, swim in the icy water, plant more flowers, and just plain relax, without him gnawing at me for a change. Dear God, I hope there are complications down south, that he'll be gone longer than anticipated. I need a break … time to think … do things I feel clean doing for a change. A small vegetable garden would be nice."

Either we conduct ourselves like lovers, rebuild our trust, and work on the repair of our destroyed spirits, or I'm gone…out of here. She thought of home, the State of Virginia, and her old friends there. *I do miss Arlington, the parties, tennis, golf, and my horses. I hope they're well. Can I ever feel like I belong here? Might I learn to enjoy the river, use the canoe or even learn to fish? Such a relaxing environment here; I do love it. I could move to Atlanta, also; hide in the heart of the city if I had to; anything to make a clean getaway. Homer is out of his mind to treat me like this.*

Virginia looked at the darkened area beneath her left eye, a grim vestige of the slap Claybourne wielded. There were still finger marks on her wrists, too, left when he pulled her like a wet towel to the floor. *I've had moments. Yes, when I thought of jumping ship, taking off with the money, some dream filled moments. He'd easily find me. I would never jilt that man or my father, for that matter. A double cross is not the way I want to deal with these two, much as I enjoy having wandering thoughts of the prospects.*

Can't forget Daddy took care of me when Mother ran away with William. I was nicely cared for, sent to college, and pampered beyond my expectations. For his dedication, for sticking by my side, I'll be eternally grateful, despite the mess we've created. Virginia cringed with distaste at how comparatively spineless her mother seemed. Afraid to stand up to her father, when troubles began between them, she simply moved out, and neglected to explain why, to her distraught daughter.

Finally, admitting to her affair, an irrevocable shock to Virginia; it drove her away from close relationships until she grew older, mature enough to appreciate her mother's clear justifications. She reviewed her own accountability, and how she conceded, so readily, to participate in *Operation Eastern Star.* It was easy, she recalled, to make the decision to steer her future in a surprise direction. "Homer is right," she had to admit aloud. "I'm a big girl and knew, at least impliedly, where I was headed.

"I'll stop today and make sure the forklift gets delivered next week. Homer said it's a must." The rear wheels spun in the loose shoulder and spread gravel far behind. She turned east; tires smoked on the pavement when the snappy three-fifty took hold. A gleaming red streak, the truck roared down Old River Road with more enthusiasm than old man Morris would have guessed possible. Heads turned in front of the antique store as she flew past, and wound to fifty-five in second gear, before she shifted. Straight through mufflers rumbled like rolling thunderclaps, and then purred when she rounded the curve in third, out of sight toward town.

"I'm going to enjoy this old crate. I feel like a local—a real red-necked local—in a red-painted, red-neck truck. To hell with Homer and his snooty ideas about cars. This is fun!" Virginia rolled down the windows. She loosened her bun, dropped hair to her shoulders, and let the fresh wind tangle it as it might. Homer would never have allowed that. Her cares drifted with the feeling of release that fast encircled her.

Mike worked several weekends, three years before, to build the expansive rear deck that spread from the east elevation of the cabin. An extended living area during warm summer months, he enjoyed it daily. The steep slope below, lunged right from the railing, and overflowed with birches. Poplars hungered in the moist soil at the bottom of the ravine, along the brook, and a plethora of maples on the far side harbored songbirds of every description until fall. His favorite spot for morning coffee, the addition was a station to await the waking sun when it topped the hill to the east. Shaded by the house wall, the platform cooled early in festering summer afternoons and, during middays, shielding tree limbs provided coveted shade.

Mike said to the spider, *"Argiope aurantia," as* if it understood its Latin name, "you black and yellow beauty. I like your morning jewelry … the dew drops on your web, but don't you work so hard. Smell the flowers," he admonished, with the cue Meg gave to him. He sipped again, unaware his coffee cooled so quickly; and intently watched the huge arachnid, her inch long abdomen fully protuberant from prey devoured through the night. He caught a few precious minutes here and there on the pristine perch, but just enough for transient satisfaction. Rarely did he take the time he allotted that morning; he found himself enamored, more than he would have believed possible.

Completely distracted from the first cup of his second pot of French roast, he sat idly, and watched the orbicular net in the weaving, by the expert herself. Draped from an overhanging oak limb, down to the back stairs, the garden spider's expansive web, carefully constructed the night before, already served its maker. It sported several freshly entombed moths.

A lonely crow cawed rhythmically in the distance, base section for the shrill, squeaky wheel songs of black and white warblers that hovered in the high branches. Brown-headed cowbirds fluttered immediately above, anxious to settle in other birds' nests. "The little pirates," Mike said, "they'll leave their dappled eggs, and another species will have to do the babysitting and feeding. Where did they learn that big city method of welfare fraud, I wonder?"

Woodpeckers, starlings, tree swallows, even a purple martin, he spotted without arising from the comfort of his chaise. Blue jays, by far the most plentiful, provided endless brass to complete the symphony of the day's beginning. The environment hovered close to perfection. Feeling well insulated from hurting feelings, the Morris shack and the Au Sable, Mike became lost in a rush of distracting memories.

Meg, in her senior year of high school, met him at her front door, wrapped in fluffy white. He called her twice before leaving his house to make certain she'd be ready. Her mother made the new formal she wore; her hair glistened—done up in traditional graduation curls—and her lips shone with fiery pink. He remembered; he waited on her porch, speechless; thought his bow tie would pop with pride. Words would not come. She never looked more beautiful. Flurries of sparkle graced her cheeks and bared shoulders. "I ... I ... you, oh Lord," he recalled stammering. "You're an angel and, and I ... I'm to take you with me, in this old jalopy?" He turned to the driveway and stretched his hand toward their wheels for the night, with a helpless shrug. Though he waxed it that morning, it was still Pop's 1953 pickup with the bashed-in left rear fender he never fixed.

Mike and Meg were elected Prom King and Queen that evening. It came as a complete and embarrassing surprise. Later, he recalled, he pledged himself forever devoted to her, while they stuffed themselves with after-dance Bee Burger dinners and sodas at the Yellow Jacket Drive-In.

An unforgettable night, that is, until Wayne showed up at the popular hangout, well into drinking, adorned with his hopeless grin. "Jesus crisp, he smiled like a 'possum eating bumble bees. He mustered the fake ID, bought that bottle of peach brandy and, proud of his conquest, held it high for all to see." Their behavior evolved to the lamentable, but Mike laughed non-stop, nevertheless. Against wishes of their dates, the two brothers nipped too much of the cheap, sweet liqueur, and, before long—inhibitions released—their antics grew out of control. Mike climbed the elm tree that shaded the restaurant parking lot, to the entertainment of schoolmates who also enjoyed midnight snacks from trays in their car windows.

A loud snap, the crashing limb from which he hung, garnered everyone's attention as it fell with his weight from rooftop height, and tore smaller branches and twigs behind it. Mike dangled below like a frightened monkey, undisturbed, but for his shocked pride, and the long tear in his rental tuxedo.

Wayne managed to start two fights and Mike sealed the evening, when he launched the contents of his burger-stuffed stomach on Meg's new dress. "Oh, a good time was had by all that night, it was," he chuckled, when he pictured the look on her mother's face as he staggered toward the door to deposit Meg at home for the night. He couldn't swear to it, but it seemed a month passed, during which Meg was admonished to say nothing to either Gladdock, much less, not to go out with Mike. Summer fun did not begin so brightly that year.

An almost imperceptible tussle in the leaves above drew his attention to the crown of the newly laced yellow birch that rose to his left. He shivered from the sudden chill as it enveloped him and waited for her inevitable intrusion.

"Oh, Mike, don't you remember that graduation night? Doesn't it seem only yesterday?" She laughed, as he always wanted her to cut loose, when he tried to be funny. No woman he knew could roar like Meg. One of her feature attractions, her blue eyes rolled to the side, while dimples puckered, and bright white teeth flashed. "You were so terribly handsome at the prom. If we parked by the lake afterward, in our spot," she continued, "at the water's edge, between the pines and the lighthouse—and you made one of your impassioned passes at me—I...I don't know; I might not have resisted. We might have married a few years earlier. Instead, Wayne's brandy rescued me from my desires.

"Ugh, it was so awful, I could hardly swallow it. You ruined my dress, you know. You were messed up," she snickered, "and your brother: lips swollen, and his right eye, I'll never forget. It looked like ground meat … the blood drops, all that red … streamed down his powder blue tuxedo coat. Such babes, drunk so quickly." She laughed again. "Little did I appreciate at the time that we'd soon start a family, have so much in common, so many good times in our many years together."

He envisioned tears of joy welled in her eyes. She could be inescapably sentimental when she reminisced. "Don't you think your mother hated me that night, Meg? Poor thing; she worked so hard to sew your formal gown, right up to the minute you put it on, didn't she? Your mom worshiped the ground you walked upon, treated you like the princess you were."

"As did you in those days, My Love. That night was one to remember, except for the finale, of course. Funny, how compliments, expressions of admiration, became understood as our relationship matured over the years. How seldom it was, once we married, that you said how much you valued me, as you did during the years we dated. I knew you did, but you could have reassured me a bit more often, than Christmas, birthday, or Mother's Day. Sometimes I didn't know how you felt; found myself insecure and unable to ask for your accolades. If I was more communicative about those needs, it might have helped."

At least she admits some responsibility. For a minute I thought I'd be dragged through the blame bit again. Good to hear she looks at both sides. His mind raced at fast forward to digest her revelations. *They come rapid-fire now, so I must pay full attention.*

Suppose I could use more coaching. I've never been one to lavish compliments and was always aware of that. It seemed phony to me, to wreath someone with praise. What does a person do when openly admired? Why … why they deny the qualities you just put forth. They'll do it every time.

He turned his notions outside. "'What lovely hair you have,' I might say. The woman would surely remark, 'Oh, thank you; thanks, but it needs washing.' Or I might utter to a man, 'I like your suit.' I'd get nowhere, because the reply would be, 'Just a cheapo—an old one, too—bought it for Aunt Fanny's funeral ten years ago, and haven't worn it much.'

"Throwing out shallow compliments hasn't been my bag, Meg. I can't trust people when they. ..."

She interrupted, "So that's it. You're afraid they're not being genuine? Why don't you just say so? I want to hear you say you're afraid, just once, I do. It would be good.

"OK, OK, I'm afraid. There! How's that sound byte, coming from Mike? Does that make you happy?" *Death is the only thing I have really come to fear. I'm afraid of dying before I get my hands on the Morris property. I've seen my Meg die. The reality, the vividness of death, finally, is an inescapable threat. I'm slowly coming to terms with how fragile life is, how much more so it will become, as the years creep onward.*

Everything around me seems more sacred since she left. "On one hand I want to get more done in less time, now that you're gone. On the other, I want to take more time to do less. Which is better?" he asked.

A zephyr twilled the treetops above; the spider's web bounced with the air movement and *Argiope* hesitated weaving until stillness returned. Lazily, Mike watched her progress throughout his dialogue with Meg. *What a luxury, to watch a spider spin her web. I do wish Meg stayed longer. I miss her so, should have complimented her, taken the hint. How can I be so blind? Think I'll go to the mall for summer flowers and plant the beds in front. I'll pick up some hanging pots and drape them around the deck. Soon there will be more spiders to watch.*

Mike's black Suburban threaded through the crowded parking lot at Tri-Counties Home and Garden Center. Saturday morning at early summer's start, the place filled to the brim with energetic folks from miles around, glad to have the freezing immobilization of winter behind them. A red pickup truck swung left in front of him as he slowed to make a right turn into a vacant slot.

"Gheeze, lady! Get some manners, for cripe's sake," he grumbled loudly. *Gol dern women drivers! What the heck is she thinking? Must be from New York or some big city where they'll fist fight for parking spots. She stole the dern space right out from under me.* He suddenly mellowed. "Wait a minute; that's the '57, the old Chevy, from the shack. He chilled and elected not to allow room for another encroacher to cut in front. "Guess I better wake up a little and recognize the usual sunny day rat race at Tri Counties. I'm still moving like a snail."

She waited by the rear of the truck, one foot on the bumper, hands on her hips; head cocked in a friendly pose. The lavender shorts she wore accented her slender, creamy tan thighs and drew his eyes down from her polished smile, to the skimpy stretch top that covered a pleasingly narrow strip of her torso.

"Hey there; how y'all?" Virginia's words flowed forth in the most delicious, though whiny southern drawl he ever heard. "I didn't steal your space, did I? Didn't see a right hand turn signal, so I just. ..." She made a sliding gesture with her hand, *It's Claybourne's wife, girlfriend, whatever she is, the female with him at the Paul Bunyan—the one he slapped at the shack, for cripe's sake.* Shocked, Mike withheld a response for too long and simply stared. Stunning, she looked a bit taller than Meg. Her silky hair: fine, clean, and shiny, rustled with the light breeze. Her face glowed. *That lipstick! What a wild color, and those legs; too, too wild.*

"Oh, oh, not at all; it was ... that is ... I'm really not in a, ah ... hurry," he stumbled. "Nice truck ... I mean ... I admired your wheels. That was my last year in high school, 1957 ... good year for. ..." He remembered Meg's advice earlier in the morning, and before he could contain himself, the words shot forth. "Your hair, it's lovely, pitch black, and that captivating, magnetic smile to go along with it. Whew. I was lost there, for a second. Sorry. You know, when I see a beautiful woman, I can freeze up something terrible."

"Well," she said, as she opened her smile to picture-perfect, "well, thank you; that sure made my day. First compliments I've had in, oh well, far too long, I suppose." She reached out her right hand. He took it in both of his and shook heartily. Virginia's the name, Virginia Blakes." Her handshake was firm. Her breasts pulled his eyes downward again. She felt the admiration. Her eyebrows arched in approval.

"Oh, yes, Mike's the name. Last name's Gladdock, I grew up over in East Tawas," he spewed, and blushed noticeably. "I have a place … little gardening today. He blurted it out then blushed again, that time to a bright rose. "A real sexy outfit you've got there … if I may, real … cute. I meant that … I like. …" He stopped in his tracks. *Cute? Cute, Mike? What's cute? You've never in your life used the word, cute.*

He stood aghast. Her eyes penetrated his, for the awkward sentence to be completed. "I like short shorts and small tops, nice combo on a balmy day like this." *Where did that come from, for Lord's sake? I'd better shut up. Just a few days ago, Claybourne was trying to find me. What the Sam Hill did he want? My God, what am I doing, babbling like this? I let the cat out of the bag, mentioned my full name, and East Tawas. Now they'll be able to find Wayne over there; he's listed in the phone book. I said, 'Gladdock,' as plain as the nose on my face. Brother's going to love me for that!*

Mike came to his senses and reverted to his more covert side. "We … ah … er, sort of met on the road, there on Highway 55, just west of the Paul Bunyan Café, late at night a while back. It was a little embarrassing. Then, we. …"

"I thought you looked familiar. Yes, that was you in the restaurant, wasn't it?" she asked cheerfully. "I do apologize for my husban … my fiancé's obstinacy that night. He's been stressed, just retired from the army, and can't get used to the fact that civilians usually act decently with one another. He is a good man, deep inside, but he has been difficult since we moved to the woods, still needs to chill, adjust … you know … cool down some. Homer is away for a week or more, so I'm elected to do the planting, veggies and flowers, if I can. I'm from the south; it comes easy for me."

Mike melted with her smile. "Well, I'll do that today, too. I want to start fishing this trip if I can." He played dumb and went on, "I love the Au Sable. You might know of it: the big river … runs to Lake Huron from up past Grayling. Best stream in the area for browns, brown trout, that is. I fly fish for them in the early summer, especially when he bugs come out. It's nice then." He could not shake his nervousness.

"Gosh, you'll have to come by our place. We have a delightful view right on the water, on the Au Sable. That's our river, the Au Sable."

Mike fumed, his face flushed, and his fists reflexively clenched. Anger rose like a rocket. *Their river, hell! What would she know about the river? Their river? Not ever! It's my river, dern it all!* "Where would that spot be?" he queried with an innocent look and feigned interest, barely able to maintain control.

"We bought some acreage off Old River Road. It used to be called the Morris Estate, we were told, but Homer changed it to Claybourne Farms."

Estate? It's a shack, for cripe's sake. "Why ... what a ... why that's a coincidence! I know the very house. I've fished there for almost fifty years. Always drove in and parked at the clearing. We ... that is, I ... we ... my deceased wife and I, used that road since we were kids, and my Pop before us, most of his life. That part of the river is like the back of my hand. Caught my first brown there, know every danged hole in it." Mike beamed proudly.

"It's private now," she jabbed just a little too quickly for his taste. "Homer put up a gate to restrict hunters and four-wheelers. There was lots of vandalism damage to the house after Mr. Morris' death, burglars, too. Yes, someone was there just recently and took Homer's gun. We felt a little intimidated, so we have increased security. There will soon be personnel watching our woods. Sure hope they can discourage further intrusions."

"Yep," he responded patronizingly, "you can't be too careful. Lots of weirdoes come up from the cities these days."

"I'm sure Homer wouldn't mind if you drove down our road to fish a little. That could hardly be a problem as far as I'm concerned. Mike's your name, right? You say your wife is gone?" She gave him a thorough top to bottom check-up when he momentarily glanced away to gather a response. "I'm very sorry."

"Yes, she died recently. I'm still trying to get my head together."

"I hear you. Well, you seem real nice." Her smile glowed again as she stood up straight and fluffed her hair behind her ears with both hands. "Just drive on over, anytime, if you want to fish. There's a button to open the gate on the right hand post. You'll see a silly stuffed deer cross on a track just inside. Wait for it to cross back again, and then drive on through. If the deer stays in the center of the road, then we would like to be private, OK?

"The general's idea to use the dumb thing for a security camera. Just disregard the cable. We don't usually secure the lock. Feel free to park out by the barn; you know the area, and fish all you want. Watch out, though; there were some damned crazy hunters shooting out there."

"Thanks, I will. Fishing's always best after nine or so at night. You know that, don't you?"

"Do now," she called, turning toward the store. She slung her purse over her shoulder and giggled like a teenager. "Nice talking and, by the way, we have three dogs: Jack, King and Ace. Think of the face cards to remember their names. They run loose most of the time. They'll eat from your hands like puppies if you give them a little time to get friendly."

Virginia looked surreptitiously over her shoulder at the back license plate on the Suburban: *MEG 099*. She repeated the number to herself several times until she reached the curb at the storefront. When Mike passed through the nursery department door, she hurriedly jotted the license number on a shopping bag scrap, folded the small piece of paper, and stuffed it into the outside pocket of her purse.

CHAPTER 17

Mouth dry from a long, open-mouthed, speechless spell and more than astonished, Wayne sought relief with a second beer, and guzzled half while Mike caught his breath. The tales of Mike's eavesdropping session at the river, and the surprise encounter with Virginia that morning at the Mio Mall held him overwhelmed. Wayne sat close to Nell at one end of their dining table. Frozen with interest and concern, their arms stayed tightly clenched as Mike's stories wove onward.

"The big limo took off down the path to Old River Road; the general and the girl, Virginia, inside with the Arabs," Mike concluded, as if he finished reading a bedtime classic to his grandchildren.

Dinner with Wayne and Nell, always an event—food supply on overload, and quality at its best; all three gladly opted for the break. The roast golden pheasant, naught short of mouth-watering, would have tickled the palate of the fussiest Epicurean. Two large birds nearly disappeared before the threesome's eyes, along with a stack of Nell's special cornbread, wild rice, and cranberry stuffing. Roasted baby russet potatoes, bathed in olive oil and sage, rhubarb garnished, and two helpings of blueberry pie completed the bill and left the overfed attendees well satisfied. The serving platters before them, lay nearly vacant.

Mike saved his recitals until after dessert. The family's custom to discuss business ... their father's protocol, dated as far back as he could remember. *Pop's special time ... no one would interrupt, when punishments were thoughtfully aired, contrived and dolled out to those deserving. Serious interrogations, too, were conducted then, when Pop wanted answers. He got them fast; no holding back when the old man demanded the truth; absolutely no escaping from it.*

"We didn't mess with Pop after dinner, did we?" Mike asked, oblivious to his divergent thinking for a moment.

"Hey, you were talking about this, this Virginia," Wayne barked, anxious for him to continue, "and, now Pop? Are you confused, Dear Brother?"

"Dern, I was just day dreaming there for a second. Remember Pop's business talks?" He went on to complete his thought, "after we finished dessert? Then, later, he'd dish out our whacks."

Wayne willfully joined Mike's reminiscing. "I sure won't forget the whipping I got when I shoots that old bull coon, skins it in the woods and tells Ma…heh…that it was a big rabbit. I still think she knew, when she battered and fried it, but she kept it to herself." He laughed. "She hid it well until we told the old man, but, that occurred well after he devoured all four stringy legs."

Mike chuckled, leaned forward and patted his own behind, while he responded. "You couldn't sit on that rear of yours for a week, could you? There were coat hanger marks across it like a tic-tac-toe game. I dern near got nailed, too, just for knowing of the prank, and for laughing aloud. Cried like a baby in our room when your licking went down. You were out there, back of the garage, just bellowing like a sick sow. That hurt, Buddy, must have hurt. Somehow, Pop didn't see the humor of eating raccoon instead of fried rabbit. No appreciation at all, for a good joke.

"'Shouldn't happen to a hard working man,' I remember he said."

"So, this is a classy woman, you say?" Wayne asked with one of his sneers. "Good grief, what a pushover, Mike! She got to ya with a little flattery, heh? She looked that good? C'mon, really, Bro? I know you're lonesome, and maybe you've some small horns a growing', but that little flirt might cost us some serious sleepless nights." He looked toward Nell for a nod of approval.

"Suppose she follows ya to the cabin? She knows who you are, and where the cabin is. Well, that'll be just no problem; now will it?

Claybourne wanted to find you, Mike. The bastard was asking Ina, for Christ's sake. He was looking for ya at the Bunyan, and now he'll know, won't he?" Wayne angered at his brother's naiveté. "He's likely after your younger brother, Wayne, too." He gestured toward Claybourne's M-16 rifle, which lay on the living room coffee table, wrapped in a towel.

"And you say she tips you off to the switch at the gate and lets on that the cable lock isn't closed? Sounds like the black widow spider luring the unwary gent into her tangled web, I says. Maybe she's the one with the growing horns, not gettin' enough from the old general, heh?" Nell jabbed Wayne painfully in the ribs, but kept her thoughts to herself.

Wayne continued, "Could it be that she didn't recognize you from the shooting spree, that you were hidden by the reeds when she approached Claybourne on the bluff? It was dark, Mike. She might not have, all right. I disagree, though; she sounds way too smooth, says I. She's on to ya, big time. Don't be stupid, thinkin' she found you charming. Sheeit! Your chain was pulled by a pro. She's sharp, moves a mile a minute, and you're in a damned blur," Wayne finished, to Mike's consternation.

She's beauty personified. Smooth, yes, but sincere, and I could tell she liked me. My compliments melted her; she seemed happy to talk. What's Wayne know about women anyway? He's been with one lady all his married life. When I go up to the shack to. ..."

Wayne's query broke his wanderings, "So, where'd the limo go after the two of them gets inside with the turbaned camel jockeys or whoever they were?"

"Well, when I saw them winding so slowly along the path, I figured I could run like heck to the car, race down North Cabin Road, wait a ways up, toward the bridge, follow them and see what's happening. Sure enough—though just barely—I beat them to the gate. I could see the bright security lights on the path, flickering through the trees, and there they came.

Claybourne got out at the gate, the door slammed, and the rig high-tailed it west. I took off in a minute or so, and found the limo at the power line road apron. They turned off, parked right there, and were barely visible in the shadows. I watched from a distance; nearly two hours passed, and no one got out. The limo finally returned to the Morris gate, drove all the way in as far as I could tell, and returned twenty minutes later. Then it ripped out of sight to the west, pedal to the metal. Never saw Claybourne get back inside. He must have walked the way to the shack. Why?"

"Oh, Mike, can't you imagine what that foray was about?" Nell inquired with a wink at both men. Is your new lady friend a hired hooker?"

"Of course not!" Mike retorted. "She's dignified, articulate, smart as a tack, and double lovely. Hookers don't come like that! Er, ah, do they?" he added with a blush, and an element of doubt in his eyes. "She must look like a million when she's dressed up; cuts a beautiful figure. What does she see in that high-minded, hard-nosed army type, for cripe's sake?" Wayne shot another disapproving glance at Nell, but held his tongue.

Mike shifted their talk from the curious woman. "We've got to return the gun, Wayne. It's a must. Top priority for us to. ..."

The loud phone ring muffled his words. Wayne jumped to answer and anxiously prodded Nell for a pencil and paper. Roger Thorsen, his old classmate from high school, a Lansing Police Department detective, with narcotics, called from Michigan's capital city.

"Yup, buddy, I hears ya and do appreciate the effort. I know you've stretched; of course it's illegal. You never said a thing. I know nothing, and no one will ever know ya called. This is very, very sensitive. Trust me, I can't say a thing at the moment, Roger. But mark my words, when this blows over; we'll talk. You're not going to believe it. Get on up here this fall and let's sit in the duck blind, freeze our butts, and chew the fat, OK? Maybe some salmon fishing on Mike's boat during the summer, eh?" Wayne winked, and raised Mike's curiosity with the one-sided discussion. "All right, then, and yes, I do appreciate this. It's a bombshell, to say the least, and you may hear from us sooner than you think."

"Holy Ghost!" Wayne yelled when he hung up the phone. He threw his hands toward the ceiling like a pleading evangelist. "This is out of control, completely beyond all imagination. What the hell's going on?" Mike and Nell looked on anxiously as Wayne slowly seated himself, finished the last of his beer, and slammed the emptied can down hard on the quilted placemat.

"Roger did a check on the license you called me about from the river—the limo plate. His inquiries led to Washington D.C, because it's a frigging U.S. diplomatic license: red, white and blue, like you said. Roger almost got caught doing the check." Wayne recovered his breath. "How's United Arab Emirates sound for size?"

"Who are they," queried Nell. She never heard of the U.A.E.

"Why, why they're always in the news," Wayne snapped. "It's a huge bit of barren desert real estate on the Persian Gulf, sitting above bottomless pools of oil. Might as well be gold. I just read that Abu Dhabi, one of the emirates, contains almost a tenth of the world's reserves, and it's just a postage stamp in dead center of nowhere. "Yep, that slick limousine is registered to the diplomatic service for the United Arab Emirates.

"What the hell are Arabian diplomats doing in the Michigan woods, for heaven's sake? What are they up to in our forest? I'll tell you why they're here, damn it! They came to see Claybourne and, as we suspected, he's up to something illegal. I guarantee the general's not buying oil. The Arabs, they're here to buy something; Patriot Missiles, maybe?" Wayne leaned across the table and whispered: "This Claybourne is a real bad boy, Mike. He's selling to them, for later movement to the Palestinians. How 'bout that for an idea? It's getting a mite more real, isn't it?"

The ramifications were chilling; the tenor of their conversation drew more serious as they passed the next two hours to look at options. If they notified police, they'd be in trouble for burglary, and maybe, for starting the shooting, too. That did not bode well for making a report.

"Wayne cried out, "What I did, fired my pistol; that's assault with a deadly weapon, Roger reminded me. We'd face years of hard time and he, the general's off with a self-defense excuse, for shooting back at us. 'I was just protecting myself and my little woman,' he'd claim. If we call Washington, D.C., the F.B.I., D.O.D., who knows where we'd get transferred? How far ya thinks we would get, if we tried to spark someone's interest in the alleged illegal activities of a retired brigadier general? Without a lobbyist who knows insider D.C., that would be a damned dead end, too."

Mike thought deeply and spoke less at times like this. He finally chimed in. "Look, as much as Meg … as … er, I … er … I … I want to bail from all this, we're in it up to our necks. Fearing further involvement, though I do," he stammered, "we have to stay connected … no choice, really, until we can see a clear way out. Claybourne has us clamped up, and I'll bet he's pompously unconcerned, because he knows we can't report him without incriminating ourselves.

"I need to go to the shack. She invited me; said the old boy's out of town for a week. I'll chat real friendly like with the young woman, and find out what I can.

She'd like Meg's fly rod, a real lightweight. Virginia seemed interested to learn a bit about fishing. That'll give me a chance to see the dogs, get to know them, and peep around some. How's that set with you, Brother?"

"I says, I go with ya openly, or I sits back across the river, and watch, like you did. I'll make damn sure she isn't the spider I thinks she is."

"No, nope, that won't work. I complimented the daylights out of her. She seemed shocked by what I said. I don't know where it all came from, but I didn't argue with the words. They just flowed. Flattery did the job and she smiled like a proud kitty. No, I'll go it alone the first time. I've got no one to worry about, now." He looked affectionately at Nell who seemed grateful for Wayne's extrication, that the risks would not be his this time.

"I'll figure out something to cover return of the gun. Maybe I can stash it by the water and we could find it, together, so she'd not be suspicious."

"The M-16 stays here," Wayne insisted. "It's one less weapon we'll have to deal with at show time, God forbid. He has lots of guns in there, on a rack by the stairs. You need to talk, sweet talk your way inside and case the place. We have to know the full layout and how many more firearms they have. That's your mission: snoop as much as you can."

Goose bumps burst on his arms. Mike grimaced, looked at his brother with concern, and cradled his chin on his fists while considering potential consequences. *Wayne may be right. I can't be swallowed up in my pride, just because this Virginia woman seemed interested to see me again. She's twenty years younger—maybe more, for cripe's sake. Claybourne's about my age, though. I may look a little younger, who knows? What would Meg say about all this? I have to do exactly what we've decided, no options, unless she's got some bright ideas.*

Mike raced to the cabin, anxious for input from Meg, uneasy she might feel slighted, and would not appear. He spoke above the low volume stereo music, hoped it would take him to Meg and her sage thoughts. "What alternative action might she offer, except, what she's already put on the table? She'll simply tell me to stay away from there. That's not the solution. How can we not stay with it? Wayne and I have been through the options already, and it's not going to work for us to abandon further activity. I want that property. What I do in the face of a possible crime, may have everything to do with my eventually getting hold of the place.

"Now or someday, I can and will wait." Mike imagined his name on the title, Gladdock at the top of the tax bill, and his own fly tying gear in the front window, just as he dreamed before. He mused, too, about fishing at the pool, unrestricted, and without worries or dogs interfering, as he did for decades. Claybourne's presence didn't change things. They would just be delayed.

The thirty-minute drive from Wayne's house to the cabin went uneventfully. At least Mike thought so, for he was mindful only of the heavy lug tires that whirred loudly on intermittent stretches of the road in the midst of repairs. Gravel spatters in the fender wells sounded too much like winter ice. The cold would return all too soon for his taste.

Silent to his ears, but beeping a short repetitive code of dots and dashes every fifteen seconds, a signal emitted from beneath his Suburban's rear bumper, a continual drone that would endure up to thirty days if it operated to specs. Transmitted on a very high frequency band, the homing device sent a discreet message. A magnet held the sender tightly in place, right where Virginia planted it, when Mike left the vehicle in the mall parking lot. It spoke audibly only to its companion antenna, affixed to a portable direction-finding receiver that sat on the living room table at the Morris shack.

Beneath the dim light from the lamp in the ceiling stairwell, she listened with satisfaction, to the familiar, and repetitive *dah-ditt-dah-dah, dah-dit-dah-dah*, which, though static-filled because of the distance, spoke well of her success. She swung the receiver around while she danced in stocking feet on the shiny hardwood. The noise disappeared, then returned each time the antenna pointed due south to southwest of the shack. "Well, he's not too far away," Virginia Blakes pronounced. "Looks like he's on the move. Yes, he's moving." The signal sounded loudest when its bearing read one hundred sixty five degrees. This time, Virginia noted it changed ten degrees to the west. The beeping remained most notable at that heading.

"He's either stopped or he's now moving south. The heading isn't changing, but the signal is getting weaker. He is going away; I'll just bet. Guess I should move out; see if I can find him. This might not be easy, but it's something to do.

Homer wanted me to locate those two at all costs."

The security fellows will arrive next week. We will need to familiarize them with the layout of the river, start a close watch for snoopers. It's getting very serious now, and we don't want to mess up in the finale. The red truck bounded south on Highway 33, out of Mio. Every mile or so, Virginia stopped, stepped out on the moonlit two-lane road, and swung the receiver in an arc toward the south. The beeping still came from that direction. She reached Rose City and the signal grew stronger. It swung to the east, but absent any roads off-shooting in that direction, she was unable to follow it. She studied the map and returned attentions to the antenna.

"Let's see, that's Highway F-28 there, goes due east, and so does the signal. Don't know where this'll lead, but onward and upward." The moon was still bright. Its soft glow melted into the nighttime cool, but the pavement beneath her feet held warmth from the heat of the day. It remained in the mid-seventies. Humidity dropped after the brief thunderstorm passed. The balm excited her.

"I wonder what that Mike is like?" she asked herself. "I must have impressed the hell out of him. He could hardly speak at times, and those compliments. They were so nice. The way he looked me over, focused on my breasts. Why doesn't Homer do that anymore? I like it when men take notice, and undress me with their eyes. Wouldn't any unattached girl my age like that?" She flipped on the dome light and took a moment to assume a pouty expression. Lower lip pushed out, she clenched down on it lightly with upper teeth, tipped her chin up, nodded slowly, and looked approvingly in the rearview mirror.

Signal is still to the east—almost due east. I'll keep on this way. Beeps grew louder as she approached Long Lake and wound around its south shore to Lakeside Way. Radio checks every block suggested no improvement in signal strength; she reread instructions, which told her she was nearly on top of the source. Virginia followed the sensitive directional needle, turned left into a heavily wooded area, and wound downgrade onto a rough gravel road. The sign read Meadowlark Lane. Virginia crept more slowly, until the needle stayed centered.

Nearly to the bottom of the hill, she paused on the steep shoulder, and froze in amazement when the needle suddenly reversed. A quick survey of her surroundings revealed the black Suburban, parked in the driveway behind a stocky two-storied structure, at the rear of which sat a large barn and a three car garage, down grade, about one hundred feet away.

M-E-G, the first three letters on the rear plate, confirmed the sighting as the vehicle to which she attached the homing device after she met Mike Gladdock at the Mio Mall.

"319 Meadowlark: that's it! This little baby worked like a charm; sure did the job. Homer will be delighted. *Now that we know where he lives, what's next? What's Homer going to do to the guy? I'm sure he's clueless about our project. There's no conspiracy here; just a couple locals, determined to fish the river; that's all. I don't want them roughed up or involved any further. A big mistake for Homer, violence would only dig us deeper into potential trouble and increase our exposure.* Virginia had misgivings. She liked Mike, appreciated his manners, and hoped he'd show up to fish. After all, she realized, he was practically given an engraved invitation.

"Nice place he's got there, a huge barn and garage, too … probably built them himself. He is a big man," she continued, "very strong, the kind who solves his own problems and who is good to have around. I saw someone honest, loyal, and responsible, if not a little boring, under that bashful skin; but a gentleman who'd stick with his woman no matter what. She just died, he said. And then," Virginia whined, "and then, there's Homer: everything a woman wouldn't want, topped off with an immutable hunger for the almighty dollar, and no scruples how it's acquired."

Shamefully, she was of the same genre when it came to money. *OK, I admit I wanted to be rich and have the independence good funding provides. Now that I have tasted the possibilities, gone this far; am I no better than Homer? He better back off his recent moves toward physical abuse, damn him. That's where our personalities diverge. He thinks I'm fair game, as if he needs to show excessive horsepower to keep me in line. Little does he know the depths to which he's taken our sinking ship of romance. Could it ever be refloated? Is there any hope he'll merge back to the sweet man I met that night at the Officers' Club? Or, with millions in his pocket, will he likely grow more unseemly?*

Meg did not come to him in the night. Mike felt frightened when he awoke and wondered why, as soon as he collected his senses. He lay still in the dark, enough to wait for the rustling of curtains, or a tell tale breeze; but he sensed no movement. The trees outside stood placid in the pre-dawn, ebbing moonlight. His bedroom remained still, vacuous, if not almost hostile. He had to arise; the clock ticked four. Yet he felt ill without Meg's comfort.

Mike rushed to make coffee. The day's agenda, irrefutable, compelled the long commute to Flint, and requisite arrival at the plant by 7:30, followed by a full workday, and another lonesome night at home. Continued time alone lay in store for the rest of the week, an ominous thought in the face of so many, almost welcome, distractions over the preceding days.

He weighed options and with little trouble, resolved the dilemma, dialed the illness notification line, and left a brief message on the voice mail. His supervisor would pick it up just before the shift began. *He'll understand. I only took two days off after her death, for cripe's sake.*

"Mike Gladdock, here … Electrical Services. It's early; I'm up north, feel very ill and felt badly through the night. I won't be in. Put me in for a sick day, maybe two. I'll call tomorrow if I'm not improved. Thanks, Paul. Hope all goes well for the crew. Call me if you need further info. It's Mike—over and out." Mildly guilt ridden for letting down his boss and the men on his detail, he also knew the day at the river he quickly designed, would prove far more interesting.

No hesitating, he set to his mission and assembled fishing gear. "An afternoon at the Au Sable for Michael Gladdock, a dern nice one, too. A canoe trip west would be good, for a change. and stretch the muscles a bit. I'll take a swim, and drop some flies in the big pool tonight, if all goes well and the caddis show."

The sun forced its way through resistant breaks in the newly emergent foliage on the hill, and cast gleaming new day rays across the back deck where he sat, relieved that work no longer loomed in the picture. He labored over a new task, instead: to oversee the large garden spider at work once again, to repair a tear in her web, likely left when a large moth or small bat darted through in the final hours of darkness.

"She goes from one catastrophe to another and thinks nothing of the continuous interruptions. Make a web, eat, fix the web, mate, lay eggs, eat, make repairs, eat, and so it goes through her short life. What the heck's the difference between her and us working stiffs, when it all settles?" Waxing philosophical, he went on, and spoke to the trees as if they listened, "The difference is: smelling the flowers.

"We smell the flowers, or at least we should. It we don't, what's the difference between us and spiders, bees, ants, and the rest of the workaday little creatures that never stop moving. Their story is strictly survival, while we have opportunities to do more than that, if we adequately exercise them. Meg caught me short, sure did point out how I played the spider role too dern much. Well, that's going to change, and I can do something about it today.

"I'll go on over to the Morris place later, Black Widow or not. The little lady deserves some more compliments. What a fireball. Maybe I'll stop for some flowers, too—just a small showing of my appreciation, to thank her for letting me in the gate. It would be no more than that," he lied to himself, "just a token."

As the heat of the day passed, and afternoon shadows grew longer, Mike left; boyish notions filled his head. He grew giddy as the morning dragged, simply wondering where, en route to the gate, he might find cut flowers to fill her heart.

Meg hovered but said nothing to Mike. *Flowers? Flowers for that hussy?* He wouldn't listen, not just then, at least. She knew him too well. With goodness in his soul, Mike was a train tugged by too many locomotives, a jet plane driven by fifteen engines, a wagon drawn by an added fresh team of draft horses. "No stopping a man when he smiles like that. I know Michael Jules Gladdock when he's on a mission," she lamented to undiscerning ears. Mike wore his best smile on the way to his car from the flower stand.

CHAPTER 18

"Ginny … Ginny!" Claybourne, practically shrieked over the phone. He sounded like an elated child who strained to tell his curious parent the latest tales from summer camp. "I've got news, and it's all good, Virginia Baby." She hardly heard his words over the river's many voices and the drum of late afternoon breezes that stubbornly wove through the trees. "Outdoor equipment sets, if you know what I mean, are all assembled. They've passed final operational tests. The gear is boxed, in the warehouse, already off the base. Today the crates will be painted and labeled for shipping. By the weekend, they'll be on our truck, *en route* to our, er, north facility." He took no chances that their conversation might be overheard and continued with his circumspection.

"The men driving the load east, they're, ah, they're technicians, qualified as a ah … a … ah … highly skilled in their specialty, and they'll stay with us for, ah, ah … security reasons … former Army Rangers, you know. They'll be perfect. They are interested in earning bonuses, too, should they be called upon to serve any extraordinary duties while there. Handling … er … delicate personnel problems will be their main forte."

Virginia nodded approvingly as she listened. She sat on the beach towel and carefully untangled her wet hair, cool and sweet smelling from her swim in the river. The report was a good one; final payday appeared much closer. His mention of "technicians" frightened her, however, for she knew by his stammering that the men were trained killers, tough guys Claybourne hired to camp in the woods and scour them for intruders, until the buyers carted everything away.

He assured her the security types were accustomed to digging in, completely at home under survival conditions, and would only be seen or heard from if protective tactics were required. They were probably rejects, she thought, too mean for their own good, certainly for peacetime conditions. The general recruited them from the Army Air Defense Artillery Center at Fort Bliss, a Patriot training facility just outside El Paso, where a large company of U. S. Army Rangers based. Their hand-to-hand combat capabilities, "second to none," he boasted, could prove useful.

"Virginia, their very special qualifications bring to mind the two men: those fellows we tangled with, whose activities, er ... ahem ... may need to be neutralized. The dumb one we encountered at the café; he and his crony who took the pot shots, will cause us no further difficulty. Our new assistants will assure that. They will be discreet. We haven't seen the last of those two locals. I can smell trouble a mile away and we. ..."

"Homer!" She broke in, and ignored what he said, "I've news, too. I found the black Suburban, his house, also. It's just a few miles south of here, east of Rose City. Only a vacation retreat, he actually lives in. ..." The general's words about the hired killers suddenly stuck home and, in that instant before finishing the sentence, she hesitated, fearful she revealed too much. "He lives there, but, er, only part time. I planted the beeper you gave me. It's under his rear bumper. I saw him and the car at the Mio Mall and tracked it to his home on Saturday night. The little baby worked perfectly. The directional antenna did just as you said. Now what?" she asked. "Now that we know he's there, what else do we do?"

"You've done well, My Dear, very well. I want you to find the other character, and identify him. Let's get a transmitter on his vehicle. Do that immediately," he admonished. "We've three more units in the box, my closet, in the bedroom. We'll decide how to handle the situation when our boys arrive with the equipment. We can't have local yokels poking around once the goods are in storage."

She dismissed his implications of threatened violence, and asked, "When are you coming home? Will you drive with the men or fly? Will you call me before you leave?"

"When the trucks are off, I'm on a plane, more than likely by next Sunday. Is everything OK there? Weather nice and hot, skeeters out at night?"

"Yes, yes, it's warm," she replied passively, uninspired to speak of her earlier nude swim off the sand spit. Erotic chills filled her with desire throughout the afternoon. She warmed herself to a full tan in the baking midday sun, bikini conveniently crumpled on the sand next to her. Homer would turn inside out, knowing that.

"It's real nice here: thunderstorms pass briefly in the afternoons, much as we see them in Virginia. The winds have more gusto, but they moderate before dusk." Reclined on the warm sand, bathed by the slight breeze from the west, she closed her eyes, and imagined basking on the beach in St. Martin. Her favorite Caribbean island, it lay in tourmaline waters, smothered with French food, white sands, and cooling winds that whistled twenty four-seven, day after day. She and the general spent a week there during the winter, but that was before increased pressures of *Operation Eastern Star* tightened romantic reins.

Claybourne rambled on with more disguised talk of the missiles, while her mind drifted. She thought of Mike, wondered if he would follow her lead and show up at the property to fish. *He's a curiously attractive man … sensual, yet distant in a way that makes him inviting as hell.* Virginia always felt challenged by a man who maintained his self-control in her presence. Emerged from the riverbank just after the general's call came through, she left her swimsuit off, and wrapped herself in an oversized bath towel, half-hoping Mike would drive in and see her that way.

She let the towel fall to the floor and stood before the mirror on the wall next to the gun rack. Turns to the right and left, with pauses every few moments, she admired her own shapeliness, and how alluring she still appeared. *It's been too long since Homer has shown interest.* She rotated the other way. *Where is his sensuality? What happened to that magnetism he had for me and my body?*

This Mike, quite attractive, awfully good shape, hardly any gray hair.

Virginia swirled around playfully, and looked over her shoulder at the rear profile again, pleased she maintained the trim figure.

"And, just after the goods arrive from Texas," Claybourne continued minutes before; once again he failed to capture her full attention, "the large trailer from Alabama will arrive. That'll be the operations center, and it's all in order. I just verified it's now off base, if you know what I mean." She understood; he completed arrangements through his contact in the Alabama National Guard. The bulky launcher and its control center were now completely appropriated.

Claybourne knew the 69th Air Defense Brigade just returned from a major exercise in Israel. Dubbed *Operation Juniper Cobra,* the Patriot training and efficacy-testing effort was to better prepare Israeli troops for anti-missile defense activities. That extensive array of assets, became the rich vein the general mined for the embezzlement.

Claybourne, however, might have talked to a wall. "The Brigade Commander had the impression that one launch unit would be sent back to El Paso on its return from the Middle East. Just a small bit of confusing paper work steered the high dollar package off course, and up our way.

"Yes, it's just a matter of paperwork in our military. You fill out the right documents and a nuclear weapon can be yours. El Paso will never know what happened," he chuckled. Their copies of the faked transfer documents were never faxed. They've no idea what isn't going to them and Alabama thinks they received all of it. God! Someone's head will roll big time on that one at inventory time, unless paperwork already shows it as expended."

More than distracted, Virginia paid but peripheral attention to his final comments, relieved she'd have the remainder of the week to herself, undaunted by the isolation. "I'll sign off now," he concluded, "I miss my Virginia. Yes, I really do; but there's work to do. Y'all take care and we'll talk when we talk, heh?" He showed little affection in the perfunctory conclusion, nor did she.

All too soon, Homer, as far as I'm concerned, no hurry. She tried without success to quell contemptuous thoughts that filled her mind.

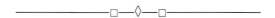

Mike stepped quietly to the Morris shack doorstep from the wood porch. He cupped hands around his eyes to reduce glare and peered before knocking, through the closed screen door and into the dark entry. Simply instinctive, a move bent on curiosity, he was not being circumspect or snoopy.

Just inside, Virginia stood, clearly recognizable by her ebony hair. Her back faced him, but that didn't matter. Unclothed, she stood to admire herself in the full-length mirror at the foot of the stairs. His squinting gaze stopped at her buttocks—beautifully crafted, he thought. Then it moved to her athletic legs and to the floor. She stood on her toes, shuffled her feet as though dancing with a tall man to an unheard rhythm. Hands on hips, she twisted her torso to the imaginary music. Her breasts bounced in concert with body movements. *Will you look at that! Thank God, her eyes are closed. I'll just move off the porch, ever so quietly, and redo my approach, more noisily next time.* He felt immobilized, however, as one would after receipt of an injection of curare. The muscles of his arms and legs would not answer their call and his vocal cords failed to vibrate. Paralyzed, partly because of the delicious sight before him; but also, because he feared what she would do if he announced himself. He felt faint, rendered, and feeble. *I'm going to be caught standing here at the door like an idiot—a voyeur. I've no time to think what the heck to do.*

In lieu of driving onto the property as she instructed, Mike launched the canoe upstream, on the north bank, a half-mile to the west. He approached without the warning she thought would occur from the gate alarm. Relaxed, he ran down river with the current, on a leisurely cruise, stopped along the way to sun himself and prepare his fishing gear for later use at the big pool. As silently as an Indian brave, he climbed the bluff by the spreading maple, and shuffled soundlessly to his present position, helpless—mouth agape—at her front door. He could not respond to the screams inside his head to do something and do it with dispatch.

Then it happened. Her eyelids lifted lazily when an unexpected jingle of change in his pocket made the announcement. Loud speakers at a ball game, artillery fire, even a train whistle would have been less invasive, he thought. His jaw dropped. Unconsciously, before the alarm, he leaned toward the screen, to view her better. Virginia swung around, her eyes widened, and she came close to unleashing a warning shriek. Before the reflexive action took place, though, she recognized Mike silhouetted against the outside brightness.

Quick of wit, Virginia turned slowly toward the door, and much to his surprise, made but a cursory effort to cover herself: poised as the classic sculpture of a modest Grecian maiden, one hand partially across her breasts, the other gracefully over the apex of her thighs. The young woman spoke first. Surprisingly calm, she said, "Why, it's … it's … Mike, isn't it? Forgot your last name already. Sorry, I didn't hear you there. The dogs must be down at the gate. They watch for horses and bark like hell at them. I'm so sorry. I hope I'm not embarrassing y'all, standing here, naked as a jaybird." Mike turned his head toward the river, apologized similarly, and helplessly glared again through the screen, more unabashed than he might have figured.

"Came down the river this afternoon, took a nice paddle from up west. I didn't mean to surprise you. I won't do that again, you can count on it; nope, never again," he went on hurriedly, looking at her the while. *The dogs! The dogs, for cripe's sake, I didn't hear barks and thought nothing of them at all. How stupid can a man get? They could have eaten me alive.* Mike remembered their names, Ace, King and Jack, and felt lucky he didn't encounter the Rottweilers as he climbed to the clearing from the river.

She stepped like a model and sat on an arm of the couch. She covered her upper body with the towel, crossed her legs and replied in a low, gravely voice, "Well, you've now seen Virginia without clothes. What else is there, when that happens? C'mon inside," she said with a wave and patted her hair dry at the ends. "After all, I invited you and didn't say to fire a warning shot. Who's to blame here?" She giggled in the same silly way she did in the parking lot and doing so, her eyes rolled and her teeth sparkled. It reminded him of Meg and her unique belly chuckle, the one he missed so much.

Entry into a house occupied only by a beautiful and comely young female, sans clothing, was not something to which Mike was accustomed. Incredulous over his initial introduction to Virginia, Mike knew his brother would never believe the continuing saga. Fantasies painted like that, appeared at times in the past, but Mike never imagined himself a star in the actual play.

Not only that, he thought, when he opened the screen door; *the little beauty could be a criminal. Wasn't it Virginia, though, who put an end to the shooting? Could have saved our lives. She must have wrestled with Claybourne for the M-16. That's likely how he got hurt. She yelled for him to put the gun down just before that last shot rang.*

Mike quickly rationalized Virginia's involvement in the missile business. *She may not know. It could be his game and he's keeping it from her. Could she be that naïve? The computer displayed the curious letter about Patriot Missiles, in the midst of the shooting incident. Surely she saw the screen or others like it at some point.*

Despite trepidation, Mike entered the front room. "I'm terribly, er, sorry for barging in; thought I'd say hello before I headed down to the big pool. There might be an early hatch tonight. At least it's possible. A caddis hatch, I mean; the fly hatches and swarms over the quiet pools on the river; draws the big browns up from the depths. It's an irresistible time for me, as it is for them.

"I've never missed fishing the big pool at this time of year—not once, since Pop showed me. I was just a kid. Brought waders and a pole for you, that is, if you were inclined." Mike glowed when he spoke of the near record twenty-eight pound, seven-ounce lunker he caught a few years before, in front of the shack. "That's one heck of a fish, for a small river—one big brownie for that matter. Even my dad, who knew this section better than anyone, wouldn't have believed that spotted jumper until he saw it for himself."

She smiled; it seemed his comments met with passive interest at best.

Virginia felt restless, looked him over with increasing frustration and finally spoke, though hesitatingly, "Mike, if I asked you … if I wanted to know … whether you found me … a … alluring right now … or even pleasantly attractive … exactly how would I do that?" She allowed the towel to slip just below the tops of her small nipples when she awkwardly tugged at her hair.

Jesus crisp, alluring is the understatement of the year; she's downright screwable, right here and now, that's what. Mike never visualized those words before. "Screwable," was not within his vocabulary; it never was. *Where did that come from? I sound like Wayne.* Hesitation was not the answer she wanted and he sensed her consternation.

"Oh, I can answer that, very easily," he said, blurting out the words as if they were held under pressure. "Ask no more. I … I …find your legs, your rear end … oh, I apologize. My mind … where is it? In short," he kept the pace going, "you were a ten out in the mall parking lot, and you just went off the scale, there in your birthday suit. Very nice—irresistible, indeed—if I do say so."

Testosterone spewed into his circulatory system in a full-scale, rapid-fire, body distribution effort, and he felt the glow. Hastened toward excitement, knees wobbled and, though faltering, words came forth he never before used with a woman, much less a new acquaintance. "Alluring? You bet. Sexy beyond my deepest imagination … sure as can be. Do I need to get the devil out of here? Yes, ma'm," he emphasized, and upped his voice another octave. "Yes, I think I need to get down to the river and cool my arse. A cold shower probably would not work for me. You see that. …"

Virginia stood, the towel sunk to her feet; she took two short but stealthy steps toward Mike and unbuttoned his shirt before he could utter another hard fought word. Her hands were cold. They slid deftly under his large arms and around to the small of his back. Though disbelieving, he couldn't resist. While he shivered with delight, prying fingers coaxed quivering skin around his belt line. They found the belt buckle which fast dropped open, as did the button behind it.

Hovering above her, mouth buried in her damp hair, his hands busied, keenly concentrated on the escalation of her arousal. She purred involuntarily when he found her warm and waiting inside, trembling with anticipation. She smiled wide, with his deep breathing. Wanting fingers gripped him tightly, urged him to the couch, and smothered his excitement. She was on him in a heartbeat, moaning rhythmically with hurried movements of her lower body, nearly singing that she conquered a man she first thought unconquerable.

Mike's lips found hers again and again, and vice versa. Far too long since he embraced like that, his concerns stopped when Virginia's gyrations began. She lost all interest in anything but self-preservation. He well understood, comforted her as empathetically as she wished, but a veritable void ensued, nonetheless.

That vacuous space was quickly filled with each appreciative whimper, with every determined thrust, as Virginia awakened Mike's senses with renewed vigor, relapsed into calm, and fast regenerated herself into repeated fervor. His passion, though experienced more succinctly, extended beyond measure, well outside the bounds of recent memory.

Meg ... oh, Meg. His mind silently screamed into the black space, where only her voice affirmed her presence. *It's been so long.* His lips and hers clashed in wet unity. *This reminds me so much of the time, that time on the blanket, just off the road that night. It is you here beside me, isn't it? It's you looking at me.* He spoke to himself with assurance. *I smell your damp hair, the fresh scent that's always been you—after a shampoo—your perfume, too. It's my Meg; I know it.* He felt himself being rolled under the body next to him, warm breasts pressed to his chest. *You like it better this way, don't you, Dear, my holding you down?* His unanswered communications continued. *Tell me when you're ready.*

The figure above him finally fell limp with exhaustion. He heard a deep sigh, and then, "I loved that, Mister Mike. I simply loved that. You're more than the animal I suspected you'd be."

Another exhalative sigh and all was quiet, save the low drone of small caddis swarms on their short journey, away from sheltering conifers, toward the big pool. A speckled fin ruffled the surface. Then a flashing eruption of chilled water followed, through which the torso of a huge brown reached to the sky and inhaled a small cluster of unwitting insects as an appetizer.

"Mike, wake up! Wake up, damn you. You've been acting crazy as hell tonight! What do you think you're doing? It's not me, naked next to you. I swear; you must look at her, now! She is not your Meg. Darn it! You didn't smell me, or kiss my lips. She's not your Meg," the voice seemed to yell almost in desperation. "You're in trouble, Mike. Get out of there!"

Those weren't Meg's words. She doesn't speak like that ... must be someone else. His consciousness began its return. He looked at Virginia, eyelids glued together in a peaceful daze, lips slightly parted from their last kiss, bent in a glimmering smile. The woman seemed a stranger. *That was Meg calling. She said the woman ... the woman ... this woman ... was not. ...*

Could Meg have spoken to me? She hasn't appeared for days. The language wasn't hers. Recovered fully, he lifted his head from the soft cushion and looked out, through the open screen door. He felt the Au Sable's brisk evening, downstream wind. Completely dark, his watch read ten o'clock. "That's impossible," he said aloud, enough to disturb Virginia. "Where did the time go, for cripe's sake? Two hours disappeared in the time it would take for one flick of a fly across the riffles."

"Oh, it's possible, and the time did pass," Virginia replied, still half dozing. It went so quickly, so beautifully, and so much fun, too."

Meg's words began to sink in. "Look, Virginia, I … I don't know how this happened. Good Lordy! I hardly know you, and we're here: bodies sweating next to one another like this. It's not like me, I can assure you. I want you to. …"

She placed a finger against his lips to stop the kind of chatter she hated to hear after lovemaking with a near stranger. "Now, Mike, let's just enjoy the moment, not make a career of our passions. How about that? Just file this away as a great bit of moaning and groaning— nothing else—at least for the present. Is that all right?"

He thought about Meg's harshness and turned attention back to the object of his two-hour delight. "Sure, sure. That's it, for the moment, it's fine." Never before did he experience sex "for the moment," not with anyone; he felt it a strange, if not unnatural concept. *It's better than hearing she's in love, for cripe's sake. I couldn't handle that right now.* He stayed quiet a few minutes, and then spoke with words that should have been muffled.

"Say, Virginia. We were originally introduced under peculiar conditions, an argument on the highway, and words with your friend, on the road, later in the café, the arm injury, and, I think. …"

She cut in abruptly, tightly grasped his shoulder and looked into his eyes inquisitively. "How the hell did you know about Homer, the general's injury? How did you know?"

His mind raced to respond covertly. "I didn't for sure, not until you said so, I didn't. The waitress told me your friend Homer asked about me at the Paul Bunyan Café; said he was sporting a sling on his right arm, that he seemed in pain. He had no sling when I saw him in the café, the night he nearly hit me, so I put two and two together, and you just confirmed it."

"Damn you. You were such a lover. You weakened my truth chords. That's what you did. She squeezed him affectionately and pressed supple lips to his neck. "I'm to keep the shooting real quiet. If you ever meet the general, say nothing of the gunshot." She hesitated to continue but her remaining inner warmth provided the persuasion and, too, she felt inclined to trust Mike.

"I had to take his gun away. He might have shot both men, in cold blood, right there on the riverbank. Homer is a man who will stop at nothing when he's on a mission, and, trust me; he's on a mission, which. ..." She stopped abruptly. *Must keep my mouth shut, have to keep it quiet from here onward, no more talk of the shooting spree.*

"So, what's the mission? Why is he so spaced out? Where is he now?" Mike persisted.

"Oh, away on business, retired you know; he has new financial interests that keep him away from time to time. Yes, he flew out to Texas," she said with a benign expression. She pulled the towel over her shoulders, goose-bumped from the incoming breeze.

"So, what's he into, oil?"

"It's silly; I don't even know. He doesn't say much. Something to do with the army, I guess. Homer's out to visit Fort something or other, near El Paso."

"It's been bothering me ever since I saw the gate across your path out there on Old River Road. I'd like to know; what the heck gave him the idea he could install fencing, that the property by the road was his, and the river bank, as well?"

"Oh, the realtor, John Simmons, listing broker, said the long driveway was ours, that we could privatize it from the entrance to the bounds out here in the woods behind the barn. I was there. We took him at his word. Homer had the gate built as soon as escrow closed. There was so much vandalism damage to the house; we thought it best."

"Well, I've been fishing here all my life." Mike felt his old temper flare; the one from younger years, rise up from the depths, beg to be heard, and he began to broil. "I don't think that was proper. He can't keep people from the river. It's an illegitimate use of government property." *Whoa! Have to cool down, or I'll never learn anything more.*

Must canvass the house, see the dogs, and get acquainted. That's why I came, before I was so beautifully seduced.

"It's kind of maddening to think those of us," Mike pressed, "those of us born and raised here, can be denied access like that. The Forest Service agrees, but they're still awaiting receipt of title papers." *That'll be it; no more tough talk. I'm not going to scare her.*

"It can all be worked out. We may not stay up here long. Who knows what will happen? I do understand how you could love the river, though. I went down to that pool and flaked out nude in the sunshine all afternoon. It was as nice as any tropical beach. That's when I got all hot and bothered, thinking about you stumbling on me. Who should appear later, but y'all, come a knockin' at my door?"

Dogs barked in the distance. Their cries grew louder and, in a few minutes one whined at the screen. "Sure hope he can't talk. I'd be in real trouble. They're his, aren't they?"

"Oh, yes, his angels, the dusty little mutts. I won't permit them in the house. Nice guard dogs, but they get under my nerves, and quite quickly. Let me introduce you; they're sweet, really."

"I hate to leave, but I must get going. I'll drive back south in the morning, I suppose. Although I'd still like to fish, maybe show you a little, too. May I use your bathroom?"

"Sure, top of the stairs, turn left. It's off the far wall in the master bedroom."

Mike dressed, leapt up the steps, and, despite his haste, admired the grain of the colorful black walnut wood treads and risers. He spotted the bathroom, but hesitated. *Nightstands. I have to check for guns.* Carefully he opened the top drawer in the small antique stand on the window side of the bed, and spotted trouble. *Whew, that's a big one—loaded with hollow points, too.* A Colt .45, shiny chrome, it lay in a quick draw holster, beneath Claybourne's socks. *Wouldn't like a smack in the side by that one.* He softly closed the drawer, and found one box of cartridges in the lower one, but no more weapons. Hidden beneath a disheveled pile of women's panties, crammed full of long rifle rounds, in the center drawer of the maple stand on the other side, lay another gun. *It's an old Ruger .22 semi-automatic, magazine loaded with ten shots, I think.* Hoping for more time, he ran to flush the toilet, whisked back his hair and rinsed his face. He looked quickly in the large dresser drawers before returning silently to the stairwell. She sang a familiar melody in the kitchen.

Sounds like she's making drinks. I have a little more time. Need a moment to check the closet; might be some arms there. This guy's got a small arsenal in the living room. Mike foraged through hanging clothing, around shoes and boots on the floor, and then shuffled through Claybourne's stacked hunting garb.

He saw nothing more, but became curious about three radios in a box, on a wire shoe rack in the general's section. *These look like model airplane controls or something ... small antennas on each ... two buttons and a dial. Oh, here's a label.* He spoke aloud to himself, to spur his memory. "Must remember ... Alert Investigations, Arlington, Va., transmitter-model # 677. What the devil are these? I'll have to find out." He heard steps approach, the sound of ice tinkling in glasses. Panicked, he felt his heart jump ahead; his forehead stretched like a drumhead. Mike exited the closet and tiptoed to the window, where he stood gazing toward the river, when she walked in with the tray.

"Good grief love, you take as long as I do to dress and polish up. Brought us cool drinks. How does lemonade sound? Must have lost a gallon of water. Quite a workout in this humidity."

He stayed standing, aimlessly peered across the *cul-de-sac* and tried to compose himself. His heavy breathing nearly brought him to discovery—much too close for comfort. "Always wondered what this place was like inside. I've always wanted it, and would have bought it if you two didn't come along. I'm feeling very sad inside, that I missed the opportunity of a lifetime. I was just taking in the lovely view from up here.

"Do you mind showing me the rest of the place before I go? I've pictured myself in this bedroom, oh, so many years." He guzzled the lemonade, and poured another from the green glass decanter she handed him, thankful his near panting respiration rate dropped to normal.

"Maybe you'll be there sometime soon, I hope. I had no idea, when our paths crossed, that I'd be confronted with lovemaking, such kindness, yet such remorse. You really love this place. I can tell by the look on your face."

Stark-raving fear, not sadness, he masqueraded it well. "Meg: she's my wife, sure loved it, too. We thought we would manage to live long enough to find old Morris' weak spot, and dreamed we'd be there at the critical second he made the sell decision. We felt sure the day would come sometime; just didn't know when. Meg failed but tried so hard to survive and see it through." He dropped his head sadly, felt a covering blanket of guilt as well, for standing in the general's bedroom after enjoying sex with his girlfriend.

Fitting his designs perfectly, Mike toured the house, played with the dogs on the way out, and made certain to leave his scent with all three— particularly Ace, the alpha male. He knew the largest one would make aggressive moves before the others, if things ever got out of control.

Dressed only in a large T-shirt, she watched him amble to the bluff. Her legs shone like white columns in the rising moon. "Say, Mister Mike," she called, "y'all take it easy. See you soon, I bet."

He stopped and turned back for one more look. "Bye for now and … and thanks for the lemonade and everything," Mike stuttered. He peeled a broad grin, jumped to the water's edge, boarded the canoe; and, with a few deep strokes, passed beneath the overhanging cedar limb, on to the west, and into the darkness.

CHAPTER 19

Two does fed in the tall grass, raised their heads, turned ears toward the house, and wiggled their tails before darting back a few yards. They fed less than fifty feet from the porch where Wayne and Mike, reclined on lawn chairs, sipped ice tea, and enjoyed the coming dusk. Though a welcome sight at day's end, Wayne's loud voice finally spooked the timid animals. They dashed toward the nearest cover.

"My Lord, Brother, if it was anyone but the Mike I know, I'd never believe it happened. Christ, you've the *huevos* of a water buffalo, and if she's anywhere near as gorgeous as you say, I salute you; yes sir, I do. You're nothing short of incredible. Jesus, Mike, you just meet the lady, after a major gunfight, and you're in the sack, having lemonade in the master bedroom afterward—General Homer P. Claybourne's boudoir! What a riot, and it happens not long after I busts in, and prints a letter off their computer. It's too funny."

"Hey, hey, you're talking too loud," Mike snapped, seemingly unaffected by the accolades. "The little deer are skittish tonight. They moved away." Wayne's house faced a woodlot some three hundred yards to the south. Hundreds of acres of thickets, swampy ground, and dense tree growth beyond, provided shelter for a plethora of local wildlife that made his expansive field their twilight dining table.

"The woman seduced me, Brother. I can't take credit for any of it," Mike went on, while he pleasantly relived the experience he related. "She was just there by the door, without a stitch of anything, admired herself in the mirror by the staircase, while I looked through the screen and drooled on my boots. She took over from there, and my duds were off before I could yell, 'Meg.'"

Wayne expressed elation with the news, for the sake of Mike's sanity, if nothing else. *What good fortune for him. This lady, as long as she lasts, should help Brother break his ties with Meg—help him let her go. It could be lots easier with the little spitfire around.* He collected his thoughts and spoke, "I talked to Donnie the other day. They had a fire over the hill to the dam, got it stopped quickly, though. For a change, the Forest Service didn't have to call on local volunteers. He was happy about that.

"Don said, too, that the title papers for the Morris property arrived from D.C. headquarters. There was no mention, and I had him look very careful like, no mention whatsoever about any rights to build a gate across the path. The papers were silent about that and, importantly … no deeded exclusivity to the riverbank, anywhere along the property boundary.

"The line, Donnie says, goes along the bluff above the river and not to the water, with exception of the smallest sand spit. There, Don thought the general could argue a valid waterfront title; but only at that single spot. It doesn't give the SOB leave to do any fencing, in any case. When he gets time, Donnie will call Washington and confirm with headquarters, that it's appropriate for him to intervene."

Wayne beamed with the news, while he read his notes. "He'll serve a Notice to Demolish and post the property at the gate. The frigging barrier comes down, Mike! Claybourne will have thirty days, and if it's not gone, the U. S. Forest Service will pull it and the stupid deer down and bill the cocky SOB for costs. If he doesn't pay, 'cause I asks Don; they lien the property, and it can go up for sale. So there you have that bit of good information to mull over. Maybe you still have a chance at it."

Mike filled his glass and turned to Wayne with a broad grin. "That's the best info I've had yet today and I needed something favorable. I called the plant and got the wringing of my life for using a sick day again, especially when I told the boss I'd be at the cabin, to repair myself, for a change. When I bailed out on Monday, I did feel emotionally torn and that's certainly cause to take a break. It teed me off, though; he took it personally; knew I was at the cabin. Two years or less, if I wish, I'm done with the insults. No gratitude whatsoever, for forty years' service."

Mike slid deeper in the chaise cushion and squinted through the binoculars toward the forest's edge. He watched with interest; a six-point buck proudly stepped into view, and handed the glasses to Wayne for a check. "Seen him here before? Big feller, isn't he? A whole lot of steaks on that one."

Mike cleared his throat and moved the conversation to a more serious note. "Wayne, I'm worried over Claybourne and his antics out there. He's up to no good, no good at all. I poked around in his bedroom after … after … er …Virginia and I finished. Found three weird little boxes in there—electronics—but I couldn't tell what they were. Today, I called Alert Investigations in Virginia, the company's name and address … printed on the labels.

"I was careful, asked lots of questions, and learned they are transmitters, beepers for a matching homing device. Strong magnets allow them to be quickly placed under a vehicle frame, well out of view, for surveillance or tracking purposes. They sell the units mainly to law enforcement and private investigators. One hundred eighty bucks each.

"The homing device is nothing more than a radio direction finder much like I had on the old boat before GPS navigation technology came along. A directional antenna pinpoints the mobile transmitter's line of position. Only a matter of tuning the antenna while it beeps, getting a few bearings with a map or just driving around, and following the strongest signal. Then you can zero right in and find the vehicle."

Mike's look was grave as he hesitated, looked to the field and back to Wayne, who still greedily eyed the stately buck. "Guess what I found when I checked the Suburban, on a whim, really, after learning the purpose of those devices. I was curious because there were three in the box, but space enough for a fourth unit. Sure enough, Wayne, there it was: right behind my rear bumper. Yes! Stuck to the frame cross member, was the fourth sending unit, beeping its silent signal out there, for anyone with a mated receiver tuned to that frequency. I freaked.

She must have put it there at the gol derned mall on Saturday, while I shopped inside."

Wayne seemed genuinely shocked. "Do you thinks I have one under the truck?" he asked. "I certainly don't want Nell driving that crate while it's beepin'. No sir, surely don't."

"We'll check, but I'm sure they don't know who you are. She asked me. I figured she'd been told by the general to identify and locate both of us, before he left on his, 'business trip,' to Texas, where he now is, supposedly. In case you don't know, you're a good friend from down south in Lansing. 'Slim Jim,' I believe I called you.

"They don't know we're brothers, but that'll come soon if they do much more prying. Bud's Chevron at the edge of town, would be a logical place to nose around, and old Jeb, the lube guy—gol, he'd spew it all out—tell 'em every story about us he'd ever heard. Nothing will come from the Paul Bunyan, though. Ina assured me. It won't be difficult to chase down the Gladdocks around here, for cripe's sake. We've been around too many years."

"Mike, I've a thought. Suppose, now just suppose, we takes the same approach. We hang devices on their vehicles to see where they go, what they do, where they shop. Could we learn anything of value? I'd be willing to split the costs just 'cause I don't like the guy. I didn't appreciate becoming an M-16 target."

"What are we likely to gain?" Mike replied. "We already know who they are and where they live. If we want them, we know where to go. Claybourne did this because he wished to identify and locate us, maybe even eliminate us if he found we knew something we shouldn't. His motives were a whole lot stronger, seems to me."

"Just the same, I wonder if we might do it for drill, for whatever we might learn? If we called the firm in the morning, we could have them air freighted overnight, plant the damned things in the next few days, and I could do some follow-up in the evenings next week when he gets back. You could stick one on his Excursion. It's probably sitting in long-term parking at the airport in Flint. I'd bet on that. You leave yours in place, unless, yes, until we might need to deceive them for some reason.

Then, you can take it off, plant it on some car headed into the woods, maybe a long haul truck headed north on the Interstate. We don't want them to know we know about it right now, do we? Later, that little baby could come in real handy."

"I removed the transmitter and took it in the house" Mike replied. "I like your idea, though. It makes more sense. We could really confuse things when we needed to do so. I'll replace it tonight and you keep checking the old truck."

Wayne stretched, yawned and grabbed his brother's shoulder firmly. "We'll make another trip to the shack, stake the place out again and get inside whenever we sees her leave. You're here all week, so timing's perfect. I want to search the barn, if we can get in, and I'd like to take it to the next level with the dogs. We'll get to them, get real cozy-like. You've made friends, but I have to do that, too. The critters could make or break us as the plot thickens. We don't need a pack of hundred pound Rottweilers as enemies."

Barefoot, Nell glided to the porch with a large tray, and playfully licked her chops. She set before the men a simple but sumptuous desert, one of her favorites, beside fruit pie. "There you are my sweet men: fresh local blueberries, iced honeydew chunks, a spritz of limejuice, and a sparkle of candied ginger to make your hair curly. That'll do it, won't it, Mikie? Might even work on somethin' else." She leaned over, grinned, and whispered in his ear, "What's this I hear about the new little girlfriend, Mister Don Juan?"

Mike pulled away, gave Nell a questioned look, and followed with a stern glare toward Wayne. "If I'm Mister Don Juan, then your overweight husband, the chubby one stuffing his jowls over there, is Mister Big Mouth. Can't you keep my personal business under wraps for heaven's sake? Why do I tell you these things, Wayne? I've asked myself that for too long."

"Now don't you worry at all. Tales like that, the whole bit with the Morris place, shall go no further than our property lines; I can assure you. ..." Wayne yielded.

Nell interrupted. "You needn't fret. There's too much seriousness, even danger for land's sake. We'll keep it 'tween us."

"Well, I did discuss our recent suspicions with Donnie, just a bit, I did." Wayne shifted worried glances between Nell and Mike. "We talked about it—had to, Mike. I wanted Don to know we developed information that suggested criminal activity, and ya know what he said? Just exactly what we thought. 'Well, how do you know?' he asks. 'What did you learn that led to that conclusion?'

"Talked just like the cop he used to be. I had to clam up about breaking in, no choice. Finally, as I might have figured, he asks once more, 'and what, may I inquire, have you guys been smoking?' That did it for me. He wasn't interested in looking into a crime that occurred on government property. There was no firing him up. That's why he quit the P.D., for Christ's sake. He grew sick of law enforcement, and got lazy, too."

"Virginia did let a few tidbits out as we talked—makes me think she's the innocent side of the general's doings and. ..."

"A fox in chicken feathers, I says," Wayne cut in. "Just take what she has to say, for now, with a grain of salt. Won't you please?"

"As I tried to get anything I could from her, she told me there are some security people on the way to the property, whatever that meant, supposedly to help them control vandals and burglars. They think the window was broken, the shack entered by someone looking for money or guns, because, as we know, nothing but the gun was found missing from inside. Security people will help them establish protocol, and improve existent systems for increased protection, she claimed. Of course, I didn't believe that for a minute. I'll bet the so-called 'hired help' will be there for tough guy tactics, not security in the usual sense of the word. She didn't speak convincingly on that one."

"So, when do these thugs arrive?"

"Don't know," Mike replied; he swatted a flock of mosquitoes on his cheek with a loud clap, "quite likely after the general returns next weekend. If we're going to snoop, we'd better do it real soon. We came too darned close to becoming targets last time. We don't wish to be around there with trigger happy bodyguards from out of town."

Wayne finished the last of the berries in the large bowl and lit three citronella candles on the table. "These fumes will chase away the blood sucking little nuisances. Should have done it earlier. They're getting bad already." The mosquitoes dissipated within a few minutes as the scented candle smoke wafted about the table in the stagnant night air.

"I want in that house again," Wayne continued. "I need another peek at the computer and I know right where to go to explore their activities further. We'll review the latest correspondence the general has received or sent. Don't ya agree?"

"That—yes—and I'm even wondering if it's practical to remove firing pins from his shotguns and rifles, the ones on the rack in the front room. Could we disable them and reduce his opportunity to nail one of us? I'm not inclined to empty the .22, though. That's her gun, I'd guess, there in the bedroom drawer with all her panties. As for his big .45, what do you think of exchanging his rounds with casings from which we've emptied the powder? I've got a .45 caliber jig for my re-loader down at the cabin. I'll buy a box at Mel's, remove the charges and exchange them with those in the cartridge box, and the magazine."

"Good, good, I like it, and now for timing." Wayne made hurried notes as he talked. "Getting in should take two minutes. I'll bring my lock picks. Didn't waste that training, now did I? You head upstairs and do the pistol: two minutes, maybe, no more. I waits for the computer to locate the file. I'd bet, being ex-government, they leave the computer on all the time. If not, and a password is required, we may have missed our only opportunity. If it's off and not locked, three minutes, and you should be back downstairs, unless ya searches a little more up there. Five minutes to review directories, and files, bring up, and print what I need—no more than that, and we're done with the computer. Then both of us sets to work on the rifles and shotguns. We'll ask Mel what we can do to disable 'em. I remember the one M-16. I can handle that one. The Browning over and under shotgun we saw in his Excursion, a mean twelve gauge, can be altered. There was a Winchester Model 700, the old double barrel twelve, and the Remington pump. It was a beater, a Model 870, I think. What else?"

"The AK-47 wasn't loaded, I don't think, but we sure as heck don't want it rattling away at us."

Wayne cocked his head when Nell cleared the table and left for the kitchen. He leaned closer and whispered to Mike, "Let's not forget the foxholes we saw in the woods. We may see some thirty calibers being installed, if these dingbats are into real security, and that's not good. I want access to the barn, the basement, too. We could easily burn up five minutes searching there. Ten minutes go by before we fix the guns. And, say fifteen, screwing with firing pins or other disablement efforts. Wow, that's a lot in the scheme of things, but we've got to do it. Then five or ten minutes for the remaining search, and we're the hell out of there. Bottom line, at best; we need a half hour inside. Can we, should we, dare we?"

"As far as I'm concerned, yes," Mike said. "How would Nell feel about watching the gate from Old River Road? We'll take a VHF radio, and give her one, for a warning shout. That allows, at least, a ten-minute notice. No matter where she goes—to town or across the bridge north—it's twenty minutes to get anywhere. We've a comfortable margin if we're there to watch her leave. We'll lock up, cover our tracks on the bluff, and get away in the canoe. It has to ... we'll make it work," Mike assured his somewhat doubtful Brother. "We can see this through."

Nightfall dropped suddenly as darkness with its soggy-looking clouds moved in to obscure the sky. A light patter of droplets scattered on the deck, ushered by distant thunder clashes on their way northward, though away from them. Undaunted by the emergent dampness, for it cooled the ground noticeably, they continued in conversation until humidity and temperature sank enough to sleep comfortably.

Wayne thought more about the electronics and was worried about Claybourne learning of the order they would place. "How do we know he isn't in contact with the firm? They're in his hometown. Maybe he knows someone personally. We'll be real careful, have them shipped to the United Parcel facility in Grayling for a will call pick-up ... cash ...

COD … no traces. We'll use the name Jake Langferd; how does that sound?"

"Well, my brother's a red light thinker tonight; a brilliant idea if I do say so."

"I gots us another, even better one Mike, and this'll steal your heart. The Alert outfit probably has bugs, concealable microphones and recorders, for sale, too. If we can get inside again, how about planting a bug or two? One under the computer, in there behind the switch plate, another near their bed, and let's see what the hell they talk about upstairs. No cop in the world would ever officially want to listen, and they'd scoff at recordings as evidence, but we could—and I emphasize—we could save our own necks by what we learn. Damnit!" Wayne stomped on the old front porch until dust flew. "Let's fight fire with fire. However, I don't want to listen to Brother Mike panting and puffing; a female riding him like a wild Mustang. Spare me all of that."

Mike smacked Wayne on the shoulder with clenched fist, snickered, and said nothing as his brother grimaced from the blow. "I'll call you with COD information and shipping details. Then we plan the stakeout. Tomorrow I'll reload .45 shells without powder. You keep checking your Chevy for a beeper, and we move onward."

"Don't forget to order bugs, super sensitive mikes, if they have them." Wayne bid Mike farewell with a mock salute and returned inside to practice a quick disassembly of Claybourne's M-16 before retiring, assuring that the firing pin could easily be removed. It took six minutes. *Too long for that task, way too long. I'll practice at Mel's Sporting Goods in the morning until I gets it down fast with the other guns, too.*

Mike's back deck served as a good place to melt down after the intensive planning session. The poplars almost sang with the draft that slid down through upper branches, and the air suddenly grew crispier.

"Well, we have some catching up, Mister Gladdock, now don't we?" Mike tugged his shirt closed at the neck and waited, arms tightly locked across his chest. "Don't you want to tell me something, Michael?" Meg asked, almost in a cant. "Isn't a little frank and forthright *tête-à-tête* in order, here? I may have nothing to do with your choices, but I'll not be an observer to the likes of your bizarre activity the other night—with the little hooker—if I may call her that. No sermon from your Meg, though, just wise counsel for the love-struck. Though you've not yet asked for it, the advice is: back off! I'd never have imagined you so gullible."

Mike clenched his eyes tightly. He felt a bitter taste in his mouth, cramps in his lower abdomen, and began the litany of defenses he found himself practicing on the way to the cabin from Wayne's house. He snapped as he intervened. "How do you know what she's like? How could you feel what I felt, being there, making love as I've … I … did … at. …"

He realized he'd tear her apart with a recount of the ecstasy he experienced. Silenced by good advice from within, Mike withheld all efforts to participate. Lips closed, he dropped his head in shame, and fell silent. Unwittingly, though, he chose an attack for the retort that followed. "You've never done what she did. You never stood naked like that in the living room, danced and admired your own body. You always wore a nightgown. She had no qualms, nude as a rock, totally unembarrassed. A new experience, yes indeed, and I want more. I'm suddenly impatient for more exposure to such satisfaction, afraid it might not happen much in my remaining days, months or years. She gave me a workout I never thought possible."

Meg knew, but she understood also, what lay behind that *façade* of tender young, supple skin, Virginia's tailored breasts, thighs, and her oil-black hair. "Mike, even Nell sized the little hussy up for you. Don't you remember? Simply hearing of the limousine parked at the power company gate for so long, prompted her to view your little plaything as nothing more than a glorified wildcat. Have you forgotten what your perceptive sister-in-law realized? The young woman, and I use the word loosely, is big time trouble. However, don't worry; I'll not tell you again. And your plans to invade the shack—have you boys lost your minds?"

"I don't get it," Mike whined. "I don't understand how you see so much, hear everything, know all that has happened to me…too unreal for me to absorb. You come back and chastise me for what I think is right, Meg. National security we're possibly dealing with, but there's nothing abnormal happening in the open just yet. We can't get law enforcement interested. It's up to us to gather evidence, get things into focus, and then tell the authorities when there's something for them to see. We're going through with this, Meg or no Meg," he asserted, concerned he'd not hear from her again. "Above all, I want that shack! As for the woman, she can wait. We'll see what fiber she's made of, as time goes on. How about that?"

The tallest poplar by the back steps to the ravine shook almost defiantly. A good many new spring leaves flew downward in the swirl that encircled it and its closest neighbors. Then a muggy stillness reeked.

"Meg? C'mon, Margaret Gladdock. I know you're there. Meg?" Mike questioned repeatedly in a whimpering voice, as encroaching tears clouded his vision.

CHAPTER 20

———◆·◆———

Midday heat stifled and easily drew sweat from those along the Au Sable River that Wednesday morning. Wayne and Mike—poised on a cushion of cooling damp leaves beneath low-hanging boughs of a large maple—intently watched the Morris shack from upstream, on the opposite bank, some fifty feet closer than Mike's previous spot. Second day to stake out the place, the day before produced no notable results, a bust; Virginia never left the property.

Tired of the interminable wait on the main road, Nell complicated things with her reluctance to again serve as their lookout. That would have seriously compromised their safety, in case Virginia left. How would they know when she returned to the premises? They departed early.

Wayne and Mike sensed the new day would bring them better luck. The electronics arrived in the meantime. Everything could be accomplished with one break-in, a great reduction in risk. "Damn, she's got to leave for something: dog food, groceries, booze, contraceptives … heh, heh," Wayne said, and then thrust an elbow into his brother's rib cage with a sneer. "I emphasize the latter." Mike ignored the crack and maintained his watch with powerful game spotting binoculars that swiveled on a sturdy tripod stand at convenient height for extended viewing comfort.

"Still nothing; no dogs, either. She might have them in the basement, again. She gets angry when they whine and scratch at the front screen, doesn't like them in the house. She is in bed for all we know. The front door hasn't been opened." Mike chattered as he stared into the lenses.

"This reminds me so much of that winter, a particularly cold and snowy one, when we both got those nice binoculars from Pop. Christmas, probably 1951, maybe it was '52. We nearly froze our tails out there, below the dam. Remember waiting for starving deer to pop out from the tree line? Cripes, we lay prone on the wet snow, nothing but the old wool dog blanket to keep our skinny bodies warm; shivered, we did, like dead trees in a gale, but pellet guns were at the ready."

"Sure, sure; I couldn't forget. We hitched a ride on that blue stake truck, used to deliver firewood in the area," Wayne replied. "It slid all over the icy road, scared hell out of us. The wind chill that day, oh, it must have been thirty below—worse in the open truck bed. By the time we hiked to the gate at the dam, we were blue as a late spring sky. How long did we stay there, waiting out the animals? Three, four hours, or more? I don't know, never been colder. Your idea; my Big Brother always led little Wayne astray, with his adventurous plans.

"There we went, into the Valley of the Shadow of Death. I trusted you, damn it. I didn't know we were the only human beings outside that day. Do you remember the look on Mama's face when we finally got home, half dead?" Wayne laughed, shook his head emphatically and continued, while he tugged at, then bit off, a chunk of homemade jerky. "It took an hour in the hot bath to thaw our chilled bodies. She was in a state of panic. I can still. …"

"Shhh … shhh, hold it! The screen door just opened. Wait! Here, look; you can see why I had such a good time." Mike could not conceal a shy smile as he spoke and passed the binoculars to Wayne. Virginia wore only slippers, and the new tan she acquired sunbathing on the sand spit over the weekend. She swept the porch, shook the throw rug, and leaned on the broom handle, apparently to admire the meandering Au Sable for a few moments.

"My God, Mike! What a beautiful body. I feel like a pervert, but so what; this is amazing. She's without inhibition. Look at her: rubbing lotion on her breasts, hips and thighs, just a standing' there before the Almighty and us, for God's sake. Don't stop, Virginia; don't stop. Just relax and enjoy the morning sun." Wayne's eyes stayed glued to the oculars. "Hey, she's going back in, left the door open, just the screen, now. And here come the Rottweilers, 'round from the cellar, probably. They're off to the woods behind the barn. What a show!"

Thirty minutes passed with no further activity. Nell called twice on the radio. Bored again, she talked of leaving … short on patience. Would it be like her post the day before, nothing for her to do but work on her knitting in the discomfort of the steamy car seat? Would she be useless once again?

"Tell her to hang in there, Wayne, just a little longer. At least Virginia is up and around, a good sign for a change. We'll cross our fingers she's restless," Mike mumbled during the radio chatter. "Beg Nellie to wait at least one more hour. Whoa! Wait a second. Virginia put a bag on the porch. Looks like it's filled with empty bottles. That spells a trip to the market, for a deposit refund, maybe groceries, too; doesn't it?"

"Sure does, yup. Sure does. Wayne to Nell: hang in there, Baby— more action out here. Let ya know when it gets crankin' and we'll. …"

"Wayne! Here she comes, has her keys, the bag and her purse. She's going; yes, no question about it. She is leaving." The red Chevrolet pickup exhausts bellowed, a cloud of blue smoke filled the space between shack and barn and, without benefit of a warm-up, Virginia chugged out of sight toward the gate.

"Man, they got ripped off on that engine rebuild. Burning oil already. Wonder which shop took the Morris' money? Only three in Mio. Probably Charlie's, I'll just bet that. Nell: Wayne here," he cut in on his own thought, and hurriedly pressed the transmit button, "Nell: Wayne, here. Are you back enough not to look suspicious? Here she comes, '57 Chevy, fire engine red. I'm. …"

A fuzz of static spewed forth, and then her voice reported loud and clear. "Nell, here: it's about time. Yes, I am looking in the rearview mirror, faced away from the gate, toward the bridge. I can see the apron just perfect. Hope she's not out for the rest of the day."

"Likewise," Wayne said. "Nell, if, for any reason, when you call to warn us—should we not answer—lean on the car horn. Do a test as soon as she's past the first curve on the main road. We might hear it. Try it, just for drill.

I'd like to check, have that warning horn as a backup. She'll be there in five-ten minutes or so. Wayne, out."

"That's it, Bro. Let's pack it up and hit the river. There's some time we didn't take into account—to close things here and the short paddle—another ten minutes. Our time in the shack just got sliced back."

The canoe disappeared into a cluster of rushes and out of view from the bluff in front of the shack. No danger of setting adrift, it would be secure and put them on open water in a jiffy, in the event of a needed fast exit. The men glared at one another; each silently expressed doubt, if what they were about to do, made sense, any sense at all.

"We're not breaking windows this trip, Wayne. Do you understand that? They'll be no property damage," Mike admonished, "no forcible entry. I plan to see Virginia again and I don't want that coming up. I'm not a good enough liar; dern it."

Wayne held up the small, tooled leather case that contained his lock picks.

He smiled and replied, "No problem. Show me the door and I'll show you how these work. I'll only need. …"

He stopped mid-sentence to the alarming cacophony of barks and snarls that came from the rear of the shack. The noise advanced quickly. The dogs, were not in the cellar as before, would be on them in the flash of a fast pulse.

"Quick, Wayne, the meat," Mike called.

"Thweeth, thweeth." Wayne spat repeatedly and tossed the plastic bag to Mike just as the three Rottweilers bounded toward the porch.

"Ace, come," Mike commanded, "King, Jack, here dogs. Good boy, Ace." The big male showed teeth, but dropped his hindquarters to a perfect sit. Then he hunched down, back bristled, and again he snarled viciously. Ace crawled his way toward Mike, who did not show a speck of the fear that tumbled his insides. The other dogs stood their distance and chanted ferociously. They watched their leader intently for a signal to strike.

"Atta boy, Ace. Good boy." Mike winked at Wayne who remained motionless, yet shaking inside, and vulnerable, crouched by the steps. The excited dog took the meat, and fell silent while the others took smaller morsels, yet to their clear delight. Mike extended his palm for Ace to smell. His scent still lingered about the shack, and Ace remembered. Suddenly playful, the dog rolled over on his back and whined, while the others followed and extended the same gestures to Wayne, when he fed them again. The animals were theirs. They nuzzled and pushed each other away, vied for pats and scratches, and soon lost interest. Minutes later, two bushy-tailed gray squirrels, which ventured to the ground in search of acorns, lured the threesome away. The dogs romped after them, into the tree line.

"It's off to work, Bro. We're home free, for the present, anyway."

Wayne set to the locks and more quickly than even he imagined, the door swung open, closed behind them, after they stepped safely inside. Mike unlocked the kitchen door as a possible escape route to the trees in case of Virginia's early return. The quiet shattered with a crackle of the radio. "Nell to Wayne: Honey, come in." The call sounded frantic. Wayne hesitated, about to search the computer. He sensed concern in her voice. Mike already climbed the stairs and turned to disable the pistol he previously found in the general's nightstand.

"Nell, what's wrong?" Wayne nervously held the radio.

"She's here. The gate's opening ... I see that mule deer crossing the path. She's waiting for it. There; she's out and the gate is closing. She's turning, oh, God, please go west. C'mon, c'mon. There, OK. yes. She's headed to Mio, being a woman, most likely to the mall. Truck is out of sight now. I'll lean on the horn. Can you hear it?"

"Hardly, Nell, just barely. Try short blasts. That might. ..."

Mike called from the bedroom, "Hear the horn? Got it real well up here. Virginia left the dormer windows open."

"All right, let's see," Wayne remarked aloud to carry himself through the search process. "Here's the document directory, lots of files, but nothing; nothing I want. Hold it. What's this?" He brought up a folder named *Eastern Star,* loaded with files bearing many unusual names, such as *Arafat, Abbas, Al Bin Im Mahooud, Patrioit Launchers.* Stunned, Wayne shook in disbelief as he noted details in one e-mail sent to General Blakes:

> *Rod,*
>
> *Your daughter Ginny and I admire constantly and humbly, the validity of your contacts and the accuracy of your predictions. The Arabs arrived within minutes of the time specified in your memo, with the first two million installment. We're paying off now, for all the goods and contacts. I'll leave for El Paso soon, to handle final assembly of the units. They are to be taken off base within the week. Our man there will be paid in full. A quarter mil is a lot, though a pittance of what we would have paid, were we pressed harder. There were huge risks, as you know; over one hundred million in replacement value. Not bad. Virginia says she loves you, and I wish I could say the same. You did it Rod. We have all done our jobs well, so far.*
>
> *Off for now and regards, H. C. P.*

"Units? Must be the missiles. What else could be worth that much? We're getting exactly what we needed. We've really nailed this, Mike. Looks like Virginia's father is in this little caper; Rodmend Blakes, General Rodmend Blakes. What a den of thieves!"

He closed out and the computer screen dulled. Wayne looked at his watch. "Twelve minutes, way too long. Time's running out and too much left to do."

"Well, the bugs work. Both are in place," Mike exclaimed. "We do have to get out of the house." He concealed the two small transmitters beneath wall socket plates, one in the living room, below the computer, and the other next to Claybourne's side of the bed where sat the telephone extension.

Rifles and shotguns were disabled. So terrified he was during the effort, his hands and fingers continued to tremble. Each weapon he checked outside with a live round, to assure it no longer fired. "All units are officially dysfunctional, Sir," Mike said elatedly. The last rifle he placed back in its place with the others. They locked the kitchen door and secured the front door behind them. Their search of the cellar proved a waste of valuable time.

Carefully, they scuffed pine boughs over the ground in front of the shack to obscure footprints, and made their way to the barn. The side door there was easy. Wayne slipped a plastic credit card past the tumbler and it popped open. "Sure as hell, they do need increased security. Saved two minutes here. Still way overtime, though. Jesus Louise," Wayne complained, "I'm sopping wet."

Both men perspired profusely. The air was still and muggy, sun too hot for such exertion; the barn even warmer. Empty but for a bench piled with tools on the far wall, a snow blower and the big auger snowplow extension for the John Deere tractor, parked outside. Both pieces of equipment were covered with large, heavy-duty tarps. Wayne propped an extension ladder against the loft, which overhung more than half the barn's ground floor footprint. He climbed upward like a frightened monkey.

Lots of boxes up here. Damn it, no time to look inside any of these. New movers' tags on all of them; probably junk they couldn't throw away, from Arlington. His thoughts skidded to a halt. He called to Mike whose search below thus far produced nothing. "Whoa, Billy! Mike," he called. "Didn't you say the Arabs came with two leather briefcases, real large ones?"

They hung from the very back rafter, in the center of the deck, and almost escaped Wayne's vantage.

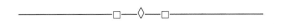

"Mike! Jesus Christmas ... oh ... oh, my God ... Mike! Help! Oh, sheeit, Mike!"

Mike thought the worst, a booby trap his primary concern. He searched at ground level and foraged through the contents of several cartons when he heard Wayne's panicked, blood-curdling yell. Frightened to the core, he knew immediately; his brother found trouble. He pictured Wayne with a knife, maybe a sword through his back, impaled somewhere, a hatchet buried in his forehead.

His chills ran deep, pulse pounded like wildfire, and his subconscious resisted the urge to move. Breathing became labored. He stopped to regain composure. *I knew it. I knew we stretched this too far. Wayne is badly hurt. I'm afraid to look. The fear in his voice, and that scream: no jokes here.* "Meg," Mike called aloud, instinctively. "Meg!" His loud cries brought no reply.

"Mike, get your ass up here, and fast. This is ... I ... I don't know what to ... oh, sweet sheeit, Mike. ..."

He peered with due caution into the darkened loft as he reached the top rung of the ladder, and saw his brother, prone on the plywood floor. Next to him was a black briefcase exactly like he saw the Arabs bring that night. Tipped to its side, it brimmed with bundles of cash, and several were cast about the floor.

A bright aluminum crossbow bolt—very stout arrow about sixteen inches long, with red feathers at the nock—pinned Wayne's leg to the wood deck.

"The sonofabitch; the dirty thieving sonofabitch, could a killed me. He sets that crossbow up there in the rafters." Wayne pointed to the weapon, secured in a yoke of two by fours at the front gable. "He aims it here, ties a trigger string to the bags, and it fires when I grabs one. Thweeth, thweeth." He spat, shook his head in disbelief, struggled to recover from the surprise and spat again: "Thweeth, thweeth." Mike rushed to his side and pulled the razor-sharp, three-bladed hunting tip, a frighteningly lethal projectile, from the cut in Wayne's pants.

"I'm afraid to look," Wayne remarked in alarm, as he raised the cuff. Well, lookitey there." He gasped with relief. "Got me right alongside the Achilles tendon, but it's just a scratch, nothing serious." His panting subsided. He breathed deeply a few times, spat again and continued, "We need to reset the damned thing or he'll know someone has been here. We don't want him suspicious; not yet. We'll replace the cash, too, except for two bundles. They'll cover our expenses. No arguing. We'll take a little and get out."

"Not so fast, no, Wayne. No stealing."

"Hell, Bro, this isn't their money. It's from the Arabs; you told me yourself, and I've got confirmation right here." He patted his shirt pocket with the folded computer printouts and smiled broadly. "Claybourne could have killed me, Mike. That, alone, is worth a few grand, isn't it?" Mike could not disagree.

A blur of static on the radio startled them. "Wayne to Nell: come in." There was no answer. He called again and it brought no reply. "Wayne to Nell...Wayne here. Goddamnit!" he yelled after releasing the button, and then he called again. "Wayne to Nell: come on, girl." The radio fizzled but no voice could be heard.

"Mike, we're gone. I say trouble is on its way. Just a hunch, but I don't like this. Nope, I don't likes this one bit. How many more booby traps has he set."

They cocked the crossbow, raised its trajectory up some, loaded the bolt, and restored the brief case to the rafters, exactly as Wayne found it. Wayne tied the trigger string as it was before, and all but two bundles of cash they replaced in the briefcases. The remainder, Wayne stuffed under his shirt. The brothers dropped to the barn floor and hastily hung the ladder back in place. Wayne stopped in his tracks, cocked his head, grabbed his brother's arm and held tightly. "It's the truck, the damned pickup is coming back. Hear the pipes?"

The red Chevy rounded the last turn to the *cul-de-sac* and chugged to a stop between the two structures, almost next to the barn side door. Wayne clicked it closed, locked it, and they stepped into the shadows beneath the largest tarp, out of their wits with what might come next.

"Good God," Wayne whispered, "we're trapped in here. Let's hope she didn't go to the nursery or the hardware for outdoor supplies. She'd unload that stuff inside here, with us! A moment's relief, they heard the crackle of paper shopping bags. There were groceries to unload.

"Hey there, boys and girls," Virginia cheerfully called to the barking dogs.

They ran from the woods, with the truck's approach. "Did y'all all stay out of trouble? Hmmm, now did you?"

"Wayne, listen; there's Nell honking the truck horn. Listen. Quick, turn down the radio, we don't need that dern thing blasting, giving us away."

"Sure. Wouldn't that be nice? Wait, she's in the house," Wayne said. "I heard the screen door slam. We've got to go. Hold on, it's the door, just slammed again. Christ, she's coming back out here."

Virginia's key slid in the lock. She turned it one way, then the other, and the side door opened. Miraculous she didn't hear their hearts pound like snare drums; both thumped hard against trembling ribs. The dogs headed for the rear of the barn. They hovered by the plow; tails wagged vigorously while she reached through the door. She dropped a squeeze bottle of insecticide and a new pair of clippers to the floor, and called, "C'mon boys and girls; here dogs." Her body blocked most of the outside light. "Do you smell one of those big rats? Hmmm, do you? C'mon y'all; let's go." The men dared not breathe. Perspiration beads effused about their foreheads, cheeks and around the napes of their necks. A haunting eternity, but the animals reluctantly turned away, and followed the woman outside.

Mike crossed himself twice.

"Thanks to the Almighty for that little favor," Wayne whispered, and released a deep sigh of relief. The shack door slammed again, and they heard water run in the kitchen sink.

"Out of here. Doesn't the kitchen window face to the west, Mike?"

"Yep, we're safe, I'd say, to beat it through the woods, behind the tractor and into the tree line. She won't see us from the window. We'll loop around by the big cedar, down the bluff and we're off with the canoe.

CHAPTER 21

—◆◆◆—

"Tomorrow night," Mike affirmed as if Meg were with him, "tomorrow—dern it—I'm fishing, if it's the last thing I do this week. I'll go alone, no Wayne." A flash of headlights from ahead distracted him. He dimmed his high beams and found his thoughts pleasantly fickle.

He smelled her freshness; he felt Virginia's cool skin, and shook with the thought of her muscular legs tightly entwined with his, locked in one of the many embraces they enjoyed. The thrill of being with the woman, the possibility of repeating the experience, still alive, wildly stirred inside. Desire almost overtook his gnawing compulsion to lure a brown trout.

"She's like a magnet, all I've thought about. Mind's been on single track, as never before. It seems so impractical, though." He reluctantly mediated; hated the admission as he shrugged shoulders to his own image in the rear view mirror.

"How could she be interested, seriously interested, in me? Who is she, really?" He turned the wheel sharply to the left, and avoided a concrete column at the base of the ramp to the third level. "I have to get my mind back where it belongs: find Claybourne's car and plant the beeper. One hundred eighty dollars for the derned things, six hundred more for the bugs we planted. Cripes, the stuff didn't come cheap! Hope we get our money's worth before we're done."

A slow cruise through the long term parking lot several blocks from the Flint terminal failed to reveal the bronze SUV. No sign of the general's Excursion in the first two levels. Mike's last hope, the third and final floor, finally produced what he wanted, Claybourne's SUV, ripe for planting the Alert beeper. One of the large flood lamps burned out. The north corner, deeply shadowed, appeared more sinister than the rest of the deck—dimly lighted with an eerie orange glow in the night mist. He screeched to a stop the instant he spotted it and quickly assured himself. "The Roof rack's the same. Yes, gun rack behind the front seat and the D.C. license. It's his. It's Claybourne's." Before getting out, he carefully canvassed the lot. "No one is around," he whispered nervously. He peered over his shoulders once more, slumped to the task and placed the instrument, about the size of a pound of butter, on the back side of the front frame cross member. "I'm clear. Far worse in the planning than the execution, it went too easily; I worried needlessly." Mike hustled back behind the wheel in seconds, turned on the receiver that lay on the front seat and dialed in the frequency, 156.115 megahertz. The Morse code letter "O" came in perfectly. *Dah-dah-dah,* followed by a five second delay; it cycled over and over. "Perfect," he exclaimed. "I'm off to check our house, and then hit the road north to the cabin. I hear the caddis flies a calling. I'll miss the swarming little fish attracters if I'm not careful. Just can't do that." He shuddered in his excitement, at the thought of going through what Meg endured; so many months of bed-ridden confinement, never to recover enough to fish the river again.

"I could be sapped of my agility just as easily," he lamented and inhaled deeply to assure he breathed clearly. "Sure glad I quit the smokes in my early twenties, drinking, too, when I eventually did so." *Just can't let death come like that. Not yet. Patriot Missiles, Palestinians, the Israelis, our army and now, this woman? So much to learn about.* He thought to himself with trepidation then voiced continued concerns aloud once again. "What if the woman is a serpent beneath that lovely covering? If her old man's involved, and he must be, as the printouts suggested, her bad blood could have deep roots. Is that any reason not to wish for more time to live than Meg received? Wayne may be right. The wrapping on that package may be too good to be true."

Despite the negatives, pictures of Virginia continued to envelop his senses. *There's a chance, too, a slim one I have to admit, that she's got a good heart, that she was victimized into this scam for some reason. Does she owe Claybourne a serious debt? Is she beholden to him for some reason, or in fear of her life?*

"I saw the way he smacked her. *That was no love pat on the cheek. Is her father holding her hostage?* He voiced and ruminated so many concerns, his self-generated confused thinking bordered on chaos. He wondered about Virginia's upbringing. "She said nothing of her childhood when we talked on the couch after lovemaking." *Is she in this just for the money, or is it some benevolent cause she's supporting? Does she have a criminal record? Is she a real con, and do I wear a sucker's mark?*

Virginia's infective and innocent laugh, a cheerful tatter, endlessly reverberated in his head. He played it back repeatedly, but the record was close to worn out, and needed reconstitution. How easily she dropped her towel to the floor, how quickly she took him, before he could say, "No."

Fewer cars clogged the freeway out of town at the late hour. Return to the cabin would be easy. He felt relieved. His hands no longer quivered as they did when he entered the airport gate, ready to search for Claybourne's Excursion. Clandestine activity was not in Mike's nature, and did not come easily. He slapped the wheel to the rhythm of Merle Haggard's *That's the Way Love Goes,* played it for the third time, and got up to speed on the northbound Interstate.

"That's the way love goes," Mike said wistfully, "just like the song. Here one moment, gone the next. It seems so distant, now. Will I ever see it again, like it was with Meg? 'Love,' Pop once said, 'is meant to happen just once.'"

He would look at Mama across the table as if he really meant it, though he never said the three little words in front of us. It was hard for Mike to view himself in love again, having the energy to input as much as he did during courting years with Meg. *How could that be possible? Where will those old feelings come from, all that energy I had when I was young?*

Wayne's call interrupted the tunes and his loose chain of darting deliberations. Almost resentful of the invasion, Mike came close to pulling the plug. Then, after the third ring, he lifted the cell phone from the seat and reluctantly responded. Panting hard, Wayne could barely speak. Mike was concerned. "What's wrong,

Brother? Go ahead; take a minute, and get yourself together."

"As I tried to say, I went to the river, up on the north bank, to listen in; had to get closer to pick up transmissions from the hidden mikes. Well, she's in the bedroom; heard her on that unit. I tunes it in, and she's right there. Works perfectly." He still gasped anxiously, and found it difficult to express himself. "Yup, clear as a bell, I hears her speaking to the general—Claybourne, that is, a talking on the phone."

"What did she say, for cripe's sake?" He turned the stereo volume to a low hum and closed the crack in the driver's side window to stop the whistling wind. "C'mon, Wayne; out with it. What happened?"

"It's still a happening'. I'm listening now. There's hell's afire between the two of them and she's about to have a kitten. I wanted you to know, she's trying to weed herself out of the deal; said she was through. She mentioned her share … yup, payment of five million plus change, Mike; that's six zeroes after the five."

Fascinated with the report, Mike could hardly keep his eyes on the road, with images of Virginia, probably in bed as she spoke, and unwilling to take guff from the general. He found it impossible, though, to perceive her in the intimate company of Arabs; he shuddered uncontrollably at that notion.

Composure returned, Wayne breathed deeply and continued his monologue without added pause. "Then she gets real quiet, only says a few short words like, 'but, I … I … I, that,' and so forth. She doesn't get in a word edgewise. I figures, least it sounds so, that he's giving her bloody hell. Finally she starts to talk again, and you can pretty well guess what he must have been saying in between. It's why I called you right now. Hope that's all right, with our cell bills so high nowadays."

He gave Mike no chance to reply. "Damn it, I wish I could have recorded this. I made a few notes, as best I could. Wanted to call while it was fresh. Maybe with two of us, we've got a better chance of recreating the confab.

"After some quiet—she's listening to him—well, she pipes up a scream, almost blew out my eardrums. That damn transmitter is real sensitive, and, now, so are my ears. She says, 'There won't be any killing; absolutely not, while I am involved in the operation, and so long as my father stays in it.' Now she's got my attention, Mike. 'Cause you and I know who it is she's talking about, now don't we?

"She screams again, 'I said, no!' she yells, 'That will not happen, and I will not set them up for it. Are you crazy?' she asks him. 'Have you completely lost your chips?' There's a pause. She must have used the bathroom. I heard water running for a second and she comes back.

"'Have I met the man? Of course,' she says, 'yes I have, and he is not only a very pleasant local, he is a perfect gentleman, and has no clue what we're up to, Homer. That I promise. He's interested only in one thing, fishing with his flies, at the bend in the river, in front of our place. He's been going there his entire life,'" she says. "Sounds to me as if she likes old Mikie, just a little."

Wayne chuckled and continued with no change in his enthusiasm. "The girl then says, 'Oh, he doesn't know. He … he's just too … er … too … innocent to think I am a … a. …' Claybourne must have interrupted. She utters nothing for a while, two minutes at least. Then, 'the shooting?' she asks and answers, kind of sassy-like, 'that shooting was a random matter, started with your dogs. He told me we have no right to use threatening animals at the riverbank and certainly not in the water. He said the information came from Forest Service people he contacted, when he first saw the gate. They told him that the gate must come down, too, that we didn't. …'

"Mike, that cheery little note must have really wired up the general, 'cause she gets real quiet once again, and for the longest time says not a word … nothing. Then I gets scared again, when I imagine what he's telling her.

"'Those soldiers won't do anything of the kind, and there will be no machine guns on this property. What do you mean two of them?' she asks. 'Two thirty calibers?' she inquires again. 'Who do you think will threaten the unloading and the final loading processes? We're out here in the middle of nowhere. Have you gone completely paranoid? This is the forest, Homer; deep in the forest in northern Michigan. We planned well for this isolation. Get your head screwed on properly. It's not Vietnam.' I shakes all over again, like a retriever jumping from winter lake water, when she speaks."

"'His name is Mike and his buddy is … a … ah … Jim something. No, I don't know Mike's last name and I will not get it for you,' she says. 'No I won't. You're not going to touch him, and neither are your drivers. Drivers!' she yells, 'drivers? They're nothing more than paid gunslingers, and you know it. I've not met the other man, but he lives in Lansing and without his last name, how would I find him anyway?'

"Mike, I really trembles when she goes on, 'How can he trust me after such a short encounter at the Mall? I will not lure him to the house. He will not get Sodium Pentothal. No way, not by me, or in my presence will that happen. I don't care if you bought the drug on the black market. I won't sacrifice my professional background to knock out a fisherman.' He's a tellin' her to drug you, maybe kill ya, probably get you to spill the beans, and see what you know."

"Sure sounds that way, doesn't it? Wayne; now get to the other details. I'll stop to gas up real soon." Mike had less than a quarter tank, and the number of open stations dwindled by the mile as he forged north. Soon he would exit the Interstate and leave most all of them behind. *The two-gallon emergency tank in back is empty, too. I'd better be careful.*

"'Well,' says I, 'this is a fine kettle of fish.' I listens more and hears her say, 'It's your baby, now, Homer, your problem. I'm telling you, he and his buddy are not threats. Are you calling me a liar? Don't you talk like that. You bastard. I'll eliminate you before that would ever happen,' she snapped. 'You so much as touch me, and this time Daddy will hear about it. He finds you've placed a heavy hand on me; he'll take you out all too fast. You know him. He'll never quit the search, and he will find you.

"'No place of hiding would be beyond his grasp. Army Intelligence would shoot you on sight, at his behest. He'd see to that. He's three stars above you, you small-minded underling, and he'll not be happy when he finds out what you said tonight. True colors are flying, aren't they, General?'"

Wayne continued, still almost breathlessly, with his detailed account. "She's convinced, I think, that we're babes in the woods. Those hidden microphones paid for themselves, didn't they? Looks as if we have a mother's wing over us chickens; thanks to you, Brother, and your antics with the new lady friend."

"All right, let's keep that out of the discussion, I'd. ..."

Wayne cut in, "Hey, that little love-in experience of yours might have saved our behinds, old buddy, could really have cut us some slack. You had a good time, too. She dresses down the general and it goes quiet again. He was probably livid with her threat. We should find out what we can about her father. The more we know about all the players, the greater our safety factor. You can find out a little more about him on the net: where he is, what branch of the U.S. Army he commanded. Most anything you learn could be of help to us, if you're going to ... er ... see the little lady again."

Mike stayed mum on his plans to fish the river. He needed the solitude, a break from the stress. Wayne would be excluded from that venture.

"One final comment she made, and that was it, so far as I absorbed it. She asks him, 'just where and when are these killings to take place? What if they have had enough at the river, with the shots and all? Yes,' she says, 'I found his house, tracked the Suburban there. That was before you told me the men were slated for execution. C-4? Isn't that plastic explosive? Blow up their cars? Never get me to do that, either. A car bomb out here? You're crazy! It would attract the attention of authorities like a Las Vegas revue at the Mio Mall. 'Homer,' she says, 'we shouldn't even talk about it.' There it ends, Mike, as far as I can remember, anyhow.

"Pentothal, shooting, and C-4 explosives and thirty calibers," Wayne went on, "the sonofabitch means business, real big, serious business. We have to watch our tails and we had best monitor his whereabouts when he gets back. Let's see exactly what he does, where he goes. Shortly, there ought to be missiles lining up outside that barn. This whole program is racing to a head, and if we're not real careful, the heads might be yours and mine.

"We still have nothing solid for the cops. Even though we recorded all this talk, they wouldn't do anything, because it's probably illegally collected evidence. As yet, there's nothing illegal for them to see on the property. We'd be a laughing stock. We have to get the authorities out there once the missiles arrive, and, preferably, when they're being picked up, so they get the crooked Arabs, too. Ah, what would the newspapers do with this one?"

Mike involuntarily shook with the ramifications of his brother's account. "Incredible, Wayne. That's invaluable information, a dern good piece of luck you were there to overhear it. We do need to start recording anyway, because, evidence or not, we're going to need whatever backup correlation we can accumulate when we present this to the F.B.I., State Police, or whoever may eventually listen. One of us may have to go to Washington D.C., considering there are two big gun generals involved. Not just anyone at the Pentagon will give the cops, F.B.I., or us, an ear. We'll need photos of the barn when it's loaded with the goodies, some proof to do the talking for us. Aren't we faced with a repeat trip, another break-in?"

"I'm in if you are. We're too deep not to keep swimming, I says."

"I'm becoming more worried about our safety, depending on who these men from Texas are," Mike added. "I think the general wants someone else to do his dirty work—too smart to pull the trigger himself, I'll bet. So we may need another beeper.

"Should have called you in the morning. The signal is working on his Excursion. I found the Ford on the top floor at the airport, just like you figured. Good call. I was as nervous as a wet hen, but it took just a second and it tested fine. A mile or two up the Interstate, it was still going."

While he spoke, Mike thought about fishing, and Virginia, too. "I think I need to see the woman again, for follow-up. I'll … ah … a … let you know."

The service station's lights at the Highway 61 turn-off shone brightly. A full tank and he would take the lonesome way, through the woods. *Should be lots of deer out. It's late. Meg would have suggested the longer route, too. Meg! She's been so quiet; no contributions, none of her well-meaning admonitions.* He listened for signs, a sense of her hovering presence. Now that Wayne was completely tuned out of his consciousness, her smile, her tolerance, and patience pervaded his thoughts. But she did not speak. "Meg?" Mike finally pleaded aloud, "anything you'd care to offer, here?"

"… And, then she says to the general, 'Homer, this conversation is. …'"

Mike missed Wayne's last sentence. He turned into the expansive truck stop lot. Several tractor-trailer rigs were parked to the side of the lube rack in the rear. From behind one of them, he could swear he saw the blur of a red 1957 Chevrolet pickup truck, streaking east on the crossroad.

CHAPTER 22

Claybourne called her again the next day. "After our last conversation, Virginia, I certainly got the message: you were more than just a bit fearful and still very angry. I slept on it and realized you had every right. You knew from the beginning that you'd have to be salacious at times, er, ah, hospitable, if you will; that you would attend to many … ah … female oriented administrative duties. You understood we might see impediments to our progress, risks of arrest, trial and conviction, but, I must admit, neither your father nor I ever suggested ah, taking someone out, might be among our responsibilities. I sensed your infuriation at that thought. Am I correct?"

She found his demeanor unusual, a bit too solicitous, almost fox-like. He spoke too smoothly, in part, from the lingering after effects of too much scotch, whiskey in the hotel bar the night before, but with clear designs to placate her, as well.

Claybourne knew he had to be careful with Virginia. It became a new and top priority, to curtail her threats. General Blakes could not be included in their disruptive personal affairs. Fearfully, Claybourne pondered the wrath of his former superior's potential for retaliation while Virginia continued where she left off. Still perturbed, she tore into him without relent.

Christ, I don't need her old man on my case, Claybourne mused. *No sir, not now. He'd find me in the Bahamas in no time. He knows of my boat and … and, he knows … God, I've made a mistake, telling him of the offer I made on the house. I thought I could hide in George Town, get a slip for* Miss Mahi, *and live my life, fishing, boating, and basking. No chance! Hell, he'd have an Intel thug waiting at the American Eagle ramp, when I got off the plane. Exuma International Airport would be my last appearance on this earth. It would be far easier to take me out in the Caribbean, than at home.*

He'd probably note my death as a "tragic diving accident," my remains, naught but cheap feed for those hungry reef sharks. It would not likely get past the small, local TV news. Blakes is high man in our food chain and always gets what he wants. I can't tangle with the bastard, and I cannot mess up with his daughter. It's become too complex. Virginia's the love of his life. Stunned with the reality of his neck in a noose, he trembled in a moment of regret, from the mix of business with pleasure. Claybourne unconsciously uttered aloud, "You filthy little gutter snipe; you're. ..." The dangerous slip erupted from deep within his soul.

"Homer, what did you say? I'm a little what? Why were you so quiet? I thought you hung up on me."

Startled, he fast swallowed his words, apologized, and went forth with more appeasement. It would have to work. Blakes could not hear of his abusiveness, and he knew there was no other way to define the recent liberties he took with Virginia. "Ginny, I want us to go the Bahamas, together. You loved the Caribbean last time, and George Town is even better. It's so ... so out of the way. Life's quite simple by comparison.

"When *Operation Eastern Star* is concluded, escrow on my place at the beach will close. We'll have permanent help; we'll play, play, and play. You'll have to trust that I've not been myself lately. The stress has pulled me apart, the only reason I have been so unpredictable, and apparently uncaring.

"Please listen to me," he blabbered on, "do I have to drop down and beg?"

She interrupted several times to remind him of his violent problem solution methods.

"OK, I'm aware of what you said. I wouldn't have called you to talk if I weren't remorseful." *How do I put this so she won't impulsively jump to it?* "Now, now; there's no need for Rodmend to be brought into our recent differences. No reason at all, is there? Can't we work out the little squabbles we've had, and resolve them ourselves? We could spend the hurricane season back home in Virginia if you wished." He felt himself melting. "You'd have the horses. We both love Arlington. I'll keep the farm. Or we could stay in Michigan for the summer? It's such a beautiful place there by the river. If we pooled our new resources, we could enjoy the luxury of all three."

Virginia looked around the *cul-de-sac* and at the dense forest beyond—from her perch on the double chaise lounge—soon to be shaded from mid-day heat by sheltering maples at the edge of the bluff. While cool that morning, she eagerly sapped energy from the low, early sun on her exposed body. Nude, but for the straw hat she wore, she lay faced to the east, toward the dirt path.

Claybourne's platitudes nearly shut out, she fantasized Mike's Suburban rocking over the last ruts, into the clearing. *I'd tear him up today…make him well aware of his age, and how different a woman of my years can behave with such deep cravings. Though, he did put me through some paces I didn't expect.*

"C'mon, Virginia, speak to me. Don't be so stubborn and please, try to understand my own distaste for the way I've behaved. I cannot go on without you. I am deeply in love with my Ginny. I have a little something for you, too, which I bought in Dallas. I think you'll like it … a … them, actually."

That lightened her up. She playfully asked, "What is it? What are they?" Laughing for a change, she inquired again, "Just tell me what store, where you bought them. I'll wait for the rest until you're home." He did have a way with her. She knew how easily she could be manipulated. Was it another diamond, maybe a sapphire? She liked them both.

"All right, all right, I've listened to your promises, and I'm glad you'll be back soon, but I need more than feeble assurances, proof this frightening trend can be reversed, that it won't worsen with time. That can't happen, Homer. There's no future to such psycho conduct, not with me, or any woman, I should think."

"Ginny, I assure you, things will be different when I return. Within two weeks we'll be millionaires many times over, and it's all cash, My

Dear. No taxes to pay, it's all ours. I don't deserve the break, and I hope you'll give it to me. I've had a week to think on this. You snapped me out of it during our last conversation."

"Then, stop thinking you're free to simply eliminate people who get in your way. You already spoke of that. Do not entertain the idea that we can operate as if we're Mafia or the C.I.A. My life and my father's life will not work like that, not even once. Is that understood?"

"Yes, yes, understood; sure it is. We will use … er … a … other … ah methods, scare tactics, particularly if these men are as uninvolved and peripheral as you say. That's probably all we'll need to do: forever frighten them from the place, and our section of the river. We can talk about that when I get home. In the meantime, get the other fellow's name and address. That's critical. Your father would want to know that. I can tell you right now."

Claybourne kept the rest of his thoughts to himself. *Hell, Blakes would take them out immediately—in a heartbeat—given half the chance. How many times has he done that before, beneath the drapes of the military? I couldn't count the bodies that have floated down one river or the other, unfortunate souls, at the behest of your father; just for minor mix-ups with that crafty man.*

"Just … let's keep Rod out of it," Claybourne then said, "trust me; there will be no orders for anyone to be killed. Roughed up? OK, maybe. We'll see about that. Can you wait until I'm home? Please Ginny? Would you?"

She held the phone away from her ear as he spoke his last words, and grimaced angrily. Virginia felt better with his contrition but, deep down, she knew he was not a man to be beaten. "Watch out when he gets the money. Watch out, big time," she said aloud. She pushed the disconnect button, relieved she'd have to hear no more of his desperate verbal massages, at least for several days.

Adrift in a relaxing morning nap after a final sip from the small goblet of California Chardonnay she nursed, Virginia immersed herself in pleasurable daydreams of horses. She missed the beautiful trails at home—tunnels almost—beneath overhanging trees, along mile after mile of white rail pasture fences. *Laser*, her favorite riding horse, a retired dark bay thoroughbred, dominated the brilliant imagery that pervaded for nearly two hours until she awoke with a start. The gate alarm sounded its loud report from the speaker beneath the barn eave.

Virginia rushed to the house and, excited with her suspicion, confirmed Mike's entry on the surveillance video screen. "It's him." She stopped herself in the run upstairs for clothing. Paused instead, before the mirror, she brushed her hair, tied it back tightly with a mauve silk scarf, applied fresh lipstick, and retreated to the soft chaise beneath the tree. Her wrists still bore the scent of orange blossoms, vestiges of perfume she applied after the early shower she took following breakfast. Feigning sleep, she lay still until breathing returned to normal. Anxiously, she awaited the man whose smiles and gentle touches filled lighthearted fancies in the final minutes of her morning siesta.

Tingled with delight, as the black Suburban rambled around the last turn and skidded to a stop by the main barn door, Virginia maintained her supine position, hands clasped across her stomach, all but her navel openly exhibited for Mike's benefit. The dogs followed after him, and ravenously devoured the chunks of meat he dispensed. As before, he gave the first and largest piece to Ace, the dominant male. "Not so much as a whimper from the three of them," Mike quipped, as he shuffled toward the chaise.

The animals seemed a bit too friendly, considering the one introduction she knew about. Virginia stretched out her arms and yawned, opened her eyes and looked dreamy with the luscious smile she wore. Then she thrust forth that same laugh, the one that captivated him before … Meg's contagious titter. He loved it for nearly half a century.

"Hello there," he almost whispered. He leaned over her with more bravado than he thought possible. "I say hello. You are gorgeous, no, beyond belief, just laying there, nothing on but your sexy grin, and that sweet perfume." He inhaled deeply, planted kisses across her forehead, around her left ear, and beneath her chin. Eyes closed, he found her cool lips, parted and waiting, while hungrily, he caressed her torso. Virginia was not shy. She pulled his hands to her hips and brought them together where her anxiousness waited. Little more stimulation was needed before she rose above the bluff, into the trees, above their lofty tops and into the lingering scuds of dawn's overcast.

Mike was above her when eyes opened and his mind, too, returned to ground level once again, starved for breath, in synchrony with his pounding pulse. Less respite than she counted on, he soon settled down with the weight of his body, to induce into action again, her untiring source of pleasure. She gasped, almost desperately, and, expended past her usual capabilities, begged for mercy and acceded to defeat as if scripted. They laughed, kissed profusely, and slept in the merciful buds of toasting shade until mid-afternoon.

CHAPTER 23

"Say there," Virginia said quite unexpectedly, and brought Mike to his senses. Hardly aware of his unclothed state, he arose with a start, and rested his head on one elbow. "You'd think Mister Mike was a regular here at Claybourne Farms, the way the doggies went to you.

"They aren't near as playful with the carpenters or the plumber. They've all been here many times. Even the painters who worked daily for several weeks, weren't given such respect. Ace didn't act that way. Kind of curious, knowing them as I do."

Mike blushed, but maintained a perfect poker face just the same. He felt his forehead turn warm. A good liar he was not, and he knew it. Without stammer, though, he took a breath, gathered his wits, and replied, "Sure helps when a hungry mouth is stuffed with good venison. Nothing quite like it for a doggie. It's the gamey taste, I guess." Practically passed out from his near flub, he curdled when he almost said, "It worked so well last time I was here. ..." *That, stupid, was when we picked the lock, helped ourselves to the shack's interior. How close could I have come to such a grave error? I'm simply too darned honest for deceit.* "I fed them while ... er ... getting ... a ... out of the car." He tried to close the spaces between his words. "Brought a whole bag full of the stuff—frozen since winter before last. My two retrievers love it. Gave the big piece to Ace and smaller ones to the others, who watch his every move. Settled right down. Yessir! Nothing like the lure of raw deer for a hungry hound."

Chuckling with his cleverness and sensitivity to the animals, she brought him close, grasped his shoulders and longingly looked into his eyes. Virginia assured that the dogs would be getting much better acquainted with him in the future, if she had her way about it.

Then, with earnest desire to convey her concerns, yet with needed restraint, she issued a warning shot that came as no surprise. "At this point, Mike, you should know; there … there … ah … may be potential danger. You could be at great risk, if you come here again. I invited you, I know; but as I thought about it, the idea was too selfish, too inconsiderate of your safety. My boy friend, the general—Homer, would hardly be a sport about it. You've seen his temper. Merely for trespassing, he might have killed you and your friend. What's his name?"

Mike almost said, "Wayne," before catching the word in the back of his throat. "Jim, Slim Jim, I call him."

"What's his last name? Even yours, I don't know yet and look at us—two nudists—baking in the Michigan sun together, wrapped like octopuses. I don't even know your last name."

"Eckert," he lied. "E-c-k-e-r-t." He spelled it out for her and for himself, so he would not forget. "Mike Eckert. Now you know. My buddy, Jim's last name is Medlow, he's from down in Lansing and doesn't get up here much." *Where did I get those names? Never heard of them. How the devil will I remember? I have no choice. I'll say them repeatedly in my mind, whenever there's a blank in conversation. Just can't forget. If she remembers, asks me later, I could be doomed.*

"That's it, then, Mike Eckert, a nice name. A good man, and a real man, I can plainly see." He could tell she withdrew. She pulled her knees to her chest, tipped her head and gazed westward toward the overhanging cedar and the bluff beyond. "Tell me, Mike; have you ever struck a woman, your wife, perhaps, or another, any time in your life?" Her eyes turned to his, and they penetrated deeply for the slightest hesitation in his reply.

This is easy. No lies, no stories, no fabrications needed here. "I assure you, no. My daddy—Pop, I called him mostly—told me at a very tender age that if I ever struck a woman, he'd hunt me down like a criminal, and make me pay for it. That warning came when I made the mistake of hitting my sister, from across the dinner table. She tattled on my brother and me for going fishing at the river mouth. We were to baby sit for the afternoon and were told not to leave the yard. In a jiffy, though, soon as Pop and Momma took off, we snuck away like escaped convicts.

"We didn't say we were going, fished for two hours, and returned to find Sis on the back porch; sobbed uncontrollably, she did. It wasn't a pretty scene. Thought we regained her confidence until after dinner, and then she spilled it. I got a lickin' like I never received again, mostly for smacking her on the arm when she broke the story. Believe me, Pop's words never left. Nope, never struck a woman and, certainly, not my Meg. Forty years, we were partners, through thick and thin, too, at times; but never did I lay a hand on the woman.

"Any man who would strike a lady, no matter her make-up, should be horsewhipped, tarred, feathered, and sent out of town on a rail. That's from Pop, too, and I believe it, as though the words were mine. Why? Why do you ask?" *I know full well, why. That crazy general hits you as if you're a cloth doll, the sonofa. ...*

Mike nearly spoke aloud. *Have to control myself, can't be too careful.* His jaw clenched tightly, to hold back what he thought. "Why do you ask? Is the general doing that to you? Is he?" Mike asked as if he didn't know. Tell me. Does that man hit you? Is he physically abusive in any way?" *Maybe I can distract her from inquiries about my brother. Why the heck did I have to mention I even had a brother? She's likely to ask his name. That could spell trouble.*

Virginia remained mute at first. Mike felt tears drop to his shoulder. She trembled, whimpered, and fell into a deep, and disturbing cry. Cradled in his arms, he rocked her limp body until she regained her faculties and tentatively replied. "Yes, to be honest, he's recently become careless with his hands and mouth. We spent more than a year together— never a problem—but I'm afraid he has lost control. He'll swear at me, threaten me, even put a knife to my throat once, before he left, when he ... that was just before he left. He wielded his hunting knife, grabbed my hair, pulled me to the floor, and really hurt me several times. Slapped me real hard." Again she cried and related details, but never alluded to the underlying reasons Claybourne rationalized the behaviors.

"He can be so damned mean, yet kind, too. Much of the time he is decent, but when he angers, I want out. I can't keep exposing myself to the ups and terrible downs. I've never been treated that way, by anyone. My father never spanked me, not in my entire upbringing. I needed it at times, but, much as he wanted, he never put a hand to me. My father has his problems. He is a good man, though not without his own streaks of larceny, I'm afraid." She withdrew the near-empty bottle from the ice bucket and filled her glass with the last of the wine. Her chatter loosened as she felt its effects.

"My father and Homer, close friends in the Army, stuck together throughout their careers. Father helped Homer gain his rank, more than once bailed him out of a desperate pinch. They just missed each other at West Point, five years apart or so, they were; but they've managed to serve in the same units throughout most of their careers. The Pentagon was their last duty assignment. For quite a few years they worked on anti-missile defense systems. Whoops, I need to shut up…not supposed to speak of that." She grinned, nuzzled close to Mike, and thanked him for his empathy. "Just giving a listen is so important for men. It's a gift they can give to a woman they care about. Why don't more males handle a lady's upset as you just did for me? How kind you were.

"I must warn you and your friend, Jim. Can't say why, but you shouldn't drive, uninvited, on the property again. Homer considers this land private, and is likely to take some kind of armed action, should he see you as he did before. If he drove in and there's your Suburban, it might not be a pretty sight. I'm afraid—knowing how he's reacted to me—what he might do if he saw you here."

"I hoped for exactly what happened out here today, but I've been dreaming, too, of some after-dusk fishing." Mike pointed affectionately to the big pool. "Brought all my gear, some for you, if you want to try. I've waders, a creel, vest, the whole bit, even a mosquito net for your face. Meg always hated the bugs around dark. Drove her nuts, they did."

"Sure, why not? He's gone for now. It's safe and you're here. Why not? Let me fix some dinner, and we'll dress for the occasion, much as I hate to put on clothes. She stood up, paused with a wry grin for his admiring stare, and walked like a model, crossing one foot before the other, in a slow and delicate prance to the porch.

Upstream from the bend, Virginia received her first lesson. Mike avoided disturbance to the big pool with practice casts, until the caddis flies emerged. He explained the need to sneak on all fours to the river's edge when casting in close, coaxed her into the waist deep, faster water, and handed her age-old caveats while she followed. "Shuffle cautiously on the bottom and never step blindly. Just shuffle, to avoid holes or the occasional sunken snag. You'll feel them that way. Swim toward a bank or downstream if caught in the swift current, but never up river." Fatigue in the cold water, loaded heavily with waders and gear, he explained, was an open invitation to drowning.

"Never trust the bottom where you've walked without incident before. It can change in just minutes. Bear your weight down slowly and if the foot sucks in, back out, and do it fast. Quicksand patches are found anywhere on this bottom," he continued, when he sensed her keen interest. "You look too gorgeous for words in that outfit, hardly like the fishermen I know. They have whiskers and they're ugly as bulldogs."

She held his elbow tenaciously, and admired the ease with which he cast the tiny fly. Four back swings, it flew past the river's center, and popped about as live ones did, when Mike jerked the pole tip with almost imperceptible wrist movement. "Look, a fish jumped," she came close to screaming in excitement, "right at your fly."

"Another lesson, Virginia," Mike whispered with slight sarcasm, though softly and patiently. "We never yell on the river. The big ones down deep in the pools: they feel the vibes of a twig snap or any strange sound, and they'll know. Just remember to whisper. The smarties won't bite unless the river feels right to them. Very sensitive, those big old brownies."

Embarrassed, she hugged his shoulder just the same.

Mike retrieved his line, brought in the small fish, when she spotted the three animals. "Oh, look," she called, at shriek volume once again, "a mother beaver and two little beaver puppies, not far from me. They're beautiful, never seen them in the wild." Her excited words bounced through the forest.

"You're yelling again," Mike reminded Virginia, astounded, though inwardly pleased with her excitement. "Sure, there are lots of them around here. That's an active beaver dam just upstream and another down past the fallen tree. All that debris is their work product. River's too deep here, though. They wasted lots of time. Just look at all the trees they felled, to try and build the dern thing." The little water animals paddled slowly with their broad tails, only their noses and ears above the surface, made it seem easy to buck the force of the river.

"They were down there in the grove of fresh saplings, gnawing new bark, their favorite food. Probably going home to do some work on the dam ... mostly nocturnal."

Mike remembered some of the words to a poem he wrote, to chronicle an evening just like this—years behind, but nearby, on the Au Sable. He recited without hesitation, while he wrestled with the trout:

> Crouched beneath the trembling pines,
> Dusted softly with powder from their faces,
> The river's magnetized my mind.
> Thoughts fall like summer rain
> And settle in from many places.
>
> From verdant bank with grassy beard,
> Tumbling toward a swift embrace,
> A bullfrog croaks, slicing night,
> Searching for its mate this eve,
> Swims the current for a taste.

Songbirds fill the sleepy glade,
With throaty bluster, shrill refrain,
Twill to one another from the birches,
Blinded by the velvet dark.
A whisper comes from velvet rain.

Fireflies dance to blend the dusk,
And bejewel the inky deep below.
I listen; hear a distant splash
And, from the sullen dark appears,
A beaver and her pups on sentinel patrol.

The eldest lead the stalwart troops,
Without a sound they came,
Upstream so softly, yet so fast,
Determined in the stream they passed,
To let us watch their evening game.

"Mike, you wrote that? Did you? How perfect. You must have seen those little critters many times to write a poem about them. I've done some writing too, but Homer, well, he's not into poetry, I'm afraid. Sometime, I'll read a few to you, maybe. Oh, he's a small fry," she laughed as Mike netted the pan-sized brown. "Wouldn't make much of a meal."

Mike shook his head, held it in the water until sure it would swim, and gently returned the iridescent fingerling. "Bye, little guy. See you in a few years, I suppose." He looked plaintively at Virginia and went on, over filled with sentiment.

"Yes, I suppose I'll see you, too, depending on how General Claybourne and our laws might resolve the privacy he's tried to create here." *Privacy, my rear end. This river's my last hurrah. I'll be here every year until I die, to fish these pools. Yes, it will be the very last thing I do.*

CHAPTER 24

———— ◆◆◆ ————

Two o'clock on a damp, drizzly morning, the clanging wigwag signal, one of its red-flashing warning lights out, needlessly labored at the rail crossing. At that hour, there was no traffic. The lone vehicle stopped at the otherwise deserted intersection, a battered white 1988 Ford van, enshrouded in plumes of its own misty-white exhaust, blushed a soft rosy red when its red light flashed with each swing of the oscillating disc.

The van driver, a Mexican national who carried U. S. Army Ranger identification, lit a cigar while his two home country *compadres*, similarly credentialed, followed less than an hour behind. Each man drove a brand new Kenworth ten-wheel tractor. Neither pulled semi-trailers. Highly trained in Patriot Missile operations, the threesome spent several frenetic weeks, while they tested, repaired and reconditioned missiles and support equipment in a sweltering warehouse, on the outskirts of Waco, Texas. They beat their deadline by nearly two days, and earned a bonus of five thousand dollars for their extra efforts.

Before loading, the crates were painted and re-marked to indicate they contained outdoor recreation equipment components. Though well camouflaged with the benign sounding labels, General Claybourne hedged even further against possible detection at the many state border crossings they would pass along the way to Michigan. Eliminating that risk, the crates were placed on two semi-trailers and, in turn, piggybacked on a Mid-West Railways flatcar, number BCT-599876. It rolled forty-ninth in line, behind three locomotives that slowly nudged the long train in the last leg of its northeastward journey.

The flatcar, soon to be sidetracked on the short spur at Bancroft, Michigan, a very small town with a seldom-used depot, not far off Highway 69, and less than twenty-five miles from Flint. Claybourne wisely arranged offloading at Bancroft, before the train reached its final destination in the big city, to avoid unwanted scrutiny. Soon to overtake the freight train, the two tractors were set to tow the trailers—over discreet back roads for the remainder of the trip to Claybourne's barn— to be stored there until the Palestinians took possession.

Solario Mendez, the Ford van driver, exercised extreme care to adhere closely to the train's schedule. He stopped to rest where it stopped for loading or car release, and he drove continually when the train did not pause. How many times, he wondered, did he wait at a country crossing to watch the train speed past, simply to assure Claybourne via a cell phone text, that the car with his precious load, remained intact? Hundreds, maybe more, he was sure. This time, outside of Bancroft, and eastbound on East Winegar Road, he greedily inhaled a dose of acrid cigar smoke, and checked the detailed schedule, confident he would soon see the freight train pass a stop again.

Yes, we're just west of the Looking Glass River, he assured himself. The railroad route map confirmed the time and location. He saw the light of an approaching locomotive and could tell by the distinctive blast of the horn, that it was his train. So close he was to the track, the van shook.

He felt proud; hand picked by General Claybourne, despite the nefarious services he performed. The general watched him in many a battle situation, and considered him among the best of field soldiers with whom he worked. Cool-headed under the worst of conditions, calculating, and lethal with his hands, firearms, a knife, or explosives, Mendez had all the qualities for the job at hand.

Dark-eyed, with a low, rippled forehead, he conveyed a look of anger and innate meanness that evoked fear in those who opposed, or served with him.

The lifer soldier, who tried hard to live up to such perceptions, with his heroics and unending stealth, was an unashamed braggart of many kills. He and his two men, also U.S. Government-trained killers with comparable backgrounds, were brought on to assure protection of the missiles until takeover time, to handle any "personnel situations" that required their attentions. They would also serve as Claybourne's bodyguards in case of funny business with the Arabs.

Mendez brought a .45 automatic, his own from active army days, with which he was a crack shot and for which he had a concealed and carry permit. Parts for two dissembled thirty-caliber machine guns, about one third of them, he secured for the trip, behind wood paneling in the rear of his van. The remaining components were equally split between the two tractors. Should one of the vehicles be searched for any reason, possession of a complete unit could never be assumed.

Twenty kilograms of C-4 plastic explosive in the back of the Ford, he masqueraded within two hollowed out, eight-inch diameter pine logs, each about three feet long. Bundled in the midst of a stack of similar pieces of "firewood," he would say he carried the logs for camping along the way. No one knew what the general planned to do with the highly destructive substitute for dynamite. Claybourne thought of every possible contingency; the most finite, if not ridiculous details. Consequently, Mendez felt secure that he and his men operated well within their practiced ability parameters, considering the liberal monetary returns they were promised.

So this is Bancroft! This is the one horse town he described to us, all right.

Reminds me of old Mexico ... one gas station, one market, one of everything. He laughed when he passed the sign at the outskirts. *Population: five hundred ninety four.* "What the hell do they do here, for fun, or work? No bars. No open bars anyway," he said, as he passed a small club called the Wolverine's Den on the same piece of property as the Grand River Family Motel.

"Sure could use a cold beer. We have to keep going, though, until we get the trailers off-loaded. There's the spur; the railcar's there. *Sangre de Cristo!* "Not a soul around. Where the hell's the tow motor? *Que paso?* It's as dark as a Cambodian jungle trail out there." He looked at his watch and sized up the scene. "Nearly four o'clock, my tractors are due any time; so is the railroad crew from Flint. The flatcar will have to be pulled or pushed to the loading dock, through that switch. The tractors will back up the ramp; we'll hook up, and be ready for the highway before dawn. I have to be out of the city before then, and don't want to use this."

He patted the semi-automatic beneath his belt, when he heard the roar of engines from behind. Crouched down in the seat, he peered back, in the side mirror. "Quintano, Miguel; they're here. Damned if they didn't find the place, too." *Homer did everything but drive us here. Global positioning and all; how could we miss? It was one hell of a lot easier than finding our way across the spreading arteries of the Mekong Delta.* "Now, that was navigation," he proclaimed when the first unit pulled to a stop alongside. "*Amigo,*" Mendez called, "*esta bien? Su viejo, es bueno?*"

"Sure, hell yes; the trip was great fun," Quintan Lopez responded with evident sarcasm and a sneer. He yawned deeply, before he continued. "It's been a long drive, a long time, too, since this segment began. We'll be ready for the sleepers."

"*Sus siestas*! Catch your catnaps while you can, *compadres;* we'll have to be off with our loads the minute the tow motor arrives and we can hook up the rigs. It's due real soon."

A shrill horn awakened Mendez from a light doze. He rubbed his eyes to recover from the twenty-minute rest, and saw the bright oscillating headlight of a diesel-powered handcar approach on the track from the east. It squeaked to a stop at the spur's switch. The engineer leaned on the stubborn manual lever, opened the switch, and continued toward the stopped flatcar. Mendez and his men waited in dark shadows nearby. One waved a flashlight.

"Ya want that thing over to the ramp, do ya? Hell, do ya knows what this overtime costs? More'n two hundred an hour per man." There were three of them. All wore blue and reflective white striped jackets in spite of the night's warmth, having run in open air from the train yards in Flint. They pushed the flat car to the butt of the spur, bumped it against the loading platform and set the brakes.

"That figures about six hundred an hour for all of you, eh?" Mendez confirmed, part of the agreement between your boss and mine. Why should we give a damn, eh?"

"Yup, guess we shouldn't care, so long as you don't," the foreman said, as Lopez backed a tractor up the dark ramp, connected with the first trailer and nudged it onto the dock. "Your paperwork … let's get formalities behind us, afore we pull the cargo away. I need a copy of the new Bill of Lading. Here's yours from the rail trip," he went on and handed perplexed Mendez a sheaf of originals and carbons.

Claybourne told Mendez in advance, that the documentation he had, all of it, perfectly forged, would get the goods past police checks or through any weigh or state border stations. The railroad foreman, however, asked Mendez to produce something he didn't have, and he didn't like being placed on the spot. He decided to get tough and bluff his way through. *Claybourne would do it loud and to the point, so why not us,* he mused.

"Why the hell," Mendez yelped angrily. He contorted his face into the frightful look that scared most people, "why you ask me for irrelevant papers, useless information, at four in the morning in a God forsaken spot like Bancroft? You don't need papers, I don't have. You're not getting any. Now, move that poor excuse of a switch engine out of the way."

The second tractor stopped backing when its fifth wheel slipped under the remaining trailer and locked. "If you don't like it, bitch to your boss when you get back. I was told to be on my way, and that's what *Senores* Lopez and Rodriguez here; that's exactly what they are going to do." Rodriguez made the connection, and before Mendez finished intimidating the engineer, the completed rig rolled down the ramp to the parking lot. "We have no documents for you, no damned Bill of Lading, no *nada,* and we're leaving. Any objections?" He wielded the tire iron he kept beneath his front seat, for just such a purpose, and walked in big steps toward the railroad workers as he spoke.

"No ... prob ... problem," the foreman stuttered, "We'll ... a ... jus ... just ... be a headin' east about now." Before Mendez could carry through, the handcar engine whirred, and the machine rumbled into the distance. The railway men never looked back.

"Let's roll the wagons, *amigos. Nos vamos? Vamanos, al norte!* We have our instructions. We'll stop only if or when I say so, depending on progress. We do our job on this part and there's another bonus for us to count. We'll all go back to Texas with green stuff bulging from our pockets, eh? No toll stations on the remainder of the route; nothing to stop us but the random bored cop. Should be none of them to bother us, so long as we just take it slow and easy. We're sure to be OK, weight-wise, on the smaller bridges and byroads. OK, a*migos*?"

The two trucks, led by the old Ford, headed north on Grand River Road, a fortune waiting to be tapped, battened down inside the two semi-vans they pulled.

CHAPTER 25

———◆◦◆◦◆———

Homer Claybourne stepped off the plane at Flint, after an unexpectedly long stopover in Chicago. As usual, O'Hare was jammed; his plane delayed by more than two hours. Frustrated and a bit tipsy from the four Scotches he downed to ease tensions, his mood topped surly. A trying week; everyone in the procurement process—paid, sworn to silence, and warned severely of repercussions if they ever talked—would forever respect their agreements. In each case, threats of death or violence were made clear, directly by Mendez and Claybourne, not to threaten the potentially deceitful servicemen themselves; but to imply fates worse than death, for their family members, children, even friends; if they had no family. Mendez's tough guy infamy, and his reputation for relentlessness, left no doubt as to whether Claybourne's threats would be a reality, for any infraction.

Before leaving Texas the general felt confident that silence and secrecy would never be a problem. Each participant took more than seriously, how their involvement could never be traced to the masterminds, Claybourne and Blakes. "Should you ever talk, you would incriminate yourself, with no way out," Claybourne repeated to each participant until blue in the face. Once told the horrid details, his cohorts found themselves regretful of the greed that initially prompted their participation.

Too late to withdraw, they were not informed of the snapping jaws of the larcenous general's trap, until services were already rendered, and the goods were off base. Claybourne knew how the army worked and, more importantly, he understood and invoked the workings of the opportunistic and rapacious human mind. In every case, hunger for big money seriously overran logic and loyalty. He counted on that as a maxim for each relationship established to carry out the escapade.

7:00 AM: just after dawn, Claybourne left the top-level of the airport parking lot. Out of habit, long years of suspicion, because of his all-to-common below-the-board activities, and his past high profile at the Pentagon, he carelessly checked beneath the car for anything abnormal. Dress clothes stopped him from kneeling down to look behind the front cross member, however, where the Alert Investigations beeper silently repeated the Morse Code letter "S," *dit-dit-dit,* every fifteen seconds.

A similar symphony of inaudible dots came from Claybourne Farms. Early that very morning, Wayne successfully planted a transmitter unit behind the rear frame cross member on the red 1957 Chevrolet pickup. The dogs, asleep in the cellar, missed his Indian-quiet stalking, up the bluff from the river, then across the dry leaf-strewn *cul-de-sac,* and over the gravel surface to the parked truck.

Though graced with luck, considering the high risk of exposure, Wayne shook with fear, as he worked with no back-up cover. His only remaining task, after so many hours of surveillance almost proved futile. Virginia's absence until after midnight required a prolonged stay at his observation position across the river. Wayne sensed her restlessness while he watched the shack. Bedroom lights went off shortly after her return, but they went on and off four more times over the next two hours. Assuming she had trouble sleeping when he finally saw activity in the kitchen, he dozed off until almost three o'clock, to allow plenty of time for her to settle, and finally, to complete his task.

"The evening went perfectly, Wayne," Mike related cheerily. "You couldn't have done it up any prettier than I did. I was so pleased with myself, yes, very pleased. She, Virginia, this woman, could be a Goddess, and she enjoyed the fishing, too. I never imagined such unfettered inhibition, so little concern for modesty, showing herself to me, everything she's got, and no shame at all. Why are we taught that it's so wrong? Meg wasn't comfortable like that, and neither was I, for that matter. How long has it been since you and Nell … well, don't look at me that way … really … how long?"

"Let's just say, too long, Brother. Hell, what married couple, twenty years or more together, acts that way, I'm sure, you're thinking? Not many," Wayne said, while he blushed with embarrassment. You don't want the details, thank you."

"She's probably had too much practice, as you said before," Mike replied. Call me naiive … well deserved, I know. I can tell by the facetious look on your jealous face. I get it; you don't approve. You'll never be able to hide that."

Paul Bunyan Café was crowded at noon. Dead tired from his late night exploits at the shack, Wayne guzzled cup after cup of their trademarked, bitter and hair-curling-strong coffee. He sat across the red plastic laminate table from his brother and lazily leaned on his forearms. His large right hand encircled the cup as if it might jump. He looked cautiously toward the front window as he spoke; he did not wish the conversation overheard. "Get yourself together, Mike. I should say, get that thick skull in line and start thinking with your brain, not that hot spot below your belt, for a change.

"I hate to say it, Brother," Wayne went on, "but the girl has been with who knows who, in her exploits with Arabs, and God only knows who else, before them. That's more than scary. You've overlooked the basics: her character flaws. Too much love in those lonely eyes of yours. Get rid of the crazy notion that she's good for you or that you're good for her. Doesn't need ya, Mike; really don't need your help, not a tinker's damn, I'd wager.

"Remember Pop's admonitions, the ones he always gave us when we started out with a new girl? First date: he wanted to know all about her, didn't he?"

"First date?" Mike retorted, "I pretty near only had one first date, never had a new girlfriend. It was always Meg, and she could do no wrong by Pop. She certainly was. …" Mike stopped and looked forlornly at his empty plate. "She was Pop's idea of perfection, so I never got the warnings, the funny character lectures he bestowed on you. Seemed so old fashioned to us at the time, so irrelevant, but you've apparently never forgotten the talks. It was always Wayne who got the little heart-to-hearts about character, what with your rather liberal standards in the selection of females in those days."

Wayne showed some regret but a tinge of pride, too, when he mused over his innumerable conquests, as a young and single suitor. He shook his head in deliberation, laughed, and acknowledged that he chose some of his temporaries for reasons other than brains and loyalty. "Well, I gets some experiences where I gets 'em, didn't I? That's exactly where I'm coming from. I've a much, er, deeper background than you, than my older but less-than-wise brother has accumulated. He spent his life, from puberty to where he is now, with one woman, for Christ's sake."

Wayne went on with his unsolicited reflections. "The old man said that going to the right church was most important. Good Catholics, they'd have to be, or else. That proved their worth, and it didn't matter from there so very much. If he saw the damsel in Mass or I could vouch for the Catholic Church she attended, he was OK with it, remember?

"If the poor thing was of some fundamental background though, I'd never hear the last of it. 'Hell, fire and brimstone to 'em,' Pop would say, 'if dese damned off-the-wall religions just preach damnation they say we face, not the goodness that's available to those with contrition in dere hearts. No Sonny, ya doan wanna lock yourself up for life with a woman who doesn't see that,' he would say, and shake his finger in my face."

"Pop worried, too," Mike responded, "about the ones who weren't local, right there from Tawas, as if that spelled any kind of quality. When you'd slip out of town for a date, he stayed up late to talk when you got home. He always applied Mama's high standards as the measure of character we were to use. 'She get good grades? Her father and mother still together? Her daddy work in Flint or Detroit?' "He didn't like the idea of folks laboring at the auto assembly plants, thought the work too sporadic and didn't much care for unions.

"What a father's occupation had to do with a daughter's character, only Pop knew. He brought it up often enough that I was embarrassed, even as an adult, to tell him that day I moved out and got my first job at General Motors. I hated that moment," Mike continued, and finished his dessert.

"Pie was great today, Ina, unusually good. Did you make it instead of that weird night cook with the bad attitude?"

"All right, boys, no more insults to our chef ... you finished?" the waitress replied, while she swept crumbs from the table with a coffee stained rag. "Thought I might see you fellers this weekend. Did you cross paths with that obnoxious southerner again, the one who bought the Morris place?"

Mike answered as if he forgot about Claybourne. "Nope, haven't tangled with him and don't want to; do we Wayne?" Wayne nodded briefly but remained pan-faced and mute.

"Heard from Mister Shanks," she said. "He owns the lawnmower shop, you know, the one on fifty five, out east. His daughter works in surgery at Grayling Hospital. They live outside Mio; heard rumbles about shooting on the river. Put two and two together, when Gwinn, his daughter, tells him about a guy they treated with a gunshot wound in the armpit. Turns out it's this former army man, a retired officer— yep, the very jerk we had in the restaurant. He hasn't been back since he came in to ask about you, but the girl stops by at times, by herself. I wonder how he got shot?"

Increasingly uncomfortable, Mike began to fidget, and winked at Wayne that it was time to go. *Cripes, that's all I need, to meet up with Virginia in here some day. Sure don't want anyone thinking we're acquainted. Be too easy for the general to hear about it. Probably should avoid the place, for a time, anyway.*

Their conversation continued after Ina sauntered away to tend to other patrons. Wayne added, "Grades were important, too. The old man always asked about them when we brought 'em home, 'Well, Missy; so how ya do in school?' He'd inevitably get to the subject of work, too. Speaking of which, what's this Virginia do. Does she have an occupat. …?"

"Sure as heck does," Mike cracked before Wayne could finish. "She spent years as the head scrub nurse; she's an RN, with one of the most prominent heart teams in Arlington, the ones politicians and top military people go to for complex operations: bypasses, transplants, new valves, and so forth. She quit, though, when Claybourne suggested they move north."

"Apparently more interested in Patriot Missiles than surgeries, heh? Speaking further of character," Wayne persisted, "what the hell's she doing—making it with you, when she's in some sort of relationship with the general, stupid as that one seems on its face? After all, she's two timin' as fast as she can."

"I can't agree more. That's real frightening, but for some reason, my present standards have allowed me to go with the flow, despite warning signs. Once a cheater, is one always a cheater, or might they learn by their mistakes?" Mike listened anxiously for Wayne's validation.

"Learn? Learn what? They'll only learn if they recognize the error of their ways … when they or someone else gets hurt from it. If a cheater enjoys the experience and no one is hurt, why would they stop? What are they going to learn from that? Seems, says I, that she's in that category, so long as Claybourne doesn't find out about it. It can't be all that fun, though, with that hanging over one's head. She'll come to terms with it and with you, as well. You, the baby, might be thrown out with the bathwater. If Claybourne, on the other hand, gets tossed, whoa boy; I could see him nailing her … yup … beating her to merciful heaven."

Mike cringed at the thought, tightly shut his eyes a moment, and then opened them to comment further. "Jesus Crisp, Wayne! Don't talk like that. He's a frightening man. We both know it! But I'll tell you, if that son of a buck touches her again, he'll answer to me. I'll stop the foolishness." He hesitated a minute and then admitted, "I want the Morris place more than ever and, now, I want her. Is that asking too much for the rest of my life? Do I sound greedy, too?"

"Gheesch, no! You simply sound like a long-time, dedicated husband who's lost his wife—lonely and a bit misdirected, maybe—but not greedy. I want you to get as much from the rest of life that's dished out to you, as much as you possibly can. When I think of being separated from my better half like you've been, I don't know, Mike, just don't know what I'd do. I sure as hell don't hold these exploits again' ya. I really don't, but I do urge caution with this little—I'll go on and say it—this little rattlesnake."

"Snake? She's kind to me, sensitive, lovely, smart, has a figure to beat all, and she seems to like me on top of that. We fished together. She cooked me a wonderful dinner. That and good loving, sure made my night complete. Why shouldn't I fall for her? No snake that I can see."

"Look, we have to plan for Claybourne's return," Wayne countered. "Didn't she suggest today or tomorrow might be the day?" The noon rush ended and the café cleared. Their talk would become more conspicuous. "Let's get out of here and finish plans at the cabin. I've got to get home soon, need to work sometime today and Nell's getting worried."

They retired to Mike's small den at the cabin. Steamy and windless, mosquitoes arrived too early to be outside. They chatted to a background of television, that blared baseball. The Tigers and Indians played. Detroit's Damion Easley struck out with Wickman's fancy pitching.

"Can't that guy ever hit the ball?" Mike asked, distracted briefly from the business at hand.

"He's a New Yorker, with a crummy average. What do ya expect?" They laughed, watched the rest of the inning, and began to brief their schedules for as much surveillance as possible. Timing became most important. If they were going to interest authorities, they had to draw them there, while some of the stolen equipment was visible. That would avert probable cause issues, Don the ranger assured Wayne. It would be that or a warrant, and the chances of the latter at the eleventh hour, they were told, would be slim at best.

"I did speak with Donnie again, Mike. The Forest Service in Washington D.C. confirmed to him that the general has no title to the dirt path that leads to the shack. No claim to it whatsoever, it's all bluff. The gate, too, is an illegality. He didn't apply for a permit and one would not have been issued anyhow. The dirt path is defined in some archive as a public easement into the woods, a former lumber road. That it happens to go to the shack is of no consequence. Don has an order to demolish; all he has to do is nail it to the fence post. They won't need to serve Claybourne personally. I'm thrilled by the news, but Donnie doesn't want trouble now. He won't confront the general yet, and chance curtailment of activity at the shack; especially after I related our recent observations. Claybourne will fume over it, maybe lose his cool somehow. The bastard. We'll get him, though."

"I sure hope he doesn't lose his cool with Virginia. She's very likely to take the brunt of his anger, which means it's necessary for us to go back there, now, tonight, to see what's up. If he's back, we'll watch his every move, and then we're in for more crafty planning."

Wayne's eyes, drooped from the late night before, still looked bloodshot and fatigued. His face had whitened. He dragged his feet in the hike from the car to their observation point on the north riverbank. Mike felt contrastingly keen, while fraught with concern over Virginia's well being. They had the essentials: binoculars, radio receiver to overhear transmissions from the hidden mikes and plenty of hot coffee. "Wayne, look; the Excursion. He's back and the beeper is still working." Wayne crouched down behind shielding underbrush, searched the compound with binoculars while Mike settled on the pad of leaves, and pressed headphones close to his ears. "They're talking; shhh. Says his trip was…

says everything is complete. I quote, 'All the payoffs have been made. Everyone has received special warnings that to talk will invite death to family members.' Cripes! What the devil's he talking about—family members?" He turned to Wayne with a frightened expression. "Says … says … wait a minute. Jesus Crisp, he's saying that the missiles will be here any time. He's going to take his drink out to the river. She's staying in, wants to take a bath, she said. I hear water running. Let me switch to the bug downstairs. Nothing but footsteps, a deep sigh, ice cubes in a glass, and steps again.

"There's the SOB, out the door, going to his car. No, he's headed for the chaise by the maple," Wayne related excitedly, as he continued his observations. "That's where she was flaked out, nude, when I drove in the other day. Little does the general know what we did, right there, exactly where he sat," Mike grinned and gestured helplessly.

"Hey, hey." Wayne said. "His remote phone just rang. He's answering. Damn, we should have done a wiretap, too. Mike, you know how to do that. He's standing up, has his drink, walks back to the house, shakes his head. Wish we knew who the hell it. …"

"Wayne, wait, hold it. We may know. Yes, it's his guys, the drivers with the missiles. Listen up! Claybourne said to Virginia, 'Solario Mendez just called. They had a bit of trouble with one of the trucks. The load's apparently too heavy … transmission heated up. They had to take it slower. I've got to go meet them," he said. Claybourne's going out," Mike continued. "I'll stay here. You follow him with the homing receiver and, when you learn something—where he's going—call me with developments. Then go on home. Get some sleep. You're going to need it and very soon. I have the feeling we'll spend lots more time minding these folks." Mike watched curiously as the general opened the front barn doors. A loud engine crackled. They saw the dirt bike when they hid in the barn, under the tarp and behind the auger snowplow attachment in the corner.

After revving it several times, Claybourne darted into the clearing, spun around on the gravel pavement, and headed into the woods. *He's rolling toward the game trail. Yes, into the trees he goes. The game trail passes through the woods to the power company road. Why? What's he up to? He told Virginia that he was going to meet his men.*

Within a half hour the general returned, on foot this time. To Mike's surprise, he then went straight to his car and left for the gate. "Why the heck did he leave the cycle back in the woods?"

Wayne picked up the beeping. While he waited several hundred yards north of Claybourne's gate, around a bend in the road and just beyond visual range, he noted the signal increased in volume. He slipped down in his seat to avoid notice when the general's Excursion exited onto Old River Road. The sound then diminished and its direction changed more than ten degrees. "He's off to the west. My luck is as good as it gets. Slow and easy; don't get riled up," he reminded himself. Then he saw it, the Excursion, far ahead, rolling west toward town, almost out of sight at the crest of a hill, a quarter mile ahead. Wayne resisted the urge to drive faster. It wouldn't be necessary with the helpful electronic tool on the front seat. He stayed in touch by periodic adjustments of the antenna, and continued onward. Claybourne couldn't lose him if he tried.

He made a turn in the road before the stop sign at the edge of the business district, and spotted the bronze SUV again. It turned left, to the south, its driver oblivious to the tail that followed. Wayne kept in visual contact often enough to validate the direction finder's operation. The signal suddenly weakened. He drove faster, but stayed on smaller side roads. "Why the hell is the general making it so difficult on himself? The main highway would be so much fast. …"

Atop the long uphill grade, his comments were stifled by the view ahead when he began the long descent on the other side. Two tractor-trailer rigs stopped at the foot of the hill, directly ahead, and a white van parked at the shoulder on the opposite side of the road, snared his immediate attention. Claybourne stood next to the panel truck, and spoke with the driver.

Owl-eyed at the sight before him, Wayne nearly swallowed his tongue when his engine sputtered, then sputtered again, coughed and backfired. A harried glance at the instrument panel, and he shrieked, "My God … gas! I forgot to fill the tank this morning."

CHAPTER 26

---◆·◆·◆---

Lack of activity at the shack since Claybourne's departure, dimmed Mike's spirits. Alone, bored with the quiet, he sought a few minutes to look at his thoughts, when the tree limb above him wavered. Its movement captured his attention, too erratic for the slight downstream breeze that barely filled the river basin with cooling night air. His eyes dropped closed. He set the binoculars on the leaves, took some deep breaths, and waited.

"Good evening, Darling," Meg whispered gently and far more solicitously than he could have expected. "Yes, good evening to you. I know I haven't seen fit to connect, to ah, sit in with you. You've been somewhat preoccupied, have you not?"

Embarrassed, Mike withheld immediate comment, no idea how to respond. *I have to watch myself; don't want to sound defensive.* Finally he replied, "I have been busy, really busy with this missile theft monkey business; yes, I have." *I'll try; maybe she hasn't sensed what has been happening.* "Yes Meg, I've missed you terribly. I never stop missing you. I keep working on this fiasco for our benefit, to fulfill our dreams."

"Our dreams?" she questioned in a hostile, chastising tone. "Don't you mean your dreams, Dear? Your own dreams would be a better way of saying it." She stayed quiet for too long. He waited until she went on, "Should I say, too, that we're now talking about her dreams?" Meg clearly referred to Virginia. "Aren't her dreams in this little picture?

"Mike, she's gorgeous, young—you even told Wayne—and her body beats all, I remember you saying. That's quite a compliment to pay a girl you hardly know. You went overboard with the young woman: sex

267

on the bluff, in the living room, with hardly a scruple. My Lord, Mike, can't you get yourself togeth. ...?"

Meg stopped short.

He was startled with the pause and felt a rush of shame creep through his edginess.

"Dear, I am brokenhearted with the sudden infatuation," she went on with some reservation. "This high school gloating is not like you; such a young woman, with no visible character at all—none that I can see, anyway. I'm devastated that I might lose you and to such a spineless little ingrate, no less. I did leave you alone. How can I make you so wrong for trying to heal your sadness, the gaping wounds with which I left you, in the best way you know how at this moment? I cannot do that to you; have no right."

Speechless, assuredly shocked, he was overwhelmed, too, with the generous way she approached her disapproving oversight. It saved a conflagration, one he even planned to face, fully expectant she could appear at any time, to tear into his escapades with Virginia. Even worse, he labored day and night over the degree to which she might have perceived his inner longings for this new woman. His mind filled with Virginia since their first introduction in the mall parking lot. Certainly, there would be no mistaking that, he feared.

Meg spared him the indignation, though, and took full responsibility for the predicament in which he found himself so deeply immersed. She went on with her surprising placations while Mike maintained a quasi watch on things at the shack. Nothing special to see, he turned his full attentions back to Meg. He invited her to continue keeping him company and felt relieved she stayed.

They talked over old times: raising the children, how fast the grandkids grew, the shack, and its ever-present allure. Still holding to his dream with her, he cried inside from the warmth she extended, also for the isolating, cold reality of being alone. Her comforting hands caressed. He forgot himself there at the river and looked down at his perch as he rose swiftly through the trees, and remained somewhere aloft, for how long he did not know. A shivering, ethereal experience with no time dimension, it was one he'd not forget, before his gentle return to the forest floor.

Though exhausted from his perceptions of Meg's unusually aggressive lovemaking, the cell phone vibration broke into his ruminations.

Wayne spoke and he was wound tight. "There I was, Brother, like a field mouse a lookin' over his shoulder at a hawk swooping down. It could have happened. Jasper—it was so damned close—greased through, I did...skin of my teeth." Breathless, Wayne called on his cell phone from a service station, less than a mile from the parked trucks he just passed. "Mike, I swear, my engine dies as I gets to within a hundred feet of them." He continued speaking in panic. "It spluttered some when I tops the hill by the horse ranch down there, south of town. I can't back up the hill, so I goes on down, coasts a bit and I loses power again.

By our mother's sweet eyes, it plum stops right there. I shoves it in neutral, coasts by three mean looking, tough guys, the general, too, and then I tries to start it up. Mercy me, the engine took hold. Must have fed some more fuel on the downhill slope; it fires once more; it did. Yup, it rattled right there and starts to spin. "I slams it in gear and off I went, like a maniac, to the truck stop over on State 33; just makes it before she stops for good. Flat out of gas, runnin' on vapors; the tank—bone dry, Mike."

"Jesus Crisp, that was too close for comfort. Those guys would have ground you into hamburger, if the general recognized you. We're getting ourselves into too dern many close shaves, Wayne. Our luck is running out and I don't like it, Mike said.

Claybourne opened the gate. Two enormous rigs slowly lumbered through. The trailers rocked precariously over the ruts, scraped noisily along overhanging tree boughs, and inched into the woods toward the shack, temporary resting place for the missiles. There, his plans dictated, the crates would be stacked in the barn, with just enough room left for the launcher and command unit trailers, soon to arrive from Alabama. Not until they made the final payment would any product be released to the Arabs, whose trucks would then transport the cargo to Consolidated Air Frame's repair hanger at Detroit's Metro Airport.

When well hidden within the cavernous structure, the Emirates Air 747, a huge empty shell designed solely for bulky cargo, would await armament loading, for a direct flight to Damascus, Syria, not the African coast as they planned from the start.

Nothing was forgotten. Claybourne rented the repair firm's entire facility at an extraordinary rate, allegedly for filming of a motion picture segment, to the exclusion of the company's employees. He paid for that in advance, but the Arabs agreed to take full responsibility once they exited his river front property with their trucks.

The final agreement in their negotiations, this one took the most time to negotiate, but the general would not relent. He would not risk discovery any farther than he already stretched. Considering diplomatic immunity the Arabs enjoyed in the public sector, he argued that it would be safer for them to take their chances on the highway.

The general followed the trucks along the narrow path. Foot by foot they struggled to round the myriad sharp turns through the thick growth. Nearly thirty minutes and scores of tree branches later, the first rig's tractor bounced into the clearing. Its airbrakes hissed it to a stop. Rodriguez jumped out, and waved Lopez to a position alongside, where the forklift could access both trailers. Mike watched intently while, what seemed forever, each of the crates was off-loaded, and stacked in the rear of the barn with the barely adequate forklift. *Outdoor equipment, heh? 'Vibrant Outdoor Toy Company!' That was the name on the e-mail Wayne found on the computer.* The vans were also emblazoned with large logos, the same as the crate labels.

Suppose we get them busted, and we find they're actually shipping gym sets. There would be no going back. Gol dern! The false arrest suits would earn the general millions. That's why we need to see more—lots more, before we give Donnie the call. Mendez removed a panel from the rear of the Ford van. He set several small canvas bags on the gravel and after them, what appeared to be two long, fluted gun barrels. The two men who drove the Kenworth tractors onto the property handed him similar bags. Mike's night vision scope revealed everything, a chilling sight he wished he didn't have to observe. "Cripes almighty! Foxholes," he said too loudly, "the derned regulation foxholes. Wayne was right, machine gun emplacements, and the weapons are now here, to install. They're not real big ones but large enough for my taste. Wayne would know what they are, if I can describe them adequately."

He made detailed mental notes, and saw belt after belt of ammunition follow as crate stacking continued. *Who would need two automatic weapons like that, to guard outdoor toys? If only Donnie could have seen them. God help us if no one else bears witness to this craziness. It's more than unbelievable.* Perspiration soaked Mike's shirt. He opened the buttons to cool himself, and hoped a calm would ensue, after the experience with Meg. He mused over the bizarre levitation he felt sure took place and brought his cerebrations back to her.

"Meg? Meg, please, Meg." Needing consolation, he waited before he observed goings on across the river again, however, she left as fast as she arrived.

Meg didn't have to be that charitable. I was half thinking she'd be tough, that she would try to talk me out of further involvement with Virginia. She's leaving it up to me, though, after pointing out the same negatives Wayne did: the woman's dubious character, and the illegalities of all that's happening. Virginia is yet a willing participant and has not opted out from her involvement. Yet, I do think she was sort of maneuvered into the activity. Claybourne's an intimidating man. She did defend Wayne and me, when we eavesdropped. "We might be alive right now, because of her. That's not bad character, is it?" he asked himself, while still packed with doubt.

Unloading completed, the second semi-trailer's doors slammed closed; the barn then secured. The three Mexicans and Claybourne took chairs and sat beneath the big maple tree on the bluff for some time; drank whiskey, and smoked cigars. An occasional laugh, they talked mostly with deathly-determined looks. While they spoke, Mendez and Lopez assembled the machine guns, piece by small piece, as though they did the task a million times, Mike thought. He watched Claybourne frequently refer to a thick manual, with a dog-eared red vinyl cover. *That must be his battle plan, every gory detail. I wish we put our hands on that. I wouldn't be sitting here right now, that's for sure, and neither would they. Maybe we should wait for an opportunity—get in there just one more time—find that book and take the derned thing. Wayne would definitely be game to try for it.*

Virginia strolled to the men with a tray of snacks at the general's behest, wearing a most contemptuous expression. Mike knew she detested the outsiders' intrusion. Two of the men eyed her ravenously, smiled devilishly, and said something Mike could not decipher. He was angered by the attention they paid her. They seemed a little too friendly for his taste. One of the men patted Virginia on the buttocks as she passed food to the other. She ignored the move but, when the unseemly gesture recurred, she dropped the tray to the metal table with a bang, and swung her right arm in a wide arc to the left. To his immediate surprise, it clashed the Mendez' face, quite broadside.

Mike heard her scream above the river's voice, "Keep your damned hands to yourself if you know what's good for you. I'll never. ..." He could not hear the rest of her admonition but Claybourne clearly did; his response was not a gentle one. He grabbed Virginia's wrist, twisted it abruptly and pulled her to the chaise where he sat. His other hand snapped in an instant to the back of her neck; he pulled her head close to his. He whispered briefly in her ear; released her as quickly, but not without a sharp tug that elicited a yelp of pain. She rubbed her neck, stood mute, and stared at the general, intolerant and enraged.

"That sonofabisquit! Does he think that's something she'll simply forget? I have half a mind to get my deer rifle and put a hole in his head. Who would know who did it, if I. ..." He considered telltale ballistics tests, though, and how effective they seemed in TV crime shows and movies. "I'd go to prison and what good would I have done? I'm going to get him, though, before this is all over. He'll pay for the hurt he's caused her. Why does she keep taking it? She is up for a large split of that money, as Wayne suggested; that has to be her rationale. Will she stay involved until the deal's done?"

The hour drew late and Claybourne left, staggered toward the shack where Virginia went earlier. The three Mexicans took large backpacks from the Ford, slung them to their shoulders and slouched off with the help of a small flashlight, deep into the sheltering trees to the east of the barn. Mike had enough. It would have been productive to overhear conversation between Virginia and the general in the bedroom, but he feared inability to control himself.

Songbirds' whistles and repetitive chattering filled the ravine beyond Mike's rear deck. Two woodpeckers hammered on the crook of a far off oak and carved small tunnels in the thick bark, to hide meals for later. The sky grayed to a dim overcast at first light and portended rain. Widespread thundershowers were confirmed in the early weather forecast, with high winds to follow in the late afternoon. It would not be a good day to watch the shack.

"So he takes that scooter into the trees, does he?" Wayne asked and sneered at the general's covert cleverness. "He takes the scooter back there? Why? There was plenty of room to stack the crates in the pole barn, right?"

"Plenty," Mike answered, "more than enough. He could have put both vehicles in the barn, still with room for. ..." They conversed on Wayne's front porch, a picture window to watch the fast moving squalls.

Wayne's mind grappled for an answer and then it came. "I'll tell ya, Bro. I know just what the hell he was doing, and so did he. He hid the damned thing out there in the woods, likely just inside the tree line, off the power company road. Ya know what? He's getting real nervous and has planned a personal getaway, just in case anything goes wrong at the shack—should things blow up for some reason. Suppose the Arabs come barging in to pick up their fireworks and a skirmish erupts. Claybourne grabs what money he can from the barn, jets out through the trees, runs like hell to the bike, and takes off down the power company road.

"The chicken neck! He makes a quick escape and leaves poor Virginia to fry for him. This guy, I tells ya, is nothing short of real bad. What do you think?" Mike knew his brother's logic reached a higher level than first appeared.

"I know what you're thinking. That's something we can do in the rain: take off with his escape machine, like shooting ducks in a barrel. We'll approach from the south, push it back to the truck, store it in my barn, and he's out of luck should he try to leave the party. Let's step to that task today.

Should be able to find the foxholes, too. We can pinpoint them for authorities if they ever come out here. God forbid! Those sites have to be disabled before any invasion takes place. It's going to take some commando tactics, with those bruisers I saw talking to the general last night. They don't look at all like Boy Scouts earning merit badges."

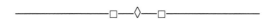

Wayne's truck whirled around in a "U" turn. He backed until the tailgate touched the power company fence, and then nudged it forward into the brush so it could not be seen from the highway. After strapping the gun belt to his waist, he withdrew his revolver, spun the cylinder and replaced it. Mike carried his .45. He, too, became a believer in self-defense in view of recent developments.

Both felt at home in the woods. Their stealth bordered on the incomparable; each complimented the other as they pushed back overhanging saplings, and gently let them go, to avoid unnecessary clatter. Camouflaged hunting outer garments created fuzzy blends with forest foliage. Wayne raised his hand in caution. Mike stepped close behind to hear his whispers. As would a hoot owl, he turned his head right, then to the left, to better decipher a sound that did not seem OK.

"What's up, Brother?"

"Thought I heard footsteps, noises of some kind. I don't know; let's just wait and listen."

Mike also heard something out of sync with forest clatter. "It's, it's chopping, I think. Maybe those tough guys are digging in, near the dirt path, by way of that first foxhole we stumbled upon, closer to Old River Road. That's where it's coming from. Speaking of digging in, it makes me think that a few discreetly placed big game snares like the old Chippewa—Pop's friend—taught us … might be very wise to rig. Remember?" Cleverly set lassos, discreetly placed on game trails, a certain way to catch most any animal, large or small. They used such ingenious triggers to unleash spring-loaded nooses, methods passed down from old timers in the tribe, generation to generation."

"Sure, sure; the old Chippewa," Wayne answered. "Dark Thunder … Pop called him Joe and we starts to call him 'Injun Joe,' after Mark Twain's *Tom Sawyer* character. Yep, his snares worked like a charm and I recall most everything he told us. You recall, out there on the reservation? We were about ten-twelve or so, spent the weekend following him around like curious puppies. He snared a buck in less than thirty minutes with his cleverly placed trap."

"Oh, how we did soak up his lore of the woods like sponges. We'll need wire rope, nails, to make it easy, and a handsaw to cut quietly," Mike replied. "We've all the sodden logs necessary for deadfalls, wherever we place the snares. Let's take the bike now … get it out of here. We'll come back and put in as many snares as we have the time and gear to rig. How 'bout that?"

They continued on to the game trail, one they followed for years when hunting in the area, and stopped at an intersection with an old logging road, almost grown over with young poplars. It fell from use years before. Wayne spotted the bike first. "Lookitey there! Look over there, under the tarp—motorcycle wheels. That's it," he said, as he lifted the brown canvas cover, "just asking to be taken. Honda XR 250 just like my old one, but a 1994, maybe '95, a waitin' to be plucked."

After removing the motorbike from its temporary shelter, they cut a few saplings, propped them beneath the collapsed tarp, and left it, appearing just as it looked when they discovered it. "Even if Claybourne comes out here to check on things, he's not likely to look under the cover. We'll get the goods on him this time," Wayne said, tickled, as was Mike, with their accomplishment.

Once they secured the dirt bike in Mike's barn, the duo returned to the area where they found it. All necessary components for snares and booby traps, filled Wayne's pack frame. The 1/8" wire rope, more than tough, would handle the largest of men; but was still light enough to blend with the landscape and not be seen.

Quickly completed, the first snare encircled an open space in the overgrown trail where one would naturally crouch to pass through low-hanging vines that grew amidst the underbrush. Wayne placed a dead root within the rigged loop and moved it no more than an inch. The supple birch they both struggled to bend to a ninety-degree angle, flew skyward.

With great force, its pull tightened the noose around the heavy surrogate leg and snapped it high into the trees above. They were elated. "Now, we've got to be careful not to pass through this damned thing, ourselves. In case it's dark, and we're the ones on the run, we'll tie these small white rags on both sides, but back far enough from the trail so they won't be noticed."

"We sure as heck don't want to entrap a deer or bear in here either, for heaven's sake," Mike replied with more concern than he showed for the Claybourne bunch. There shouldn't be any hunters around here until fall, I hope."

They rigged the next trap with the same style noose. Nothing more than a light touch to the trigger, it would unleash the one hundred fifty pound, jagged log they hung high in the crotch of a hemlock directly above the trail. A force to be reckoned, it would lethally drop upon the back of a man who passed on the small trail through the woods and away from the Morris place. "Broken ribs, maybe the spine, from this one, a sure thing. If it gets 'em in the head, it won't be a pretty sight," said Wayne."

Four snares, cleverly rigged, covered the only remaining trails through the heavy forest growth, which stemmed from the dirt path toward and away from the compound. Pleased with their project, Mike and Wayne left the sets with renewed enthusiasm, onward to the source of unusual forest noise they heard earlier.

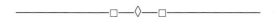

"Jesus, Mike! It's an M-60, thirty-caliber," Wayne nearly yelled when they found a heavy-duty machine gun emplaced next to the foxhole they stumbled on earlier. "You can tell by its size and the fluted barrel. That belt-fed little baby can empty one of those two hundred round ammo canisters in, oh, some thirty seconds. Look at all the ammo cans. Must be fifty of 'em," exclaimed Wayne, "That piece spits them out at a muzzle velocity of some twenty eight hundred feet a second. One wicked weapon, it is; tracers on the ammo belts ... night tracers, too. What a sight that'll be if they fire the SOB in the dark! The deer will never come back, and, we do not want to be anywhere close."

Mike looked petrified. Angered at the sight, though, he anxiously replied, "Let's get out of here, and find the other foxhole before those thugs rise and shine. They had two of those M-60 barrels when the trucks were unloaded. The big guy assembled both of them right away. We've got to find the other."

As Mike and Wayne continued to zigzag through the thick cover, impenetrable in places, the track brought them closer to the Morris shack, where they eventually found the other gun emplacement. A score of ammunition cans practically filled the foxhole. The weapon, in fire-ready status, lay cocked and pointed toward the *cul-de-sac*. They found a night vision scope, rations, and two powerful flashlights in the large rucksack also left there. "I've got my Swiss Army knife, with three screwdriver blades. You know the weapon. How quickly can you pull the firing pin?"

"How fast can you hand me the tool? Give me the knife and it's done."

Wayne fell to the task, disabled the firing mechanism, and tossed it into the trees. "We're off; dogs are stirring by the house. You hear 'em? The general may be up and around. Time for breakfast, anyway," Wayne said calmly. "After eats, we'll disarm the other gun and head to the lookout. Maybe we can get ourselves updated with the Arabs' arrival time."

"Donnie and I had a talk last night, Mike. This time I got him more than fired up. He'll come when we call, day or night, soon as he can witness something, anything, clearly illegal." While they traced their path back to the power company gate, Wayne continued: "his fly rod is always in the truck. He can testify if necessary, since he has comp time of more than a week, that fishing, not professional curiosity, brought him to the river. Sporting, not snooping would be his reason for being there. So, if he sees a crime being committed, by accident, he'd have the power of arrest.

"Something incriminating will have to be in his clear view, though, and it's up to us to set the table so he can feast on any federal law violations ongoing. He spoke with Forest Service lawyers in D.C. They finally notified the F.B.I. It would be about three hours on short notice, for a sizeable complement of agents to be on site."

CHAPTER 27

＊·◆·＊

Dishes clinked in the background, and Wayne heard some unintelligible mumbling. No distinct conversation stemmed from either bug as he switched the channel selector back and forth. Mike watched through the spotting scope while Wayne monitored audio.

"Sounds like breakfast; she's cleaning up I think … probably fed the big bastard to keep him quiet. Is she a good cook?" Wayne asked with a hungry grin.

"Salmon, steamed okra with ricotta cheese, homemade cornbread with molasses, stuffed peppers and, for dessert … sound good, so far?"

He licked his chops and patted his hungry abdomen. "Wait, wait; the phone … more inaudible talk. I can't hear details. Hold it!" Wayne held up his hands, fingers extended, to capture Mike's attention. "Hey, more equipment's coming to the shack, I think." Wayne listened with keen interest. "The general's talking about us, well you, anyways. Still doesn't seem to know who I am, quite happily." His expression paled and he exhaled with a deep guzzle. "The goddamned general," he continued woefully, "thweeth, thweeth." He spat to the side.

"Says, it's time, long overdue, he said. His level of fear became more real when Claybourne remarked that the time had come, to remove Mike from the picture.

"Virginia's crying, protesting, and threatening. "When she said she'd warn you, it got quiet, and then I heard a chair, a piece of furniture, something whacked the floor or a wall. He yells for her to come back downstairs. I hears a door slam and muffled cries."

279

"I switches back to the bedroom and, loud as can be, she's there, real upset; calls telephone information. She asks the operator, 'You have a Wayne Gladdock but no Mike or Michael?' You're still unlisted, right?"

Mike nodded and stayed mum.

"Then she asks for the number and, damn it! She asks for the address, mine, Mike. She gets my home address."

"Then she did remember my name from the mall that morning. I foolishly told her the other day that my name was Eckert." Mike interrupted himself, "The big Mexican guy is returning to the shack. Cripes, we've got our hands full now. He's carrying a couple of pine logs under his arm and a small canvas bag. What the devil is that stuff for?"

"Brother, this is not good. Claybourne says they're going to track you with the beeper and, wait; the Mexican has blocks of C-4, real bad stuff, a powerful plastic explosive. He's dern well going to plant the stuff on your Suburban, and use a remote detonator to set it off. We've got to keep my pickup truck out of this, with Nell using it around town so visibly. She wouldn't know what to look for. You'll have to check very, very carefully, every time you use the Suburban.

"Before ya opens the door, turn the key in the ignition; turn on the lights, anything electrical; you check carefully for sure, the front and rear cross members, side rails, and fender wells. They may follow you and detonate at will. If Claybourne had the slightest inkling what we know, there'd be no chance of our being spared. Our bodies would be shipped out in a missile crate." Little room remained for glimmer in their eyes, with such reflections.

Mike spurred the stifled conversation. "Claybourne is off to the Excursion. He's leaving, Wayne; you've got to tail him. You do have a full tank, now, I hope. Cripe sake, I'm. ..."

Before Mike could finish, Wayne was off through the trees, with nary the crack of a twig, to take on the chase as he did before. Mike waited and kept up the electronic eavesdropping. He slapped a mosquito from time to time, sipped lukewarm coffee, and hoped for reassurance that Virginia was not in the path of the chair or table the general apparently tossed.

Claybourne called him Solario, as they exited the front door. They exchanged a few words, and after the general drove away, the heavily built Mexican jogged from the porch at a fast marching pace, around the barn and into the woods. He carried the AK-47 they saw on the general's gun cabinet. Mike recognized it by the red leather shoulder sling.

"That's one weapon we don't have to worry about," he muttered above the rustle of birch leaves above him. "He'll be one surprised tin soldier when he pulls that trigger and hears a death-defying 'click,' just a silly, toy gun thud and nothing more." The weapon numbered among those disabled by the brothers. Mike scanned the dirt path with the scope and saw another one of the general's soldiers, armed with a pistol, and a large knife on his belt, seemingly on patrol toward Old River Road. Outfitted in a crisp fatigue uniform, properly camouflaged to blend with local forest colors, he looked battle-ready. They were clearly getting organized.

The third Mexican emerged from the tree line west of the shack, similarly attired, walked into the clearing and then moved, all too catlike for Mike's comfort, toward the river. He stood stoically at the bluff, just past the overhanging cedar and swept both banks with binoculars. Mike flattened himself on the leaves, tipped the spotting scope on its side and pushed his backpack behind the tree, to assure he'd not be seen.

Motionless, the dark skinned soldier stayed in position by the river for close to an hour and finally moved slowly across the clearing toward the west wall of the house. The dogs playfully followed a few feet behind, waited for sticks he periodically threw for them. He looked down, scrutinized the dusty surface. Every so often he dropped to his knees for a closer examination. *These monkeys prowl around like pros; we have to watch ourselves, mind our backsides, too. We will have to know where they are at every moment, if we're to cross the river again for any reason. They're not here to play around and act like this is real serious business.*

When the man disappeared back into the woods, Mike resumed listening and continued surveillance with the scope. Virginia's voice blared over the receiver. She spoke from the master bedroom. He turned the volume down. "Geeech, must be right next to the derned thing. We either hear something and it's too loud, or nothing … no betweens." His hand cupped over the other ear to block outside noise, he listened and found her side of the phone conversation more than enlightening.

"Daddy, it's you! We've not talked for so long … yes … yes … oh, yes, we … we … are doing fine." Mike sensed the reservation in her stammered reply. voice. "I'm worried Daddy; the Arabs are soon to arrive for the exchange, yes Tuesday, in the afternoon. Then, thank God, we'll be over this nightmare and I can get out of here. Homer—I've not wished to tell you this—but, Homer. …" Mike heard sobbing, no talk, only sobs. "He's crazy, Daddy; he's a crazy sonofa," she whimpered again, "and … and I can't go on with him."

After a long pause, she continued, "Of course he's hurt me, all too often. He's abused me since we arrived here and lately, lost it completely. I've no idea what provokes it, but he goes off the table any time I disagree. He wants to kill the men with whom we had the shooting dispute. That spat, though, is far behind us now. They're harmless local people, just resentful of his fencing the road to their fishing hole; that's all. They haven't been here since, and he's going to have them killed? I heard him assign the savage looking character, Solario or something like that. Mendez, yes, that's the man, a real mean looking one. He's been told to take care of the men, to blow up their cars.

"Daddy, I can't have murder on my conscience, and neither of us can afford to be accomplices. That's what we'll be, if word gets out. Homer's just the type to pin it on us. Oh, I know he's an old friend of yours, but he's a lying scum with no scruples and he'll get us in big trouble. I smell it coming. I'm even worried for my own. …" She cried again, while her father evidently spoke. "My life is at risk," she went on. "He told me he'd drop me on a moment's notice if I interfered. I threatened to notify the fishermen that their cars were set to be bombed, and Homer told me right then; he'd, 'cut my throat, hog tie me, to rot in the sun by the river,'" his very words. She bordered on the hysterical.

"No, no, it's too late to intervene, way too late for that. I don't want you hurt, Daddy. I don't want you to bring out any thugs either. Someone is sure to get shot with all the damned firearms Homer has accumulated up here. They now have machine guns, already in place, in foxholes. That's how serious this has become. We should have known. Automatic rifles, pistols, C-4 explosive, even a few hand grenades; I saw a canister full of them in Homer's closet."

"Dern, this is not good," Mike whispered, "I sure didn't see grenades when I searched the wardrobe—only the Winchester and the electronics."

"Yes, Daddy, I'll be careful; I will handle things. We'll get by all the confusion. This Mike is a very nice gentleman and I don't want him hurt. Why I led Homer to him, I'll never know. At the time I thought he simply wished to rule out any connection with the law. That's clearly the case. Maybe you can explain that, yet I don't want him to know we've discussed it. He'll beat me for telling you; really, he will."

"Yes, next Tuesday, the Arabs are to pick up everything, two o'clock, I think, and they'll pay the full amount due. So far they've stuck to their schedules so I'd bet that's the day. We should net more than five million each, possibly a bit more. I should take your share when the money is exchanged or you may never see it. Can you tell Homer, send a sternly worded e-mail and remind him of his obligations and responsibilities to you and me? Homer is unpredictable, could screw us out of it, if not entrap us in the aftermath. I tell you he's not trustworthy. He's whacko, overwhelmed with the pressure and the loom of big bucks around the corner."

Mike felt an almost irresistible urge to follow Claybourne. He could intercept him on the road, take him into the woods, shoot him once in the groin for Virginia's benefit, and let him beg for mercy before the death knell. Virginia's recounts of the general's behavior made it easy to visualize. Mike felt the rising anger in his gut. It was more than anger, though, a rage up-welled that tightened his abdominal musculature, quickened his pulse, and blushed his face near red. He began to pack his things, intent on a confrontation, but paused with the low volume cell phone chime. He sat back on the leaves once again, to listen.

"Yes, Wayne, I've got an earful here, too: the arrival date is this coming Tuesday ... the Arabs. I overheard Virginia tell her father on the phone. What would we have done without the listening devices? We need Donnie here for this. If. ..."

Wayne broke in, "Brother, we're in luck, major luck. I have the trucks, big suckers, must have barely cleared local bridges, even with the lowboy trailers. All covered with canvas tarps, which means ... yep ... right. When that cover comes off, the equipment should be visible for Don. You're damned right he's got to be there. Get him! Get him now, and keep calling until you do. He has to see the stuff unloading to get the F.B.I. on fire.

"The convoy is about to leave the truck stop on Highway 33. Looks real innocent with the toy company logos all over the cover. What a bunch of ... wait a minute, we're off. I'm splitting. I'll let them go forward. Claybourne is ahead of the pack; he won't see me way behind. Be there in an hour or so, I'd expect."

"Wayne, be dern sure they don't have a car, a rear guard, lagging well behind for security purposes. The Mexicans are still here, but more people may be assembling for the final show down, and they could be some distance behind the trucks."

"No problem. I'll do as I did before: stay out of sight and use the direction finder, not my eyes. Tuesday, eh? We'd better get our rifles loaded, and greased up if we're going to be there. Two snipers from across the river could be lifesavers for the rangers. That's what we're going to do, right?" Call Donnie; I have to go ... leaving now."

Mike scanned the spiral notebook in his pack for Don's numbers and soon connected with his Forest Service friend. Donnie knew the trail to their lookout spot, agreed to be there inside of thirty minutes, and for as long as necessary, to see the unveiling that would soon take place.

□—◇—□

"Well I'll be dang busted, corn-fed and tattooed," the ranger remarked, while he peered excitedly through his powerful binoculars, at the huge draped trailers in the clearing. The two men who drove in were long gone with the tractors. Before arriving, Don called in the license numbers of the remaining trucks and trailers and the Ford van, too. Mike gave him the information by phone. He whispered his perplexing, but hardly unexpected findings.

The plate on the Ford actually belonged to a 1998 Chevrolet sedan reported stolen, and totaled in an accident during a police chase in Texas. Strangely, the tractor licenses traced straight to the U.S. Army at the Pentagon. Vibrant Outdoor Toy Company, a fictitious address in El Paso, Texas was the registered owner of the trailers that toted the missiles. "This information is already indicative of criminal activity, of certain interest to the Feds, but not enough to put anyone away very long," Don said, while they discussed implications.

"That, now, that's something I'm damned concerned about!" Don pointed to the heaviest trailer. Crouched behind adequate cover and more than bewildered, he watched the unveiling with glee. A sight to behold, it was exactly what Mike and Wayne wanted Don to observe. While Claybourne stood to the side, arms folded, and content looking, the three Mexicans removed the drapes from the camouflaged tandem axle trailer at the rear of the flatbed.

Having served in the artillery, Don affirmed it was an Engagement Control Station, brains for the operation of the launch system. It still bore the white-stenciled U.S. Army designation, AN/MSQ-104. Then came the clincher, as it was un-draped: a six-wheel trailer, bearing four launching tubes and two control consoles. An M-901 Launching Station, it bore similar labels. "Look at that: enough firepower, coupled with those Patriot Missiles in the barn, that we've got 'em. The Army will sure as hell want in on this arrest. Christmas, we'll have every law enforcement officer in the state wandering through our woods. They'll be shooting each other!" Don's comments brought some levity into the otherwise grim picture. They both laughed.

He continued while he dialed his cell phone for the Forest Service's D.C. Headquarters. "This is the biggest thing the department has dealt with since that huge drug bust in Colorado a few years ago. It'll be the first international missile smuggling case ever. I can see the bulletins now, and the papers … a veritable shark feed for reporters."

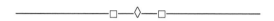

The stifling late morning sun kept many inside. So long as churches stayed filled, few vehicles plied the local roads. In fact, Mio seemed unusually isolated. Canoeists out for Sunday cruises down river on the upper reach of the Au Sable, passed through town earlier, to permit as much downstream travel time as possible before dark. Boutiques and antique shops that flourished with mid-summer tourists, were not yet open. A single engine plane groaned above. The pilot practiced stalls over the woods, as it climbed and dove like a balsa glider, close to the ground in the windless sky.

Seemingly out of nowhere, the stillness broke with a shudder—a staggering, enduring blast that shook the quiet valley for miles around. It came from the south of town; sounded like dynamite in the quarries of yesteryear, a reminder to a few oldsters who could recall the powerful explosions that shattered weekday mornings of their childhood. Artillery shelling, it resembled to some; for others, nothing more than an incidental throbbing noise that spurred only mild curiosity or concern. For the black Suburban, though, small remnants of which spread over southbound State Highway 33, it was a burst of unnerving magnitude. It catastrophically separated every part, and decimated the SUV into jagged, unrecognizable bits. Within minutes, State Police arrived to begin their search for evidence, and expected remains.

CHAPTER 28

"Nell! Nell! Damn it, Nell. Oh God, there you are." Wayne bent over and struggled for breath after his run from the barn, unaccustomed as he was to sprinting. While at work on his tractor, he listened to music on WAVC FM, the local radio station. He nearly collapsed from the shock of an intervening newsbreak. "Nell! … Nell! It's Mike. I just know it."

"Oh, sit down, now; you'll have a coronary gettin' all red like that. What's happened, Honey?" Her attentions returned to the cookbook open on her lap.

"The news, radio news, a black SUV southbound on thirty three… blown to smithereens. I just know it's him. Didn't want to tell ya … but that heartless Claybourne has three killers working for him at the river. We heard the general tell one of 'em to get rid of Mike. Mike and. …" He thought better of continuing.

Can't let her in on the threat to both of us; just cannot do that. Not until I kills the dirty bastard. Nell faded to pale, and then reconsidered. Now, just a minute, why not call Mike? Just dial his phone, the cabin, too. I'm sure it's someone else and probably just an accident." Nell always reacted to impending drama like that; rarely became upset without good cause. She began to whimper in a low level of hysteria, however, with Wayne's carryings on, forcing a stern look to reality.

Wayne collected his thoughts and dialed from the kitchen. "No answer on the cell," he said, nursing back tears. He tried the cabin and, again, met with no success. Finger poised to dial State Police, he dropped the receiver down. "No way," he whimpered, "I'm not giving myself away to them yet. I want the general's hide for this. He collapsed to the tattered oak chair by the phone and began to weep, face buried in his hands. "Why? Why in heaven did we take it so far? Why, Nell? It was becoming kind of a game to hassle the general."

Wayne entered the first stage of hysterics and again covered his flushed face after a quick glance toward his wife. She collapsed prostrate on the nearby couch, unable to comprehend. First they lost Meg, and now his older brother?

The couple merged to abject sorrow, a sorry sight, when a persistent telephone ring brought them to their senses. Wayne knew it had to be the coroner or the cops. They would want him for body identification. It was all he could do to answer. He slowly lifted the receiver to his ear.

"Now, is this some sick prankster out there? Who is this?" Wayne turned pale. "Mike? Mike, is that really you?" A long pause ensued. Enlivened by his brother's voice, Wayne grinned, gagged several times, and finally caught his breath. "Good grief! We were practically dressing for your funeral, Brother. Honestly; the broadcast on FM, the black Suburban, plastic explosive; it all fit. I heard the patrolman being interviewed, too. He said it was a terrible sight; nothing left at all. Who could it be, but you?"

When Wayne settled himself, Mike explained. Despite Wayne's warnings, he omitted checks under his car for explosive plants. He drove it three times that morning and the precautionary inspections slipped his mind. It happened on the way to the nursery.

When alerted to the danger, he stopped, bounded from the vehicle and rolled into the roadside ditch. He ran like a spooked turkey, and spread himself flat on the freshly plowed ground. Thirty seconds, a minute, five minutes, and nothing happened. About to get up, Mike related, a deafening white blast knocked him from his crouched position. When he composed himself, the car was gone. Only a cloud of smoke, and a pile of debris occupied the southbound lane where he left it.

"Well," Wayne shrieked without restraint, "don't think I don't knows what you were thinking when the smoke cleared, right? Am I right?" His knees shook from the revelation. Nell rubbed his shoulders, but he could not be calmed.

Thinking his life still endangered, Mike crawled almost two hundred yards along a deep irrigation furrow, to the next road, and hitched a ride in the bed of a pickup, to town, where he placed the call. Wayne assumed correctly. Mike wished the would-be killers to conclude he was in the vehicle at the time of the blast; thus he stayed well clear of the scene.

"Let's just keep it that way for the time being, Mike. I'll come get ya. We'll fetch the old Volvo wagon from the shop, and you can drive that rattletrap for a few days. They'll never figure it out. It's perfect, couldn't have planned it better. Far as they're concerned, you're plum dead and gone. Now, you stay away from the girl, in case she's as bad as I think she is under that sweet, peachy southern skin of hers. You're one problem they now think they've handled. Only one more obstruction for them to eliminate, and that's probably me. Right?"

Wayne called Don Johanssen to explain what happened. He agreed to warn the F.B.I. and troopers, who would withhold release of the Suburban driver's identity on the strength of an intensive investigation currently under way. Radio newscasts confirmed the Bureau's intervention. The explosion mutilated driver and possible occupant beyond recognition, they said, to go along with plans for temporary obfuscation. The Suburban, so badly demolished, local passers-by would never imagine it had been Mike's pride and joy, and the perpetrators would think him gone.

Don mentioned in the course of conversation that the F.B.I. would dispatch a slew of officers, backed by others from the Treasury Department's Bureau of Alcohol, Tobacco and Firearms, just as soon as on-the-scene evidence confirmed the apparent conspiracy. U.S Army investigators were to be dispatched, as well.

Wayne gloated over his success, when he persuaded the ranger to enter the foray with so much assistance. He drove his old Volvo to Mio, and finally admitted he should have had the foresight to adjust the timing. It attracted far too much attention, back firing every block or two. One explosion that day was enough.

Tears welled in his grateful eyes when he spotted Mike standing off the main drag, around the corner from the Huron Realty office.

"Get in, dead man," Wayne yelped, as he skidded to a stop against the curb. "C'mon, and let Daddy Wayne take care of you, and may I say, that's another fine mess you've gotten us into. Sure glad the news wasn't what it appeared, Brother; awful glad. It could have been grim. What was the signal to bail out of the car, in the middle of a two lane highway?"

"You remember how I said Meg and I speak from time to time?" Mike blushed with embarrassment but Wayne ignored it. "We'll, the windows were up tight, air conditioning on full tilt, yet I felt a colder, whirly wind coming from the back. Somewhere behind me, I thought a window slipped down, and then I realized it was Meg. She was there with me.

"Quite calmly, she said only five words, 'Get the hell out, Mike.' She was determined and I knew she meant it. I wanted to talk—even tried—but she wasn't conversant. 'Get the hell out, Mike,' she said again, in the same cool tone ... no shouting ... just like Meg. Then I knew what she was telling me. I stopped in the middle of the road and, well, you know the rest."

Wayne looked stone sober, grayish in color all of a sudden, and his voice crackled. "This'll be one for the books. Way too spooky for me, Mike. Thinks we better go back to church, real regular-like."

"So," Mike continued, "I waited in the dirt, just across the ditch a ways, unaware what next would happen. A breeze swept over the cut sprigs of last year's wheat stubble along the field margin, and she calls, ever so softly to me. 'Mike, move back; it's terrible. The Mexican fellow has placed a. ...' Then, *kaboom*! All heck breaks loose, mushroom cloud arises, and my baby, the Suburban, is absolutely finished. She knew, Wayne. She knew. But," Mike said sadly, "she didn't return in the aftermath.

"There were cops, plenty of Lookitey Lulus ... bystanders accumulated there in a heartbeat. I watched from the next road to the west. That's why I didn't call you right away. Stunned beyond comprehension, I was. Sure sorry for the fright, though."

"You're marked, or were. You've got to lay real low, until show time. You'll stay with us in the spare bedroom, and that's an order. Don't want lights in your place giving you away. Do not use your cell phone. We'll drive over there now, real careful-like. Get your things and come back to Tawas with us."

"Let's hide your Chevy truck in the barn," Mike suggested, "it's a bet they've already cased your house trying to find me, and they may know your car. If we're not on our toes, you'll be next. Get the old Buick loaner from the shop. You drive that one. Maybe customers complaining of its shoddy condition will be listened to a little more," he added with notable sarcasm.

"We've got to lay low tonight, pick up on our rest, and think about what happens tomorrow, just one day from missile delivery time. Then we'll resume surveillance, and make dern sure there are no more hang-ups like this one."

"You did it, didn't you? You're a murdering liar! You promised he'd be left alone." Virginia screamed feverishly, and spun clenched fists on the general's chest while he tried to hold her at bay. She felt the startling concussion when the Suburban bloomed into smoke and shards, and overheard the three Mexicans and Claybourne a short while later, tout their success when they joked by the bluff, and spoke of how the next one would be demolished with an even larger charge. "It didn't take Einstein to figure out what that one did." She pointed to Solario Mendez, whose expression was unruffled and arrogant. "So, how many does that give you; how many kills? You low-living slime of a. ..."

That was enough for Mendez. He took three long steps across the room, grabbed her shoulders, and lifted Virginia from the floor like a stick. He shook her until her neck could take no more, and dropped her to the floor, trembling, and terribly close to a dizzy faint. "Mexican women know better than that, you little *puta*. You've been warned, and I only warn once. The next time," Mendez threatened with a serious grimace, "the next time, I break that pretty little neck when you show me no respect. *Comprende?*"

The general stood by, helpless, flabbergasted, and unable to speak, fearful of increasing Mendez's wrath at that moment. He was not one to tangle with, most certainly. "You've proved your point, Solario. She understands now, don't you Ginny?" Mendez wasn't through making his point. He pulled Virginia to a sitting position by the back of her denim shorts, and shook her again. She pleaded for him to stop, apologized to both men at Claybourne's behest, and struggled sullenly up the stairs when the Mexican released his grasp

Mendez and the general resumed their review of the day's activities as if the distraction amounted to nothing. "General, you asked me to plant the C-4, so I went right out and did it. Ain't that why I'm here, to handle requests like that? You could have hired any driver to bring the trailers, but you couldn't find another me. *Verdad*, General? I slipped the detonator and half the plastic under the car when he stopped to buy milk and a newspaper. I had to wait until he mowed his damned grass and used a leaf blower to clean the entire property. It was getting late. I risked my neck. But you're paying us for risking necks, aren't you General?

"Your little lady ... quite a spirit, no? Could you arrange for her to have drinks with the boys and me, later in the evening?" Mendez asked the general with a smirk. His upper lip curled menacingly, and then a full grin ensued and exposed his broken incisors.

Claybourne instinctively reached for his gun cabinet as Mendez spoke, withdrew the revolver he previously kept in the bedroom nightstand, and pointed it at the surprised man. "You'll leave the girl out of this if you know what's good for you, and that goes for the two goons you brought with you. She is off limits," the general growled. He cocked the hammer.

Surly, but benumbed, Solario relented, shrugged his shoulders, and retreated out the front door, without comment. He murmured under his breath that he'd best never catch Claybourne in one of El Paso's dark alleys.

Still quivering from the tumult, the general read his e-mail, pleased to receive confirmation that the trucks would arrive two days hence. "The Arabs are coming. The Arabs are coming," he bellowed and tossed his hands high. He poured a double shot of his treasured Glenlivet and read the printout again, from top to bottom:

My Dear General:

We have a great deal of money to hand you personally. It is all bundled, and the bills are not sequentially numbered as you insisted.

Our Palestine friends gave us clearance to trade the dollars, fifteen million two hundred thousand, for the following equipment:

Twenty PAC3 Patriot Missiles with U.S. Army Certificates of Upgrade and Repair, Form number GSA 55-62UNR, spare parts per prior agreement.

One AN/MSQ-104 Engagement Control Station on a trailer, with the same certification.

One M-901 Mobile Launch Station for four units, including two consoles and the command station with radio relays, similarly certified.

Two transport vans, marked Vibrant Outdoor Toy Company for missiles and parts.

Two flatbed trailers, to transport command and radar modules and launcher.

Your men will assist in the loading, and we then take over for the drive to the airport, where our plane will await in the hangar reserved for the night. Our driving directions have been received, for which we thank you.

We arrive with three tractors, a limousine, and six men, at exactly 1400 hours Tuesday, the seventh of August. When the goods are underway, on the small road outside your property, the last man out will deposit the money with you. You need not worry. Do not hold up the procession to count the funds.

We have a critical deadline to meet and will not delay departure for your verification. We are assured details have been worked out between you and our friends. Do not reply to this. Delete it.

Do not print a copy. It has been a pleasure, and our compliments to the young lady. Both of us hope, once again, to exchange pleasantries with her.

Our abundant thanks to you,
Abdul Shal al Badizai and Alwoud bin Nadahlawi

"Damn, I'll never be able to talk her into accommodating the Arabs again. We're through if they expect her favors for dessert that day, absolutely through. I can't possibly agree to a post-transaction interlude. Perhaps the machine guns will encourage them to make a more hasty departure than they planned." Claybourne burned the printout in the fireplace, deleted the e-mail as instructed, and decided it would be best to ignore a response to the final comment in the missive.

"As to final tasks awaiting completion, if we can find that Jim fellow, we'll give him the same treatment as his cohort in the Suburban. Never did like General Motors cars." After several stiff drinks, his breath reeked of whiskey, blended with the stench of two cigars he chewed and smoked. He snacked in the kitchen, and then sought to retire upstairs. Virginia's body began to dominate his thoughts. She danced in his mind for days.

Desires were temporarily shattered when repeated knocks on the locked bedroom door brought no response. Fists clenched, the general resorted to heavier banging on the door, the frame, and even the wall around it, which shook with his persistence. Still, Virginia did not respond.

She sat in the center of the king size bed, irritated with the clatter, propped against four pillows, and two silk covered shams. Clasped in shaking hands she held her small though lethal .22 pistol, loaded with long rifle cartridges. Jolted by each bout of door pounding, she contemplated the lesser of two evils: whether to shoot the general when he entered the room, or to turn the weapon on herself. Inevitably, he'd gain entry at any moment. She knew he was not one to reject. A quick decision had to be made.

What good is all that money if I have to live in fear of my life every day? A man of Homer's nature is no longer my idea of a long-term mate. I won't even try to cope any further with his irascibility, and how terribly lecherous he has become. He's morphed into an ogre, nothing short of it.

The banging continued, augmented by pleas that ranged from friendly, if not downright comely, to demanding, and threatening. Claybourne kindly whispered, and then angrily shrieked alternatively, both efforts to no avail.

She looked at her reflection in the gleaming chrome finish of the pistol, withdrew the magazine to confirm its full load of ten cartridges, and snapped it back. Virginia cocked the hammer, pushed off the safety, and suddenly felt secure, even warmed by the thought of bringing peace to herself, either by putting an end to her life or the general's, right then and there. *It would be fun to have the money—five million or more—to play with it, squander some of it foolishly, but, I've no one with whom to spend it. Could I do it alone? Could I do it with Homer, a man who has just ordered a successful killing, a killer himself? My God! What woman would tolerate such tough guy stuff? How could they have done that to Mike? He was the perfect man—so gentle, attractive, even with his thick glasses. Intelligent, too, and above all, he was loyal. I've long dreamed of those qualities in a man, but have never before found them.*

She pointed the muzzle to her temple, to see how it felt facing imminent death. No discomfort, no distress, no worries, or concerns;

it felt comforting. Only relief pervaded her thoughts. The muzzle's coolness on her skin brought a marked tenseness for a moment. As her grip tightened, though, and her index finger found the trigger, she glided on a wave of relaxation as she increased pressure against it.

"Ginny!" I thought I heard a pistol being cocked, the snap of its magazine." His slurred words interrupted the banging. "Ginny … Virginia? C'mon, Ginny. You don't have that .22 in your hand, now do you, Virginia?"

She closed her eyes again, and moved the gun's muzzle between her breasts, down to where it pressed, point blank, against her upper abdomen, just below the sternum's xyphoid process. She knew her anatomy. The apex of her heart lay just beneath. Fragmenting bone would not stifle the bullet's pathway at an upward angle. *It would take longer to die this way. I may be conscious for some time. The temple is better, but will the small slug do the job, in the one shot I'd have? Oh, how I wished to see Mike again, to fish with him, to see the look of delight when he taught me the ropes. I'd have enjoyed meeting his daughters, too. How will they cope, losing their mother this spring and now Mike, in such a traumatic explosion? What about his brother, in Tawas?*

Claybourne almost broke down the solid core door with lowered shoulder, when a shot rang out behind it; just one blast. He heard glass shatter. Total silence followed. Face buried in his hands, he stood in the hall, frozen in veritable disbelief.

Don Johanssen listened to the turmoil from across the river. He turned to his assistant for the night's observation, but found himself wordless, unable to describe what they allowed to occur by not intervening when the tempo of the discussion in the cabin suggested impending violence.

"Good, God. I think she's … ah … the woman has gone and shot herself," the ranger finally articulated. "There was lots of noise, muffled pleadings by the general, and then gunfire. It's all quiet now. Maybe, just maybe, on the other hand, she shot him." He held the headset to his ears with both hands, anxious for an explanation.

CHAPTER 29

The door fell from its hinges and, Claybourne atop of it, landed with a resounding crash on the bedroom hardwood floor. Shaken but unhurt, the effort did not help his healing gunshot wound. He picked himself up and peered toward Virginia, petrified he would see her reclined on the bed, bloodied, dying, or dead.

Instead, she sat propped against the pile of pillows, and wore one of her better smiles, a .22 pistol held tenaciously in both hands, arms extended, finger pressed to the trigger, and steady as a rock for the next shot. He looked hurriedly and saw no blood, nor sign of injury. Only a small hole in a windowpane, near the top of the closest dormer window and the smell of spent gunpowder suggested a shot was fired. The general approached the bed and she stiffened, extended her arms a bit more to emphasize her earnest.

Though calm when she spoke, her eyes were fiery, and her face stretched taut. "I nearly killed myself a few seconds ago, Homer. I came ever so damned close, and you pushed me to that edge. I hung there, without direction. Death probably would have felt better than I feel right now, but I could not decide whose life to take; mine or yours. I decided to volunteer you. Figured you'd force your way in sooner or later, so I just advanced things a bit, with the pot shot I took at the window. And, it worked! Here you are, nothing more than a target in front of me. It's your turn to be humiliated."

"Ginny, please. Get yourself together," the general begged, "what do you want from me? I'm falling apart with this pressure; can't take much more." Almost snarling, ruddy with superimposed anger and fright, and weary, too, of the growing dissonance between them, he stretched out his right hand in a gesture of atonement. His left remained high, as she instructed.

"Get it back up! You think I'm just sitting here ready to let you off the hook, you sick bastard. No! Not that easily, I'm not." His good arm snapped straight toward the ceiling again. "This is no Simon Says, game, Homer. I've never meant what I said in a stronger way. Never!" she shouted, but forgot it was her desire to maintain complete control.

Beads of perspiration emerged on Claybourne's forehead, dripped to his eyes, and to the floor with a light patter. His back soddened and his shirt showed dampness at the belt line. "Virginia … my dear, I have. …"

"Don't you even think of saying, 'my dear,' after that misguided Pancho Villa worked me over, and you stood there, stupidly. You didn't ask him to stop. Who is working for whom? I thought we were paying the man, and plenty, at that.

He's already received twenty thousand. How much did he get for killing my … er … ah … the fisherman."

She bit her tongue for almost having said, "'my friend,'" quickly continued, and prayed inside that her blunder went unnoticed. "My successful find," she corrected herself. "He was my find. I tracked him because he was to be warned, only warned, Homer, not disintegrated. How do you think his death is going to be handled by friends and relatives, as though nothing happened?" Virginia exhaled sharply. "When his absence is realized, the cops will put two and two together. It's a gruesome homicide."

"You've said, already, that the waitress at the Paul Bunyan knew him, and covered up when you asked her for information. She's one witness who will point to you. How about this guy Slim Jim, who was with him at the river that night? He's still around. Who did they tell about the shooting? They've talked to the Forest Service about the gate, and the signage. Many folks could be snooping around? You're crazy! What were you thinking? You've wrapped my father and me up in a mindless killing. How do you know Mendez won't try blackmail? If he'd kill like that, he'll try anything; threaten to talk, ask for more money, hurt you or me."

The general knew she was right. *What was I thinking? Somehow, I must figure a way to handle Mendez, to dispel any connection with us.* His mind tore ahead. "Somehow, we have to get him away from the property for as long as it takes to finish our business here. He won't bother us, I promise. Look, Ginny, this has got to stop. I'm soaking wet. I'm real afraid, and don't mind saying. I have never seen you quite like this. You're breaking; don't care if you live or die. I can certainly see, too, that we're through. How the devil can we go on, with so many upsetting incidents stacked up like this?"

"I'm out of bounds, Dear, er, Ginny. I know that. I'm also afraid of Mendez, and the way he shook you like that. You didn't see me afterward. When you rushed upstairs, I pulled my gun, cocked the hammer, and told him to leave you alone, never to bother you again. He left the house in a huff, mumbled that he would see me in an El Paso alley, eventually. I don't like it. The man is completely without conscience.

"Why would I have hired him as a bodyguard? Boy Scouts would not have worked for his ... ahem, area ... of ... of ... expertise. You know that.

"Don't worry; I'll be kept honest to the end. I don't need to be hunted down by General, by Rodmend—your father. I wouldn't think of screwing with him or you, if for no other reason than that. Should you think of me as mean or uncaring, try crossing your father, for God's sake. Virginia, you only know the half of him. I could tell you tales, frightening stories of many a man he's ruined, if not brutally murdered with the help of others; entrapped, even imprisoned, and, for doing nothing close to what he's dished out. They've done nothing more than stand in his way. The list goes on and on, Virginia."

"OK, OK, I don't wish to hear of it. He's my father and I love him; that's what matters to me. What he did or reportedly did in the army is his business, army business, not mine. Don't bring it up again.

When this is over, we'll go our separate ways," Claybourne went on, almost believably. "If you want this property, take it. I'll sign it over to you. The lifestyle out here isn't for me, in the middle of nowhere. Can't even get a good cigar, and in Arlington they practically grow on trees." He smiled feebly.

Virginia didn't flinch; she heard enough. "Sit down General Claybourne. Sit down on the floor, and cover your eyes, if you don't want to watch the meeting with your maker. If you wish to stretch it out a bit more, be seated and be quiet, please. Don't make me shoot you standing up, sweating like that. You're a disgusting, pathetic mess."

He obliged, quickly. He saw her determination and began to sob. Her complaints sounded too legitimate. "Dear Ginny … Dear Virginia, I loved you … really I did. I still do, but what do I know about love? I'm a seasoned, old army man, taught to be tough, and knew only the military, my entire adult life. I'm not a classy person, only acted that way." Embarrassed with his carryings on, Claybourne wiped his eyes repeatedly. "My father was a violent one, disciplined me severely, and sent me to military school, where I got the hell kicked out of me for the slightest infraction. My background made me what I am. I am so sorry it didn't fit with yours.

"Please give me a chance, just a brief chance to use the money I've worked so damned hard to get, for more than a year, day and night at times, putting it together for the three of us. Don't end my tale of living, not like this, please." He fell to the floor, and wept again, just as she did for hours.

My Lord! I can't pull the trigger. It's simply not in me. He'll retaliate if I don't follow through. He'll get his gun downstairs, shoot me, probably bury my body, and tell Daddy I backed out. Now, while I'm as depressed as I am, would be the best time, I guess. I'm through; I just know it. "Get up, she ordered, "get up and get us a drink. I can't go through any more of this babbling. I can't shoot you or anyone."

"Yes, yes, drinks," he said, encouraged by her attitude change,

"Glenlivet, two large glasses. We'll get drunk. I'll get the bottle, and ice, too."

He stood shakily, stumbled from the room and, to her surprise, returned with a tray of cheese and the promised fixings for drinks. His clammy hands, clasped her wrist and he mumbled, "Thanks; thank you for seeing it my way. There will be no more trouble, I can assure you. I want to go home, but not in a box, Virginia. I want to fish in the Caribbean, see escrow close on the place down there, and travel.

"If it's not with you, all right; but I do want those things for myself. What you do from here on out is your choice. Your point was very clearly made, and I did see your limits just now." Claybourne inched his way onto on the bed. Jostling around until comfortable, they spoke little, finished the bottle and, soon found each other's arms, collapsed in Stygian slumber.

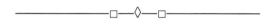

The forest rangers took turns to overhear the drama as it unfolded in the master bedroom. When it quieted, Don expressed sarcastic regret that Virginia didn't finish off the general. "Shouldn't say this, but I was pulling for her to do it; weren't you, Josh?"

"Damned tootin', I was. When you think of the way he's treated her, according to the Gladdocks, and what we just heard on the bug over there. It'd be justifiable homicide, wouldn't it?"

"Well," the Chief Ranger continued, "to their mutual good fortune, both are alive, apparently drunk, and they'll be hung over tomorrow, if that was a full bottle he brought from downstairs. Sure glad we don't have a death to investigate. Hasn't been a murder in the forest since 1984, best I remember. It's late and the both of us don't need to be here. I'll call you, though, should anything happen. I know you wouldn't want to miss the fun. We should all get here early tomorrow, for the will call." Don stretched out on his sleeping bag and set his wristwatch alarm for two hours. Josh hiked through the trees to his truck, for the short drive to his small government quarters behind the Forest Service office building.

Mike checked his rifle at the cabin, proud of the many deer he harvested with it, over the decades since Meg and the girls gifted him for

Christmas. What a present it was. They seemed so proud. What was he doing with it off-season, though? Why was he fingering it anxiously, the same anticipation with which he handled it on deer season opening day, hoping to get the shot of his dreams? What provoked his determination to use it on the general, or anyone at the compound, for that matter?

Wayne related in their telephone conversation, that he cleaned and reloaded his Weatherby rifle only minutes before. "We're going on a pigeon shoot tomorrow," his over-eager brother said, "just like old days in the cornfield." Wayne's flippant comments struck a dissonant chord, however, the reason Mike began to question the propriety of their plans. After he gave what was coming careful reconsideration, he slipped the Winchester back in its case. Resigned to use it if necessary, he stood the rifle against the front door, slung his pistol belt over the doorknob, and made sandwiches for their lunch and dinner. A long surveillance vigil lay in the offing.

Sure hope no fireworks are required. Cripes, it seems like a western movie—Gunfight at OK Corral—*something like it, anyway. Assuming the Feds come as expected, they sure as heck won't want us in their way. I don't want to miss the fun, however, seeing the general apprehended. I want that moment something awful, just to catch the turkey's expression, watch his eyes bulge when he sees federal officers closing.* "If we have to observe from up on the bank, our lookout spot will be perfect." He finally spoke encouragingly, though with lingering apprehension, as if Meg were there at the dining table, listening like she did while he talked, and did the dishes for her.

He closed the back door leading to the deck; he was sure, yet the breeze that swirled from the service porch defied short-term memory. He knew there were no breaches to permit such drafts through the well-insulated structure. Realizing she might have made her entry, he turned off kitchen lights, dimmed the chandelier over the dining table, and switched off the table lamp in the adjoining front room, to recline in semi-darkness on the couch. His eyes fell closed. A rinse of cool air poured across the room, over his face. Soft lips pressed against his; the gentle grip on Mike's shoulders felt familiar. Kisses about his throat followed. She moved to his forehead, and then to his chest where she opened the top four buttons.

"Meg, ah, Meg. It is you. I can tell, the tip of your tongue between your lips.

Always liked that, Dear, always."

"I came to ravage you, Honey; it may be our last night together, at least like this. I don't know how it will be if we're both in the beyond … together."

Mike knew what she meant. She didn't have to continue. "Honey, you two, Wayne and my loving husband, are taking rifles and pistols to the river for a showdown, a shootout, better said. What in heaven's name are you thinking? You have the F.B.I., State Police, Forest Service, and even Donnie, who's an ex cop. What can you Gladdocks do besides needlessly getting maimed, or killed? Mike, listen to me," she admonished. "Listen up. You have that look in your eyes, to suggest I'm off base … don't know what I am talking about. Oh, I can tell."

"I hear your warning. My red flag waved furiously, too," he replied, lips pursed and eyes dulled. "We're going to see this through, Meg, see that SOB arrested, and jailed for what he's doing. Then, I think of the shack. I still want that place for us, remember?"

"I came to the cabin to spend the night with you tonight. I've missed you and you've missed me, I know, even with all the babysitting time with tha…that Virginia, if I may say so. The Suburban, Mike, our nice Suburban is gone; nothing left but a dump truck full of jagged pieces. You could have been inside. That should tell you what kind of people they are."

"It should, and it does. That's why I am committed to complete the task. How do we know the authorities will show? Until now, they've sure not been very interested. Maybe they won't be in the area when the Arabs arrive for the pick-up. It could be completely up to us. Donnie and Josh, his assistant, and several other armed Forest Service folks who will be there."

"You can't do it, Mike. Your lives are in too much danger. If there were any possible way I could tell Nellie, I'd spill the beans. Wayne hasn't informed her of the exposure, and that infuriates me. Nell would never allow your brother's participation, knowing the dangers, the real threats you face. It's not fair to Nell and you're not being fair to me, our children, and grandchildren."

"We have a plan to take over," he argued, "and place everyone under arrest.

Some may run; Claybourne himself might. He stashed his dirt bike in the woods next to the power company road, to use for a last ditch escape."

Mike added some levity to the otherwise grim picture, and laughed heartily. "He'll have a long dern walk. We found the cycle and took it to our barn. A little scary, but we disabled their guns, too, and those snares we set: anyone who tries to escape through the woods will face disaster. They'll swing from the trees like swallows' nests in a winter nor'easter. One of the machine guns will misfire, and the other…well…we just have to stay out of its way. We've covered all the bases." Just before the back door slammed hard, Mike felt an icy zephyr surround his body. He shivered, opened his eyes, and found himself alone in a void, suddenly filled with confusion, absent the affections he wanted and needed.

CHAPTER 30

After a fast breakfast at the coffee shop by the bridge, they parked Wayne's old sedan loan car across the road from Claybourne's gate, at the edge of a turnout several hundred yards away. Just in case something happened to the Volvo, which Mike drove, the Buick would be their back-up means of exit. Canoe on top, for crossing the river if necessary, the brothers piled into the wagon, and headed up the crooked dirt road to the trail on the Au Sable's north shore. "Nervous?" Mike asked. "Aren't you nervous at all?"

Wayne seemed cool as a cucumber on the outside, but admitted he twisted with guilt beneath. "I should have told Nell; should have given her the full story."

"If you did, Bro, you would not be sitting here right now.

Well, we didn't inform her and, now it's too late, isn't it? Thweeth, thweeth."

He spat out the window as Mike drove past extending tree boughs that scraped along the car sides with shrill, ghost-like screeches. They fell quiet while setting up the scope and electronics. The noise of brush breaking behind them, stood hair on ends. Their guard was down. More caution was needed.

"Mornin' gents," Don Johanssen whispered with a wide grin, a toast to his success in approaching without detection. Mike envied Donnie's youthful enthusiasm but, even more, coveted his silent stalking ability. He sneered while his friend sat by the radios. *Donnie could sneak up on any buck in the forest for a close arrow shot. Few are so capable that they don't need a blind.* He felt gratified that the passive, risk averting, Forest Ranger developed enough interest to join the sting effort.

Depending on the support they might receive, tactics and plans for options were hammered out for a full understanding by all. Don advised Mike and Wayne that, before two o'clock, Feds from Detroit would swarm the woods. Mike listened intently, aghast at the story of what happened in the bedroom, and wished, like Don, that Virginia shot Claybourne when she had the chance.

"Five hours to go," Don reminded them at 9:00 in the morning. "Let's make the best of it and gather more evidence, usable or not. He brought a recorder and patch cord to convert conversation in the house to tape, while he continued to monitor the headphones.

Opting to be the listener for a spell, it wasn't long before Wayne burst with excitement. "Oh boy … Brother … Arabs are coming early … twelve o-clock … two hours before they were expected. Claybourne just confirmed the change in arrival time; he's on the phone with someone, right now. The government will need to know with whom. They'll want this tape, Donnie." Wayne flipped the recorder switch, ceased further reporting, and listened anxiously for several minutes before he relayed more subversive discussion to the others.

"He's telling Virginia that the caller complained: the airport hanger would have to be cleared two hours earlier than planned. It fouled up the works. Claybourne says the 747 is there, waiting on the apron. This guy is a planner; give him due credit for that. For every plan, though, there's a crow bar just a waitin' to pry it apart, eh?"

"What happens if the Feds don't make it in time?" Don asked, fearful of their next move without the heavy government support they planned on having. "The crooks will be gone before our mini-army arrives. This definitely isn't what I wanted," he said. "We could be in deep muck, without serious backing."

Mike planned on that very possible eventuality, and offered a detailed alternate strategy they willingly considered. Anyway, few other offerings existed at the late hour. "If the Arabs don't show by the time most of the loading is complete, it'll be up to us. We'll need some men deployed as decoys to divert attention to the woods behind the shack. Don, you call for four, six, maybe more armed Rangers to infiltrate that part of the forest accessible from the power company road, all the way west to the abandoned maintenance building. Poised along the path every twenty-five to fifty yards or so, they will hide in the thick brush, and be prepared to fire toward the road. That crossfire will draw Claybourne's paid fighters away from the one operational machine gun.

Gunfire from the woods behind their positions would spook them no end. They'll take the quickest routes out, along the game trails, where they'll be captured, shot, or snared." Agreement was unanimous. Don used his radio to summon help. Wayne offered to direct the men, to assure snares were avoided as they found their spots.

"Don, when Wayne returns, You, Wayne, Josh, and I will paddle across in the canoe, and cut through the thickets to the west of the house. Claybourne will surely be outside to supervise loading of his precious missiles, and the armed Arabs will be wandering close thereabouts, as well.

I want to warn Virginia. No doubt she'll stay out of the fray, in the house. I'll go inside anyway, tell her to stay put, in case trouble erupts. Maybe she can even avoid arrest, Don. She's done nothing, herself." Wayne looked at Mike quizzically, raised his eyebrows, but stayed silent.

"Once you three have taken cover in the trees, wait until I rendezvous, then we'll carefully maneuver ourselves to where we can see the barn, and what's going on around the clearing. We'll direct your men by radio, to coordinate diversionary shooting from the woods."

"Thweep, thweep," Wayne spat, nodded in approval and assured that his four magazines were properly stacked with shells. Don's concerns were somewhat alleviated with the Gladdocks' confidence that one machine gun would not fire, that Claybourne's .45 pistol, and all his rifles were dysfunctional.

"Damn, you guys had the nerve, screwing with all the guns in his house. Why? What prompted you? Have you no pride?"

Wayne grinned slyly. "We thought we'd be alone in this skirmish, didn't expect big-time government assistance. It started because Mike was bummed over the general's purchase of the property. The fence, though, and that damned gate were straws that broke the camel's back. We figures we'd do whatever was necessary to get Claybourne out of there. Look what we found: a battery of missiles, selling out to the Palestinian Liberation folks. We had no idea!"

"Nope," Mike added, "not until this clown fell through the derned front window, when he tried to read the computer screen. He opened Pandora's box, when he helped himself to an inside inspection." Mike grasped his brother's shoulder affectionately.

Don and Josh shook heads in disbelief, exchanged shrugs, worried glances, then gazed at the brothers incredulously. "If you two were half the hunters that you are criminals, we'd be afraid to compete with you on opening day," Don joked. "I hope that. ..."

Wayne interrupted, "Hey guys; listen up. The trucks are real close. The general just took a call. He's heading out to unlock the barn and place the three goons on station. He told Mendez to send Rodriguez to the far gun; the one we disabled. Lopez was left with the other, closer to the shack. Mendez stays with the general, probably to cover his rear if there's trouble.

"Let's do the deal; Mike's ideas are as good as any. Wait for me, maybe a half hour to forty-five minutes or so. Trucks are coming ... Claybourne said so ... no less than an hour away. They are ahead of schedule."

Ten o'clock, straight up, a fierce forenoon sun steamed the forest. Plenty of songbird chatter supplanted the river's rustle. Two large hawks circled above the treetops, eyes peeled for inattentive fish that might venture too close to the surface. Thoughts of big browns deep in the pools drew Mike's musings to the caddis flies. It was early, yet, they began to swarm in the trees, teased him, awaiting a twilight call for their over-the-water dances. Canoe hidden in the reeds close to the section of rushing water, the three men nervously awaited their river crossing, upstream from the shoals, and well out of view of the shack.

"Hey Don, it's Trask here. Switch our channel six." Don Johanssen's code enforcement supervisor called. "Hiking west on the power company road now. Our trucks are safely hidden from view, and Wayne is on his way back. Will advise when the last man reaches the old clapboard building. Be ready soon. Bill's closest to River Road … already found the deadfall trap. Said to tell the guys, 'it's one hell of a set and will surely knock a man's head off his shoulders.'"

"Advise when positioned half way through the woods. Touch base when you have the path to the shack in sight, and stop there for now."

Mike's cell phone vibrated quietly. He snapped the earpiece open, and relayed the message from Wayne, who was frantic. "The trucks are just behind, Brother. The first is white, a brand new tractor with two men inside, both dark complected, maybe Arabs. It's towing a long flat bed, empty right now, except for a pile of rolled tarps. That'll be for the launcher and command center transporter. Two more tractors are trailing close behind. All have diplomatic plates, just like the limo out in front. He can't see through the limo windows; no idea how many men might be in there. No other vehicles, but he'll stay put for a few more minutes on a side road, to insure that a truck full of back-up commandos isn't behind them, to serve as an afterguard.

Faces on the bluff paled, and little discussion ensued. He peered through the scope Mike supplied; Josh saw Claybourne and Mendez open the barn doors. The general operated the forklift, and pulled the two trailers outside.

Don called his F.B.I. contact again. Their men began briefing in Detroit. It might be as long as three hours—possibly more. Don was shocked. The missiles could be gone by then, and Claybourne could disappear with more than fifteen million. Absent other options, their hastily planned, last minute moves had to work.

Wayne slipped from the thicket behind where the others waited. "This is frightening. I'm … thweeth, thweeth … scared out of my shorts. You guys, too?" All nodded solemnly. "We'll wait until the trucks pull up to the barn. There won't be time for worry."

10:48 AM: another ten degrees piled on the thermometer. Everyone sweated profusely as forest humidity climbed. An increasingly loud reverberation from the east attracted their attention. The black Mercedes limousine rounded the last turn into the *cul-de-sac,* followed closely by the trucks that rocked perilously as they traversed the deeper ruts. Mendez directed the driver while Claybourne, without hesitation, towed the first trailer into position, to be pulled up the ramp with a winch cable.

"Oh, oh," Wayne remarked. They looked over their shoulders and sighted six Arabs in dark blue fatigues, each with an AK-47 in hand, bail out of the limo to station themselves around the equipment. The three Arabs they saw before, decked out in dress white garb and turbans, similarly armed, milled about and watched every move made by Claybourne and his Mexican gunmen. One Arab hastily checked ID numbers of each component and the labels on box after box of spare parts stacked high on four pallets.

The Gladdocks' canoe slid into the river. Rushing water lapped alarmingly at the gunwales with its overweight load: Don, Josh, Mike and Wayne. Dampened from cross-stream spray, the four men narrowly made it past the shallow, turbulent stretch, when the bow scraped the sandy beach on the shack's side. Josh and Don concealed the craft in the reeds along the bank. Mike moved stealthily toward the house, rifle slung over his shoulder, pistol in hand, while the other three rushed into the cover of underbrush west of the shack.

Unseen, with all the activity in front, where the dogs, too, congregated, Mike slipped though the open kitchen door, and tiptoed up the stairs.

She lay prone on the bed, reading a magazine spread on the floor, and nearly passed out from shock when he appeared from the hall.

"My God ... Mike!," Virginia exclaimed, completely dumbfounded, cock-sure she saw an apparition. "What in the name of heaven are you. ...?" She cupped both hands to her mouth and nearly screamed aloud. She heard steps, and expected Claybourne. "I thought they killed you ... the car ... I ... I. ..." Virginia flushed, began to shake and burst into tears. I ... I thought you died. I couldn't handle it and almost shot myself over it. Yet, I had a strange feeling that. ..."

Mike pressed an index finger to his lips. He begged her in a low whisper not to cry out, and to stay down. He bounded for the east window to assure he was not seen entering the house. The men were busily engaged in the loading effort. He turned abruptly and with hands outstretched, said, "No, I got out just in time, but the car was absolutely destroyed. Have only a minute, Virginia. I came to keep you from getting hurt, maybe killed, and to prevent your arrest, if at all possible. There's a good chance you can avoid it."

"Are you a cop, Mike? I thought. ..."

"No, not a cop, just a local who stumbled on some scary criminal activity in my woods. Can't tell you now, but it all started with being pissed off at the fence the general put up, being shot at; his purchase of the property and, finally, those Patriot Missiles."

"Patriot miss ... you know? But, how? Virginia jumped from the bed, stepped toward the open window, but he grabbed her wrist, and pulled her gently to the bed. "If you want to go down, take your chances with the risks of life in jail—for a few million dollars—just tell me, and I'm out of here. Otherwise, I think I can convince the F.B.I. and the Forest Service who will be closing in, any moment, that you're an innocent victim ... coerced to participate." She turned white with the news.

"Hopefully, your father, too, might get off the hook by testifying as to the general's activity. So far as we know, Claybourne's done all the stealing. All the evidence we have collected, all of it points to him; even the computer."

"You've been in here ... on our ... er ... his computer? My God, but how?"

"Can't talk, don't have enough time." Mike said. He shook increasingly with excitement. "Please, I think about you, every minute and wouldn't wish to visit you in federal prison for the next twenty years. Kiss off the money, Virginia. Stay in this bedroom and lay low. After the bust, I'll help you through this. Assault team people will be here in no time ... probably some shooting, too. They want the Arabs and they want Claybourne. Wayne, my brother and I, removed the firing pins from the guns."

"Not from my .22, you didn't. I was going to shoot myself. At the last second, though, I hit the window instead. She pointed to the small hole."

"I know. I found that one in your drawer, and thought you might need it for protection. Figured I'd take the chance that you were a good person under it all. Homer's pistol, however, has dummy cartridges. The box of ammo, they're dummies, too. I removed the powder and replaced the slugs, so nothing but the primer will blow. It's futile—the deal's over—I can assure you. Have to go. Can I count on you? Can we try to stay friends, possibly more as time goes on?" He strode to the door. "I wish you luck, hope to God you go our way, and trust that you'll do right with your conscience. It hurts me, pains me terribly, to know of the beatings you've suffered. Not right … just weren't right."

"Mike," she called as he passed out the door, "Homer's got another gun. a .45. He kept it in his car and he's a damned good shot. Be careful, it's a big one."

Confident she'd not interfere, Mike gave her a grateful smile, disappeared down the stairs in a few long steps, and ran behind the cabin for the woods.

Virginia thought about the five million, Mike, and then Claybourne. She made her decision In a heartbeat. *What choice do I have?* Hurriedly, the bewildered woman grabbed her pistol and the box of long rifle shells, and made for the cellar. After locking the outside door, she hid herself well, behind a shelf filled with old Mason jars of canned fruit and vegetables. The small window there allowed her to see part of the cleared area behind the barn. She heard men converse in the *cul-de-sac*. Loading of the crates began and moved along faster than they calculated. Mike met up with the others, who waited impatiently for him before each established his pre-planned position.

All were glad the woman would stay clear of the fracas. Don spoke first. "I've called the F.B.I. again, Mike and, instead of driving, in view of the delay in aggregating forces, they're on their way in a Blackhawk combat helicopter. Though the airborne invasion force is *en route* and several vehicles are now on the road, they said we'll have to make the arrests if it appears anyone is about to leave."

"Let's go, then," Don muttered anxiously. "They're not going to sit here waiting. We'll fire one or two shots at the first tractor. The Arabs will think Claybourne's men are sabotaging them, and they'll fire into the woods, toward the shots. We lay real low. Next thing we'll hear is the operational thirty caliber, probably shooting at the Arabs, and we'll let them hammer it out. When the dust settles, we move in. Much of our work will be done by the Arabs and Claybourne's men hashing it out with each other, if we're lucky enough.

Quiet reigned in the trees. The last crate slid onto the second semi-van. The Arabs began to wrap the flat bed load with tarps. Don made the call to his men in the woods. "Rick, you see that white cab-over, the one towing the flat bed with the launcher and command module?" The reply was affirmative. "Take a clean shot at the driver's door, if you can see it."

The men froze with baited breath while the ranger positioned himself. *Blam!* Then, *blam … blam,* again. The forest rocked from three loud rifle shots that found their marks—shattered impacts on the truck's door. Window glass splintered. Echoes rang along the river. Bewildered, all the men dove for cover; none knew from whence the initial shots came. Contrary to instructions, but helpful to increase the shock, another one of Don's men fired, this time the left front truck tire took the hit. A gasping hiss followed. The front end slumped to the ground on the driver's side.

The Arabs were first to respond to the initial rampage and recoil, they did. All of them crouched low and strode in the direction from which they heard the shots; they leveled their AK-47s and emptied magazines in seconds, as they swept the trees with an aimless barrage of automatic rifle fire.

Lopez panicked, and let loose with the unmistakable staccato *rat-tat-tat-tat-tat* of the thirty caliber that was not disabled. Twenty seconds and true to its capacity, the belt emptied. Two hundred heavy slugs seared through trees, the barn and everything in their way. As though his platoon suffered an attack, he opened a second ammunition canister, inserted the belt, cocked the gun, fired again, and struck four of the Arabs who shot in the Mexican's direction.

While the bullets whistled, three of the uninjured Arabs stayed prone on the ground, as did Mendez and Claybourne, shielded by the cover of several boulders. Rodriguez, alone in his foxhole, struggled to fire the non-functional machine gun he manned. One ammo canister after another failed, the gunner thought, which left no choice but an arms-up surrender. Quickly subdued by three Forest Rangers, who gagged him and cuffed his hands around a tree, he begged for mercy.

An Arab who crawled toward the bluff and dropped to the river, sought to approach the snapping machine gun from behind. Following the ear-splitting racket that continued from the foxhole, it took him but seconds to make contact. He fell upon the Mexican with a razor sharp dagger and slit his throat with a single swath. Mendez ran to the site and surprised the Arab. The fast shootout between them dropped both to the ground, to bleed furiously from fatal chest entries.

Mike, Don, and Wayne saw two Arabs turn from the shootout and run for the woods. Confident of their snares, and the armed Forest Service men who waited in the thickets beyond, they were unconcerned and remained positioned.

Minutes later, they heard the first scream. Yanked by his feet into the low-hanging tree limbs as the noose took hold, the man left *terra firma* swinging head down, and unconscious from the sudden jolt. The next noise was a gratifying, though agonizing yell that permeated the woods above the noise of crackling gunfire. "The deadfall," Wayne whispered with a devious grin, while he shook his head regretfully. "Too bad, isn't it? Probably lost his face on that one."

The remaining Arabs wanted the general, convinced he planned the betrayal and the initial outburst. They both saw him scurry low to the ground, toward the lead tractor, when the first shots began the sortie. Across the open clearing he lay hidden, pistol in hand, face down in the leaves. Two more Arabs appeared, armed to the hilt. They waited in the rear of the limousine until there was some relent. Claybourne had to be their target. They separated and each headed toward his last known position from different directions.

The general saw them coming, got up, and broke into a panicked run toward the side door of the barn. Mike advanced from a thicket behind the building, and peered toward the trucks from behind a large oak. Pinned behind the tree, temporarily immobilized by cracking rifle fire, he winced from a hail of bullets that sheared through the trees around him, and dared not move from his protective spot.

Claybourne rounded the corner of the barn, recognized Mike through a cluster of small birches, took too quick a bead on him with one hand and fired at his back. The general carried a U.S. Army .45 semi-automatic, which Wayne and Mike didn't find in their search for weapons. The first and second shots missed Mike by inches, and spattered bark just above his head. Mike dropped to the dirt and out of the corner of his eye, saw Virginia peer through the basement window at ground level, an enraged look on her face. She screamed in horror.

Startled, Claybourne turned to he sound of her voice, swung back around, leveled his pistol at Mike again, and ignored Virginia's pleas to give up. Absent any sign of his submission, she had to act fast. She cut loose three rapid shots with her semi-automatic .22 long rifle pistol, the second of which struck the general's right thigh with a slap.

Claybourne fell to the ground.

My God! She saved my life. "Get down! Virginia, get back," Mike yelled instinctively, in horror of what would have come next, if she were not there.

The general screamed in pain, dropped his gun, and limped toward the side door of the barn. He propped a ladder against the loft rail and struggled up the rungs, panting from the stiffness and pain of the bullet wound. He would get the money he hid there and make his getaway on the dirt bike.

"To hell with Virginia. I'll go it alone … take care of myself," he snarled. "Have to get what money I can and get the hell out of here." He struggled to the rear of the loft. Claybourne grabbed for the large briefcases of cash. A harried moment of cerebral disarray passed; he remembered the booby trap he set, a nanosecond too late.

He tugged at the black valise. That pulled the rope, and the rope jerked the crossbow trigger behind him with a sharp click. *Thwoop!* The one hundred fifty pound aluminum bow cast loose its fury. A fast forward streak, the heavy bolt twirled clockwise on its axis, due to the angle of the tail feathers he carefully fletched. As a rotating rifle bullet, it sped accurately to its mark.

General Homer P. Claybourne, Retired, turned just in time to see the razor-edged hunting tip, before it launched and buried itself in his neck. Mike heard the general's tortuous gasp and, without hesitation, knew the man's fate. Claybourne tremored; his arms jerked three times, then dangled down like a scare crow, as he went limp, impaled by his cervical spine against the plywood wall.

The two remaining Arabs made for the limo, spun the wheels in a wide arc, and raced toward the dirt path. Wayne and Don wasted no time. They ran wildly, made it to the foxhole and let the thirty caliber do their talking. Fifty or more holes appeared in the right side of the vehicle. Its engine clattered hopelessly, a cloud of steam arose, and it was over.

The turbaned duo stepped out with hands extended. Both bled badly, from thirty caliber wounds to arms and legs; they collapsed to the ground. Gunshot racket ended with the *blap-blap-blap-blap* of the C.I.A. helicopter that swooped over the river in a low hover, to expel its mixed load—agents from four federal agencies—on rappel lines.

Smoke, dust, the unmistakable smells of gunpowder, and death, slowly cleared from the *cul-de-sac* with the incipient breeze, and the songbirds resumed their mid-day symphony.

Men in black assault gear infiltrated the area, called to one another as they cleared the shack, the barn and the vehicles. They dragged Claybourne down from the loft, stone dead. Wounded and dead, they pulled to the dirt path, and lined up on their faces like logs in a pulp mill storage lot. A fast body count said everyone was accounted for, except the Arab who drooped from the pine, motionless, and his cohort, whose face seemed glued to the jagged end of the heavy log deadfall in the woods.

Virginia emerged from the basement and into Mike's arms. Hysterical, she quivered incessantly, would not let go.

"It's OK, Virginia; it's all right. He's gone, Virginia. He planned for you to take the rap, was up there in the barn loft, to get the money, and take off on his dirt bike. Days ago, he hid it out there in the woods, to aid his escape if things went sour."

She shuddered and dropped to her knees. Faint and in disbelief of what just occurred, she held tightly to Mike's legs. "It's fine," he assured the two Feds as they looked upon her skeptically. "She's with us; just saved my life … shot the general in the leg when he took a bead on me from the backside with this .45." He looked down at Claybourne, still and crumpled, his precious fifteen million final payment still in the bullet-ridden limousine.

"You poor dead sonofabuck." Mike waited for that unusual yet comforting cool wind, for the telltale rustle of treetop leaves. They remained still. She did not appear. *Meg must have heard this turmoil. Would she have words of advice?*

He listened for her, but heard only the forest's birds, the silence of the watching trees, and the beckoning rumble of the river. This time Meg did not come back.

Affectionately, Mike rubbed Virginia's trembling shoulders, turned to her and uttered softly, "Tomorrow, Virginia. Tomorrow the caddis will move in massive swarms. I know they're ready. The big browns are hungry. I'll teach you once again … to … to cast a fly."